THE FINAL DECREE

SHAMI STOVALL

CONTENTS

Published by
CS BOOKS, LLC

The Final Decree
Copyright © 2021 Capital Station Books
All rights reserved.
https://sastovallauthor.com/

Cover Design: Darko Paganus
Editor: Nia Quinn, Amy McNulty

IF YOU WANT TO BE NOTIFIED WHEN SHAMI STOVALL'S NEXT BOOK RELEASES, PLEASE VISIT HER WEBSITE OR CONTACT HER DIRECTLY AT
s.adelle.s@gmail.com

ISBN: 978-1-7334428-9-3

To John, who loved this novel.
To Gail, for being the last set of eyes on the manuscript.
To Big John, my family.
To Jessica Robbins, for giving a voice to the characters.
To Beka, thank you.
To Mary, & Dana, for all the jokes and input.
To my Facebook group, for all the memes and fun.
To my Patrons, especially Josh.
To Lucius Quinctius Cincinnatus, a Roman leader who inspired this story.
And finally, to everyone unnamed, thank you for everything.

CHAPTER ONE

I stumbled forward, fueled only by hate.

The soldiers of the god-king had taken everything from me, but I would be safe once I crossed the border. Denying them the satisfaction of my death would be my final act of defiance.

The winter winds rushed past, as bitter and cold as my thoughts. I walked the long road through the Kingdom of Luka alone. I was a stranger—a random woman—nothing more than some wraith passing by, devoid of purpose. People regarded me with suspicion, and I hurried along. I tried, at least, until I tripped and fell.

I hadn't eaten.

Snow provided little in the way of sustenance. It sated my thirst somewhat, but my gut twisted in agony. It felt like my stomach was consuming my insides, cannibalizing the other organs to keep me alive. I knew it wasn't, but my nightmares had been filled with such imagery, and it was all I could dwell on.

I pulled my stolen blanket tightly over my body, unable to stand. With gritted teeth, I continued at a crawl. I should have found shelter and rested, but I was on the edge of town, by the first few houses that lined the road.

When merchants rode by on horses and carts, I glanced up, hoping they would spill something edible. They didn't, of course—no successful merchant would—and I contemplated my situation with dreaded realization.

I might die here. In some town whose name I didn't even know.

"That's a nice blanket."

The tone put me on edge. It wasn't a compliment, but an appraisal. I tilted my head back to stare at the speaker, still unable to stand. The man who had spoken wore thick winter garb. Similar men flanked him on either side, each with a full beard and light satchels. A woman stood next to them, a bundle of firewood in her arms. I suspected they were leather workers.

I scooted up against the wall of the nearest building, holding my wool blanket close. My throat was too raw and dry to offer a verbal response.

The man leaned down, grabbed the edge of my blanket, and yanked it from my grasp. I tried to hold on, I really did, but hunger killed my capacity. I couldn't keep it.

The instant the man took it, he and his companions jumped back, their gasps a painful chorus in my ears. I had trousers and bindings over my chest, for when I had pretended to be a man, but I wore no shirt—it had been cut off by my pursuers as a cruel joke, leaving most of my skin exposed.

I covered my left shoulder with my hand, but it was too little, too late. The black cascade of spiderweb markings that stained my skin was visible for all to see.

"You're cursed," the man said, dropping the blanket to the dirt road.

I closed my eyes and huddled against the cold stones of the building. What could I do? I wished the group would leave. I wielded magic unlike anyone in this backwater town, but even that was useless when hunger dominated my body.

"No wonder she's a vagabond," the woman with the firewood muttered.

"She's a monster."

"We can't let her roam around."

I heard the familiar sound of a knife leaving its sheath.

The man intended to kill me.

Townsfolk congregated on the edge of the road, their eyes wide and their postures stiff. They didn't look at the man with the knife—the man poised to gut a stranger—they looked at *me*, their brows wrinkled in silent disgust.

I was a Lord of Flame and Cinder. If I had had the strength, I would have burned the whole town to the ground.

Perhaps the men were afraid, or perhaps they wanted to take their time, but they didn't stab me right away. One got close and kicked me in the side, just below the ribs. I would have said the kick hurt, but it didn't compare to my aching stomach. Another one joined in, stomping on my legs, and I bit back the urge to cry out.

I wished they would get it over with. Life was nothing but a parade of struggle, suffering, and disappointment. I didn't want a prolonged finale.

"What're you doing?"

The new voice cut through all the others with a commanding edge that demanded attention. The men beating me ceased their aggression, but I feared it was too late. I would surely die, bruised and starving.

The clink of metal stirred dread in me. It was the sound of sollerets—the plated metal boots of soldiers. They had come to take me back. They had come to torture me and throw me at the god-king's feet. A death at their hands would be a thousand times worse than a death in the winter streets.

My tormentors ran, and the crowds dispersed. I shivered with each clink of the boots drawing closer.

Please, gods of old—please, not this. I didn't want to go back. I would apologize for my transgressions. I needed the blanket or else I never would have stolen it. *What else have I done to anger you?* It wasn't my fault I was born cursed… *Please, let my end come quick.*

The soldier knelt next to me and placed a gauntlet on my shoulder, the metal so cold, it burned. I cringed away and forced out a growl, unable to speak and conducting myself no better than a rabid dog.

Kill me. *Do it.*

The soldier stood, and for some reason, walked away, the clink of his boots fading with each step. I didn't know why, and I wasn't sure I wanted to. Even if he didn't know my identity, soldiers of the god-king were rewarded for killing the cursed. What possible reason could he have to stay his hand?

But I didn't have the energy to dwell on it.

I crawled away from the street, through the dirty alleyway between hovels, and back toward the wilderness beyond the town's limits. I had forgotten my blanket, but it wouldn't do me any good where I was going.

Once I reached a patch of iced-over shrubs, I eased myself into the detritus beneath them. I would die here. In nature. Away from everything I had grown to hate. It was how my father had died, after all. I supposed I deserved no better.

Before my wish was granted, the clink of metal returned. I closed my eyes, hoping to feign death, and I listened as the soldier easily followed my furrow through the dirt. He pushed the branches of the bushes aside and stepped close to my body. I couldn't help but shudder.

He knelt again and turned me onto my back, his now bare hands warm and powerful. I opened my eyes, confused by the gentle way he lifted my head. My vision, blurred with hunger, took in a young man with a hard, neutral expression. Calm brown eyes, dark chestnut hair, red maple leaf scarf—or maybe I was looking at a tree, I couldn't tell through the delirium—and I relaxed a bit, amused by my own skewed perceptions.

Knowing I would die had removed the stress of trying to live.

The soldier placed the lip of a canteen at my mouth and poured. I gulped down the water—warm water, not hot—and the heat coated my insides with comfort. It was only after a second gulp that I realized it was soup. The fragrant herbs and shreds of meat were like distant memories returning to me after having been long forgotten. I had never tasted anything so delicious in my life.

"Everything will be fine," the soldier said.

If I could have cried, I would have. His confidence was undeniable and infectious—I had never heard anyone reassure me like he had. I wanted to thank him. I wanted to tell him that, if I died, at least I would have known comfort for a moment before passing. I wanted to tell him that his single act of kindness meant more to me than anything else I could have experienced.

But I couldn't.

I coughed after the third gulp and shook with dry sobs.

He hung his canteen on his belt and wrapped me in a thick cloak. It was warm and smelled of sweat. It was his.

With one effortless motion, he scooped me up into his arms. I didn't protest as he walked out of the wilderness on the edge of town and carried me back to the main thoroughfare. He continued beyond, walking at an even pace. I rested my head on his shoulder and closed my eyes.

Finally, sleep took me.

When I awoke, it was to the glorious crackle of fire.

I loved the brilliant glow brought about by the flames. Fire had a special meaning to me. No force compared to the heat and radiance, and while fire could be a tool, no man could conquer it. Sure, it could be snuffed, but the blaze of the sun reminded us that it would never be beaten.

I stared at the stone hearth. The small flames licked at the black logs, a gentle glow brought about by their dance. The sofa I rested on creaked with my movements as I turned to get a better look. I sat up and examined my new blanket—a woven cloth of moons and stars, perhaps a child's aid to learning the night sky.

"You're awake."

I flinched and held the blanket close. I hadn't bothered to examine the rest of the room, and I cursed myself for such folly.

"It's all right. You're safe here."

Shaken and confused, I stared at the man standing by the far wall. He was tall and gaunt, but wiry. He had curly chestnut hair, but the curls were so small and tight, they clung close to his head. I would have guessed his age at eighteen, maybe nineteen, and he offered a smile. I pressed myself against the armrest of the sofa. He wasn't the man who had carried me off the streets. He sounded different.

"My name is Wulfric," he said, his voice boisterous.

He walked over to the sofa with excited energy in each step. My grip tightened on the blanket, my nails indenting my palms through the fabric. I offered him a glower and nothing more, my heart beating hard against my ribs.

He stopped a few feet from where I sat and examined me for a moment, his eyes narrowed. "Uh, don't worry. I'm not a nobleman. My father just likes to name his kids after dead royalty. He, uh—" Wulfric chuckled and folded his arms across his chest, "—he thinks it'll help us to *aspire to greatness.* Odd, right? You may call me Wulf."

I didn't speak. Instead, I examined my surroundings, taking in the details I hadn't before. I was in the front parlor of a modest home, one made of wood and worked stone. The window, while large, was covered in a thick drape, blocking most of the midafternoon sunlight, but a small sliver sliced through the middle of the room. Trophies from past hunts adorned the walls. I stared at a pair of antlers mounted above the fireplace.

Wulf fidgeted for a moment, tilting his head from side to side. He looked confused, and I suspected he didn't know what to do with himself amidst the silence.

"I'll go get my brother," he said. "And something to eat. Wait right here."

I said nothing as Wulf hurried from the parlor, leaving me with the fire. I stared at the flickering blaze. It danced, hungry, like I was. Although I knew I shouldn't—no one should discover my talents—I held out a hand and called a part of the flame to me, just to make sure I still could. A wisp of fire twirled through the air and I grabbed it. The heat soothed my sore skin.

Floorboards creaked. I glanced up to catch sight of a much more imposing man than Wulf. He was thick with muscle and tanned from the sun—a warrior if I ever saw one. I shrank down into the blanket, keenly aware of our difference in size. I was much shorter than the man and emaciated from the long trek.

"I'm glad to see you're awake," he said as he entered the room with a slow gait.

It was him! The man who had carried me from the street. Already his voice was ingrained in my mind. I would know it from a thousand other men in a busy tavern.

He took a seat on the opposite end of the sofa, the furniture straining under his solid frame. I almost missed the fact that he held a mug of water and a half loaf of bread. Without words, he motioned for me to take them.

I kept the blanket up over my body as I grabbed the food. I waited, half expecting him to say something, but nothing happened. Without wasting another second, I bit into the bread, my dry and cracked lips bleeding from the range of motion. I washed back the blood and pain with several gulps of water.

"You shouldn't eat so fast," the man said. "Not if you want to keep it down."

Although I wanted nothing more than to consume everything all at once, I forced myself to relax. How cruel was life that even eating was torture? But he was right. I hadn't eaten in a while. And my body had suffered enough.

The man stared at the fire, his gaze set and focused. "My name is Rylion Nasos."

Rylion.

That was the name of the first god-king to rule over the Kingdom of Luka. Stories made him out to be a conqueror unrivaled on the battlefield. If Rylion's father wanted him to aspire to greatness, he had picked a large pair of boots to fill.

"What should I call you?" Rylion asked, never looking away from the flames.

I sipped another mouthful of water and took in a breath. Could I speak? I coughed and forced out a few sounds.

"I, uh," I began. "My name is…"

My voice had a rusty tone and it pained me to say even four words.

Rylion waited. I gathered the fortitude needed and continued.

"My name is Artemisia." I held the mug close. "Artemis. You may call me Artemis."

That was what my father had called me when we had been alone.

"You don't look like you're from here."

I stared at him, and he glanced over before motioning to my hair. I touched the disheveled locks hanging long enough to reach my shoulders. My mother had said I had hair like coal, and eyes as gray as ash.

"Did you leave your home because you were cursed?" Rylion asked.

I finished the bread and tucked myself back into the blanket, the mug held between my legs. I hated that we were discussing the fact that I was cursed. It brought back the loathing I felt for the world—the hate that would never leave me. I wished the curse would vanish, rather than consuming me at every moment of every day.

But I knew it would never happen.

Rylion exhaled. "You needn't worry. You don't have to run anymore if you don't want to."

"Rylion," Wulf shouted as he entered the parlor. He panted once. "Soldiers are at the door. They've come for—" he glanced at me, and then back to Rylion, "—well, I told them you would speak to them."

Were they not aware? Surely, they were. All citizens of Luka, not just the soldiers, were offered a reward for killing the cursed. But there was a chance—a small chance—Wulf and Rylion were oblivious to that fact. And that was the only reason they had helped me thus far.

Would they kill me once they knew? What a cruel twist of fate. But it wouldn't surprise me.

Rylion stood. "I'll speak with them."

He exited the room, his brother close behind. The heavy slam of doors echoed throughout the house.

Wulf was the younger sibling, and I suspected Rylion was six or seven years older. They had the same impressive height and broad shoulders, but while Wulf had a rambunctious spirit, Rylion had a calming presence.

The simple thoughts kept my mind off the terror that lurked in my heart. I tried to continue thinking of their family, but my mind returned to the possibility of death.

After several long minutes, I heard the squeak and slam of doors. I stayed huddled on the sofa, knowing that escape was futile. Whatever they decided would be my destiny.

Rylion reentered the room, his quiet confidence a reassurance. I didn't even need to ask. He had sent the soldiers away. Wulf paced behind the sofa, his long legs taking him farther with each step. Rylion returned to his seat, and I stared at him, confused.

"I thought you were a soldier," I murmured.

"I'm a hunter," Rylion said. "But I know the soldiers of this area well. They won't ask questions while you're here."

A hunter? When I had met him on the street, he had worn pieces of plate armor. No hunter wore half-plate—the loud clink of metal would scare the animals away for miles. But I had no room to comment, nor did it matter. If he said he was a hunter, even if he was a terrible one, I believed him. He had given me no reason to doubt.

"She talks?" Wulf asked. He walked around the sofa, smiling wide. "What's your name?"

I took another gulp of water, unwilling to repeat myself when energy was in short supply.

Rylion turned to Wulf. "Her name is Artemis."

"Really? She'll talk to you, but she won't say a word to me?" Wulf threw his arms up in the air. "It's the handmaidens at the market all over again! I'm the one to initiate conversation, yet they speak to you."

The brothers shared a laugh, and all the anger I had thought Wulf harbored toward me disappeared. I was surprised by their jovial attitude, considering everything that had happened. How could they be so relaxed around me? *Me*? I was cursed. They knew. It didn't bother them that their lives were in danger?

Their laughter waned until the crackle of the dying fire reigned supreme. Wulf resumed his pacing, his attention jumping from the window to the empty doorframe. Rylion watched the flames consume the last of the logs, his gaze unfocused, as though deep in thought.

I wanted to speak to him, but the words never came.

"He's still not back," Wulf said, breaking the silence between us.

"He will be," Rylion stated.

"What if he's injured? He might need help."

"He's tough."

"He's *old*."

"Not so old that he can't handle himself."

Wulf sighed. He stopped his movement and placed his hands on his belt. "I'm worried. It's almost sundown. We should look again."

Rylion stood and nodded. "Very well. We'll look again." He turned his attention to me. "We have a room. You can rest there until we return. That may not be until morning."

I glanced around the front parlor. A small house couldn't have more than two bedrooms, maybe three, if the carpenters were competent. They would give me one? Even for a night? I stood, keeping the blanket over my shoulders, and followed Rylion as he led me deeper into the building.

The room he offered was a simple bedroom. A mattress on a light wooden frame. A nightstand with a basin for washing. A single candle. A chair. One window. Rylion motioned me in.

"You're leaving?" I whispered, staring into the room. "Even though… I could turn?"

Surely, he knew? He knew why the cursed were shunned and killed? He must have known. Everyone knew. Everyone knew we were twisted by fell magic, eventually losing ourselves to our dark markings and transforming into wretched monsters. Beasts with no mind. No control. Some worse than others—some with claws and horns and venom— some so malevolent they hunted down children and feasted on their flesh.

And the cursed could change at any time. I had worn my curse mark for my entire life, all twenty years, but some transformed immediately. Some transformed in a few weeks. Would I change tonight? Tomorrow?

Most killed themselves before they turned.

Rylion motioned to the room a second time. "Right now, you're still a person. I won't treat you as anything but."

His confidence rocked me. I didn't know what to say.

I shuffled into the room and stared at all the amenities.

"Consider this your home," Rylion said as he stepped away from the door. "My brother and I will return by noon tomorrow, perhaps sooner. I suggest you rest. I'll bring more food with me then."

I nodded. He closed the door, leaving me to my new space. For a long moment, I stood and listened, keeping track of Wulf and Rylion until the front door shut and I knew I was alone.

I could run. I could take what I needed and flee to the next country over. Maybe then I could start a new life. No one would know me. No one would know I was cursed. But what would I do then? How long did I have before becoming a monster? Was there even a point to trying when everything could end in an instant?

Dying sunlight streamed in through the window, but the frost at the edges of the glass betrayed the chill of winter. I hated the window. I didn't want to be seen.

With frustration building, I stormed over and pulled the heavy drapes closed. Still, light shone through the cracks. Someone could still see in if they wanted. I walked over to the bed, pulled off the top quilt, and threw it over the drapery rod, further covering the lone window until all was darkness.

I waved my hand and lit the candle, pleased to see the fire spring to life as quick as it had. I had feared, perhaps irrationally, that I might have lost my connection to magic. It had been so long since I had used it... Father had never wanted anyone to know.

The bed invited me to rest, but I was still uneasy. I didn't want anyone to find me. The thought of being out in the open, on top of a mattress, was anything but comforting.

Instead, I pulled off the last blanket and flipped the bed onto its side with a bit of struggle. The light cork wood and thin straw mattress shouldn't have been a problem to move, but in my weakened state, I was surprised I even managed. My body ached from the effort, and I promised myself I would rest once I was satisfied.

I dragged the mattress off and pushed it into the corner. Then I tilted the lightweight bed frame up and against the wall, creating a mock cave. I placed the blanket of stars inside, and used the sheets to create the fourth wall of my enclosure. I crawled inside the tiny space—a space devoid of light—and curled up into a ball, my breath warming me with each passing second.

The confinement reassured me. No one could see. No one knew I was here. It was safe.

I snuffed the candle with a thought.

Before I rested, I whispered a prayer to the gods of old.

"Please," I said. "Not tonight. If I must turn, if I must be a monster, be it some other time—some other place. I do not want to harm them."

I closed my eyes and gave in to sleep.

CHAPTER TWO

The sound of doors closing pulled me from my sleep.

Although I couldn't see the sky, I knew it was the dead of night. The darkness of my makeshift cave comforted me as I listened to the movement throughout the house. Muffled voices drifted into my room, but I couldn't understand their words. Rylion's tone was among them, and that fact reassured me.

I crawled out of my hiding place and stood. The small amount of food, coupled with the rest, had done wonders for my energy. I was still starving, but I was no longer on the edge of death.

Unable to see, I grabbed the star-covered blanket and shuffled forward, feeling along the wall until I made it to the door. Once I exited my room, fire from the parlor illuminated the hall with a dim orange glow. The black shadows that lingered in the nooks and crannies shifted with the flicker of the light, moving like they had a life of their own.

I walked down the hallway and stopped at the threshold of the parlor door. The sofa rested up against the wall, allowing for a wide space in the middle of the room, but I didn't venture in. I waited, half-tucked behind the doorframe.

"The mountain will have a considerable amount of snow," Wulf said.

He and Rylion stood near the back of the room, their attention on a man in front of the hearth. The man—who was everything sturdy and stout—had a thick beard, trimmed neat, and disheveled mud-brown hair marked with gray and white. He was older, beyond his prime, but not yet done with life. His arms bulged with muscle, and even through his heavy clothing, I could sense his strength.

"It's nothing we can't handle," the man said, the gruff timbre of his voice similar to Rylion's. He held his hands out, palms open, and warmed himself with the heat of the fire. "Mountain training will do everyone good."

Rylion crossed his arms. "You're sure she's up there?"

The man nodded. "I've followed the trails, and the traders up north say the mountain is swarming with birds. Some call it an infestation."

"We'll have plenty to hunt then."

"My thoughts exactly."

The floor creaked with my weight, and I ducked around the corner, my heart rate high.

"Who's there?" the older man asked. He unsheathed a knife—I would know that sound no matter the blade—and I couldn't bring myself to answer him.

"It's all right, Father," Rylion said, calm as ever. "She's the one I told you about. The one I picked up from the streets."

"The one who's cursed?"

"Yes."

I held my breath and rested my forehead on the hallway wall. I hated that Rylion had told someone else. I didn't want the information of my curse spreading, especially when some would come for my life. Why had Rylion told his father?

The man sheathed his weapon. "Come out here, girl. I didn't mean to startle you."

After a long exhale, I pushed away from the wall and

stepped around into the front parlor. Through sheer force of habit, I kept the blanket tight around my shoulders, hiding my curse mark and the rest of my body, ashamed anyone would see any part of me. The man stared at me with calculating dark eyes. His beard half masked his expression, but I swore it was a look of pity.

"You're young," he said with a grunt.

I ran a hand through my shoulder-length hair, knowing full well it was pointless to argue. Everyone assumed my age was far lower than the reality. I wanted to tell him how wrong he was, but I doubted he cared. I had the youthful appearance of a child, my mother had said. I should consider myself lucky. I didn't feel "lucky" when everyone patronized me, but such details were irrelevant.

My mother had always compared me to others, especially when family had visited. Snide remarks, mostly, all of which had been meant to showcase her disappointment with how I hadn't grown into a proper woman. I probably dwelled on my appearance more because of it.

"Father," Rylion said, drawing me out of my thoughts. "This is Artemis. Artemis, this is my father, Osmund Nasos."

"You made her wear a blanket?" Osmund asked. He waved his hand out. "You know Bryn kept some of his old robes in the back. Go fetch her some."

"I will," Wulf replied as he jogged from the room, eagerness in his flight.

I stepped toward the doorframe and leaned into the shadows. Not only had they taken me in and given me a room, but they were also providing me clothing? Why? I doubted even the selfless saints would have been as accommodating to one of the cursed.

Wulf returned with two sets of robes, one white and the other black. He walked over to me and held them out, like I should choose. I spotted the gleam of metal on the collar of both outfits—small, copper rings pierced through the fabric.

They were the robes of a scholar. The number of rings signified the number of years in study.

I took the black robes. Five rings adorned the collar.

"My uncle doesn't need these anymore," Wulf said. "They might be a little long, but you can keep them."

I held the clothing close and nodded.

"Maybe you should change and see how they fit. There's a tailor in town, we can get them fitted for a woman."

Without saying a word, I stepped back and returned to my room.

The darkness greeted me with open arms, but I didn't want its company. I lit the candle.

Once certain I was alone and the door was firmly shut, I removed my blanket and ratty trousers and then changed into the robes. The rope belt for the waist and the cuffs on the long sleeves meant I could adjust the fit. The hood fell back between my shoulder blades, and the matching trousers went longer than my ankles, but I liked the outfit. The soft fabric reminded me of home.

Of course, nothing would feel completely right until I bathed, but that would have to wait.

The three in the parlor resumed talking. I snuffed the candle and cracked open the door, curious as to what they talked about when they believed they were alone. Was it about me? Were they secretly worried I would turn?

"We should leave by noon," Osmund said. "I've already informed the others. It'll get too cold to make the trek if we wait even a single day."

"This is sudden," Rylion replied. "Is the mountain lodge even prepped with supplies?"

"Some."

"Enough?"

"We'll make it work," Osmund said. "Bryn is still there, after all."

"You don't think you're being rash, Father? We can catch her come spring or summer."

Osmund grunted. "I've hunted her for years, and I'm not getting any younger. One injury and I may never recover at this point. I don't want to risk missing my opportunity."

"What about Artemis?" Wulf asked, interjecting himself into the conversation.

"I will ask her to join us," Rylion said.

Again, Osmund grunted. "Good. I will round up the others and secure us a cart. Meet me on the western road when you two are ready."

Good? He had said *good* to me joining them? Not even a word of worry? A word of doubt or uncertainty?

Their odd acceptance of my presence filled my mind with hesitation and speculation. Why were they so accommodating? Why didn't they fear me? I wanted to know, but I dreaded the answer, certain I would regret asking.

The stomp of someone walking down the hall sent a shiver down my spine. I jumped away from the door and hid in the shadows out of habit. When someone finally entered, I remained still and quiet, unwilling to reveal my presence before I knew who had come to speak to me.

"Artemis?" Rylion said.

"Yes," I replied, my tension waning. "I'm here."

"My father wants us to travel to Mount Regel for a hunt. I said you wouldn't have to run from soldiers or pursuers, and I mean to stand by my word. If you join us, I can make good on that."

He meant to protect me? A stranger?

"Why?" I asked, probably sounding more ungrateful than I felt.

"We could use another hand on the hunt."

"No, I mean, why do this for me?"

"If you had a destination you were traveling to, by all

means, continue on your way. But it didn't look that way to me. And like I said, we could use another hand."

That was it? I was a wayward soul, so he offered to give me purpose?

No one was that altruistic. My suspicion grew deeper with each moment, but a part of me wanted to believe him—gods, I wanted so much to believe him!—because if there were men like him, then I might be wrong about the cruel nature of the world.

"What would you have me do?" I asked. "I'm no hunter."

"There's always work to be done outside of the hunt. Meat to cure. Fires to maintain."

"Fires?"

"Mount Regel would be uninhabitable without them, yes."

I shuffled out from the shadows and stood at his side. Before I said anything, Rylion sifted through his pockets. He withdrew something and held it out, the faint light from the parlor outlining him enough for me to see his silhouette.

"Here," he said. "Jerky from the butcher. You should eat plenty before we make the trek."

My mouth watered at the mere mention of food. I took the meat and unwrapped the linen binding. I wanted to believe the situation was real. I wanted to believe he was a kind man helping me with no ulterior motives.

"I'll go," I said.

"Good to hear," Rylion replied. "We should get you cleaned up and we'll gather some things for you to take on the journey."

"Do you need more water?" Wulf asked me.

He offered his canteen.

I took the container and guzzled another round of liquid.

So delicious. I had been eating and drinking all day, but it all tasted wonderful. I was full, then hungry, then full—everything in short bursts, like my body sped through each process to consume as much as possible.

Rylion walked out of his quaint home suited in heavy armor. When he had taken me from the streets, I had thought he had worn full-plate mail, but I could see now he wore half-plate: metal pieces covered vital spots, held in place with adjustable leather straps, rather than covering his whole body from head to toe. His chest and legs had some protection, including thick greaves that guarded his shins. He wore gauntlets, sollerets, and a pauldron—a curved piece of steel armor strapped over his left shoulder.

It must have been a burden. That much weight would have prevented me from walking.

Wulf, on the other hand, wore leather in all the same places, cutting the weight of his gear to a fourth of what Rylion must have had. Wulf's was more practical, I thought, but it offered less protection.

Still, why wear such extravagant armor for hunting? It was rare for a buck to stand and fight.

Rylion secured a dark navy cloak over his shoulders. The garb covered him completely from the shoulders down to the dirt. When he walked over to join Wulf and me, the clink of his armor and the harsh rustle of his cloak followed his movements. His cloak looked like cloth, but it didn't flow with the wind or his movement. It hung straight, like it was weighted.

I stared at the garment. Rylion lifted an arm and allowed me to touch the edge.

The moment I felt the material, I knew why it defied the wind. There was chainmail woven on the inside. The cloak itself must have weighed an extra forty pounds. In total, I would have said Rylion dressed in a hundred, perhaps a hundred and twenty, pounds of metal. Could he truly expect to fight in such conditions?

Rylion looked me over. My bath had done me wonders. "You look like a scholar," he said.

I released his cloak and nodded. "I studied for thirteen years."

Wulf lifted both eyebrows. "*Thirteen years?* That has to have been expensive! Where did you study? Who instructed you?"

"It doesn't matter," I replied, curt.

Wulf went to say something else, but Rylion shook his head, silencing his brother. The conversation died. Better than talking about my past. It was best they didn't know who I was, or where I had come from. I would rather be a new person, anyway. Free to do whatever I wanted.

A fresh start—until I became a monster.

Rylion motioned with his head. I followed as he walked to the main road, Wulf on the other side of him. The warmth of the winter sun offered some comfort from the chill, but not enough. I shivered and crossed my arms tightly over my chest. I could only imagine the weather on Mount Regel.

"We keep warm gear in the lodge," Wulf said, like my thoughts were out in the open for all to read. "I'm sure we'll have something for you!"

His energetic voice was odd, considering the innocuous topic. I dwelled on that and didn't answer.

Rylion withdrew a red scarf from his satchel and handed it to me. "Here."

I recognized the piece of clothing. He had worn it the day he had taken me from the streets. I took the scarf, and without delay, I wrapped it around my neck. The vibrant color reminded me of embers.

"Thank you," I muttered.

It didn't take long for us to reach Osmund and his cart full of supplies, covered in heavy blankets. Five horses and four other people awaited our arrival. It was an awfully large group for a hunting party. Did they mean to run down a whole herd of animals? I kept my sarcastic comments to myself, but I couldn't help but wonder.

Rylion nodded to his father and then glanced over to the cart. "Do we have enough?"

"I got salts and spices," Osmund replied, tapping the wooden vehicle strapped to a large workhorse. "We'll catch the meat we need. I didn't bother with any of that."

"I guess if you're ready, we should depart."

"Indeed."

Osmund waved his arm, and the group urged the horses down the western road, toward Mount Regel, seated not so far in the distance. The white cap, visible thanks to the clear skies, was dappled with evergreen trees. I hadn't taken a moment to enjoy such sights in a long time.

Everyone walked—even Rylion, despite his gear—and I attempted to ignore the blisters on my feet as we marched forward. The road made it an easy trek, though. The rattle of the cart was a pleasant white noise that distracted me from darker thoughts. I liked having others close by, even if I didn't know them well. I could pretend I was a normal person.

I turned my attention to the four I had never met.

One man. Three women.

The man had blistered hands and dark stubble on his chin and neck. His oak-brown hair, pulled back in a short ponytail, was slick with sweat.

"Look what they have me carrying," the man murmured, walking close to a lean woman carrying a quiver. He motioned to his overstuffed pack. "They treat me like a pack mule."

"You're the handsomest pack mule I've ever seen," the woman replied. The smile on her heart-shaped face dispelled misery. "Handsome enough to take to bed."

The man huffed and fussed with the straps of his pack. "Shush, woman! What if the others heard such talk?"

"Would you prefer I treat you like an actual mule?" She cracked an imaginary whip.

"Enough of this silliness! The others will stare."

She laughed and leaned over to graze his cheek with a feather-touch kiss. The man blushed red enough to be seen from the mountaintop, but he didn't push her away or protest.

Wulf must have noticed my staring because he jogged to my side and pointed to the man and woman. "That's Steen and Lydia. They're married. Steen cures leather and cooks. Lydia sews and fletches arrows with the best of them."

Married? It explained their odd relationship.

Lydia's dirty blonde hair, held back in a tight braid, betrayed the fact she was a foreigner—or at least, not someone from the capital. Her bright blue eyes lit up whenever Steen spoke, though his gruff mumbles never seemed pleasant or joyful.

Another woman, small and frail, held the reins of the lead horse. I wouldn't have expected to find someone so delicate among a group of hunters. She kept herself swaddled in three heavy cloaks, but her narrow wrists were plain to see.

"That's Thea," Wulf said. "She cares for the animals. They all listen to her no matter how agitated they get. She has a gift, she does."

Thea's tiny frame, coupled with the light step of her walk, made me think the animals could easily topple her over if they wanted. The lead horse didn't try, however. It nickered and snorted when urged forward, but it never misbehaved.

Her beautiful caramel hair fluttered freely behind her, but she kept her head down, preventing me from seeing her eyes or facial expression.

The last woman had long ebony hair down to her waist. It hung straight, without flaw, and shone in the winter sun. She walked with her head held high and her gray eyes glued to the sky, almost as though she were lost in her own thoughts, wandering a path unseen by everyone else.

I would've said she looked like me, but the woman was much taller and willowy. She wore scholar's robes, however—six copper rings hung from the collar.

"And that's—"

The sounds of a hard gallop cut Wulf off before he finished. A rider up the road, near a fork, barreled toward us. The horse panted with each gallop and a dreadful feeling twisted in my gut.

No one rode that fast to deliver good news.

Thea stopped the horses and Osmund walked beyond the lead, waiting for the strange rider to draw near. Once she was close, I could tell it was a woman, and the more details I took in, the more I knew my intuition was proven correct.

She was covered in blood.

"Travelers," she cried, her voice half-cracking. "Up the road! It's up the road!"

Wulf and Rylion jogged to meet their father. The unfamiliar woman galloped to the group and reined in her mount, slowing the sorrel horse to a stop. The animal pranced and turned in place, its eyes wide and its brown coat spotted with dried blood.

"Osmund," the woman said. "Thank the gods! It's beyond the hills. It attacked the merchants. They didn't stand a chance."

The woman's quick, breathless speech left me anxious. She was so panicked, she could barely get her thoughts across, and most of the blood she wore likely wasn't her own. I stared for a bit longer, hiding behind the cart. She was missing a few fingers from one hand, and a fresh injury along the top of her scalp kept her brown hair wet with crimson.

"It'll head to town," she said, her hands shaking as she brushed clumps of hair from her face. Then she stared at her hand for a moment, as though noticing her injury for the first time.

"Is it one of the Forsaken?" Osmund asked.

"Yes. It's Forsaken."

"You're certain?"

"No doubt."

I ducked around the cart completely, terror filling me with a chill far worse than the winter.

The Forsaken. It was the name of the cursed once they had transformed into monsters. And one waited for us up the road; perhaps it was already on its way. No one enjoyed the sight of the Forsaken. Their twisted features filled my nightmares.

That would be me one day.

"How far from here?" Osmund asked.

"Half an hour. Maybe a little closer."

"You should get home, Frema. Take care of yourself."

"Be careful, Osmund. The beast... It—It was so fast..."

Her broken words pained my ears. What had happened to her up the road? I supposed I would never know. Frema rode her horse past our group, urging it into a full gallop. Never once did she look back.

"Rylion, Wulf," Osmund called out. "You heard her. Get the chains!"

His sons complied with his command. They walked to the back of the cart, and I stepped aside, curious about their behavior. Weren't we going to leave? Shouldn't we at least clear off the road? The Forsaken would surely kill us all if we gave it the opportunity.

Rylion and Wulf threw back the blankets covering the supplies. Half the cart carried barrels and boxes full of edible goods, but the other half held bear traps and wicked weaponry. I caught sight of chains with spikes, long stakes, and flails—objects crusted with blood—too large to be used against a man. Wulf struggled to haul some of the heavy equipment, but Rylion took the brunt of it and threw a long chain across the road. The others went about preparing the area, pulling the horses back and unsheathing weapons.

They meant to fight the beast.

I caught my breath as stunned realization gripped me.

They were hunters. Not *normal* hunters who sought caribou and elk, not with tools like theirs. They were hunters of the Forsaken. They hunted the monsters born from people cursed.

Of course! How could I have been so blind?

Half-plate armor for a hunting trip? A whole group of people for the hunt?

And that explained why they weren't afraid of me. They *wanted* me to turn. The god-king offered a reward ten times higher for the corpse of a Forsaken over the corpse of a cursed man. All they had to do was keep me around until I fell victim to the curse. Once I shed my old body, they would strike me down and collect their prize. Their kindness all made sense when the reward was the equivalent to six months of paid labor.

I turned and walked back toward the city, my breath short and shallow, and my steps quick and shaken.

Good—that was what Osmund had said when Rylion had told him I would accompany them. *Good.* I was sure he had imagined their next payment when he had said so. *You're so young*—that was what he had said. Now I knew what he had meant. *So easy to kill.*

All the signs had been there.

"Artemis!"

I picked up my pace and continued toward town. We weren't far. I would reach it soon enough. Then I would walk to the next kingdom, like I had planned before. I didn't want to be someone's bounty.

"Artemis!"

Rylion's voice. I stopped and waited, hoping I was wrong.

Hoping this wasn't the truth. He caught up to me, the clink of steel dredging up memories of the soldiers who had chased me all the way to his town. I could trust no one to be my ally —they were all out to manipulate or kill me. Every. Last. One.

Rylion walked to my side and placed a heavy hand on my shoulder. I jerked away and gritted my teeth.

"You hunt the Forsaken?" I asked.

He hesitated, perhaps confused. "Yes."

"And…" I took a moment to inhale. "And you plan to kill me once I turn?"

"Yes."

Gods, damn me. He didn't even deny it!

I knew it. Darkness and greed dwelled in the hearts of all men. But I had hoped. I had hoped Rylion and his family would be different. What a fool I had been to think such things. Like a child—a child who wanted to deny reality because it was too harsh and cruel to handle.

Without another word, I marched forward.

"Artemis," Rylion said.

I ignored him.

Would he kill me now that I was about to leave? Better some money than none. I wouldn't be surprised if he stabbed me in the back. The thought burned more than it should have. I had been a fool. A trusting, naïve fool.

CHAPTER THREE

"**W**ait," Rylion commanded, an edge of authority in his voice that hadn't been present before.

I froze.

Rylion once again walked to my side. A cloud passed overhead, washing us in shadow. I clenched my hands into fists and held my breath, ready for the confrontation. I was still thankful for his assistance on the side of the road, and a part of me wished I had never discovered it was all a ruse.

"Do you want to hurt people?" Rylion asked. "After you turn, I mean."

Yes.

That was what I almost said, but I bit back the answer.

I hated them. I hated the people who tried to use me for their own gain. I hated the people who wanted me dead. I hated the world for its rules and its curses. Maybe, if they knew suffering under the heat of my fire, then they would be sorry.

And sometimes I tasted the rage as it boiled beneath the surface of my thoughts, threatening to dominate my actions.

I had to remind myself I didn't want to harm anyone. I didn't want to become the very thing I hated. My loathing was born from a lifetime of mistreatments—I knew that. It tainted my perceptions, like a dark veil forever covering my eyes. I didn't want to despise myself, but some days I found it difficult.

I felt broken beyond repair.

"Artemis. Do you want to hurt people as a Forsaken?"

"No," I forced out.

"Then wouldn't it give you peace of mind knowing you won't? Knowing that we'll be there when you turn? That you won't live life as a monster?"

I stared at the road, watching the wind carry flecks of dirt into the shrubs.

I hadn't given it thought—the fact that I might live a life of twisted agony as a monster. That I might harm more people with my savagery. I had thought turning would be like dying. That I would cease and the monster would take my place. I didn't know for sure, and Rylion's point stood.

"That's how Thea and Steen feel," Rylion continued. "That's why they travel with us."

"Thea and Steen?" I whispered. Their hunting group was made of people who were cursed?

"Yes. When they turn, we'll be there to slay them too. And in some ways, hunting the Forsaken brings them a bit of redemption."

All the new information got me pensive. I didn't know there were bands of hunters made of cursed individuals. There would be a sense of security knowing my end would come quick.

"And if I decide to leave?" I asked.

"I won't stop you."

I choked up.

Really? He would let me leave? Did that mean he really saw me as a person first, and a bounty second? How would I ever know?

I unraveled the scarf from around my neck and held it out.

"Keep it," Rylion said.

With unsteady hands, I wrapped the garment back around my neck. The road stretched out before me, and I exhaled before continuing forward. I listened as I went. Rylion didn't move, not until I was more than a hundred feet away. When he turned, I heard the clink of his steel armor and the rustle of his chainmail cloak.

He was letting me leave. After giving me so much.

And he hadn't asked for anything in return.

I stopped and clung to the scarf. People had always expected things of me. My mother had wanted me to look a certain way, act a certain way—use my magic for her. My father had wanted my mother's favor, so he had trained me in magic and done as he had been told, manipulating me when I had come to him upset. My other family members had wanted my magic for themselves. The god-king and his Holy Guard wanted me dead. Hunters wanted my mark so they could collect their coin.

And the world wanted me to become a monster, if my curse was any indication.

Yet Rylion asked nothing of me? Not a single thing?

I turned around and jogged back down the road, the burning of my blistered feet momentarily subdued by my determination to be with him. I had to know what made him different.

When I reached his side, the cloud passed, and we were once again bathed in the glory of the sunlight. He smiled and welcomed me with a clasp to the shoulder.

But a heinous screech shattered the peace.

I knew the sound. It was the Forsaken, coming our way.

Rylion raced back to the cart, his focus on the far end of the road. I followed behind, hesitation in my step. Another soul-rending screech and my heart rate doubled. At the fork in the road, where the path disappeared behind a foothill, a merchant horse emerged, chased by a wicked creature running on many legs.

No, the creature didn't "run," it flew across the ground with lightning speed, far faster than any animal or man. And of course it would. The Forsaken had ten spindly legs with sharp claws that tore through the dirt and propelled it forward. It was a black reptile, elongated like a snake, but with the weight of three stallions. Its malevolent golden eyes, unblinking, focused straight ahead. The slits of its irises reminded me of a snake.

The monster ran with its mouth open, its maw soaked in blood—flesh and dismembered human limbs hanging between jagged fangs.

The Forsaken never slept. The Forsaken never grew full. They hunted for flesh, not because it sustained them, but because their fell magic compelled them to.

The reptile monster chased the stray horse with a bloodlust beyond comprehension.

The worst part—more disturbing than its speed or slithering movements or insatiable appetite—was the human face jutting out of the monster's skin. Every Forsaken had it… the face of their human self… somewhere on their body. It was a face frozen in time, twisted in horror and agony. This Forsaken had a man's face bursting out of its forehead, right between the bulging eyes, and the face's mouth hung agape in a silent scream.

Oh, gods, it was close. I took a few steps back, uncertain of my role.

The Forsaken caught the horse with a powerful crunch of its jaws. The mare lost her back legs from the force of the bite —the whinny that followed pained the ears. With only two legs, the horse writhed on the road, attempting to flee. The Forsaken lunged forward. With six of its ten legs, it vivisected the mare, ripped out her intestines, and gobbled down the innards with a sick gurgle as it filled its gullet.

Rylion moved forward and unsheathed a short sword from his belt. He stood behind the spiked chain and secured the top of his cloak to his shoulders, creating a heavy cape.

It didn't take long for the Forsaken to finish its victim.

The thin woman, Thea, led our animals to safety.

Wulf and Osmund climbed on top of our now horseless cart, a good seventeen yards from Rylion. Wulf held a short yew bow nocked with an arrow, while his father knelt and uncovered the last of the cart's cargo. He hefted a large compound bow, one with axles and a complex string system for powerful shots. It was nearly five feet from top to bottom, and the entire bow, even the axles, was carved from pure white bone. The silver bowstrings, taut and thin, glittered in the sunlight. I had never seen such a majestic weapon outside of the god-king's armory.

The Forsaken dashed toward the cart, stepping over the last shreds of the mare's fresh corpse.

"It's coming," Wulf announced as he took aim with his smaller yew bow.

Half a second later, he let loose an arrow. It whistled through the air and struck the Forsaken deep in its left golden eye. The organ popped, like a swollen pimple, spewing pus and blood across the dirt road.

The monster screamed, its long tongue thrashing out of its mouth, but it barely slowed. Wulf nocked a second arrow, drew, and fired. The arrow slammed into the other eye, ripping through the soft flesh. The eyeball ruptured, leaving the creature blind and infuriated.

And yet the Forsaken continued forward. It rushed over the spiked chain, tangling four of its ten legs in the dubious trap. The beast persisted, bleeding and cutting itself as it went. It snapped its fangs and was close enough that red spittle splattered across Rylion's armor.

Rylion stepped forward and swung his sword up with both hands. He cut into the Forsaken's throat, slicing through twisted scales and severing arteries. Despite the massive gouge in its flesh, the monster fought on. It slashed Rylion with two claws, but the metal pauldron on Rylion's shoulder protected him. When the Forsaken snapped and bit, Rylion ducked under its jaw and stabbed into its shoulder, pinning it back with his weapon.

Unable to see, the creature thrashed and rolled, lashing out at every angle. It struck Rylion twice in the process. His cloak and armor held fast, but the bash of the creature's limbs left Rylion bruised and bloodied in a matter of seconds. Still, he withdrew his sword and stabbed again, keeping the beast from charging forward.

Rylion was protecting the cart.

Wulf continued firing his arrows, but they never pierced the monster's scales.

I gritted my teeth, unsure of what to do. The four other hunters in our party stood with the animals far from the fight. They watched, rapt, and held their weapons close. But none of them looked like they could face the Forsaken. I had my magic, but how potent would it be in my weakened state? Then again, how long could Rylion stand against this monster?

Rylion dug his heels into the dirt, holding the Forsaken in place despite the creature's ravaging attack.

Osmund nocked a bone arrow in his massive bow.

When he pulled back on the draw string, I heard the strain of the weapon—Osmund's arms shook, and he clenched his jaw in solid concentration. The draw weight of the bow must have been intense. Normal bows required five to thirty pounds of strength behind the draw to send an arrow flying. Osmund's bow must have needed seventy to a hundred pounds, and that was just to get it fully extended. He held the string at full tension for two seconds before releasing.

The arrow pierced the air, not with a whistle, but a screech.

Perhaps the arrow would have torn through the monster's body, had Osmund not missed. The arrow continued far down the road, barely losing height as it traveled at a disturbing speed. Osmund cursed under his breath and nocked another arrow.

He had missed? *At fifty feet*? He must have had the gods' disfavor.

The Forsaken bashed Rylion and sent him hard to the ground. Rylion got up—one foot, then a knee, then the other foot—his fatigue plain for the world to see. He was strong, not many could match stances with the Forsaken, but the brief encounter had left him drained.

With one snap of its jaw, the monster ripped Rylion's cloak from his shoulders. The Forsaken thrashed its head from side to side, attempting to rend the garment through sheer force. The cloak never broke, or even tore, and Rylion used the distraction to pick up his sword and ready himself.

I couldn't stand it. Osmund struggled with his second arrow, and Wulf's continued shots hit the Forsaken, but without effect. Couldn't they do something more? Would they let Rylion die to this monster?

I rushed onto the road, despite the cries of the other hunters for me to halt. I got close to the Forsaken, its foul odor of blood and rot stinging my nose. When Rylion swung again, the creature deflected the blow with a swipe of its claw, slicing open Rylion's arm in the process.

He dropped his sword, and I knew he would be ripped to ribbons. I lunged for the blinded beast.

"Artemis, stay back!" Rylion shouted.

I slammed a single hand on the creature's side; the pulse of the monster throbbing under my fingertips.

My magic was divine—a gift straight from the gods of old —and its divinity overwhelmed the fell magic the Forsaken were made of. Even a brief second of my fire was enough to melt the hide of the beast, destroying organs and bones alike.

Flames erupted from my palm and washed straight into the monster's body. If I were stronger and not starved, maybe I could have done more, but the short burst of fire required all my energy. The flames liquefied a fourth of the monster's body, its blood boiling and spilling onto the road by the bucketful.

I fell to one knee afterward, my breath shallow and my hands shaking.

The Forsaken lashed at me with its tail, like a horse swatting a fly. I hit the bloody mud on the road, my side burning in agony. I took some satisfaction in the pained cry the monster let out. The hole in its side continued to gush blood as it curled in on itself to protect its new vulnerability.

The screech of Osmund's arrow cut through the Forsaken's screaming—and then the arrow found its mark, piercing so deep into the creature's monstrous skull that only half the shaft was visible once it landed. For a strained moment, the creature froze up. It twitched twice, stumbled around, and exhaled a putrid breath.

The Forsaken crumpled into a puddle of its own blood, its body massive enough to cause a splash. After a groan of agony, it died. Silence soon followed. Even the clouds in the sky held still as the creature settled with a slump.

I staggered to my feet, shaken, but relieved.

"Artemis!" Wulf jogged over. "Are you hurt?"

I glanced at my blood-soaked clothing and cringed. It took me a moment to remind myself it wasn't my blood—it was the monster's. I would be bruised from its attack, but I wasn't wounded.

"Out of the way!" Osmund said with a grunt.

He pushed me and Wulf aside and walked over to the corpse of the Forsaken. Rylion joined him, and so did the last woman—the tall one with the long, ebony hair whose name I hadn't heard. Osmund turned the creature's head and examined the frozen human face jutting through the scales.

The woman placed her palm on the forehead of the face, her thumb over one eye, and her fingers over the other. "You have paid for your sins, and now the gods will take you. May your good deeds be remembered."

"May your good deeds be remembered," Rylion and Osmund intoned in unison.

I was surprised to hear them offer a prayer. Most just burned the bodies of the Forsaken, not a hint of deference in their actions.

The woman removed her hand and motioned to Rylion. Despite his bleeding arm, he hefted his sword and plunged it into the forehead of the Forsaken. The monster's flesh around the human face sunk in and sputtered blood. After a quick circular cut, Rylion dug his hand into the creature and lifted out the skull of a man, the face affixed and stretched over the bone.

Not white bone, but black bone, a sign of the cursed.

Wulf took the skull and ran it back to the cart. The black skull was all that was needed to claim the bounty for killing the Forsaken. The rest of the creature was to be disposed of. It was the same with the cursed—taking the skin stained with the spiderweb marking was enough, the body needn't be intact.

Wulf placed the bloody object in a thick leather sack and closed it tight. Osmund whistled for the others and they returned with the horses.

"Will we bury him on the side of the road?" Rylion asked.

"We don't have much of a choice," Osmund replied. "If the god-king has a problem with it, he can come dig the thing up himself."

I stared at the gruesome corpse. "You won't burn it?"

"No. It's disrespectful. We always bury the bodies. They're back with nature then. Back to the true mother."

"But the god-king has decreed them evil and without redemption."

Osmund grunted and turned away, his lips pursed. Had I offended him? Without another word, he walked off. I didn't ask any more questions, but a piece of me wondered why they followed the ways of the old gods. Ancient teachings spoke of the curse being a punishment for otherwise good people, and that once a Forsaken died, they were once again a person worthy of joining the gods in a divine kingdom.

But the god-kings and god-queens claimed the opposite. All those who broke the decrees were forever damned. There could be no redemption.

Rylion stared at the monster for a moment and then turned his attention to me. I held my breath, ready for when he would confront me about my magic. He had been the only one close enough to witness the fire erupt from my palm and sink into the Forsaken. Even if he hadn't seen, wasn't he curious? I had obviously hurt the beast, but I carried no weapons...

His staring left me guilty, as though my continued silence was an act of subterfuge.

"I'm sorry," I muttered, unable to think of anything else. I couldn't tell them. No one was supposed to know.

Wulf jogged back to us and glanced between me and Rylion. "What happened?" he asked. "What caused the Forsaken to curl up like that? Everything flew by so fast."

Rylion shook his head, dismissing the comment. "We should focus on cleaning up and then be on our way." He held up his bleeding arm and showed Wulf where the Forsaken had sliced part of his metal gauntlets. The beast's razor claws had known no equal.

He had kept my secret. Rylion had helped me at every turn. I hoped my attack against the Forsaken was, in some small part, the start of my repayment for his kindness.

"Rylion!"

I turned and spotted Thea riding a horse to the road, her caramel hair practically glowing in the afternoon sunlight.

The animal stopped before it was within twenty feet of the fallen monster, and I didn't blame it. If the skull wasn't removed from the body, the Forsaken were known to rise again, sometimes empowered by the rage of their counterfeit death.

Thea leapt off the saddle and rushed to Rylion's side. She took his injured arm and immediately withdrew bandages from her satchel to tend to the bleeding.

"I was so worried," she said, her voice gentle and demure, but laced with a breathless anxiety. "These monsters get more perilous as the years go on. I've never seen one that big, or fast."

"I'll be fine," Rylion said. "Thank you for your concern."

He placed a hand atop her head—their difference in size highlighted. He must have been a foot and a half taller than she was, and three times her weight in muscle mass alone. As if aware of those facts, he touched her gently, stroking the length of Thea's hair with his knuckles.

I couldn't articulate why, but I disliked the sight. I turned away, my chest tight. Anger was a familiar companion. I hated how often it took hold of my thoughts, however. I tried to calm myself by walking away.

"Come!" Osmund shouted from the cart. He threw shovels to the other hunters. "We have a hole to dig! We need to get this done if we're going to continue to Mount Regel."

***

The setting sun engulfed the sky in a blaze of orange and red.

Our hunting party continued on the road, already half a day behind schedule. They had dug fast, even Rylion, despite his sliced arm, but the Forsaken was too big for a normal grave.

I faced Rylion. He fiddled with his heavy cloak while Wulf walked along next to him. Both brothers had dried blood stains across most of their clothes and skin. Everyone wanted to press forward, however, rather than bathe, so we did.

Wulf caught me staring. "I'm surprised you got involved," he said with a smile.

I nodded. It occurred to me I hadn't spoken much to Wulf, despite his pleasantness. I took a deep breath and said, "I'm impressed with your aim."

My statement came off stiff and forced, but Wulf smiled widely regardless.

"Thank you. I practice every day."

"Your father should as well."

I hadn't meant to sound so harsh and judgmental, but what else could I have said? Osmund had jeopardized Rylion's wellbeing with his faulty aim. He *should* have practiced more.

"My father has bad eyes," Wulf replied with a shrug. "Things are blurry for him, he says."

"Why don't you shoot his bone bow, then? It seems more effective than your tiny one."

"Me? Wield his bow, Calavandi? I can't. It's much too heavy. I tried, but I can't draw the strings."

That made sense. Wulf was smaller than his father, albeit taller. I turned to Rylion. "Why don't you shoot your father's bow? Surely, you would have no problems."

"My eyesight isn't much better than my father's," Rylion replied. "Things are blurry at a distance. It makes for poor aim."

Wulf laughed. "I'm the lucky son. Perfect eyesight, just like my Uncle Bryn. I can hit a bird midflight up to a hundred yards away."

Impressive. Still, it was unfortunate that one son would get the brawn and the other clear sight.

Through the shadowy sunset, a glimmer of blue light caught my eye. My heart sank the moment I recognized the King's Stone. They were stationed all over the Kingdom of

Luka, but I had hoped to avoid them. The King's Stones were tall pillars of black obsidian with the god-king's decrees etched into the side. The words glowed with a faint blue light once the sun set. Anyone could see the glow from half a mile away, even in harsh weather.

As we approached, the group turned toward the stone. If we wanted to make the best time, we should have headed straight for the mountain, but alas, we did not.

"What're we doing?" I asked.

Wulf pointed to the King's Stone. "We should pray here and check to see if the god-king has issued any more decrees."

"He doesn't make new decrees often," I said, curt.

"Yeah, but you can never be too careful. We need to know what they are so we don't get cursed."

I knew he didn't mean to insult me. Still, it irritated me, even if the fear was completely rational.

If anyone in Luka broke any decree, they became cursed. And then, be it fast or prolonged, they transformed into one of the Forsaken. The punishment was unwavering. No exceptions.

The horses drew the cart to the base of the black obsidian pillar. The structure was fifteen feet high and four feet wide on every side—the perfect square pillar with corners rounded enough not to cut. The glowing blue words shone with the god-king's decrees, in ascending order from when they had been given. At the base of the pillar was the first decree uttered by God-King Eliezer—the same first decree made by every new god-king.

Cursed be the man who commits regicide.

And the next two decrees were similar to other god-kings, but not always repeated.

Cursed be the man who disobeys the god-king's direct command.
Cursed be the man who emigrates from the Kingdom of Luka.

If the citizens couldn't kill the god-king, or disobey the god-king's orders, and couldn't leave the god-king's realm, he had total control until he died and the next god-king took the throne, or so the reasoning went.

The next two decrees were also standard fare.

Cursed be the man who commits matricide.
Cursed be the man who commits patricide.

I once had asked my tutors why the god-king didn't craft a decree that forbade all killing. The tutors told me that was too rigid. No one would want to serve in the god-king's armies if there were a decree that forbade killing. I supposed the tutors were correct—and so the only three people a person could not kill were the god-king, their mother, and their father.

Cursed be the man who lies with another before marriage.
Cursed be the man who lies with an animal.
Cursed be the man who lies with a corpse.
Cursed be the man who lies with the Forsaken.
Cursed be the man who lies with a child less than the age of ten.
Cursed be the man who commits adultery.

God-King Eliezer had always been disturbed by odd stories of the bedroom, especially the thought of unfaithfulness. His decrees on the matter didn't surprise me in the least.

Cursed be the man who steals from a member of the god-king's court.

Very specific, but it, too, didn't surprise me. He couldn't forbid *all* stealing, not when the punishment was on par with death itself. A simple stolen thimble wasn't worth the rise of a Forsaken. The roads of Luka would become clogged with corpses.

Cursed be the man who herds another's livestock and sells them for money.
Cursed be the man who does not make good on a debt within five years' time.
Cursed be the man who drinks in a tavern after pledging himself in service of the god-king.

All god-kings and god-queens had civil laws meant to keep the kingdom in functioning order. They weren't always as specific, but God-King Eliezer had made it clear he thought his citizens should trust each other when it came to sheep, cattle, coin, and his personal servants.

Cursed be the man who hunts the summer lioness.
Cursed be the man who hunts the pronghorn.
Cursed be the man who hunts the golden warbler.
Cursed be the man who hunts the moonlight starling.
Cursed be the man who hunts the silver hare.

The last five decrees were gifts. God-King Eliezer uttered a new decree for each subsequent wife he took, giving them each the power to forbid one animal from being hunted. The silver hare was his current wife's favorite animal, and the beast was mounted on all her family's banner flags.

I wondered how long the list would grow. God-King Eliezer seemed to be running out of patience when it came to his wives bearing him a child. He didn't care about the gender or health—he just wanted a child. His previous queen had only lasted eighteen months.

Osmund walked to the pillar and placed his hand against the side. Divine magic coursed through the cold stone—reading wasn't required to understand the decrees. Once an individual placed their hand upon the pillar, the intent became clear, straight to their thoughts. No word games or semantics could be played to get around it. When the decree stated a man could not "lie" with another, the King's Stone conveyed the sexual intent, not the physical act of lying side by side. When the decree stated a man could not "hunt," the King's Stone conveyed the requirement of killing the animal, not just stalking it through the woods. And when the decrees stated "man," it meant all of mankind, not restricted to a specific gender.

Once Osmund had his information, he pulled his hand back and ambled to the cart. Rylion and Wulf gave the King's Stone a long stare before joining their father. I stood a bit longer, staring at the text.

"You're cursed, aren't you?"

I tensed. The man standing next to me was a member of our hunting group—Wulf had said his name was Steen. His oak-brown hair was slicked back, and the stubble on his chin and neck seemed to have gotten thicker over the course of the day. I had yet to say a word to Steen, and *this* was how he greeted me? Talking about my curse? I narrowed my eyes and returned my gaze to the pillar. I didn't have to answer him.

"I know you are," Steen said under his breath. "Rylion always treats us cursed a little differently than he treats normal folks."

Again, I remained quiet.

"You know I'm cursed, too, right? I'm sure one of the others has told you by now."

I glanced around. The sun crested the mountains in the distance, and purple darkened the height of the sky. A few peddlers and travelers rested not far from the King's Stone—forty, fifty feet away. Less than ten people, but still enough to spread rumors. Steen kept his voice low, and I doubted anyone had heard, but I wished he wouldn't even voice his thoughts.

"I stole from a man," Steen said as he laced his fingers together and placed his hands on top of his head. "I didn't know he belonged to the god-king's court. That was five years ago, back in the City of Gourna."

I held the red scarf close. Steen shared Wulf's lean frame, but he didn't hold himself like a warrior. I vaguely remembered Wulf saying something about him being a crafter or a cook, but the details eluded me. I wished Steen would leave me alone.

"What did you do?" Steen asked. "To become cursed, I mean."

"I don't know," I said, hoping the man would be satisfied.

Steen glowered. "You don't know?"

"No."

"Was your crime that bad? So awful you can't talk about it?"

I offered the man a glare. "I was born cursed."

Steen snorted and then laughed once. He shook his head. "That's rich. You must think you're real clever. I should start using that too. I didn't break any of the god-king's decrees—*I was born cursed!*" He chuckled, though in a mocking, cruel sort of way that got under my skin.

I had touched ten different King's Stones and read over his decrees more than I would have cared to admit. Nothing offered me an explanation for my cursed state. Nothing. It was a mystery that had plagued my thoughts since I had been old enough to grasp the situation.

Steen's response wasn't a surprise. No one ever believed me, save the people who had known me all my life. But that number dwindled with each passing day.

The heavy beat of hooves accelerated my heart rate.

The nearby peddlers and travelers pointed to the far end of the road.

A man ran toward us, but he didn't last long. Soldiers on horseback chased him down, the lead soldier going so far as to slice open the man's back with the edge of his halberd. Once the man hit the dirt, the warhorse stomped down, crushing bones and splattering the road with gore.

The soldiers weren't local city soldiers, militia, or even hunters, like Rylion—they were the god-king's Holy Guard, the most elite soldiers in all of Luka—soldiers tasked with killing the cursed and the Forsaken.

The merchants backed away from the sight, but a few cheered for the violence.

"Kill the cursed," one woman said with a chant-like tone. "They're evil!"

"Evil," another merchant agreed. "Vile!"

The soldier who led the Holy Guard, the one who had cut down the fleeing man, was someone I recognized. Alexavier

Lowell—the kingdom's *Scourge*—a warlord in charge of carrying out the god-king's punishments.

He was the one who had led the hunt for me after my father had been killed.

He was the man who had cut off my shirt and told me I could "have a head start" before he would come looking for me.

Unfortunately, my divine fire didn't burn his flesh, no matter how many times I had tried.

I jogged back to the cart, sweat soaking my blood-stained clothes.

I hadn't thought Alexavier would find me here. I thought he had gone in the other direction, toward the bustling cities along the trade routes.

Wulf and Osmund glared at the Holy Guard, tense in every regard, but Rylion looked me over with a keen eye. "Don't worry," he said. "Nothing will happen while we're around."

"They've come to kill me," I whispered, almost tripping over my words in my haste to speak. "Me *specifically*. They know who I am. That's why they're here."

CHAPTER FOUR

Rylion turned his attention to the god-king's Scourge and frowned, seemingly unimpressed, almost dismissive. Without saying a word, he removed his heavy chain-mail cloak and threw it over my shoulders. The garment was too much for my frail frame, and I almost tumbled over.

"This won't be enough," I whispered. "The Scourge knows me. I must hide."

Rylion glanced around at our barren surroundings. "I want to help you, but we might draw attention to ourselves if we leave now."

What could we do? If he couldn't come up with a plan fast enough, I would have to.

"The cart," I muttered. "Maybe with the weapons. Please."

Rylion walked to the back of the cart.

"Wulf," he called out. "Come here."

His brother hustled over, a slight smile on his face. "Yes?"

"Stay here and tie the weapons down but don't finish with the task until the Holy Guard has left."

"Why?"

Rylion motioned me onto the cart. Then he pulled the

weapons close—the long chain, three swords, a pike, a quiver of arrows, and two spears—and gently pushed me back until I was sitting next to them. He used his cloak to cover me completely, with only the weapons sticking out at either end.

"Is this what you meant?" he asked.

I replied with a single nod.

"You mean we're to hide her?" Wulf whispered.

"Don't let the soldiers know," Rylion said. "She's small enough to fit in among the weapons."

Wulf stared. "Perhaps…"

I hated my smaller frame for a myriad of reasons, but I supposed the ability to hide made it an advantageous trait at times. The faint musk of blood irritated my nose, however. It only became worse as Wulf tied one end of the cloak and then started with the other.

I peeked around the other edge of the cloak, trying to keep an eye on the Holy Guard's activity.

"Do you need assistance?" the tall woman asked.

"Thank you, Caprice," Rylion said. "Please help my brother tend to the equipment. I'll be right back."

I had never spoken with Caprice before, but the prayer she had offered to the dead Forsaken still rang in my ears. She took a seat on the edge of the cart, dignity in her posture, her white robes cleaner than the rest. She fumbled with the ties Wulf made, undoing everything so she could do it all over again.

The chainmail cloak weighed me down, and I soon found it difficult to breathe deeply. Restless energy flooded my veins. I wanted to get up and run, but I remained motionless, as Rylion wanted. The whinny of our horses didn't help my mood. They grew ever more anxious as Alexavier and the Holy Guard drew near, and everyone knew why. The Holy Guard didn't ride normal stallions or mares—they rode twisted hybrids, the offspring of horses and the Forsaken.

Sinister Beasts, or so they called them. Abominations.

A shudder ran down my spine when I contemplated such a breeding session.

The sinister horses had black coats and sharp cloven hooves, much like deer. And their faces… it took a man with a strong amount of willpower to look at them. The Sinister Beasts had two sets of eyes. One set was normal in every regard for a horse, but the second set was a pair of *human* eyes. They stared with an unblinking intensity that sent shivers down the spine.

The beasts stood a foot taller than most horses, and their breath smelled of raw flesh, no matter their diet. Truly, they were terrible creatures unfit for the world.

Alexavier spurred his fell mount toward the cart, and I held my breath. His full-plate armor, styled with the god-king's heraldry of thorns, refused to reflect most of the setting sun's light. It was crafted from King's Stone and then dipped in black oxide, muting all reflection and giving his armor a matte ebony finish. Same with all the Holy Guard's armor. The men appeared to be shadows of warriors—dark apparitions that followed the god-king's will.

Despite his attire, Alexavier and I shared a handful of physical traits. His black hair, tied back and visible without his helmet, was the same coal shade as mine. Even his bronze skin was the same hue as my own. But his dark eyes matched the inkiness of his pupils, and he had the physique necessary to wear his metal armor.

To my surprise, Alexavier urged his animal to a halt and stared straight down at Rylion's father.

"Osmund," he said. "I did not expect to see you on these back roads. What a pleasant surprise."

Osmund straightened his belt and gave Alexavier the once-over. He sneered at the Sinister Beast and then met Alexavier's gaze with a glower. "I live in the town of Ludlow. I have for some time. It's you who is out of place here."

"You reside in Ludlow? That backwater slum? My, how the mighty have fallen."

"And here you are, running down men without a second thought."

Alexavier narrowed his eyes. "That man would've become a monster. And it's the god-king's will that I slay all monsters. Surely, you don't want innocent people harmed, even by accident."

The nearby merchants nodded at the sentiment, but no one uttered a word.

Rylion walked over to his father and took a position at his side. He offered Alexavier a nod, but he kept his words to himself. No greeting. No smile. The tense atmosphere thickened with each passing moment.

"We're ready to leave, Father," Rylion said, breaking the silence. "Once we finish securing all our weapons, and Steen finishes tending the animals."

Osmund and Alexavier stared at the back of the cart. I made an art of stillness as I held my breath, even while Wulf took his time tying the ends of the sharp weapons with thick cloths. Alexavier's gaze lasted half a second before he returned it to Osmund. He dismissed Wulf and Caprice tending to the weapons as unimportant. My panic waned, but I refused to take even a shallow breath.

The rest of the Holy Guards dealt with the corpse of the cursed man like most would. They stabbed and defiled it before readying a quick fire on the side of the road.

Alexavier offered a forced smile. "You've grown old, Osmund. You should have stayed in the god-king's service."

"I've grown wise, boy," Osmund said with a grunt. "The same can't be said for you."

Alexavier clenched his jaw. He was old—older than me, at least—but he had retained a youthful appearance, whereas Osmund had the gut and gray beard hairs of a man his age.

And I knew Alexavier well enough to have experienced his hubris. He wouldn't care for Osmund's disrespect.

"I see you've taken to the role of backwater peasant quite well," Alexavier said. "But I would have the tongue of a peasant who didn't address me as Knight Captain Alexavier Lowell, Scourge of the God-King Eliezer. So know your damn place, Osmund, or I might be forced to put you in it."

"My father meant no disrespect," Rylion said, interjecting himself into the conversation. "We've had a long day and we'll be traveling through the night."

Alexavier examined Rylion's bloodied armor. His sinister horse didn't whinny or nicker—it snarled and shook its head, its human eyes drawn to the splatters of crimson as well.

"You help your father hunt the Forsaken?" Alexavier asked.

"That's right."

"Perhaps you can help me. I'm looking for a young woman. Thin. Black hair. Someone who looks like they hail from the capital city."

"What of her?"

"She's cursed." Alexavier pulled a piece of parchment from a satchel hanging off his mount's saddle. "And she's dangerous. God-King Eliezer will pay ten times the standard reward for her corpse. Look here. Can you read? It's a message from the god-king himself." Alexavier handed the parchment over with a flick of his wrist.

Rylion took it. "I see. Dangerous, you say?"

"That's right. She killed five of my men."

"Of the Holy Guard?" Rylion asked, surprise in his tone. Wulf glanced at his brother. Osmund grew tense. He folded his arms over his chest, and his frown deepened.

"Yes. Men of my Holy Guard."

"Because you were hunting her?"

"Because she is unstable," Alexavier said. "Don't think to

pity her. Beware those who know remorse, boy. Good men have no need for the emotion."

"Of course," Rylion intoned. "And what name does this woman go by?"

"If you can get her to speak, she would introduce herself as Artemisia, but the woman is quiet. You'll know her by the curse mark over her heart and shoulder."

I held Rylion's cloak tightly. Perhaps I should have taken a false name, or maybe conducted myself as a mute. Either way, I couldn't take back my actions. I had told Rylion my true name, and now they knew a fraction of my crimes against the god-king.

"I don't know the woman you seek," Rylion said as he handed back the parchment.

His lie on my behalf stilled my thoughts and slowed my breathing.

Alexavier exhaled. "If you do find her, I guarantee there will be a position on the Holy Guard waiting as a further reward. You have the look of a warrior I could rely on."

"Thank you, but I'm content in Ludlow."

"Only fools are content in a place such as Ludlow. Do not scorn ambition."

"If I find the woman you're looking for, I'll keep your offer in mind."

"Good," Alexavier said as he urged his mount away from the cart. "Finish that," he shouted to his soldiers. "We've spent far too much time here."

The soldiers hastened their actions, and the few who weren't busy joined Alexavier as he rode by the cart. The Holy Guard had just killed a man for being cursed. They didn't wait for a person to become one of the Forsaken. If Alexavier had known Osmund harbored so many cursed individuals, I assumed the encounter would have turned bloody.

Steen urged the horses toward Mount Regel. The Holy

Guard left in the opposite direction, but I couldn't watch them go for long, not while wrapped in the chainmail cloak. I waited for several minutes afterward before sitting up and removing my cover. Wulf smiled and Caprice brushed off some of the dust from the cart.

A chill breeze washed over the land. Plants curled in on themselves and woodland creatures scurried into warm dens. I huddled in Rylion's cloak. The blue fabric was ripped—no doubt by the Forsaken—but the chain mail of the garment was completely intact. No harm. Not a single link dented or scratched. I squinted to get a better look at the material, but it was much too dark. Something about it wasn't normal…

"We shouldn't be travelin' these roads at night," Lydia said, startling me. She walked to the back of the cart, an earthen quality to her braided hair. She wore dirt-stained pants under her skirt.

She continued, "Don't you know about these parts?" Her voice had a thick molasses quality about it. "Brigands watch the mountain roads. They like findin' merchants after the Forsaken run 'em for a chase."

We weren't merchants and we didn't look helpless. What was she afraid of?

Thea walked up to the group, her small frame trembling under the many layers of her clothes. Then she turned to me and offered half a smile. "Hello."

I nodded but said nothing.

"I need to apologize," she said. "I thought that because you wore Bryn's old robes, you were a man. Terribly silly of me. My name is Thea Yellahjar."

"Of course I'm not a man," I drawled.

"Well, yes, I see that now, but…"

Silence.

Even Wulf rubbed at his neck, like he couldn't decide the etiquette for the situation.

It grated on my nerves. No one had anything to say after

that? I moved back onto the cart, squeezed my body between barrels, and rested my head in the corner. It was uncomfortable, but I would rather sleep and I couldn't do it out in the open. Vulnerability bred anxiety within me.

Wulf returned to his brother's side. Caprice, Lydia, and Thea muttered between themselves. No doubt I was the topic of their conversation.

It didn't matter. Alexavier marched farther away with each second. I hoped I would never have to see him again.

The rustling of feathers woke me.

I opened my eyes and sat up. In an instant, I spotted the birds. So many birds. Dozens flew overhead in a large group that swirled and shifted with the wind, their cloud of shadows blotting out the morning sun. Some were large, some bulbous, others small. For a moment, I thought I was dreaming—a handful of birds that had six legs or three-part beaks—but the cold air stung my nose and I knew I was awake.

The birds were Sinister Beasts, offspring of a Forsaken and an animal. All of them.

Shifting out of Rylion's cloak, I made my way to the edge of the cart. Snow covered the road and the wheels occasionally slid, but the horses walked with a steady confidence, as though they had traveled this path before. I stepped down from the back and struggled to keep my balance. The packed snow had become slick ice.

The cart continued on without me as I struggled to remain upright. I turned my head and saw Wulf, Rylion, and Caprice trailing far behind the cart. I waited for them, baffled by Rylion's decision to keep his heavy armor on, despite the harsh weather.

When they reached me, Wulf smiled. "You're awake." He

motioned to Caprice. "I never managed to introduce you to Caprice. She's a priestess of the old gods from the Kingdom of Saileer."

Caprice gave me a quick nod.

She hailed from a different kingdom? And worshipped the old gods? An odd combination I had never seen before. She must have been cursed, like Steen and Thea. Most god-kings and god-queens prohibited their citizens from leaving their kingdoms.

Cawing and crowing overhead cut the conversation short. A few sinister birds swooped close, hissing with unrivaled bloodlust. Some looked like crows, others like vultures—so many different breeds—all of them swarming together. I would hate to be the target of their mass attack.

"We're on the right track," Caprice murmured, her eyes on the sky. She brushed her long hair back with her slender fingers. "There are more birds here than a week ago."

"Hm," Rylion replied.

"Your father suspects she's up near the evergreen forest, drawing all the birds with her musk."

"I hope he's right. We should find her before the beasts pour off the mountain."

I rubbed my arms through my robes and increased my gait in order to keep up with the others. For a long while, we didn't speak. My stomach churned, rumbling in a foreign language. I ignored it, but felt every syllable.

"Do you know much about the Forsaken?" Wulf asked me. "You studied for all those years, after all."

"I do," I said, holding back the chatter of my teeth.

"Do you know why this is happening? I've never known a Forsaken to mother so many terrible offspring. And the birds… They defied their migration to stay and mate with her. Their frozen corpses dot the forests."

"The Forsaken take on aspects of the sin," I said, keeping my gaze down toward the snow. "The Forsaken you fought on the road had many legs and hands. Perhaps it once was a thief—greedy and grasping at things without permission. It attacked the merchants, after all, and it had an agile swiftness to its movement."

"What do you think of… the Forsaken we're hunting?"

I stared up at the birds. "She mates frequently, and with any bird, regardless of its breed. Her sin must be of a sexual nature. Adultery, if I had to guess. Perhaps she was a whore."

"*Enough*," Rylion said, his tone thick with anger.

I turned to face him, but he didn't return my gaze. His attention remained straight ahead, his jaw tight. Wulf glanced over at his brother, anger plain on Rylion's face.

"It wouldn't hurt for me to know," Wulf said. "I can handle it."

Rylion shook his head. "It doesn't matter."

"Well, it matters to me. You and Dad won't talk about it. All I have is speculation."

"I said *it doesn't matter*. We'll discuss this no further."

Wulf grabbed his brother's shoulder and forced him to stop. "Why do you hide this from me?" His whole body tensed, and the snow around us shifted with the rage— flurries swirled about. The two brothers, while similarly tall and athletic, seemed different in that moment. The small curls of Wulf's hair were tipped with cutting ice, and Rylion tensed his broad shoulders, as still as snow.

Caprice and I stopped, then I moved away, distancing myself from a conflict that wasn't mine.

Rylion glowered but didn't say a word. When met with silence, Wulf released Rylion and stormed down the road, his breath coming out in harsh, misty rasps.

Caprice rubbed her elbows and then continued onward. She motioned with her head, indicating I should follow, but I didn't know her, and I certainly didn't trust her. I preferred Rylion, even if he was troubled and angry. Perhaps Caprice sensed my reluctance. She turned away and continued on without me.

I lingered back with Rylion until everyone was out of earshot.

Rylion didn't move. He stared at the snow—which had calmed—and I walked to his side.

Finally, he acknowledged me with a hard gaze. "Can I ask a favor?"

I held his scarf tight. "Anything."

"You haven't even heard my request."

"Alexavier would have gutted me, and although you could have gained a substantial reward for turning me in, you didn't. Is it such a surprise that I would grant you a favor?"

Rylion half-smiled. "My father has told me a great number of stories that involve Alexavier, the God-King's Scourge. I'll trust my instinct over Alexavier's word. I don't think you mean us harm."

"What is your favor?"

"Don't indulge my brother's curiosity. If he asks you about the Forsaken, especially the one on this mountain, feign ignorance or refuse to answer, I care not which."

The fell birds circled overhead. I stood closer to Rylion and shivered. "I won't speak to him about the Forsaken. But…"

"Yes?"

"Why?" I asked.

Rylion heaved a heavy sigh.

I shook my head. "Forget I asked. It's none of my business."

"You'll know soon," he intoned. "And I should have told you by now. The Forsaken we're hunting is my mother."

CHAPTER FIVE

The walk up the mountain burned my legs. My thoughts dwelled on Rylion's mother. His treatment of the cursed made more sense to me now. I wondered how long she had been marked before she had turned—and how Rylion had lived with her fear of turning.

Had she been a whore? I couldn't bring myself to ask. Rylion clearly didn't want to discuss it. But I could understand Wulf's frustration now. He was hunting his mother, but he didn't know why she had been cursed. What a terrible mystery to have hanging over one's head.

I chewed on jerky as we traveled together in silence. Once I'd had food, my body stayed heated despite my lack of proper winter clothing. I was a child of fire, and it coursed through my veins. It kept me warm, no matter the temperature, so long as I had the energy to maintain it. It was the reason I had fared so well out in the snow while Alexavier had hunted me. Up until I had reached the edge of starvation.

I glanced over at Rylion. He didn't seem to notice the cold. No shivering. No complaining. I wondered if his muscles shielded him from the discomfort or if he was merely accustomed to it.

We reached the others, despite our slow pace, due to the horses needing a rest. A snippet of the conversation broke my thoughts and dragged me back to the present.

"Can you imagine bein' the next god-queen?" Lydia asked, her accent distinct from everyone else's. "I know what I'd decree. *Cursed be the man who mistreats his work animals.*"

Thea giggled and stroked the mane of the lead horse. "I like that."

"That's the first thing you think of?" Steen asked with a huff. "The damn animals? *Cursed be the man who acts like a pompous prick and thinks he's better than everyone else,* that's what I'd decree."

Lydia smiled at her husband. "That right? What else?"

"*Cursed be the man who can't fit into his trousers.* That'll teach those fat, arrogant noblemen not to eat so much."

Osmund, sitting at the front of the cart, patted his protruding gut. "I always knew this belly would get me into trouble."

The others chuckled, their casual attitude infectious. I relaxed a bit, despite the soreness in my legs and feet.

The sun reached its peak in the sky at the same time I spotted the lodge nestled along the mountain road. The sturdy two-story building had a rustic charm unlike anything at the ironwork capital. Smoke billowed out of the numerous chimney stacks that dominated the lodge's roof, and I admired the sturdy craftsmanship. There must have been ten rooms—a rather large building for something so remote.

The horses huddled close to the outdoor wood furnace, and I understood then what Rylion had meant about the fires. The surrounding forest must have provided the much-needed wood, but my magic could work even without fuel for the fires to consume.

"My uncle takes care of this place," Rylion said. "He spends his days here year-round. You should find it comfortable."

"Year-round?" I asked.

"Yes."

"An odd profession for a man who was once a scholar."

Rylion glanced at me and then returned his gaze to the lodge. "Hm."

I narrowed my eyes, but I said nothing. I wore his uncle's robes—the metal rings alone told me he had studied for five years. It was a hefty sum of money to pay for tutors and books, even for a single year. Then again, Osmund must have made a substantial bit of coin hunting the Forsaken, so I could understand how they could afford the training, but why squander the knowledge by living in the middle of nowhere? Why not become a bureaucrat or scholar in the capital city? Talented individuals could even become members of the god-king's court.

I would have asked, but the more I got to know Rylion, the more I realized he preferred to keep quiet about other people's lives.

We walked up to the main door of the lodge. It was a solid piece of wood made from a thick trunk. Heavy wrought-iron hinges fastened the whole edifice together. We would need a battering ram to shatter the damn thing.

Rylion pushed it open with little effort and motioned me inside. I scurried in and stopped when I spotted the other members of our party gathered at a long table by the fireplace. They hushed their discussions and fell silent the moment Rylion closed the door.

I backed up to his side. I could sense it in their stares—they had something they wished to say to me. I didn't like it.

"Rylion," Osmund said, his gruff tone terse and strained. "We need to discuss Artemis."

He spoke as though I weren't in the room.

"There's nothing to discuss," Rylion stated.

The others—Lydia, Thea, Caprice, and Wulf—all turned to Steen. They were seated at a long table, their backs to the fire, like they were a justice tribunal, and Steen stood with a harsh look of judgment upon his thin and scruffy face. None of them glanced my way. I was an outsider, obviously.

"The girl said she was born cursed," Steen said, glowering. "That's what she said."

Rylion shrugged. "Perhaps she was."

"Impossible." Steen scoffed. "Don't be a fool. And what about the god-king's Scourge? I heard him. We all heard him. That *girl* is dangerous. She killed five soldiers in the Holy Guard."

"Alexavier considers all cursed to be dangerous."

"Yes, well, the god-king's Scourge is actively looking for her. That'll bring us trouble. What do you think will happen once Alexavier finds out we're harboring her?"

"The same thing that'll happen if he figures out we're harboring several cursed—yourself included."

Steen bit back his words. For a moment, he didn't respond, he simply slid back down into his seat, his cross-examination concluded.

"Shouldn't we know what she's done?" Lydia asked. She put a hand on Steen's shoulder and scooted closer to him. "I think it's only right. Everyone here knows of Thea's, Steen's, and Caprice's broken decrees. She should talk, too."

Wulf stood and shook his head. "Her name is Artemis. You can refer to her by name."

"Then," Lydia drawled, a hint of sarcasm in her voice, "*Artemis* should talk, too."

"She already did," Rylion said. "She was born cursed."

A murmur of discontentment spread through the small group as though his declaration were a stone tossed in their midst, and their agitation acted as the ripples that spread out from it.

They didn't like my explanation, but there was nothing else I could give them.

Rylion turned to Caprice. "Do you know anything?"

She brushed her long hair with her fingers. "The old gods had decrees," she said, "before they bestowed their powers onto the god-kings and god-queens. Perhaps some of them survive."

"Impossible," Steen said. "All decrees from the previous gods, and the previous god-kings and god-queens, are erased when they die. None of the old decrees have held over. Why would this situation be different?"

"Some of the old gods survived. They left this world to the hands of mankind, never to return. But they're very much alive."

The statement settled over the group like a wet blanket. I shifted closer to Rylion, hoping he hadn't changed his mind about me. Out of everyone here, he alone stood by me. Even Wulf hesitated a bit, staying on the other side of the table and only offering verbal reassurances.

I had already worn out my welcome with the others, it seemed. How much longer would Rylion tolerate my presence? At some point, his generosity would end, especially if the others continued their pressure.

Steen stood and motioned to the room with wild gestures. "That's a far-fetched explanation and everyone knows it! The old gods are dead." He gave Caprice a sidelong glance. "I'm sorry. I know you think some aren't, but Luka scholars say differently. That woman—*Artemis*—is hiding something from us. She could be a danger. A real danger."

Osmund held up a hand, and the room fell silent. I caught my breath, ready for him to throw me from the lodge. I didn't know what I would do, but I would find a way back down the mountain if I had to.

"We're not here to judge," Osmund said, his words slow and deliberate. "But we can give Artemis new purpose. I'd rather men and women work to right their wrongs than wallow in the woods until they become a monster that terrorizes good folk."

"But she's—"

"I know she's cursed, *Steen*. But she's already had enough suffering for the whole damn kingdom if she's been marked since childhood. She doesn't need any more grief from us."

Rylion nodded. "There's nothing to worry about. I'll look after her. If she turns dangerous, we'll end her."

The semi-threat chilled me, but I understood. They didn't actually owe me anything. Their kindness, their decency, their generosity—it was a gift to the kingdom, not just for my benefit. Keeping me was a form of rehabilitation. And once I died, my corpse would be their payment. Osmund didn't want monsters, either man or Forsaken, and they considered the terror of the curse enough of a punishment for most of the decrees.

The terror did take a toll far worse than a simple knife to the throat.

"I'm not here to harm you," I said, surprising half the group with my statement. They stared at me as though they had thought me mute. "I swear it."

My words seemed to ease the tension in the room. Hopefully, it would be the first step to endearing myself. I didn't want to be sent away.

"I'll keep an eye on her as well," Wulf said. "I'm sure there won't be any incidents."

Osmund grunted. "Then it's settled. We need not discuss this further." He stepped away from the table and rotated his shoulder. He grimaced, no doubt stiff from the long journey, and removed his cloak. "Tonight we relax. Tomorrow we continue our hunt."

He exited the room, leaving a wake of silence.

The others stared, and I avoided eye contact. What else did they want me to say? They wouldn't appreciate my history, and I had already assured them I wouldn't turn violent. All I wanted was to start a new life.

After a short sigh, I took in the rest of the room. The table rested on top of an animal hide rug, and a set of wide stairs led to the second story. There was a kitchen door and a cellar. The place appeared to be well-loved. And clean, which was a pleasant change. Some hunting lodges had the rank odor of dead animals and tanning leather. Few things were worse.

Rylion removed his greaves. "Let me show you the rooms upstairs. All are the same size. Small, but comfortable. You can choose one."

I nodded, and without another word, we headed for the stairs. Once at the top, Rylion strode down the hall, motioning to each room with a simple gesture of the hand. They all had a simple bed or two, as well as a washbasin. Nothing elegant or fancy, but practical. Although, I did see a pattern...

Each room had a sharp weapon by the doorframe—be it an axe, dagger, sword, or knife. Some I spotted right away, some were partially hidden. The knowledge of these weapons left me curious.

When I reached the last room, I walked in and claimed it as my own. A small dagger sat behind the washbasin.

"May I ask you a question?" I asked, staring at the bed.

Rylion stood in the doorway and replied with a nod.

"Is everyone here cursed?"

"No. Just you, Steen, Thea, Caprice, and my uncle."

More than half the group. That only left Rylion, his father, Wulf, and Lydia who weren't.

I let out a sigh of relief. I didn't know why, but I had feared that *everyone* in the hunting group might have been cursed. It was good to see that the people doing the killing would always be around to make sure it was done. And I liked knowing they would never live through the same kind of fear I went through.

I turned to face him. "May I ask you another question?"

Rylion cracked half a smile. "You needn't seek my

permission every time you wish to speak. If you want to ask me a question, ask me the question."

"Fine. Do you know of people who wield magic? They call them *lords*."

He nodded.

His response surprised me.

"Do you... know anyone around here with magic?" I asked. "Be it divine fire or—"

"We don't speak of it."

"Why is that?"

"Only those descended from the old gods can wield magic," Rylion said. "They're a dying breed and God-King Eliezer has forced the remaining few to the capital. If it were known there were individuals with magic here, he would send soldiers to collect them."

I held my breath. I hadn't known the god-king had rounded up people with magic. Even in the capital, lords of magic were a rare sight. Then again, it wouldn't be hard to hoard people with magic. It was against the god-king's decrees to disobey a direct order, after all.

But the part about being descended from old gods... that was a tale too ludicrous to believe. Only country bumpkins believed such things. It was true that magic passed through blood—parents to offspring—but the old gods had never sired children, not according to any of the tomes I had read. Magic came from their gifts and nothing more.

"Are you educated?" I asked Rylion, curiosity burning inside me.

He shook his head. "My mother taught me letters and numbers. I've never had a tutor."

Ah. No wonder he believed such things. A shame. Knowledge was key to making a man formidable.

"Perhaps I could educate you," I said. "I know a great many works by heart."

"If I have time. Hunting my mother consumes my father's every thought. I must help him."

"I will aid you in any way I can."

"I appreciate it." Then he turned for the door and said, "It might be helpful if a Lord of Flame and Cinder were at our side."

He *had* seen my magic. He had been so close when I had used it on the Forsaken that he could've counted the number of times I had blinked. Yet he hadn't said anything to anyone. More evidence he kept secrets. He seemed to collect them.

"I'll let you get settled in," Rylion said.

He walked back down the hall, leaving me to the quiet room, and I closed the door.

I mulled over the situation and realized it might be for the best.

Even if they didn't know the whole truth about me, they did know more than most people. They knew I was cursed, Rylion knew I was gifted with magic, and they knew I was on the run from Alexavier… and yet they had decided to keep me, even going so far as to give me a room and board. Reluctantly, but still. And while some of them remained skeptical, perhaps they would change their minds. For the time being, I enjoyed the feeling of being a part of civilized society again.

It was pleasant.

More than pleasant.

My insides tightened just thinking of their generosity. I didn't want to discover any tricks, games, or contingencies. I wanted to stay. I wanted to think my last days as a woman could be spent in happiness rather than misery. Were these desires selfish and unreasonable? I wondered. Maybe life punished people who reached beyond their stations. Sometimes it seemed that was the only truth.

Or perhaps I was innately evil.

That was my theory behind my curse mark. After all, the

curses were designed to punish the wicked. My heart must have been black the moment it had started beating in my mother's womb. What other explanation could there be?

The door to my room creaked open, and I jumped to my feet.

A tall man stood in the doorway. He looked familiar. Thin. Tall. Curly hair. He looked like Wulf, only thirty years older, and he shared Osmund's thick beard. His robes truly identified him, however. The five metal rings that lined the white collar only confirmed my suspicion.

"You must be Bryn," I said, my body tense. "Rylion's uncle."

He had the same hair color as Rylion and Wulf—chestnut brown—though it was peppered with gray at the temples. His eyes matched Wulf's alone. Hazel.

"Rylion just told me about you," Bryn said, mimicking my terse speech. "I came to see for myself."

I glanced over his robes. He wore gloves and full boots, and his collar went up to his chin.

"I'm sorry we're intruding on your home," I said. "Hopefully, it won't… bother you."

"No, of course not. I welcome the company. The lodge is too quiet this time of the year, and I miss the sight of people."

The conversation between us died. Bryn said nothing and I gritted my teeth. What did he want from me? He almost looked fearful. Had he overheard my conversation with Rylion? Did he know I had magic? I couldn't question him, lest I give myself away, so I remained silent.

Bryn cleared his throat. "My nephew says you're a scholar." He motioned to my attire. I glanced down and found the blood-crusted clothing to be rather disgusting, but I restrained myself from cringing.

"That's correct," I said.

"I was once a scholar."

Oh, really? And perhaps next he would tell me the sky was blue.

I held back my sardonic comments. There was no reason I should dislike the man—he had good taste in robes, after all.

He eyed my scarf and glared at the edges smeared with mud. "Here. Why don't you hand that to me? I'll bring you a new set of clothing, along with a new scarf."

I held the garment close. "I'll keep the scarf." I loved its red design and intricate stitching. I would wash it myself if need be.

"Well, the scarf doesn't belong to you."

I returned his hard look with a glower. "It's Rylion's gift to me. I'll keep it."

"Rylion gave the scarf away?" he snapped.

Bryn's response confused me. He seemed torn, half-turning for the hall, with one foot still in my room.

I said nothing.

"I'll speak with Rylion," he finally said. "It was a pleasure to meet you." He walked out and shut the door behind himself.

Bryn had all the charm of a dead fish. I shut the curtains of the room, uncomfortable with the way he had looked at me. Or maybe it was the way he had looked at the scarf. Something about it didn't sit right.

"Rylion," Wulf said. "Pass the brandy?"

I handed over the decanter, barely offering my brother much attention. Darkness filled the void beyond the window as night settled in. I stared out into it, my thoughts dwelling on Artemis. When I had left her room, she had seemed like she'd had more to say. Perhaps I should have stayed and inquired further about her past and intentions.

My father glowered at me and then snorted. "You're troubled. Out with it, son."

Wulf glanced up from his stew. "Hm? Is something wrong?"

We were the only three sitting at the small dining table, but I glanced around before speaking, my chest tightening with each new breath. I preferred fewer words when I could. I only wanted to say what I meant.

"Artemis wields divine fire," I whispered.

My father's eyes widened, but he hardened his expression just as fast as it had shifted. Wulf forced himself to swallow in his haste to speak.

"I knew it," Wulf muttered. "I could tell! She's just like Mom."

"No," my father said. "Mariana didn't wield divine fire. She was a Lord of Winter Stillness. That isn't the same."

"But Mom had magic. Everyone knows it."

"Not everyone."

Next to no one had known, except those close to her. The need for secrecy had always bothered me, but I had never wanted to distress my mother, so I had said nothing. Now that I was older, I could appraise the situation and my conclusions bothered me.

We had kept it secret so God-King Eliezer wouldn't summon her. But why must the subjects of a kingdom fear their ruler so much they would remain hidden? Such realities baffled me.

I knew very little of the world. I knew Ludlow and Mount Regel, and the trade roads from here to the City of Gourna, but that was all. Twenty-five years and I felt as though my knowledge grew smaller and smaller with each shred of news I heard from afar. My mother had said she had been the last one with magic, yet Artemis had arrived from the capital with fire and the god-king collected people in his castle. My uncle had said the god-kings and god-queens couldn't be killed, yet Caprice had arrived from the Kingdom of Saileer with news that Saileer's god-king had been murdered. And the first decree was always against regicide... All evidence my uncle was wrong.

Such bits of news shattered my reality. The world was not so small that I could stay ignorant. Even Artemis had questioned my education, as though it were immediately apparent that I knew very little.

"Maybe we should take Artemis to the Boneyard," Wulf said, his voice hushed. "If she's like Mom, she might be able to talk to the god there."

My father clenched his jaw and spoke with a strained tone. "*No.* Never. The Boneyard was Mariana's sacred refuge. I won't have others defile it."

"But there's a god there. Maybe—"

"The god is *dead*, boy. There's no point in showin' it to anyone, do you understand me? Don't you ever take anyone there. Ever."

Wulf turned to me and glowered. He always wanted me to interject, but I didn't think the situation was so clear-cut. I did, however, think Artemis would find solace in the Boneyard.

"Artemis is troubled," I said. "I can feel it. And I doubt she would disturb anything if we showed her the Boneyard."

My father slammed his hand on the table. Wulf grimaced, but I knew my father meant nothing by the gesture. He was frustrated. He hated when Wulf and I talked about our mother or reminded him of times long past. It was why I didn't want to discuss anything until we could give her peace.

"Never show her the Boneyard," my father commanded.

I nodded.

Wulf stared at his food. "All right." Then he glanced up and asked, "Can I ask her to teach us about divine magic? I know you don't want anyone to know, but Rylion and I are Lords and—"

My father shot him a glare that could silence a rowdy pub. Wulf swallowed the rest of his words.

"Mariana didn't control fire," my father said again. "You're different than the girl. You're both Lords of a different god. There's no reason to go asking her anything. Do you hear me? Leave this be. The less either of you do with this, the better."

When I was younger, I had never questioned my father's logic, but I could see now he wanted us ignorant. He wanted to protect us, which made it hard to grow resentful and angry, but I disagreed with him. He had said the old gods had given mankind this ability to govern themselves and keep the peace, yet more and more people became cursed.

Were people becoming eviler? That was what everyone believed. But I didn't. Yet it was hard to put into words what I really thought. Perhaps someone like Artemis could help shed light on the subject and give me the tools to express my contempt for decrees such as *cursed be the man who hunts the golden warbler.*

Uncle Bryn walked into the dining room and stopped cold.

My father regarded him with a long stare before standing and clearing his place at the table. Neither spoke to one another. Then my father ambled out of the room, patting me on the shoulder to let me know things would be all right. I gave him a quick nod, silently wishing him a pleasant evening.

Wulf returned to his food, and the silence persisted. It was only after my father's footsteps stopped echoing in the hall that Uncle Bryn dared to speak.

"The new girl is a quiet one," Uncle Bryn said, as though nothing strained had happened a moment earlier.

Wulf jumped up and prepared a bowl of stew. He placed it on the table and Uncle Bryn took a seat.

"Artemis is going to help us with the hunt," Wulf said.

Uncle Bryn frowned. "I don't like her. There's a shiftiness to her eyes."

"Artemis's been through a lot. She's cursed and…" Wulf hesitated a moment, taking in a long breath. "And she has magic."

Uncle Bryn held his food bowl close. He said nothing in regard to the statement, instead staring down with an intent gaze. I didn't think it was wise to tell him just yet, but Uncle Bryn *was* a scholar; perhaps he would be the best one to inform.

"Divine magic like Mariana's?" Uncle Bryn whispered.

Wulf shook his head. "No. Fire."

Bryn frowned and waved his hand. "I trust her even less. Mariana's gifts were beautiful. Nothing destructive."

"But Artemis is like her in a lot of ways. You remember how quiet Mom was."

My father had always compared our mother to an orchid, not only because of her delicate appearance, but because she had spoken just about as often as a flower. I remembered, as a child, thinking my mother was mysterious.

Uncle Bryn turned his attention to me. "The girl says you gave her the scarf she's wearing."

I had known it might become an issue, but I had no regrets. "It's hers to keep."

"*It was your mother's,*" Uncle Bryn said, dragging out his sentence with a harsh bite. "How could you possibly think to give it away?"

"My mother would have wanted it this way."

My mother never would've hesitated to help someone. There wasn't a single thing she owned she wouldn't have given up if it would have meant making someone's life a little easier. Sometimes she had given too much—I could see how it had hurt her—but she had done it anyway. She had told me selflessness and compassion were powerful, and too often rare in this world. But men could not bleed themselves dry for others, lest a new form of suffering be brought into the world.

Still, I wanted Artemis to have the scarf. For some reason, the color red suited her. Black and red. Like smoldering fire. She had the same mysterious aura my mother had carried. It intrigued me in a way few other things did. There were omens and signs in the world I didn't understand.

"You can't go giving away Mariana's belongings," Uncle Bryn said. "I house them here as keepsakes, you understand? Remembrances."

I said nothing.

I was done with my stew and I stood from the table. Wulf

watched me go, and I bid him good night the same way I did my father.

Half of me wanted to visit Artemis, but I didn't want to crowd her. She had suffered from a great injustice. She had so much hate for the world, I feared she would never be whole. When she flinched away, when she stayed quiet, when she closed herself off from others—these reactions were all manifestations of unseen injuries.

My mother had said such anguish fueled fell magic, like the kind that created the Forsaken. She would have known how to help Artemis, but the task fell to me in her stead.

I shouldn't stray too far away. For her sake.

CHAPTER SIX

Two days of sleep and food transformed me. I felt like my old self, and my magic returned in full force.

With my head held high, I walked out of the lodge and into the crisp morning of a new day. Sinister birds flew overhead in passing groups, but I paid them little heed. Divine fire would deal with them just fine.

My new robes also did wonders for my mood. My scarf still had an odor of blood, but I dared not leave it behind, lest Bryn take it, for whatever reason.

"Artemis, you're lookin' like a fresh sprout in spring," Lydia said.

She collected feathers around the edge of the lodge, smiling the entire time. She wore thick winter garb, fur around all edges, and she moved about with ease. Unlike a few days ago, when she had worn trousers under her skirt, she had rid herself of the feminine attire altogether in exchange for practical hunting pants. When she noticed me staring, she chuckled.

"I feel better," I said as I walked over to her. "I slept well."

"And for a long while."

Basically since Bryn had left my room two days ago. I had gotten up and moved around, but after every meal I had returned to my bed.

I glanced around. "I thought we would be starting the hunt soon."

"Rylion and Osmund are huntin'," Lydia said. She picked up a long, white feather and scrutinized the edges. "You, me, and Wulf will be out gatherin' some supplies." She motioned to my arms. "You ever chop wood?"

"No."

"Yeah, I didn't think so."

I pursed my lips. I had *other talents*. Surely, my worth wasn't measured in the amount of wood I could chop.

But if I were to make a new home here, I had to adapt to a new role. My role. Something I could contribute to the group. Chop wood? Hopefully not, but I needed a useful activity.

"What are Steen, Caprice, and Thea doing?" I asked.

"Steen is makin' jerky," Lydia replied. She finished gathering her feathers and stuffed them in a satchel. "Thea's tendin' to the horses. Caprice is makin' tree taps. Everyone has their role."

"And Bryn?"

"Bryn keeps the lodge. He cleans and tidies up."

"I see."

Wulf rounded the corner of the lodge. He had an energetic gait as he closed the distance between us. The moment he was by my side, he tossed Lydia a bow and a half-filled quiver. She grabbed the equipment and strapped the quiver to her hip—one belt around the waist and another belt at the bottom, near the knee. Wulf kept his quiver slung on his back. It rattled as he moved, whereas Lydia secured her arrows with a simple string. No noise.

"Ready?" Wulf asked me. "I need to show you around, and we also need to get a certain amount of supplies back to the lodge."

"I'm ready," I said.

The three of us headed along the road, away from the lodge. My feet still hurt, despite the rest, though it didn't become an issue. Lydia stopped to pluck feathers from the snowbanks on the side of the road. The birds overhead dropped them at a startling rate, and she had the cream of the crop to choose from.

While Wulf and I waited, I turned to him and asked, "Which decree did your uncle break to become cursed?"

Wulf regarded me with a frown. "He isn't cursed."

"He's most definitely cursed," I said. Did Wulf not know? Guilt ate at me a bit—I didn't want to reveal any of Rylion's many secrets.

"What makes you think my uncle is cursed?" Wulf asked, a demanding edge to his voice.

"Rylion told me so the other night."

Wulf shook his head. "You must've heard wrong. He never would have said that. Did you actually see Bryn's mark?"

"No."

Lydia lifted an eyebrow and gave me a sidelong glance, but she didn't interject herself into the conversation.

"Then how do you know for sure?" Wulf asked.

I didn't say it, but my gut instinct was to trust everything Rylion said no matter what. However, I could piece the mystery together myself if needed.

I let out a long exhale. "Fine, allow me to speculate. Bryn separated himself from civilization, though he said he misses the company of others. He keeps weapons ready in every room, for what I assume is a quick out just in case he starts to turn. And, much like everyone who is cursed, he wears clothing enough to cover his entire body, save his face. If he isn't cursed, I'd eat one of those sinister birds raw."

Lydia exchanged a look with Wulf. At first, I thought she would deny my assessment, but then she slowly nodded.

"Bryn has been on the mountain for some time. He ended his studies without much of a reason, too."

Wulf said nothing. Instead, he hefted his yew bow. I flinched, my teeth gritted. Would he attack me? He would regret such a confrontation now that I had my fire.

But then he turned his attention to the sky. Lydia readied her bow and did the same.

I glanced up. An entire flock of bulbous birds shot overhead. They flew at ludicrous speeds, zipping toward another half-peak of the mountain like they had a mission to accomplish. The beating of their wings washed over us in one uninterrupted cacophony.

Wulf nocked an arrow and fired. I suspected he was hoping he would hit something, given the density of the flock, because there was no way he aimed for a specific bird. His arrow hit one, thankfully, and it fell from the sky in a twirl.

Lydia let loose an arrow as well. Again, another bird careened to the ground. The other sinister birds hardly noticed. They continued forward, cawing and crowing.

The last of the birds sailed overhead, and the atmosphere of Mount Regel returned to normal.

"Is that for me to eat?" I quipped.

Wulf forced a laugh. "No." His curt tone betrayed his anger, however.

"I take it you really didn't know your uncle was cursed."

"No." He walked off to grab his kill as he said, "I don't understand why my brother and father refuse to tell me anything."

Lydia inspected the base of a hardwood tree, but her attention was clearly divided. She grabbed the branches half-hidden in the snow, hemming and hawing about whether she liked what she saw. Without asking me for a boost, she leapt up into the tree, an impressive display of athleticism that left me feeling inadequate.

"I'm impressed," I called up to her.

Lydia laughed as she continued her climb up the massive tree.

Wulf returned with both birds tied in tight knots. They twitched in his hands, but I was certain they were dead. "We'll be having a lot of bird this winter," he said. "I hope Steen knows more than a few recipes."

A dark, twisted piece of me wondered if Wulf thought of these birds as his siblings. His mother was the Forsaken birthing them, after all. But of course he didn't—they weren't *really* his siblings—though the thought lingered in my mind regardless.

Lydia jumped down from the tree and landed next to me with a soft crunch in the snow. She stepped out, shivering, and showed me the handful of straight sticks she had managed to collect from the tree. Perfect for fletching arrows.

"Why don't we get some lively chat goin'?" Lydia asked as we continued down the road. "Remember our musin's on the road, Wulf? Have you thought 'bout what decrees you'd make as a god-king?"

For a moment, he said nothing. Then he took in a deep breath. "Every time I think about it, I get caught in a loop. Why can't there be a decree that curses everyone who is depraved?"

"The decrees can only punish actions," I said. "You must do something to incur the wrath of the god-kings or god-queens."

"Oh. Well, *cursed be the man who thinks a depraved thought.* That's a good one, right?"

Lydia chuckled. I held back a scoff.

"Haven't you heard of God-Queen Rohesia?" I asked. "You don't want to end up like her."

Both Lydia and Wulf gave me odd glances.

"What happened to her?" Wulf asked.

Shock took hold of my thoughts. How was it possible they

had never heard of God-Queen Rohesia? It was one of the first lessons I had learned as a child about the decrees—the importance of having well-crafted rules, and how a single decree muttered in haste could destroy a kingdom.

"God-Queen Rohesia wished to purge her kingdom of evil," I said. "She made only one decree. *Cursed be the man who has ill thoughts against others.* That was all. Within the first few hours of her rule, the majority of her citizens fell to the curse. In a matter of days, there were Forsaken roaming the countryside, creating devastation in their wake. The monsters couldn't be stopped, not by Rohesia's Holy Guard or the Forsaken hunters—there were too many to contend with. Two-thirds of the kingdom devoured the final third, creating a blighted land devoid of life."

Lydia and Wulf remained quiet as we crunched through the snow.

It was a fantasy to think mankind could be purged of evil through decrees. Rohesia should've known the single decree would destroy her kingdom. Every single person harbored ill thoughts for another at some point in their life.

Evil deeds... That disproved my theory that I had been born evil and thus cursed. No decree could confer curses unless someone acted. Therefore, I must have done something. But what? I had no idea. Would the act of being born have violated some sort of decree? Then again, it could be argued that I hadn't chosen to be born.

Wulf stopped and stared down at me.

I matched his gaze, my thoughts disappearing in an instant.

"You're clever?" he asked in a sheepish manner, his curly hair fluttering in the cold winds.

"I told you I had many years of study. If that's what you count as *clever*, then yes. I am."

He laughed once, more of an amused huff. Again, he fell silent. Finally, he said, "The Boneyard is close by. And...

there's something wrong with it. Maybe someone like you can solve our problem."

Boneyard? *Our* problem? Interesting. I supposed if my plan was to stay with them, I should help with all their problems. This would be a better use of my talents than watching Lydia gather feathers and sticks.

Lydia tilted her head. "I don't think you should do that, Wulf. What would your pappy say? You know how he feels about showin' people stuff on the mountain. It's not for weakhearted folk."

"Artemis's not weakhearted," Wulf said. "I think she'll know how to fix everything."

"Still. You should tell your pappy first. Or at least Rylion."

"Dad and Rylion hide things from me," Wulf said through gritted teeth. "I don't need to share everything with them. It'll only be for a short while."

She exhaled and fidgeted with her braid. "You do what you feel is right."

Wulf placed a hand on my shoulder and guided me off the road. "You won't mind, right? If I show you something?"

I shook my head. I would rather know all their secrets than be kept in the dark. "Lead the way."

Together, we wandered into the sparse trees that dotted Mount Regel. Hardwood, pine, fir, and spruce mixed together in a pleasing sight, though the hardwood trees were devoid of leaves. We stomped through the snow, which got deeper the farther we went, and I wondered why we hadn't brought boots capable of keeping us above the slush.

Lydia trailed behind, collecting feathers. I stuck close to Wulf, my thoughts still on Rylion. Would he be upset with his brother's actions? I knew in my heart I would not hide anything from Rylion if he asked me.

The sun traveled upward. At least the snow soothed my sore feet.

A harsh snap and a burst of ice ripped me from my

thoughts. Wulf yelled and fell back into the snow. I jumped away, shaken, my eyes drawn to the harsh contrast of blood on clean white. He had stepped in a bear trap—the thick, metal clamp, lined with jagged, sharp teeth, snapped tight on his shin—though his leather greaves had prevented the trap from cutting to the bone.

Lydia jogged through the snow and leapt to Wulf's side. "Is it bad?" she asked, placing her hands on his knee. "Who in their right mind would leave a trap like this? Not with the god-king's decrees... They could accidentally kill something they ought not."

Wulf sucked in air through his teeth and lifted his leg. A chain emerged from the white powder, secured to a nearby tree. Bells rang from the branches—bells hidden behind the evergreen pine needles. The clink of their chaotic melody echoed across the winter fields of Mount Regel.

And birds lifted from the trees. Many, many birds.

CHAPTER SEVEN

I ducked down, my eyes fixed on the birds that swirled into the air. The birds swooped, and I balled my fists, ready to burn them, but they veered away and instead attacked the bell-covered tree. Each ring of the tiny bells sent the horde of fowls into a frenzy. They attacked the branches, ripped away pine needles, and pecked at the bark, all in an attempt to silence the metallic sound.

The cyclone of birds stretched far into the sky, high enough to see even over a mile away.

Lydia and Wulf struggled to unhook the bear trap. Lydia pressed on the release from one side while Wulf took the other. It strained and opened with a screech. A handful of birds dove for the metal, and Lydia released her hold in time to catch the leg of a sinister bird in the bear trap. The terrible creature—with three wings and two heads—squawked incessantly, its human eyes staring at us in terror.

A torrent of misshapen crows flew for Wulf's bloody leg, their razor-sharp beaks glinting in the sunlight. Lydia and Wulf nocked their bows and shot four of the birds before they reached their target.

Lydia pulled a hunting knife and slashed, keeping the

birds at bay. Wulf took his time picking off the rest—ten birds dead by the time he was finished. The last of the birds swooped away with a blood-curdling screech. Unlike the Forsaken, which charged for blood, heedless to their own wellbeing, a sinister animal would often revert to its natural instincts when faced with overwhelming odds.

The bird in the bear trap chewed its own leg, desperate to save itself.

Wulf gulped down a few breaths and forced himself to stand. Lydia helped him and I shuffled through the snow, concerned, but it seemed as though they had everything under control. We were a few miles from the lodge, but an injury like Wulf's would dramatically slow our travel.

We walked for a minute or two, away from the chattering of the birds, when Lydia stopped. "I knew it," she murmured.

I followed her wide-eyed gaze to a group of men on horseback riding along the narrow trails of Mount Regel. They were down the slope, but their stallions moved with purpose, hot breath coming out in bursts of steam.

"Do you know those men?" I asked.

"Brigands," Lydia replied. "This was a brigand trap."

I glanced back at the birds. They continued swarming the tree of bells, a clear indicator for the mountain bandits that something had happened. Then I turned my gaze to the snow. A trail of red followed our footsteps. A blind man could track us with ease.

Gods damn us.

Wulf pushed away from Lydia and nocked the last arrow from his quiver. Lydia did the same, her attention drifting back to the pile of dead crows.

"We should move to the tree line," I said. "If this comes to a fight… we'll want the cover. And the horses won't make it between tightly packed trees."

Wulf and Lydia agreed without comment. We hurried to the trees and Wulf motioned for me and Lydia to get behind the trunks. I complied, though with a serious amount of hesitation. Wulf alone stayed partially visible, leaning heavily against an evergreen, his mangled leg limp at his side.

The brigands rode off the trail and into the snow, their animals pushing forward with little urging. Four men in total, each with thick leather garb. My chest tightened once I got a good look at them. Black spiderweb markings covered their faces and hands—every inch of exposed flesh, actually.

For every decree a man broke, he got another mark. I had heard stories of men that had forsaken all common decency after the first sin. If they were to become a monster, why live by the rules of society? They broke every decree to make a statement. They did it because they could. And then their skin was left twisted with the markings. They became monsters long before they turned into the Forsaken.

Did Wulf mean to protect us from such men? He was touched in the head if he thought his single arrow would keep him alive against four brigands who had given up on life.

Would Rylion hide behind trees while his injured brother dealt with brigands?

I stepped out and motioned Wulf to get back.

"You have no weapon," Lydia said under her breath. "Stay back!"

To my surprise, Wulf didn't argue. He hobbled back behind the tree line, leaving me as the first point of contact with our inbound problem. He even hushed Lydia when she tried to offer further protests.

The lead brigand rode forward and pulled on his horse's reins until it halted. He waited atop his mount, giving me the once over. His beady eyes gazed down into the snow, and he counted the trails. Well, *if* he could count. I doubted men of his caliber knew much of numbers or reason.

Behind the trees, Wulf and Lydia nocked their arrows.

The three flanking brigands pulled out their weapons—

one sword, two short bows. They approached with confidence, some smiling. The lead man chortled, exposing half-rotted teeth.

"Leave," I said. "We have nothing for you but death."

"Is that right?" the brigand asked, an oily smile sprouting across his face.

"You know not who you deal with. I'm a Lord of Flame and Cinder."

"Those are some strong words from a pretty little girl like yourself." He snapped his finger. "Pass over any coin you got, and perhaps I won't defile the *lordship's* body." The brigand laughed, his men joining in the delight.

"Feh," I said, holding back a smile of my own.

My heart beat fiercely against my ribs, drowning out distant sounds. I didn't shy away from fighting. I enjoyed the cold numbness of battle—especially the way it sharpened my senses. Once caught up in the thick of it, my body craved conflict like a drunkard craved his ale.

Fighting also reminded me of my hatred for mankind, like the act of violence was a physical manifestation of anger. Men were pigs and vermin wrapped in a suit of human skin—that was what I had told myself when I had made the long march away from the god-king's Holy Guard.

"Did you hear me, lass?" the lead brigand asked. Then he motioned to the rings on my collar. "I know scribes always carry coin on 'em."

I sneered. "You're outclassed, fool. This'll be your final warning."

The brigand with a sword slid off his horse and into the snow with a crunch. The two lackey bowmen spread out, and my mind turned to Lydia. I had heard many terrible stories in the past... Stories of bandits who delighted in "spreading" their curse to others. Adultery and promiscuous behavior need not be voluntary to mark both participants, only that the act of sex took place. The way

Lydia trembled behind her tree, I knew it weighed heavily on her mind.

I didn't fear for myself. The brigands would never touch me. I would burn this whole mountain to ash before any of them managed to unhook their belts.

Such vile thoughts stirred my fire. I gritted my teeth as embers appeared on the wind, glistening with a bright orange like terrible volcanic ash.

The brigands inched closer, their boots loud in the snow, unaware of the danger they faced.

I had given them plenty of warnings.

With a quick arch of my hand, I called forth a scorching flame. It washed outward, flaring over the area. Bright white, the edges a flash of crimson red. I squinted at the intense light.

The fire blanketed the swordsman and startled the lead brigand's horse. The beast reared up, almost dropping its rider, and turned to run, its face and flesh burned so deep, it screamed. The intensity of the heat melted snow, and a cloud of fog ascended all around us.

Wulf let loose an arrow—his aim so perfect, he must have been blessed—and the arrow lodged itself deep in one bowman's throat. Lydia leaned out from cover and fired. Her arrow hit the shoulder of the last bowman's horse, spurring it into a frantic run despite the protests of its rider. A fantastic shot for someone who didn't have time to aim.

When the swordsman attempted to hobble back to his mount, I held out my hand and engulfed the man in blistering white flame. It didn't last long, but the severity of the heat reminded me of when I had killed the men of Alexavier's Holy Guard. They hadn't expected I was a Lord of Flame and Cinder. They had roasted alive in their metal armor after a mere few seconds, far faster than with normal flame or heat.

The smell of the burnt brigand irritated my nose.

A powerful wind took the new cloud of steam down the

side of the mountain. The last two brigands raced along the trails. Their hideaway must have been close. I wondered how many of them there were, but I hoped I would never learn the answer.

A whistle so powerful it became a screech caused me to jump. I knew the sound of Osmund's bow, even though I had only seen it in action once.

A bone arrow slammed into the horse of a fleeing brigand, piercing the chest and killing the stallion in one powerful strike. No doubt Osmund had been aiming for the rider, but the shot still did the trick.

The horse went limp, collapsed on the slope, and sent the brigand careening into a formation of jagged rocks. Perhaps the brigand would have lived had the corpse of the horse not crashed onto him after.

I turned my attention upward and spotted Rylion and Osmund on a nearby ridge. They surveyed the scene from above before trekking downward, across the icy rocks and steep paths. How long had they been watching?

"That was amazing," Wulf said, staring at me. "You really can wield divine flame. You saved our lives."

His awe didn't sit well with me. How had he already known? Without a word, I nodded, uncertain of what to say.

Lydia walked out of the tree line and shook her head. "That flame… You have a gift, you do. Caprice should know about this."

I held my breath, to the point I almost choked on it. My first instinct for so many years had been to deny and conceal my fire. Everything had to be kept hidden. Hide my curse mark. Hide my magic. Hide myself. Sharing information with anyone was anathema. Why did they have to spread it around so flippantly?

"I told you these parts were dangerous," Lydia said. "Brigands target the merchants who travel these roads. I'm sure we'll see more of them."

Wulf sighed. "As long as they don't turn into the Forsaken, I think we'll be fine."

"You know they will. This area has a reputation."

My stomach growled, and I was caught by a web of fatigue.

Rylion stomped through the snow in my direction. I straightened my posture once he got close, fearful he might see me as weak. He examined me for a moment, then nodded and headed for his brother. Wulf, tending to his leg, avoided looking Rylion in the eyes.

"What're you doing this far south?" Rylion asked. "There are safer places to gather supplies."

Wulf shook his head. "It was a mistake. I got turned around."

Lydia said nothing, and the gravity of Wulf's lie wasn't lost on me. He didn't want Rylion to know we were on our way to the Boneyard. I had to admit, I was more curious than I had been before. What was this *Boneyard* he had mentioned?

My thoughts came to a halt when Rylion locked his gaze with mine. I froze under his scrutinizing stare. Then he let out a long exhale.

"Thank you for helping my brother," he said.

"Of course," I whispered.

"You're more proficient with your magic than I imagined."

"I... Well, I've practiced for many years."

The statement seemed to resonate with him. He stared a bit longer, and I liked his attention. He looked at me like he saw me for the first time—as someone who could handle problems, not just wallow in them.

Lydia motioned to the water and melted snow. "I swear the whole mountain got a bit hotter there. I didn't know divine fire could be so destructive."

Divine fire could be vastly more destructive than the small amount I had used in front of them. I had read stories of firestorms made real, but no one knew them as well as God-

King Eliezer. He had stories of the arcane on display in his libraries. I was certain that was why he collected anyone he could find with a hint of magic in their veins.

And he would kill anyone who refused to serve him. I had seen it a hundred times.

Osmund finally reached us. He huffed and puffed, his breathing strained from carrying his massive compound bow on his back. In the light of the afternoon, the weapon practically glowed—the bowstring glittered, and the curved bow had been polished to a fine sheen. Carved into the arch, in small print, was the word 'Calavandi.'

"Lydia," Osmund said between breaths. "Retrieve my arrow, will ya, girl? I can't go losin' those."

"Right away," Lydia replied.

She gave me a quick glance before rushing off, an interest in her eye that hadn't been there before. I was sure she wanted to know more about the fire. I didn't blame her.

Osmund patted his eldest son on the shoulder. "You help your brother back to the lodge. Keep an eye out for bandits."

"Of course," Rylion said.

Rylion and Wulf walked together back to the snowy paths. Lydia picked up Wulf's scattered gear, the dead birds, and the materials she had gathered for fletching before she hurried toward the dead horse to retrieve the bone arrow. I turned to follow Wulf and Rylion, but Osmund took my arm and held me back.

I met his gaze and felt the seriousness in his grip.

"You took a risk," he drawled. "Next time, kill all the bandits. Corpses don't tell stories about the *lords of magic*. Do you understand?"

"Bandits don't have a reputation for doling out truthful information," I said. "I doubt they'll spread word of my existence outside of their band."

"Listen here. I don't care that you're a Lord of Flame and Cinder. Most people won't. They'll be in awe, but they won't *care.* But one man—and you know who I'm talkin' about—will pay a hefty sum to know of a fire-wielding little girl. And *everyone* cares about coin. Do you follow?"

I shifted my weight from one foot to the other.

"You mean Alexavier?" I asked.

"I do."

"Why? He went elsewhere."

"He'll be back. If the god-king sent him, he has no choice but to continue his search until he finds you."

I gritted my teeth. The decree stated: *Cursed be the man who disobeys the god-king's direct command.* I knew Osmund was correct. No doubt Alexavier had been given a direct command to hunt me down—which meant he could never abandon the hunt, lest he become cursed himself.

I hadn't thought about the level of dedication that would instill in someone.

"Men in the Holy Guard wield weapons made of the King's Stone," Osmund murmured in a low tone. "They slice clean through anyone marked by the curse, even the Forsaken. I've seen 'em cut a man's head right off." He let me go and clapped his hands together—I flinched at the loud sound, but he kept his sullen expression. "Just like that."

The mental images stewed in my thoughts.

Osmund continued, "And the god's fire won't help you. We both know that Alexavier has the same gift, girl. I saw him use it when we both worked for the god-king. Your powers will run over him like a gentle breeze."

I knew. Those with divine fire couldn't harm others with divine fire. That was why I couldn't kill Alexavier, even if I could kill the rest of the men in his service. He was *also* a Lord of Flame and Cinder. And while Alexavier couldn't use his fire against me, Osmund was right about the weapons. Alexavier would run me through with his holy lance.

"We don't need trouble on this hunt," Osmund said. "I've waited a long time and I'm *this* close to putting her down."

Ah. He didn't want Alexavier's attention for a myriad of reasons, one of which was he wanted his hunt to go off without a hitch. I nodded at his statement.

"I'll keep my magic hidden," I muttered.

"Good."

We turned to walk, but his bow caught my eye again.

"Your bow," I said. "Is that from the god-king's armory? Did Eliezer give you that for your service?"

Osmund laughed. "Eliezer would never allow his weapons to leave the Holy Guard. I've used this ever since I left his service."

We started our trek back to the others, and I kept Osmund's pace. "Why the bow?" I asked. "Why not make something more suited to your... skills?"

"Are you saying I'm a bad shot?"

I huffed. "Well, you're not a *good* shot."

Again, Osmund laughed, and this time, his belly got in on it. I couldn't help but join in for a moment, if only because Osmund seemed like he genuinely enjoyed my quip.

"I know I have poor aim," he said, mirth in his tone. "But the bone... I found... was curved. I decided Wulf would need something proper if he got good with his archery. Unfortunately, the damn thing is too heavy. I've tried to lighten her up, but this isn't the kind of material you can shave away. Wulf will just need to get stronger."

I stared at the weapon, fascinated. "And the name of the bow? *Calavandi*, right? Where did that come from?"

All joy left Osmund's expression. At first I thought he wouldn't answer my question, but then he said, "It's the name my wife wanted to give our daughter. But... life had other plans."

Guilt left a sour taste in my mouth. I shouldn't have asked.

Instead, I kept my questions to myself for the rest of the trek.

I lay on my bed, awake, staring at the ceiling.

Last night I had slept well, though I had kept myself hidden the entire time. Tonight I felt like I would sleep well again. I had helped with the firewood, watched Lydia fletch arrows, and kept Wulf company as he rested by the hearth. Rylion had thanked me a second time.

I was unable to hold back a smile.

Yes. I had been quite impressive, if I did say so myself. I was glad Rylion had seen me fight the brigands, if only because I liked the attention he had given me afterward. Soon his secret to tranquility would be mine, and perhaps I could lead a normal life among the hunters of Ludlow.

Such pleasant thoughts.

I sucked in a breath as a quick jolt of pain flared through my body.

What was that?

I sat up and scrunched my eyes closed. After a handful of seconds, I felt it again—a burning pain that coursed through my body like blood after the heartbeat. I grabbed my chest as sweat dappled my skin.

A third wave of agony came, and this time, I kicked my feet off the bed and stood. The world spun, and my legs trembled. I collapsed to the floor, my breathing strained.

My curse mark stung far worse than anything else. I slammed my hand over it.

This was it. This was the night I turned. There could be no mistake.

I tried to call out—to warn someone—but all I managed was a groan of suffering. Hot tears ran across my face and pooled on the floor beneath my cheek. Fear clouded my thoughts. Would I experience life as a mindless monster? Would I cease to be? How long would the transformation take? The pain was so great... I wished it would end.

Please, gods of old. Please lend me the strength to stand.

I should have left this place... I should have warned someone... I should have ended my own life and saved them all the hardship.

I sobbed aloud when a fourth surge of intense agony pulsed along my bones.

Why? Why right now? Why not during the years of quiet unhappiness, locked away in my mother's manor? Why not in the god-king's court? Why not when Alexavier had come for my father? Why must it be *now*? Why must it be when I finally saw the first signs of happiness?

Life was a cruel joke. Only the gods appreciated the punch line.

To my surprise, I gulped down air and the pain waned. Not all the way, but slightly, enough for me to regain focus.

Did the old gods hear my pleading? Was this their gift to me?

I staggered to my feet, sweat running off me in rivulets. I had the urge to vomit, but I swallowed it down. My curse mark still burned, and I suspected I didn't have much time.

Bryn kept a weapon in every room for moments just like this.

CHAPTER EIGHT

Stumbling across the room like a drunkard, I hit the washbasin table and knocked the bowl to the floor. A dagger tumbled through the water and then twirled at my feet. I knelt to retrieve it.

Pain returned, flowing through me, and I clutched the weapon close. Blood ran down my chin. I had bitten my lip, though I didn't know when. Could I even go through with it? I didn't know. My hand trembled, and I didn't have the strength to plunge the dagger into my chest.

I dropped the blade and made my way to the door. I should get as far away as possible. My worst nightmare was harming the others while they slept—especially after all they had done for me. I couldn't stand the thought.

My vision faded in and out as I traversed the dark and narrow hall. I clung to the wall, hoping it would steady me, but my balance never returned. Instead, my curse mark wept blood, soaking into my shirt and the waist of my trousers.

I had never seen anyone turn. Was it as horrifying for them as it was for me? Would I even make it outside?

The stairs spun, and I had a difficult time finding the railing. One foot, then the other—my knees locked up with another round of pain, like my muscles were hardening and unable to move. I staggered down the last few steps as fast as I could, my ragged breath the only thing I heard.

When I reached the floor, the front door opened. A waft of icy wind blew into the front room. I stepped forward, an urgent energy in my gait. I needed... to get outside...

"Artemis?"

Oh, gods—I would know that voice anywhere.

"Rylion," I said in a rusty, broken voice. With all my might and willpower, I forced myself to continue, "It's happening. Please... I..."

Please end it. I didn't want to become a monster. Not even for a second.

I closed my eyes, knowing I didn't have the strength to go any farther. He took hold of my arm. A dull ache washed through me, taking the pain but replacing it with an empty feeling. Was this it? Was my body dying? Was I becoming one of the Forsaken?

It must be the end.

A tranquil calm came over me. At the edge of my thoughts, I imagined babbling brooks untouched by man. The gentle lap of water. The hum of soft rain. The odd visions brought with them serenity.

If I had to die, I was glad this was what I felt.

"Relax," Rylion said. "Everything will be fine."

I opened my eyes.

I didn't know when or how, but I was on the bench in front of the fireplace. The crackle of fire rang in my ears, soothing me awake like a pleasant melody. I took a deep breath and then exhaled. A hand stroked my hair, and I was reminded of when I was younger—when my father would read to me—how he would comb my hair with his fingers.

I lay on my back, my head on Rylion's leg. I stared up at him, bemused. I slowly brought my hand up to touch my lip, my fingers trembling. The sting told me everything that had happened had been real. But then… why had the transformation stopped?

Rylion placed the back of his hand against my forehead. "How do you feel?"

"I—" My voice cracked. I gulped down stomach acid. "I don't know."

"You seem better than before."

I sat up, my head still dizzy, but the sensation quickly disappeared. I turned to face Rylion. He sat on the bench, his back against the dining table, and his elbows perched on either side of him. I hesitated for a moment and then went to stand.

"Stay," he commanded.

I relaxed back onto the bench.

"Come here."

I scooted close. Rylion placed an arm over my shoulders. I leaned against his side, under his armpit, his damp tunic against my face. For a moment, I thought of nothing—I just sat next to him, staring at the fire, enjoying the ease with which I took in air, especially with the heat. Then I thought of what it must have looked like to others if they walked into the room. Embarrassment and self-loathing filled my being.

I jerked away from Rylion and stood. My hand ran over the crusted blood that covered my curse mark. Again, he had come to my aid in a moment of weakness. And here I was, basking in his strength because mine had failed. He must have thought of me as feeble and frail.

"Has this happened before?" Rylion asked.

I bunched my shoulders up near my neck, unable to look at him. "No."

"It happened to my mother."

"It did?" I asked. Both dread and hope mixed inside me in equal parts. Were fits of torment common for the cursed? I didn't know. I mustered the courage to face him, but I still couldn't stand to meet his gaze. "Did she… turn soon afterward?"

"It happened to her several times. Sometimes at night. Sometimes out on the hunt."

"And she got through it?"

"I would be there to comfort her," Rylion intoned. "I held her until the pain faded, reassuring her that everything would be all right. She said those moments made the difference. My presence stopped the darkness."

His dolor tone and grim expression haunted me. I knew his mother was one of the Forsaken, but until then I had thought he had come to terms with it. Did he blame himself for her turning? Did he think he had failed her?

"Your presence likely prevented nothing," I said. "She was happy for your support, but her fall was inevitable."

Rylion glared at the flames in the fireplace. "The one night I wasn't there—the *one night* I went with my father to the traveling bazaar—that was the night she turned. I knew then, *it had been my fault*." He exhaled. "Trading with the merchants wasn't even important. I should've stayed, so that I could've protected her."

Had his presence been important?

I stared at the floor, uncertain. I had never heard of someone staving off the turn. Was it all a terrible coincidence? Had he just happened to be away when it had finally taken hold of his mother? Or would his presence have made the difference?

What an awful question to have lingering over one's thoughts.

I returned my gaze to him. Rylion had slipped into a state of melancholy. I sat back down on the bench and moved closer to him, wanting nothing more than to return to my earlier position wrapped beneath his arm. It was hard to deal with such feelings—I hadn't admired anyone before, nor had I ever entertained such thoughts. I had hated the company of others. And I had figured no one would want the company of a cursed girl anyway, no matter how much magic my mother and father had made me master.

Knots twisted in my stomach. "Please," I whispered. "Let me… stay with you."

I didn't want to sound desperate, but my desire couldn't be understated. I didn't want to leave his side.

"Stay with me?" Rylion asked.

"For the evening. Here. In front of the fire."

To my relief, he nodded.

Although my face burned with an inner heat, I rested against his side and settled into a comfortable position. The crackle and snap of the flames soothed me. Every moment I spent in his presence was another moment of easy breathing and contentment. I enjoyed it, especially after the harsh nightmare of almost transforming.

But my thoughts dwelled on Rylion's perceptions.

"Are you afraid of me?" I whispered.

"No," he said.

"Even though I could become a monster?"

"I've killed monsters all my life."

"I've killed men all my life."

I had almost held back from saying it, but the words left me before caution could filter the content. He didn't react with much surprise, nor did he move away.

My mother had wanted me to kill men with my fire—to prove I could—and I had spent many afternoons learning to control the heat of my flame. They had all been criminals, or so she had told me. I had believed her, though. The men had never conducted themselves with even a hint of decency or honor. But still. I had killed them. All of them. On command.

"Are you planning on killing me?" Rylion asked with a hint of playfulness in his voice.

"No," I snapped. "Of course not."

"Then why should I worry? I've more important matters to focus on than imaginary problems."

"It doesn't bother you that I could? Kill you, I mean."

He knew of my fire. He had seen it char the brigands.

Rylion chuckled as he relaxed back against the table. I melted closer to him, wishing his armor wasn't in the way. I had never wanted anyone before. But I wanted Rylion. The realization startled me, but I hid my surprise and remained still.

"Nature could kill me," Rylion murmured, his voice distant, like he was lost in thought. "Storms. Disease. Plague. But I do not fear them."

"Nature doesn't act with malice," I said. "But people do. Surely, you understand the difference."

"I believe most men act with justice."

I gripped his tunic and closed my eyes. "You're wrong."

"I don't believe you act with malice."

The comment gave me pause. How could he say such a thing? He didn't know me. He was naïve. The worst kind of naïve—the kind who trusted until proven wrong. I couldn't release my grip from his tunic. I knew then why he had treated me so well, and why he treated the cursed the way he did.

What an idealistic fool.

The epiphany almost got me laughing, but instead, I listened to the fire.

I wanted to be like him. I wanted his tranquility and acceptance from others. Did that mean I had to adopt his view on humanity? I had to believe more people righteous than not? I didn't think I was capable.

After a few moments, I stopped myself from dwelling and instead focused on Rylion's scent and presence. Even though I knew the world to be cruel and unforgiving, I didn't actually want Rylion to learn such a lesson, lest he become jaded, like me.

I would protect him from the harshness of reality, if only for my own selfish reasons. I wanted him for myself, just as he was.

What a mess my thoughts had become. Part of me didn't like the thought of depending on anyone. I needed to be able to handle my own paranoia—I had to harden my soul to the reality of becoming a monster. On the other hand, I never wanted to turn. Rylion was there for me, had perhaps even staved off the transformation. And he had been kind, when so few others were.

I gritted my teeth, determined to make a decision.

Nothing would keep me from having him.

"Are you well?" he asked.

"Yes," I replied, curt. "I am."

"Good."

Should I have told him about my desire? Admitting my newfound admiration could come across as foolish, especially after what had just happened. Rylion might think me manic and send me away.

So I said nothing.

Unease left me and I was awash with the same reassured tranquility I always had when I was in Rylion's presence. Since the first moment he had spoken to me—when he had picked me up off the streets and pulled me from Death's embrace—he had filled me with hope.

I wanted to thank him. I wanted to sing his praises. I wanted to beg him to stay with me always, to make sure the nightmare never came. But perhaps my gratitude was becoming an unhealthy obsession.

No. It wasn't. Twice now, Rylion had been there when I had needed him most, when I had given up on myself. Even if he was a naïve fool, I wasn't wrong about what he had done for me.

When sleep came, I welcomed it. Rylion wouldn't hurt me.

Never.

The lodge stirred with the life of an early morning routine.

I sat up, my heart pounding, and found myself back in my room. Rylion must have carried me. I grabbed my head as I swung my feet off the thin mattress and onto the wooden floor. Then I stood and shuffled to the washbasin, desperate to rinse away the crusted blood still coating my shoulder and side. Although I had knocked the bowl over last night, it sat back on its stand, filled with water, ready for washing. Another gift from Rylion.

Washing away the crusted fluid reminded me of the feeling I sometimes had when the moon blood flowed heavy in the night. It left me with a soiled sensation that only water could cleanse.

I listened to the sounds of the others as I took my time dressing. Some were more distinct. Steen and Wulf were the loudest. I heard Steen complain and Wulf jest over the bustle and through the sturdy wood floors. Osmund's laugh was a low rumble.

Part of me didn't want to face them. I was afraid they would know of my false transformation last night. What would they think? Would they hate me even more? Especially Steen. He didn't care for me, not one bit.

But it was too late for that. And no matter how long I waited, it didn't seem as though they were somber or questioning my presence. So, once clothed in robes, I opened my door and then flinched back. Caprice waited for me in the hall. She smiled, and I forced myself to return the gesture. What sort of dunce lingered in the hall with no purpose?

Or had she come to confront me?

She was half a foot taller than me, and her long hair was

black enough that it looked like a second shadow flowing behind her.

"Why are you here?" I asked, more demanding in tone than I had wanted.

Caprice held out a satchel with a shoulder strap. It was packed with provisions. "For you," she said.

I took the satchel and examined the contents with a healthy dose of suspicion. Jerky. Winter berries. A small canteen of water. Flint. "Supplies?" I asked.

"Yes."

She said nothing else.

I threw the satchel over my shoulder. "Thank you."

"Lydia told me all about you," she said.

Ah. Now I understood why there had been a shift in her demeanor. She knew of my divine fire.

"Think nothing of my actions," I said. "I would prefer that my abilities remain hidden."

"I'll speak of your fire to no one."

"Thank you."

Caprice nodded, turned, and walked away. I almost wanted to question her further, but I let the matter go. There was nothing to say, really. Without anything impeding my path, I headed downstairs. Steen sat in front of the hearth, spit-roasting birds, and Lydia was at the table, fletching arrows.

"You're not turning them enough," Lydia commented with a casual and amused tone.

Steen rolled his eyes. "I know how to cook, woman."

"My grandpappy roasted boar and chicken more times than I can count. He turned them often."

"I'm not your damn grandpappy."

Lydia shrugged and looked away, her attention square on the arrows she crafted. Steen glanced over his shoulder, and when he seemed satisfied that she wasn't paying attention, he turned the birds over on the iron spit, careful not to make too much noise with the squeak of the rotation. Lydia must have known at some level—the corners of her mouth upturned ever so slightly as she worked.

I made my way down into the open room. I glanced around, certain I would see blood splatters. There were some, but they looked to have been scrubbed deep into the grain of the floorboards. Someone must have cleaned up the evidence of my false turning.

Lydia stood. "There you are. We should be on our way."

"All right," I said as I followed her out the door.

"Oh, and Steen," Lydia said in the doorframe of the lodge, "you remember Bryn stores the rock salt in the cellar, don't you?"

"Of course," he replied, curt.

"Because you didn't rub the birds with any."

"There are different ways of doing it. Salt is… Well, cooking is a complicated process."

Lydia chuckled. "All right. I'll be back."

"Hm."

I followed Lydia, and as I went, I heard the faintest 'come back safe' muttered from Steen's direction.

Once outside, I exhaled a line of warm mist. Lydia examined me with a critical eye. I pulled my robes close and narrowed my eyes. "Yes?" I asked.

"You wore the same thing yesterday."

"Yes."

"The weather isn't forgiving."

With plenty of food and rest, I could manage. My divine fire coursed through every fiber of my being, and I knew the winter would never penetrate my skin. Well, so long as I wasn't lost and starving for two whole days.

Lydia walked over to the stables and grabbed a traveling cloak from a hook by the gates. She returned and handed it over. I looked at the cloak, then at her, and then back at the cloak. Lydia lifted an eyebrow and shook the garment. Was she giving it to me? People didn't *give me things*. People didn't give *anyone anything* unless they got something in return.

But then I touched the scarf around my neck.

I supposed… some people weren't like others.

"Thank you," I muttered.

I took the cloak and fastened it around my shoulders. It was dark brown and lightweight. I coiled my scarf over the top and hugged it all close. Even though I didn't need it to keep me warm, it was nice to have the feeling of being looked after. First Caprice with the supplies, now Lydia with the cloak…

Lydia grabbed a few logs from the woodpile and set them next to the lodge door. Then she clapped her hands together to clear off the bark and residue.

"What's that for?" I asked.

"So Steen doesn't have to go too far when he inevitably realizes there isn't enough wood inside to keep the fire going all day."

I huffed. "Is there a reason you married that lout?"

Lydia laughed, took me by the shoulder, and led me away from the lodge. Once we were a few hundred feet away, she giggled again and smiled. "Five years ago, Steen hid in my pappy's barn for two weeks during the rainy summer. When my pappy found him, he said, '*You no good, lout! Get out of my barn!*'" Lydia devolved into another round of laughter. "I guess it's his destiny to always be called the lout!"

"What a tale of romance," I quipped.

"Well, he saved my li'l brother from the summer lioness."

I lifted an eyebrow. "Did he?"

Summer lionesses were from the time of the old gods. They were magical beasts, but not like the sinister. They were blessed with divine magic, growing more powerful the longer they lived. When the gods of old had left this world, their creations had dwindled in number, but they still stalked the corners of every kingdom.

Legend said summer lionesses had golden coats so hot, they could burn flesh—and the elder lionesses had coats that melted metal.

"He fended it off and saved my li'l brother, all right," Lydia said, smiling to herself as though recounting the tale in her mind's eye. "It's against God-King Eliezer's decrees to kill the lioness… If I had done it, or if my li'l brother had done it, we would've been cursed. Steen risked both his life and another curse mark to intervene."

Steen had never told me about the second decree he had broken. It would make his transformation all the more brutal.

"He was very brave," I said.

Lydia nodded. "I took him to my pappy's barn and told him to hide there. I fed him too, of course. I called him my li'l piglet." She snorted and laughed. "He didn't like that. I would've let him come in the house, but my pappy didn't care to associate with the cursed, after all."

"No one does," I said.

"Yes, well, I couldn't let Steen wander off after that! And he said he once had been a chef for some noblemen in Gourna. He can cook, let me tell you what. Fish, mostly. He hasn't had much experience with mountain fowl."

Of course. The City of Gourna was on the edge of the Lake of the Damned. The fish there were huge and plentiful. It was all the denizens ate, or so I had heard. I had only ever been there once, and that had been by accident.

I waited, but Lydia focused her attention on the surroundings.

"Well?" I asked. "What happened?"

"What do you mean?"

"What do you mean, *what do I mean*? What happened after your father kicked him out of the barn?"

Lydia patted me on the shoulder and grinned. She had a pleasant face—one that smiled often—and I stared a bit longer as I took that information in. Her earnest mannerisms refreshed the spirit.

"Ah, you wanna hear the love story," Lydia said. "I didn't take you for the sentimental type."

"T-That's not what I was saying! I simply want the full story."

"Uh-huh." Lydia giggled, one hand over her mouth. "Well, Steen didn't leave. And then we started cooking things for each other. Ya see, he never had *baseborn food*—that's what we called it—and I had never had fish the way he prepared it. On the third night, I prepared him sauce from pig and fowl. It's really good. From the spit, ya know? He said it was one of the best things he had ever tasted."

"Hm."

Lydia lifted an eyebrow. "Steen isn't one of those unsavory cooks you see in the small towns. The ones who serve that gray meat. He worked for the god-king's court. I smiled wide when he enjoyed my food."

"What did he prepare you?"

"Fish. Stuff my pappy caught from the river. He said they were small and puny, and we didn't have the spices and cooking materials he likes… but he still made some flavorful meals. He treated it like an art, he did." Her last sentence came out like a dream, almost ethereal.

A culinary romance.

But then Lydia huffed. "My pappy knew of some Forsaken hunters in town. He went there and he told 'em about Steen. He was afraid Steen would run off with one of his li'l girls and spread the curse to them, too, ya see."

"So he hired someone to kill Steen?"

"Yes. That someone was Osmund."

A certain curiosity filled me when she muttered Osmund's name. Now that I was part of their troupe, I felt like a jealous new lover hearing about all the broken loves who had come before me. What happened when they had confronted Steen?

Had Osmund tried to kill him? Had Rylion extended a hand of friendship, as he had with me?

"It's ironic," Lydia said, stomping through the snow. She slowed her gait and then turned her attention to the morning blue of the sky. "My pappy didn't want one of his li'l girls running off with him. But I thought, *this'll be an opportunity.* So Steen and I went together."

Although Steen was cursed for stealing from a member of the god-king's court, he couldn't pass it to Lydia so long as she followed all the decrees. If they had married before lying together, she would remain unmarked. But why marry someone who would one day become a monster?

"I see," I drawled. "Steen doesn't seem very grateful."

"Ah, that's just because you don't know him very well. A lifetime of bein' talked down to will get a man thinkin' everyone is talkin' down to them, even when they aren't. But he always goes out of his way to thank Osmund for his new home. And I know he'd give up life eternal if I asked him to. He even helped Caprice pack your supplies. What more could you ask of a man who's tryin' his hardest?"

Trying his hardest?

Discipline and hard work went hand in hand. It was admirable that, although Steen was cursed, he worked hard and made an honest life for himself. He could have become a brigand. He could have wished for death, like me.

And he had helped Caprice pack my supplies? Maybe he had changed his mind about me.

No. That would be too good. He had probably poisoned the food—something to get me ill so he could have yet another reason to kick me from the lodge.

I shook my head, dispelling the thoughts. I just wouldn't eat anything he gave me.

We walked together in relative silence. Lydia stopped to get her hardwood twigs, and I helped her gather them. Some twigs were bent, and I threw them down, but she hurried and snatched them up.

"Don't do that," she said. "We can straighten these ones. A little heat will make 'em right."

"Sorry… I didn't know."

"Don't fret. You'll get the hang of it." She patted my shoulder again and we continued on.

The task at hand was simple, and my mind wandered because of it. Last night, if Rylion hadn't been there, I might have stumbled out into the cold and buried myself in the snow.

I narrowed my eyes, contemplating the nature of my encounter with Rylion.

"Lydia," I said. "Is Rylion betrothed?"

She twisted the sticks around in her palm. "No."

"And he's unwed?"

"That's right. Why? Do you fancy him?"

"I—" after a long breath, I continued, "—saw him last night. He returned to the lodge at a strange hour. Do you know why?"

What *had* he been doing before he had come back to the lodge?

Again, Lydia giggled. She stared at me for a long moment afterward, smiling wide.

"Well?" I demanded, heat on my face.

"He was down by the river."

"Does he go there every night?"

"He goes there when Osmund is restin'. Like right now. I'm pretty sure that's where he said he was goin' before he left."

I held the hardwood close. "Would you mind if we headed in that direction?"

She held a hand over her smile, like she was holding back another girlish giggle.

"E-enough of that," I stammered.

"All right. It's over this way."

Lydia picked up her pace and we ignored several perfectly good trees on our trek to Esta River. Although I would rather we were back at the lodge, Mount Regel had a natural beauty that was beyond compare, especially given the gritty landscape of my childhood. The pristine white of the snow mixed with a dappling of dark green pine created a glorious landscape. The capital city was nice, especially the mason work houses, ironwork monuments, and steam-powered machines, but the streets were lined with waste, and the walls marked with advertisements for show houses.

"That's the river right there," Lydia said, drawing me out of my thoughts.

The frozen water caught the sunlight and glittered. The tall banks of snow on either side lined the river's entire length. I walked up alongside Lydia, wondering why Rylion would wander around such a cold and wide open space. What if the brigands saw him? Or was he *hoping* those knaves would come calling?

Once at the top of the hill, I glanced around and locked up.

Rylion stood in the river, near the bank, waist deep in frigid water. He broke up the ice with a swing of his short sword, and then marched farther out. I ran across the snow, panicked.

"Rylion!" I called out.

He snapped his gaze to me, squinting. "Artemis? Is that you?"

I jogged down the hill, half-tripping, but I regained my footing before tumbling into a man-sized snowball. Once at the edge of the river waters, I flailed an arm to motion to our surroundings, unable to restrain my panicked energy. "What are you doing? Get out of there! The cold will kill your flesh! Irreversible damage!"

Rylion lowered his short sword and turned to face me,

confusion written into his expression. His lack of movement filled me with even more anxiety and alarm. *Why?* Why would he do this? Was he trying to kill himself?

"It's not your fault," I blurted out, jumping to the first conclusion that came to mind. "This isn't the way! Your mother wouldn't want this!"

When he took half a step around to better face the bank, my mind filled with a hundred terrible scenarios. Maybe his foot was stuck. Maybe he was trying to trap himself under the ice. Maybe he had fallen in. Maybe he was so cold, he couldn't get back to shore.

With pent-up energy and agitation, I rushed into the ice water.

"Artemis," Rylion said, his breath catching in the process. "Get out of the river!"

The burning chill fought the fire of my blood each and every step. I reached Rylion's side and then arched my hand, casting flames across the ice and melting as much as I could—hopefully, I hadn't caught Rylion in my haste. The warm steam that rose from the water floated off with the wind. I grabbed Rylion by the elbow and tugged him toward the bank.

"Hurry," I said. "We need to get back to the lodge! We need—"

Lydia's laughter overtook my yelling and I cut myself short. I stopped pulling Rylion and waited, waist-deep in the river, staring up at the woman on the top of the snowbank. She snorted and chortled, unable to contain her zealous delight.

CHAPTER NINE

Rylion stared down at me with a restrained smile. "Artemis. Get out of the river. I'm not in any danger."

I released his arm. Chunks of ice shifted around the melted patch. Hot embarrassment sluiced through my veins —but that was quickly replaced by the creeping chill of the water. I hurried to the edge of the river and stepped up onto the bank, my robes soaked straight up to my collarbone.

Lydia jumped down the side of the hill, still chortling. When she reached my side, she unclasped my cloak and offered me her own.

"You ran into the water," Lydia said with a giggle. "Right into the water! Did you think you were savin' him? That's darling!"

The heat of my face could dry up the whole river. *That's darling*? My actions hadn't been unreasonable! Rylion was out in a frigid river. How could she joke as though *I* was the insane one? Even Rylion stifled a laugh.

"What's going on?" I asked, demanding in every way.

Rylion splashed out of the river alongside me. I gave him the once-over and glared. He wore his half-plate armor. Who wandered into a river with metal armor? Did the man have the sense of the deranged? He must have had a death wish! Even if the water wasn't freezing, it was likely someone would drown.

But his exposed skin wasn't discolored. He didn't even have goosebumps, nor did he shiver.

"The cold doesn't bother me," Rylion said. "It never has."

What a mild way to explain what was happening. The cold didn't bother him? He wasn't even affected!

Lydia took a deep breath and fiddled with the sticks for her arrows. "Rylion's mother…"

I waited, but she didn't finish. I turned back to Rylion.

"My mother had magic," he said. "Much like you. She was a Lord of Winter Stillness, which means I am as well."

"You should have explained yourself sooner," I said with a huff. "All *this* and that's the explanation? Hmpf."

Rylion laughed. "You make it sound as though it's my fault you jumped into the river."

"It *is* your fault! I wouldn't have thought to save you if you hadn't been—well, er—if you hadn't been flailing about in the river!"

But Rylion did away with his mirth. "The news of my mother doesn't surprise you?"

"I've known other lords of magic," I said. "Only a few. But there are others."

"And you're not surprised to hear I'm a lord?"

"You and your brother have both done things that I'd consider extraordinary. Unequaled strength. Swift aim. Now a frozen river. I would have figured it out eventually."

"My mother told me she was the last one."

"Well, your mother lied."

Lydia tensed.

Already, I regretted my words. I had said them so quick, without a second thought, and Rylion's silence didn't help with my guilt.

"Forgive me," I said. "I didn't know her. Maybe she just didn't know."

Rylion shook his head. "I already knew she was wrong. God-King Eliezer called for lords of magic to be brought to the capital, so obviously there were more. My mother may have been misinformed."

Lydia forced a laugh. "Well, this has been one crazy mornin'. Makes for a dang good story, though. I'm sure Steen will appreciate knowin' he isn't the only one to taste the sting of the Esta River."

"Steen fell into the river and needed saving," Rylion said. "I think that's a little different."

I walked away from Rylion and Lydia, my skin covered in goosebumps. Once I was a fair distance away, I twisted a stream of flame around me, clearing a segment of snow away in a brutal burst of heat. The steam and mist circled into the air. It didn't take long for the heat to clear everything, leaving my clothing dry and my black hair frizzled. I attempted to pat the locks down, but nothing worked.

"That was amazin'," Lydia said, her mouth agape.

I shrugged off her awe. "'Twas nothing."

"I think it was quite impressive," Rylion said.

My chest tightened and I couldn't find the words to express my gratitude for his approval. I shouldn't have valued his more than anyone else's, but his praise was different. For the first time in a long while, I smoothed my coal-colored hair, hoping I didn't look too disheveled from my time in the water.

Rylion walked to a half-charred tree and kicked it over. Ash floated on the wind and settled onto the snowbank, creating spots amid the perfect white. He took a seat and Lydia joined him.

"Can you make a fire?" he asked.

A campfire sprang to life where I willed it, a few feet in front of the log. It needed no source of fuel—the fire would remain so long as I had the strength to hold it. I opened my satchel and withdrew a slab of jerky, but then I remembered Steen had prepared it for me. I mulled over my options as my stomach gurgled in defiance.

"Maybe you're cursed because you have magic," Lydia said.

I cringed just hearing her discuss my mark. What if there were brigands nearby who could hear? Or a passing huntsman? Anyone interested in a quick coin could stalk us back to the lodge and kill everyone in their sleep. It was best never to admit there were the cursed among us.

Rylion must have sensed my apprehension because he said, "We shouldn't discuss it. Besides, Wulf and I are lords of magic, but we have no mark. I think there has to be another explanation."

I held my jerky close and stared at the ground. The crackle of the new fire soothed my thoughts. "You feel none of the cool water's chill?"

"No. It washes over my skin with little effect."

"Truly?" I whispered.

He nodded.

"Why were you standing in it?"

"The water weighs me down and fighting against the current helps build muscle. I feel lighter on the land, and a little more agile because of it."

"Don't you slip?"

"I've long since become accustomed to the slickness of ice. My footing is steadfast, I assure you."

Hm. Interesting. My magic seemed more a tool to be used, but his seemed to help him in every aspect of life. Then again, the fire kept me warm, even with little clothing. Perhaps he had just mastered another aspect of magic I had never known existed. My father hadn't been the greatest teacher, after all, and my mother hadn't had the gift. She had simply used my father to have a gifted child.

My thoughts returned to Rylion. Lydia had said he came to the river at night, no doubt when the water was at its coldest, which meant he could truly survive no matter the frigid temperature.

"Did your mother do anything extraordinary with her abilities?" I asked.

Rylion nodded. "She could mend flesh. Heal any injury."

That was a beautiful power. Too bad she was one of the Forsaken.

"A healer," Lydia said. "That's impressive."

Then Rylion grew silent and still. My father had often said *still water runs deep*. I had always thought he had meant actual water, but after meeting Rylion, I could understand my father had been referring to people.

"Allow me to dry you off," I said.

I wanted the closeness—helping him, like he often helped me. At first, I thought he would refuse, but then Rylion relaxed and nodded. I stepped closer and kept a flicker of flame in my palm as I ran my hand close to his body. The heat dried his clothing, one inch at a time.

He smiled, and I couldn't help but grow red.

"What is it?" I demanded. "Are you mocking me because this process is so slow? I can use more fire, but then you'd be burned."

Rylion shook his head. "No. It's not that. I was just thinking… It's not every day a beautiful woman jumps into a river to save me, and then uses her divine fire to make sure I'm dry."

I caught my breath, my throat tight.

Beautiful? *Me?*

No. He had to be joking. He didn't mean it. I wore no elegant gowns nor brushed my hair with shiny oils. This was a cruel jest to laugh at my reaction—to make me swoon so he could say how foolish I had been for believing him.

"Artemis?" he asked, dragging me from my thoughts. "Are you all right?"

His genuine concern dispelled my previous thoughts.

Rylion wasn't the type of man to say things with the intention of harm. If he had said I was beautiful, then he meant it.

"I'm fine," I said as I jerked my hand away from him. "Just… sit next to the fire here. It'll dry you the rest of the way." With my face red, I took a seat back on the tree stump.

The last of the water on his cloak and armor floated away as steam.

Lydia had watched our exchange with an intent focus, though she glanced away whenever I turned in her direction, feigning interest in the wildlife. I clenched my jaw. Why was there always someone else around? If Rylion and I had been alone, perhaps I could've…

No. Just because he gave me a compliment didn't mean he wanted anything further. Or perhaps he did, and I just didn't know how to reciprocate his advances, and I was unknowingly rejecting him.

Or perhaps I was being over analytical. Yes. Contemplating the situation to absurdity. He wasn't initiating anything between us. There were other reasons for his actions. He was a kind man. Polite. Gentle. Of course he gave women compliments.

The crackle of fire helped calm my nerves, but my anxiety returned in full force when I spotted four men atop the hillside across the river. I held my cloak close as I eyed the strangers. Rylion and Lydia followed my gaze.

The men wore heavy furs and carried wooden traps over their shoulders. Each had a tall and full figure—none of them apprentices learning the ropes. They were hunters, but did they hunt the cursed as well as wild game? Their still silence agitated me. What were they thinking?

"Hail, travelers," Rylion called out. "Are you cold? We have a fire."

I grabbed Rylion's arm. "Do you know them?"

"No. But the weather can be unforgiving."

"You can't trust them," I said in a harsh whisper. "They could attack us in an instant. Each is armed, and there are more of them than us. I'm sure your armor alone would fetch a pretty coin at the bazaar."

"They've no reason to harm us."

"I gave you a reason," I snapped. "Money. Greed motivates a great many. Besides, mankind doesn't need a reason. It's human nature to hate those outside of one's chosen group. And there's no decree to dissuade them from killing us. They'll gut us for their own amusement, I'd bet everything I have on it."

One hunter, marked with silver on his temples, shook his head and held up an open palm. He and his men walked off down the other side of the hill, their steps remarkably quiet, despite the powdered snow.

They must have assumed we were luring *them* into a trap.

This was what I needed to do. Protect Rylion from himself. He could have easily become a corpse on the side of the river, even if he possessed magic.

Rylion sighed. "You're wrong."

I almost laughed. "I've seen it with my own eyes. You can't trust someone you don't know—and you never truly know someone."

Lydia crossed her arms. "That's mighty bleak."

"Do *you* think I'm wrong?" I asked.

She didn't answer, but I knew her true thoughts.

Rylion glanced out to the broken ice of the river. "I think everyone yearns for stability and respect."

Although I admired Rylion's adherence to his beliefs, they got under my skin like a terrible itch. How could he say such things? Had he lived a sheltered life in Ludlow?

I really did need to look after him.

I paced my room, glancing at the window from time to time.

The glory of the moon was obscured by passing clouds. The noises from downstairs had long since ended. I should have been asleep, but fear kept me wide awake. What if it happened again tonight? What if my mark burned and my body went weak?

The thoughts haunted me.

I jumped when someone tapped on my door. I took a moment to calm my breathing before replying, "Who is it?"

"It's Wulf. I have something for you."

Perhaps a quiet lad would have struggled to get his voice through a thick, wooden door, but Wulf's boisterous energy could pierce steel.

I walked over and opened the door. Wulf greeted me with a smile, a lantern in one hand and the other curled into a fist. I lifted an eyebrow. He opened his palm and showed me a collection of metal rings used in scholar's robes. He had eight in total, and I took them, if only because that was what he seemed to want.

"Thirteen, right?" he asked.

"Years of study?" I replied. "Yes." I glanced down at the rings on my collar. My five, plus the new eight would give me the correct amount. "Where did you get these?"

"My uncle had some lying around. He got new ones with each set of robes."

"Hm. I'm surprised your uncle would part with these."

"Why?"

"He doesn't need to use them?"

Wulf smiled a hesitant smile. "Well, he's not really a scholar any longer. He gave up his studies and doesn't like to admit he's an educated man."

I played with the rings in my hand. "He also seemed possessive of certain items. It made me think he was materialistic."

"Possessive?"

"He came in here the other day demanding I give him my scarf." I held the piece of clothing tightly. I feared Bryn might try to take it if I wasn't looking, so I kept it close at all times.

"The scarf used to be my mother's," Wulf said with a sigh. "My uncle likes to keep her belongings around, though I don't know why. I always thought it was for my father's benefit. He says they're mementoes."

"This was your mother's?"

The scarf suddenly felt three times heavier. How could Rylion part with something so precious?

Wulf nodded. "Yeah. She made it by hand. I'm sure she'd be happy to know someone was wearing it now."

"Hm."

"Need help piercing the rings through the robes?"

I shook my head. "No. But thank you. For this."

Wulf returned to smiling.

I mulled over the information he had given me. By the time I regained my focus and looked up, Wulf was already down the hall, walking with a slight limp but keeping a steady pace. He recovered quickly, and I assumed it had something to do with youth. Or maybe his magic.

Especially if his mother could heal broken flesh.

Once Wulf entered his room, the hallway was cast back into darkness.

With that, I shut my door.

I never would have imagined someone would part with a gift from their lost parent. How could Rylion do such a thing? Did he lack attachment? Perhaps. Perhaps he cared deeply for nothing. Maybe that was why he had no wife or family, despite his age.

I glanced at the window. Still night. Fatigue gripped me.

The bed glowed with a welcoming warmth, but guilt plagued my thoughts along with fear.

Even if Rylion had no real connection with his mother, I couldn't wear her scarf.

I removed the garment and held it in my hands.

Maybe I could give it to him tonight—a fine excuse to see him, and to ask about how frequently his mother's mark had acted up. Hopefully, it hadn't been often.

Determined to ease my fears, I slipped out of my room and into the shadowy hall. The chill of a winter evening hung all around me, but the smell of burning logs told me someone still tended to the fire downstairs.

Before I walked to Rylion's door, another person stepped out into the hall with feather-touch steps and hushed breathing. I pressed my back against the wall and waited in the shadows. Who else was up at this hour?

Whoever it was crept along without much sound, stopping once and listening, like a rabbit with its ears up. Finally, they reached a door and tapped—soft in every regard. The door opened, casting a column of light into the hall and illuminating the mystery individual.

Thea. The girl who tended to the horses.

She pushed her long, caramel hair behind her ears. Glints of light caught a few strands, and they shimmered like polished gold. "May I come in?" she whispered.

It struck me then that she was at Rylion's room. He opened the door wide and nodded, allowing her to step in. When the door shut, I regained my breathing. A million questions rushed through my mind afterward.

Were they lovers? If they were, Rylion would be cursed. It was against the god-king's decrees to lie with another before marriage. And I had specifically asked—he wasn't married, nor was he cursed.

So why would he see her so late at night? If not for a tryst, I had little idea of another motive.

Could it be that Thea was trying to seduce him?

The urge to knock on the door and demand answers was strong. Men were lustful creatures. They sought carnal pleasure as often as a cat sought a nap. Sure, some men were celibate, that had to be thanks to the god-king's decrees, but someone Rylion's age would be easily tempted. And Thea had nothing to lose since she was already cursed, only companionship to gain.

I hated the thought of Rylion becoming cursed, like me. Every day I suffered. Rylion didn't deserve such a fate.

I paced the hall, debating with myself about whether I should go in or leave them alone. I settled for a halfway solution and walked to the door with soft steps. Holding my breath, I pressed my ear against the wood and listened.

Nothing.

The room—the whole lodge—sat quiet.

They weren't even talking? Why?

Then again, silence wasn't the activity I was worried about. Perhaps Thea, being as small as she was, needed warmth. I grew red thinking of a scene in which she crawled into another man's bed for the heat. There were other ways. She could sleep by the hearth. There was no need to climb into someone's bed.

Embers shone in the air, appearing like phantom fireflies, and I realized then my hatred raged out of control. I staggered back into the wall and waited, hoping the manifestation of my magic would wane.

I jumped when I heard a floorboard creak.

Caprice hovered in the shadows, only visible thanks to the gentle glow of the fading embers. She brushed back her long hair, never saying a word.

I moved away from Rylion's door, and Caprice tracked my movement with a turn of her head. But still—she didn't say anything. The thought of admitting my insecurities bothered me. I didn't want to discuss my activities with anyone, especially not Caprice.

Without acknowledging the woman, I returned to my room.

***

The morning arrived, though I had never slept. Heat had coursed through my veins the entire evening. But I refused to become a person who dwelled on insecurity and jealousy. I had decided I would confront Thea and Rylion and learn their intentions. If they were to be wed, I would have no recourse. But if they weren't, I would advise Rylion to keep his distance. The temptations of the flesh often lured men away from the roads of the righteous.

After I had made my decision, I walked down to the front room. The smell of ash and charcoal comforted me, but the cold hearth was anything but welcoming.

Steen sat at the long table, plucking sinister birds and skinning roots. Bryn rolled up the rugs to take outside and beat. As they worked, Bryn snorted and coughed.

"Still no children?" Bryn asked in a quiet tone. "It's been years now…"

Steen growled a curse under his breath I couldn't hear.

He shot Bryn a heated glare, but they both halted their conversation when they noticed me walking down the stairs. Their tense posture and narrowed eyes betrayed their true feelings, but I already knew they didn't care for me. I held onto my cloak and returned their cold stares with one of my own.

Bryn cleared his throat. "Artemis. I need to thank you for protecting my nephew from the brigands."

His words rang with a forced timbre.

Wulf had gone out of his way for me several times. I suspected he wanted something—perhaps my attention, or my favor—but he had never demanded anything from me. And the brigands weren't worthy of the gift of life, not when they were so keen to take it from others. It was logical, and only proper, that I help Wulf when trouble arose.

I walked down the stairs and nodded, unsure of what to say to Bryn.

"So, the Holy Guard wants you because you're a Lord of Flame and Cinder, is that it?" Steen asked with all the politeness of an unruly child.

"No," I replied.

"Did you do something with your fire that got you cursed?"

"I told you. I was born cursed."

"Heh," he muttered. "What crock."

In a moment of spite, I lit the hearth with a glorious burst of flame. Bryn and Steen stumbled to get away and both tumbled to the floor. The crackle and swirl of my divine magic filled the room with heat, but I held back and lessened the intensity as I made my way to the front door. I knew such actions wouldn't endear either man to me, but I frankly didn't care. If they were callous and looking to oust me from their group, I would show them the powers I was capable of.

Maybe then they'd think twice about agitating me.

But when I placed my hand on the handle of the large lodge door, I hesitated.

Rylion wouldn't have lashed out at them. Didn't I admire his serenity? If I did, I should imitate it whenever possible.

"My flames will keep the hearth alive forever," I muttered. "No need to feed it wood or other fuels."

Neither man answered.

I continued, "I will make all the lodge's fire as such. If either of you need anything, even warm water for your bath, please come to me first. I want to be useful to the group."

I never turned to speak with them, and I didn't know their

facial expressions, but I heard the scrape of chairs and the patting of clothes.

"Very generous of you," Bryn said. "Thank you."

Steen returned to his food prep. "Just as long as you don't burn the lodge down. I don't think Bryn and I can quell an inferno."

The last bit left me with a smile. Both were men of indoor pursuits. And his jest took away the edge of my anger. Perhaps he would consider me useful enough that he soon wouldn't attempt to slight me at every opportunity.

I left the lodge and headed for the horses. They had their own furnace to keep them warm during the winter and removing the necessity to keep it fueled would be a help.

The days had been clear of clouds, save for the swarms of birds that occasionally streaked across the sky. How was it that Osmund, Rylion, and the others had difficulty finding one of the Forsaken? They were large beasts, and they didn't typically hide themselves from hunters. They didn't typically do anything in the way of strategy, really.

I contemplated the mystery as I rounded the corner into the small and sheltered area for the horses. The furnace burned hot, and the five mares gathered close to it. Walking between them, brushing their manes and tails, was none other than Thea. Her fingers grazed their coats with the gentle fondness a mother showed a child.

All tenderness left her the moment I drew near. She half-ducked behind the neck of a horse, shielding herself. The animals whinnied and neighed, each watching me as I walked closer.

"Thea," I said. "Do you have a moment?"

She frowned. For a second, I thought she might ignore my question. Finally, she replied, "I suppose I can talk while I do my chores."

"Good. I was hoping I'd see you at some point."

"Oh."

"I saw you slip out of your room last night. I know where you went."

Thea's frown deepened.

"What're your intentions with Rylion?" I demanded, my voice louder than I had intended. "I won't take silence as an answer."

CHAPTER TEN

"My intentions?" Thea repeated. She stayed close to the horse, never matching my gaze. "What are you accusing me of?"

"Don't play daft. You know full well what I mean." When she didn't answer, I walked over to the furnace. "Even though you're cursed, you should abide by the decrees. You could harm Rylion with your carnal desires. If you must be with him, and he must be with you, at least wait until you're wed. That way, Rylion won't be cursed himself."

"I have no desire for intimacy," she muttered.

"Then why go to him in the middle of the night? Can't you see how that would be interpreted?"

Thea grazed the neck of the horse, her gaze downcast. Then she whispered, "Rylion has an aura about him."

She added nothing else, fueling my ire. "Explain," I said. "I'm more than capable of understanding."

She took in a ragged breath, but never said a word. Minutes passed. I tried to hold back my frustrations. I tried. But she had to be lying. Why else feign ignorance when I had first demanded answers? *What are you accusing me of?* That had been her response, like she hadn't the faintest idea. She had known. Of course she had known. The thought drove me to anger.

"What do you mean by *aura*?" I said. "Do you mean he protects you?"

"Th-That's not it," she said.

"Then what?"

"He stops me from changing," Thea replied, louder than before. She snapped her attention to me, tears at the corners of her eyes. "When I feel like I'll transform into one of the Forsaken, his mere presence drives it away."

I held my breath as the words repeated in my mind. Memories of the night I almost turned still haunted me, but Rylion had been there to chase away the pain…

Did Rylion really have such a power? He had said his mother had magic—magic far different from my destructive fire—but I had never imagined anyone could hold back the justice of the decrees.

But he had. If Thea knew it as well, if she experienced the same thing I had, then it had to be true. It had to be.

"I go to him when I worry," she said. "I don't want to become a monster…"

And her words dug into my thoughts. I had wanted to visit Rylion for the same reason. He did have a calming presence, and with my quick temper, I had thought it useful to be near him. Thea must have had the same plan in mind.

"Which decree did you break?" I asked. What if there was something about her that still spelled trouble for Rylion? I wanted to know. I had to know.

She stepped away from me. "I'd rather not discuss it."

"Why? Is it that heinous?"

She wallowed in silence.

I glared at the furnace and the fire inside twisted into something far brighter and hotter. My magic flared along with my irritation. Flames appeared in a swirl around me—tiny flames, more sparks and embers than anything—but they caught the hay and wood, and they rang with a pop when bursting into existence.

Thea cringed back, and the horses jolted around, whinnying with wide-eyed expressions. I held out my hand to calm one, but it knocked me back with its neck and I stumbled into the wall of the lodge, painfully reminded of a horse's physical capabilities. Certain I would be bruised the next morning, I grabbed at my chest where the beast had hit me.

The fire died with my frustrations. Thea held one of the mares, calming it with a soothing voice. I opened my mouth to say something, but she looked away, her eyebrows knitted.

"You don't understand," Thea said.

She ran from the shelter, leaving me confused.

"Wait!"

I attempted to follow her, but the horses crossed in front of me and snorted. One bashed me with its long snout—nothing too brutal, but enough to push me away. I distanced myself from the animals. When I gazed out into the snow, I spotted Thea's trail, but no other sign of the woman.

Cursing under my breath, I returned to the furnace.

I paced the small space, comforted by the heat. The animals huddled together on the opposite side of the tiny shelter, each horse staring at me like I was a danger. I was certain if I approached, I would be kicked.

With a hand on my scarf around my neck, I came to a stop. I should have apologized to Thea. It was what a decent person would do, even if I doubted her trustworthiness.

Caprice jumped down from the roof of the horse shelter and landed in front of the gate.

I leapt back, unaware she had been on the roof this entire time. She stood and straightened her white robes before walking into the enclosure, her expression neutral. The horses relaxed at the sight of her.

"Do you parade around on rooftops often?" I snapped.

"Only when I'm following you," she said.

I gritted my teeth. *"Following me*? You eavesdropped on my conversation?"

Caprice smoothed her long, ebony hair—it went down past her waist, and it maintained its lush beauty the entire way down. I had known a few merchants from Saileer and each had had hair just as long as Caprice's. It must have been fashionable there, and for a moment, I admired how well-kept it was.

"Can I tell you a story?" she asked out of nowhere.

I pulled my cloak tight, confused by the shift in subject. "You're a priestess, is that right? All you do is tell stories."

"I want to tell you a story of the gods of old."

I didn't know much about the gods of old. The god-kings and god-queens often discouraged worshipping the old gods, like praising them would somehow lessen their authority. *The era of the old gods was dead*, that was what they chanted at the New Year. *The era of god-kings and god-queens is upon us. An era of mankind.*

But I was curious as to what Caprice would say. She had followed me, after all.

"Tell me your story," I said.

Caprice smiled and pointed to the fire in the furnace. "There were once six gods that ruled over every kingdom. Ravintus, the War God, was known for his agonizing fire." She motioned to the scorch marks I had created around the shelter. "His rage came quick and often, but he also knew unequaled passion. When he loved something, he loved it entirely, and without equal."

The War God?

Caprice continued, "Remind you of anyone?"

I glared but said nothing.

"And there was Vahltera, the Temperance God, known for her life-giving waters. She exuded tranquility and compassion. Never quick to decide. Never in the throes of anger. Her strength of flesh and willpower knew no equal, yet she never had the need to fight."

"These aren't stories," I said with an exhale. "Stories have a beginning, a middle, and an end. These are just statements. If you have a point, get to it."

"They loved each other," Caprice said, wistfulness in her voice. "Both the War God and the Temperance God. Unparalleled love. But when a war between the gods became inevitable… the War God and Temperance God chose opposite sides. The War God wanted to destroy mankind, and the Temperance God wanted to protect us."

"Okay. And?"

Caprice frowned as she clasped her hands together. "The war was terrible. The six gods took sides. The War God, the God of Truths, and the Despair God all wanted humanity destroyed. They hated our independence, destruction of the land, and selfish natures."

I knew next to nothing of the ancient wars. How accurate was Caprice? It made me curious.

"The Temperance God, the God of Falsehoods, and the Hope God all came to humanity's defense," she said. "They saw us as creative, innovative, and a powerful source of good in the universe."

"Even the God of Falsehoods, huh?" I quipped.

Caprice tilted her head. "Well, he liked humanity because we're the only creatures who lie, cheat, and steal. He wanted to save us for his own personal reasons."

"Lovely." I waved my hand in a circle. "I haven't got all day. Wrap this up."

"At the start of the war, the God of Truths laid waste to the land, and the War God used his magic to curse all of mankind. He instilled a deep rage into all of us—one that drove every man into a murderous frenzy. To curb his influence, the Temperance God murdered him."

"Romantic," I drawled. "A love story for the ages."

Caprice shook her head. "Heartbroken, the Temperance God buried herself alive."

What a bleak and depressing tale. None of my history tomes ever mentioned that.

"Why tell me this?" I asked.

"Those with magic are descended from the old gods," Caprice said. "That's why they're referred to as *lords of magic.* They're granted divine lordship through dynasty."

I sighed. "People aren't descended from the old gods. That's just a fairy tale. Magic is merely a gift they gave us." If I were a child of the old gods, how could I be marked by the curse? The old gods couldn't be affected by the decrees.

Caprice stepped closer to me, her eyes intense and unblinking. "You don't understand. You need to know what happened to your progenitor, so that you can avoid the same fate."

"For the last time—I'm not a descendant. I won't share any fates."

"Fire knows no age."

"What?" I asked, confused by the odd statement.

"Fire," she said. "It's ageless. That's why descendants of the War God appear so young. As a Lord of Flame and Cinder, you will always be youthful. Always."

I slowly ran a hand down my body. But it meant nothing. Youth could have been a gift from the old gods, just like their magic. It didn't mean anything else.

Priestesses of the old gods were rare. They claimed the god-kings and god-queens were nothing more than imposters —that they pretended at godhood like a thespian pretended a story. Those kinds of statements often got priestesses killed.

The old gods had granted the god-kings and god-queens the powers of decree—the right to make laws as they saw fit. The old gods had passed on their divinity before disappearing from our world. If I *was* a descendant, I was nothing more than a forgotten child, left behind on a world ruled by children. I supposed that was fitting. I was twice cursed.

"The old gods will return," Caprice said, as though she could read my thoughts. "When the era of mankind has fallen. They will return."

"Why are you telling me all this?" I asked.

"As a priestess of the old gods, I took an oath to protect their children."

"Telling me a random story is hardly protection."

"You still don't understand. I see the signs of the War God in you, and history has a tendency of repeating itself. It's my sacred duty to protect you from the same fate."

"Then you've nothing to fear."

When I died, it would likely be to the overwhelming forces trying to kill me. The curse, or perhaps the god-king's Scourge—my future lover taking my life wasn't even in the realm of possibility. Although I wanted to be with Rylion, I wouldn't allow him to harm me.

I stepped around Caprice and ignored her statements. It didn't matter who I was, or what the old gods would do in my situation. If she wanted to waste her time believing in fantastical tales, she could.

The bitter cold clung to me as I stepped out of the shelter. I turned for the lodge, but my gaze landed on Thea's footprints through the snow, and I came to a halt. Caprice watched me, unspeaking. Then I followed Thea's trail, intent on making peace with her before I headed back into the warmth.

Gods damn me.

Where had Thea gone? I had been walking for an hour, and not on the path Lydia and I usually took. There was no wind or hail or snow. I was sure I could find my way back through the furrow I had left in my wake, so why couldn't I follow Thea's?

And traveling alone reminded me of my time on the run.

I needed to find Thea. It would weigh on my conscience if she disappeared on the slopes of Mount Regel. I shouldn't have conducted myself like an inquisitor. I should have been more thoughtful.

A flock of sinister birds streaked from the trees. I stopped walking, curious as to the cause of their commotion. The midmorning sun didn't help my observation. I held a hand over my eyes and took note of the rustling trees.

A rumble—a vibration—coursed through the soles of my feet. I held my breath, dread seeping into my thoughts.

Trees dotted the area around me. I jumped through the snow and slammed my back against one, hoping to stay hidden. A terrible scream pierced the air.

The Forsaken always had nightmarish cries.

My thoughts turned dark in an instant.

Was it Thea? Had she succumbed to the transformation during my pursuit?

No. It couldn't have been that. Surely, I would have seen some indication in her trail that she was suffering—blood weeping from her mark and staining the snow. Or maybe she had turned quick? I didn't know, and I didn't have a way of discovering unless I saw the Forsaken myself.

A second scream, this one guttural and soaked in agony. Different from the first in every regard.

Were there two? *Two* Forsaken roaming the mountain? Or maybe one was Rylion's mother. Perhaps I had found her before they had.

The rumbling beneath my feet grew worse. Frost fell from the branches of the pine trees, a flurry of snowflakes coating my head and shoulders. I slid down the trunk into a sitting position, hoping to keep myself out of sight. I was in dark-colored clothing, noticeable against the ivory snow, much to my frustration.

Could I kill *two* Forsaken with my divine fire? I didn't want to try, not when a single mistake could lead to a swift death. But there was a chance I would have no choice.

Mountain creatures dashed by the tree in droves. Goats, deer, and silver hares. The silver hares were magical creatures, and they used their magic to glide over the snow without leaving prints, but the other animals struggled to run, some chest-deep in slush as they trudged forward, their eyes wide.

The thunder crash of a felled tree rang in my ears. I chanced a glance around the trunk and regretted my decision. A Forsaken rushed through the sparse forest, chasing its prey with a single-minded intensity not found in man.

The beast was hideous.

It had the form of a razorback hog, with sharp tusks that jutted from its lower jaw. The monster's hide—black as ink— was marked with tufts of white hair at its joints and down its spine. It charged forward, the size of an elephant, smashing trees as it went.

When it ran past, I pressed myself against the trunk, my nose filled with the horrid stench of death.

Four tentacles sprouted from the Forsaken's back and flailed around, each the length of a person and as thin as a snake. One tentacle lashed out and grabbed a fleeing doe, pulling it back despite the doe's frantic bleats. The tentacles trapped the animal as the hog mounted it from behind, pinning the doe under its massive body.

A barbed erection unsheathed itself from the folds of black skin under the Forsaken's body. I was less than fifty feet away as the Forsaken split the doe in twain, ripping it apart starting with the anus.

I wanted to move, I really did, but terror locked me in place.

To my horror, the second Forsaken arrived through the trench the first had made in its charge. The new monster was a snake with seven heads and many tiny arms that dragged it along the snow, like a centipede. It, like the first, was massive, the size of three stallions, but the monster's body was elongated and serpentine. It hissed and flailed about, a human skull protruding out of its back, a face of twisted agony plastered across the black bone.

A man.

I stared at the rutting hog. A human skull poked out of its ribcage.

Another man.

Neither of these monsters were Thea or Rylion's mother. Were they once bandits? There was no other explanation. They were evil men who had gotten their comeuppance, but now they wrecked the world for a second round.

The serpent Forsaken reached for the mangled corpse of the doe, its long, spindly hands grasping handfuls of flesh to stuff into its many snake heads. The boar Forsaken must have taken this as an insult, as it gored the serpent with its tusk. Crimson-black blood spilled across the snow. Steam rose from the injury in waves, and the two titans clashed with unbridled ferocity.

I stood and ran from my hiding place behind the tree, knowing full well I had to get out of the area. My feet crunched through the snow.

More sinister birds swirled in the sky, creating clouds with their bodies that cast shadows across Mount Regel. The two mammoth Forsaken screeched and spit, filling the area with their cries.

But then they stopped their fighting.

The Forsaken had spotted me. I didn't even need to turn around.

I just knew.

I felt their twisted eyes on my back as I pushed forward,

the cold air burning my lungs with each deep gulp. And then I heard them moving. Although I hadn't considered the incline of the mountain steep when I had been searching for Thea, now it felt like an insurmountable sheer cliff. I couldn't climb fast enough. The Forsaken would catch me for sure.

Shadows blanketed me. I glanced up to the ridge of the slope and caught the silhouette of horses. I gritted my teeth.

It was the God-King Eliezer's Holy Guard.

CHAPTER ELEVEN

The sinister horses charged down the snowy peaks, their black coats a harsh juxtaposition to the white of the mountain. Two of the Holy Guard veered toward me while the rest, including Alexavier, headed for the Forsaken.

When the first soldier drew close, I washed him in bluish-white flame, heating the metal of his armor and startling his horrible sinister mount. The monster horse reared up and sent its charred rider tumbling into a snowbank.

The second rider rushed by and struck me with a sword made of King's Stone. The black blade had the same lifeless hue as the horses, and it sliced across the flesh of my arm and shoulder with little difficulty, burning as it did so, like the weapon itself yearned for my death.

I staggered back and grabbed at the injury. The slash wasn't deep, but my hands shook with each second of examination. The superficial graze left an agonizing sting. If I took a deep cut, I would fall fast to paralysis.

Steeled to fight for my life, I straightened my stance and held out my hand. Fire sprang to life around me and rushed forward in a twister of unmitigated heat. The flames turned everything to cinders. The charred smell of smoke filled the area, and steam clouded the area from the melted snow. I took in deep breaths and coughed, gagging on the terrible taste of destruction.

The second rider struggled with the depth of the snow, but his steed had the strength of five horses. It leapt over a snowbank and charged back at me, spittle lacing its heavy breaths.

I unleashed a torrent of flame, but unlike the first horse, the beast wasn't deterred. It rammed into me, sending me to the ground. My fire persisted and the soldier screamed an undignified stream of incomprehensible words, pleading to someone or something.

Pick a god and pray, fool—*you* wanted us to fight to the death, not me.

My fire burned everything, including the sinister horses. When the resilient horse came a third time, I was ready. I unleashed a pyre of destruction, searing the trees and the edges of my robes. The rider fell and the horse staggered into the snow before collapsing.

Then I saw Alexavier. He was truly the god-king's Scourge. His steed leapt toward the boar Forsaken and Alexavier leaned forward, his halberd at the ready. When they clashed, Alexavier cleaved through the monster's flesh, rending a front leg from the body and coating the nearby forest in foul blood. Before the beast could react, Alexavier urged his mount away. The precision betrayed his talent. And soon he would turn that talent on me.

Determined to escape with my life, I trudged through the snow, away from the fighting. If I could make it to safety, if I could make it to a hideaway…

Alexavier waved his hand and a river of orange-white fire washed over the boar Forsaken, melting flesh. Then he stabbed again, this time in the neck. The creature attempted to gore Alexavier, but it was too late. Alexavier slammed his halberd into the back of the monster's massive mouth, and blood gushed into its gullet, clogging the throat. The beast fell to the side, its legs twitching, its brain undoubtedly pierced.

Without wasting a second, Alexavier unsheathed a sword and took the moment to carve out the skull of the boar Forsaken before it rose again. The skull of the cursed man was so high up on the boar's body that Alexavier didn't even need to dismount to complete his task.

A harsh whistle echoed off the slopes.

It was Osmund's bow—Calavandi. I had heard it so many times, it was unmistakable.

I stopped running and stared. Osmund stood atop a fallen tree trunk, on the opposite side of the battlefield, his bone bow in hand.

The snake Forsaken fought the other five of the Holy Guard, but no matter how many times it was cut, or how many heads were rent from its body, the creature fought with the same ferocity. A bone arrow jutted from one of its necks, but the thick muscles under the scales prevented it from piercing deep.

To my horror, Alexavier pulled the reins of his sinister horse and headed straight for me. I stumbled backward through the snow, knowing my magic would do nothing to him.

Another harsh whistle rang in my ears.

An arrow slammed close to my position, almost hitting me, but the flurry of snow it kicked up stopped Alexavier's charge. He jerked his head to the side and glared.

"Osmund, you fool," Alexavier muttered through clenched teeth.

The snake Forsaken screamed, its many heads flailing about. When a Holy Guard soldier got close to it, a single snake head lashed out, caught the man in its jaw, and then crunched him in half, including his armor, spilling the man's guts across the mane of his horse. Another scream and a flock of sinister birds took to the air, their own squalls adding to the cacophony.

Alexavier glanced between me and his remaining soldiers, his breath held. After a second of contemplation, he pulled the reins and urged his steed back to the second monster.

With unparalleled strength and agility, Alexavier rushed the Forsaken and planted the tip of his halberd deep into the monster's chest. It screamed and spit a line of black liquid. Alexavier ducked away and the glob struck a tree, burning it away with its corrosive acid. A splash landed on the flank of his horse, however, disintegrating a hole in the muscle. His steed whinnied, but Alexavier stroked its mane and urged it on. The creature limped, and otherwise did as it was commanded.

Arrows rained down on the snake Forsaken. Wulf arrived from the main path, forty feet from the action, his yew bow at the ready, firing as fast as his arms would allow. Rylion joined him. He pinned back his cloak, creating a cape, and strode toward the bleeding monster.

I ran to Rylion and Wulf without looking back. The cry of the birds and the Forsaken would haunt my nightmares, but there was nothing I could do about that. I focused my attention on staying by Rylion's side. His presence was a promise—a reassurance everything would turn out all right.

"Retreat," Alexavier called out to the two remaining soldiers. "I'll handle the rest!"

The multi-headed snake coughed up another glob of acid, coating the snow and road. One soldier ran through it, and the hooves of his sinister horse melted away at a shocking rate. He was thrown from his mount and landed neck-first upon an icy boulder. The last soldier rode away unscathed, but his horse appeared beaten and worn.

Alexavier ripped his halberd from the snake and stabbed it again. Before the Forsaken retaliated, Osmund fired Calavandi. The bone arrow pierced through one side of the largest snake head and shot out the other. The snake's eyes glazed and the creature screeched once more before falling, its smaller heads writhing as though without control.

For a strained second, no one moved. The chaotic cloud of birds never swooped down or interfered, they simply blotted out the sun, casting strange shadows between us.

Alexavier turned to me, his blood-coated halberd held in one hand.

"Artemisia, if you're a woman of honor, you won't involve the others," he said, his voice as icy as the snow around us. "Osmund, I'd hate to kill a former member of the Holy Guard in front of his sons. Consider your future."

Osmund nocked another arrow. "I'm not so old. Perhaps you'd better rethink your position."

I held my breath. Wulf and Rylion gave me a quick nod.

"Stand back," Rylion said. "No harm will come to you."

His confidence was there, but there was also a strain to his voice I had never heard before. Was he afraid? Was he worried? Guilt wracked me. Alexavier wanted me and me alone. And I wouldn't have been caught if I hadn't chased Thea away from the lodge. This was my fault. All of it.

Alexavier readied his halberd. Despite his steed's injuries, it growled and steeled itself, like it could read its master's intentions.

"You know I can't back down," Alexavier said.

Osmund pulled back the string of his compound bow. "I know."

A shrieking roar interrupted the scene. The storm of birds chattered and swarmed, flying together in a perfect tornado formation. Everyone turned their gaze to the sky, and Osmund lowered his weapon.

Up on the mountain, not far from our position but high enough to witness clearly, a massive form burst from the trees. It was a monster—a Forsaken—a gargantuan bird of white and gray feathers. It had four wings, two large, and two small and misshapen. And it screeched again, throwing back its head to reveal a beak made of gnarled bone. It must have been the size of a modest house, perhaps more.

"Mariana," Osmund muttered, his eyes wide. "It's her… She's finally come back to us."

Rylion and Wulf breathed deeply, their focus locked on their mother's twisted form.

"Another one," Alexavier said with a curse on his breath. "These mountains are filled with murderous bastards." He returned his attention to Osmund. "We have little time to settle this. Stand down or I'll run you through."

Mariana flapped her wings, destroying trees in the process. The birds flocked around her, crying in soft shrieks. She turned her attention to us—or, more likely, to the bloody corpses of the two slain Forsaken.

Osmund hefted his bow and Alexavier charged.

A terrible whistle heralded Osmund's shot, but the arrow flew right past Alexavier.

And then Alexavier swung wide with his halberd, catching Osmund's stomach and slicing open his gut. Organs fell from the severed membranes and Osmund crashed to his knees.

"Father!" Rylion shouted.

Wulf fired his yew bow, striking Alexavier, but the pitiful arrow couldn't pierce the black armor. He fired again regardless, aiming for connection points and the hole in the helmet, but that didn't stop Alexavier as he rounded toward us, his gaze locked on me.

Rylion, his short sword at the ready, stepped forward and met Alexavier on the icy road. When Alexavier swung, Rylion stepped aside, his footing solid despite the slick terrain. Before Alexavier passed, Rylion caught the man in the hip, slicing between plates of metal.

Wulf and I moved back behind a tree. Alexavier tried to urge his mount around, but the speed wasn't right. He took a wide turn, long enough for Rylion to ready himself for another attack.

"You'll die by my righteous flame," Alexavier said.

With a wave of his hand, the road was flooded in red and orange. Wulf stayed behind the trunk of the tree, and I pressed myself against him, not because the fire would hurt me, but because I wanted to protect Wulf as much as possible —my fireproof skin would act as a shield.

The moment the heat subsided, I whipped my attention to the road. Rylion was crouched down, his cloak swaddled around him. When he stood, he threw the cloak off. The fabric was burned away, leaving the strangest chain mail I had ever seen. Scales. It was made of… animal scales. But what animal could survive the harsh flames of divine magic?

But it mattered little. Rylion was unharmed.

A terrible shadow blanketed the area.

Mariana descended, her long legs adorned with sword-like talons. When she beat her wings, a squall kicked up around us. Through the wind and mayhem of bird feathers, I spotted her human face. A sad, twisted expression protruded from the chest of her monstrous body, her eyes unblinking and staring straight ahead.

Dozens of baby birds—half-formed and coated in mucus —wept from an orifice between her legs. Each one who landed on the ground started to form into a full-fledged sinister bird, growing a lifetime within a few seconds.

Alexavier attempted to throw his flame onto Mariana, but the wind blew everything away. Ice formed over the trees and road, becoming thicker with each second. Alexavier's sinister horse slipped and growled, and its movements grew slower and slower.

"Mariana!" Osmund called out. He held his guts like a child in his arms, but the color in his face had yet to drain. "I've come—I told you I'd come!"

Alexavier lifted his halberd to strike.

Osmund attempted to stand but couldn't. "No! I must be the one to put her to rest!"

Within the tense moment, Rylion struck at Alexavier from the side, cutting into his ribs and drawing blood. Alexavier's reaction was near immediate. He cleaved down with his halberd, catching Rylion between the folds of his cloak. Alexavier sliced deep across Rylion's chest, cutting through armor with little difficulty.

If Alexavier harmed Rylion… or if Rylion died…

I would burn this whole damn mountain to the ground.

When Rylion attacked again, Alexavier's mount slipped, but this time it fell over and tumbled down the slope of the mountain. It took Alexavier with it, and the flurry of snow and feathers became so thick, I lost sight of him after a few seconds.

"Mariana! Mariana… I'm so sorry."

As though Osmund didn't care if he lived or died, he released his hold on his wound and nocked another arrow. Mariana turned to face him, her wings beating heavily. She shrieked and lunged toward Osmund, her talons up and extended.

Osmund pulled the string back with a burst of strength and released. The arrow smashed into Mariana's chest, right into the heart, and sunk into the flesh up to the feather fletching of the arrow.

Mariana screamed, her large form shuddering after the shot. But then she moved forward regardless, her wings taking her the last of the distance. She reached out with her talons and grabbed Osmund like she, too, didn't care if she lived or died.

"Mariana!" Osmund shouted, but the rest of his voice was drowned out in the storm of birds.

Rylion slashed at the birds that flew close. I cleared the area with a burst of flame. The creatures took off, scattering in an instant. They no longer coordinated their attacks or flight, and when Mariana collapsed into the snow, the whole mountain trembled with her weight, sending the last of the birds into the sky. Mariana took in one final breath before exhaling. Her body shrank into itself, and her legs curled up to her chest, reminiscent of a dead spider.

When the birds finally disappeared into the distance, I gulped down a few ragged breaths. The chaos had left me drained and mentally fatigued. The whole encounter had lasted less than a few minutes, but it had been a lifetime of stress.

I surveyed the area.

Wulf leaned against the tree, his clothing scorched, but he was otherwise untouched. Rylion ran to his father, despite the gouge of flesh missing from his own chest.

And Osmund…

It took me a second to realize that Osmund stood tall, his shirt ripped open, but his body perfectly intact—no injuries whatsoever. He ran a shaky hand over his stomach, his mouth hanging open and his eyebrows knitted together.

In Mariana's last few moments of life—even as a Forsaken —she had healed Osmund.

Mount Regel was alive with conflict. The birds fought among themselves, the animals of the forest cowered in their dens, and the weather had an edge of malice, threatening to turn into a storm at any moment.

I hated the animosity. It stirred within me terrible memories.

Which was why I didn't want to return to the lodge. Artemis's questions had also reminded me of a past I wished I could forget. I would rather the cold weather numb me. That way, I could forget the feeling that ran down my spine when I remembered.

I walked down a long, snowy road, keeping my cloak shut tight. A whinny drew my attention, and I glanced over my shoulder. Then I gasped.

It was a sorrel mare—a beautiful horse—and I knew her well. Deana. She was the horse I had bonded with the most since Osmund had taken me into his ranks. He had given her to me when he had seen how I cared for her. Osmund was a such good man.

Deana trotted down the road toward me, and I embraced her neck with a tight hug the instant she was close.

"You ran out of the shelter," I said, half-laughing, half-crying. "I told you that's against the rules."

She nuzzled my neck. The warmth of her body brought back my happiness.

Deana must have known I had been upset when I had left. Some people thought horses were mindless beasts of burden, but those people knew nothing. Horses had personalities as big as they were, and Deana wouldn't have come to retrieve me if she were nothing more than a tool. She was my friend and confidant. I didn't know why, but horses had always understood me better than mankind.

I broke my embrace and stared into one of Deana's eyes. "Should we return?"

She nickered.

"I guess it's for the best," I muttered as I stroked her mane. "But maybe we can take the long way around, for extra time away?"

Deana had a thick coat and long mane, and her tail was fluffier than most. I knew she could withstand the chill of the snow, even if we took a few hours on our trek.

We turned and walked together as we strolled between the trees. Sometimes the snow hindered my speed, but Deana trudged forward, and I followed in her furrow. The peace of our silent partnership dispelled my anxiety. I breathed easy as I patted her flank.

But the moment didn't last long. A panicked neighing echoed throughout the forest. Deana's ears stood erect. Growling followed soon after. I had worked with horses all my life, and I was certain there was one nearby, clearly in distress.

"Come," I whispered to Deana. "We need to help."

I pulled myself onto her back. Although I disliked riding

without a saddle, there was little choice. I urged her forward and we headed straight for the commotion.

We passed several groups of trees and turned onto a narrow road. The frantic neighing never ended. It grew louder and louder as Deana and I pressed forward. Then we turned off the road and headed for a rock wall.

To my surprise, we found a black mare. Not any mare—a sinister horse. She stood a good foot or two taller than Deana, and she was clad in matte black armor. I remembered seeing this specific sinister horse before. She was a steed for the Holy Guard.

The longer I stared, the more details I took in. The mare guarded a mound of snow and feathers, growling and neighing as though her frustrations mixed together with fear in equal amounts.

Deana backed away from the sinister horse, snorting and stomping her hooves. Normal animals rarely got along with sinister creatures.

But this sinister horse didn't move. The fear in her equine expression pained me.

"It's fine," I whispered to Deana. "She's not going to hurt us."

I dismounted and examined the black mare.

Sinister animals were often despised. They were an unholy breed complete with semi-human features in places that should never have had them. The mare had a pair of human eyes under the horse's eyes. Her stare was enough to shake me, but I knew the sinister animals weren't the evil some made them out to be. They could be tame and gentle. I had once known a sinister dog that had stalked the edge of my village. He had been a kind beast until the hunters had come.

"Are you hurt?" I asked the mare.

She snorted and nudged the mound of snow with her

muzzle. Her flank had a large wound on it, like a hole had been burned into her flesh.

I stepped forward. "I won't hurt you."

The mare shoved the snow around.

"Is something there?" I asked.

When the mare didn't protest my approach, I walked over to the fresh snowbank. The feathers made everything look a mess, but I pushed them aside to search through the ice. I caught my breath the moment I stumbled upon an arm and face.

There was a man in the snow. Still wearing plate mail.

A member of the Holy Guard.

I jumped away from the body and held both my hands to my collarbone. Was he dead? He had to be. How could he survive being buried in the snow?

The mare gently nudged the man, and a line of hot breath escaped his lips.

I turned away. Deana trotted to my side, no doubt aware of my distress. When Deana drew near, I pressed myself against her side.

"We should leave him," I said. "I can't be here when he awakens."

The sinister mare bit at the man's armor and pulled. Nothing. The man didn't move outside of the occasional breath. Considering all the Forsaken in the area, I wouldn't have been surprised if he had been caught up in a terrible battle.

Crimson blood dotted the snow, adding to my theory.

He was dying.

I looked away.

For years, I had avoided people, especially men. Osmund and Rylion were the exceptions, but even then, I didn't seek their company longer than a few hours. Men frightened me more than anything else. So many memories of… of men like my father. I didn't trust them. I didn't want anything to do with them. I just wanted to be left alone.

The black mare neighed, her distress too much for me to ignore. She loved her rider and wouldn't leave without him.

I glanced back at the man in the snow. Could I even help him? He might be too far gone. But I did know of one place where he might recover.

The Boneyard. It was sacred and filled with magic.

But Osmund had told me never to bring anyone there…

"Please," Artemis said. "We must return to the lodge. You shouldn't walk around with an injury like yours."

She hovered close, fussing with the edge of my clothes, her intelligent gaze scrutinizing my every movement. She wanted to help me, but I couldn't leave my father. After cutting my mother's skull from the Forsaken's body, my father had a single goal: to set my mother to rest in the Boneyard.

My father staggered ahead of me, unspeaking, holding the black-bone fragment of my mother close to his chest.

"It's not much farther," I said.

Even that hurt. Every inhale, every movement of my arms —my wound burned, but I kept pressure on it, staving off the blood flow.

Wulf stayed nearby despite his bad leg. He had recovered fast, but the Boneyard would do him good. He said nothing, which was unusual, but there was nothing I could do at the moment. The less I spoke, the better.

We neared a sheer wall of rock near the middle of Mount Regel. To an untrained eye, it appeared as though nothing were here. To a keen observer, the rocks overlapped in a way that hid the entrance to a cave, a natural illusion born of similar colors and lack of light. Artemis had an astute mind and perceptive eye, however. She stared at the wall for a moment before she realized what we were here for.

"Is this wise?" Artemis asked. "Turmoil on the mountain could cause a rockslide, or an avalanche. What if we become trapped? In your condition—"

I placed a hand on her shoulder, and she stopped talking.

We headed for the hidden cave. The sinister birds never visited this place. No feathers. No blood. No fecal matter. They left it alone and untouched.

We entered the narrow passageway into the mountain. My father breathed deeply, and he muttered to my mother's skull, but I couldn't decipher his words. Wulf hobbled ahead to speak with him. Their conversation echoed against the walls as a blanket of ambient noise.

Darkness shrouded us for a few minutes, but then light returned to the cave. Stones embedded along the walls housed ancient magic, lighting the way like stars against the black sky.

Artemis kept pace with me, her head hanging. "Forgive me."

I took a shallow breath. "There's nothing—"

"He came for me," Artemis interjected. "And he's the god-king's Scourge—blessed by the god-king himself and a Lord of Flame of Cinder. He'll be back. He might even come for us now."

I mulled the words over. The man, Alexavier, was strong. I had felt it in the few short blows we had exchanged. Perhaps Artemis was correct, but it mattered not. I wouldn't surrender anyone in my protection to the god-king.

His decrees... I couldn't stand them.

Anger didn't come easily for me, but when I thought of the decrees the god-kings and god-queens issued, rage crept into my blood. The rules were unbending and thrust at the populace, attempting to tether them like wild dogs. They punished absolutely for crimes that may or may not even harm another, with no nuance. And the torment before the change—the animosity that went with being cursed… Some punishments were too great.

Was torture, fear, and death really the answer to a man who steals from the god-king's court? Was forcing someone to become a monster the correct response to accidentally killing a silver hare? Was it the appropriate punishment for loving someone outside of wedlock?

The decrees themselves treated all people as though they would act as animals without them. And there was no hope for redemption. Once someone had fallen, what incentive was there to stand back up?

"Say something," Artemis whispered, her gaze set on the floor. "Tell me it's all my fault you were injured and that your father almost perished. Tell me I'm a coward for not giving myself over when Alexavier gave me the chance."

I stared down at Artemis, pain flaring from my chest with each strained inhale.

She had been born cursed. In what scenario could that ever be acceptable? And here she was, apologizing to me because malevolent forces wished to snuff out her life. How warped was her reality that she would feel guilt for existing? This was the folly of the god-king and his decrees. They stifled life; They didn't enhance it. At least, not *this* god-king, not *his* decrees. Perhaps there was a ruler who knew the balance—who knew what and when to punish absolutely, but God-King Eliezer wasn't that man.

He hadn't found a suitable answer.

Artemis grabbed my arm and stopped me from continuing. Her grip was so tight, I felt her fingernails through the layers of my clothing. She pressed her forehead against my shoulder.

"Please," she said, almost inaudible. "Your silence will be the death of me."

I forced myself to speak, despite the pain. "Artemis. It's nothing. Everything is fine."

"Don't say that."

Artemis pulled me closer, her body trembling.

"You can't forgive me," she said. "You've already given me so much. I have no one left, Rylion. *No one.*" Her voice climbed in volume the longer she spoke. "They died. They left me. I'm a burden. A blight. I know it. Even the gods themselves despise me—if you need proof, I can show you my mark."

She gritted her teeth to the point I heard the grinding.

Artemis continued, "Don't lie. Tell me you hate me. I'm a monster wearing the skin of a woman. I'm nothing but a curse to those around me."

Some injuries were far worse than the physical. I feared Artemis's scars ran too deep to ever fade, and the thought angered me.

I wrapped my free arm around her despite the blood that would soak our clothes. The Boneyard was close, and soon my pain would be tended to, but for now, I had to reassure Artemis. With her tight in my hold, I leaned my head down and spoke into her ear, using as little breath as I could to save myself unnecessary agony.

"Artemis," I whispered. "You're not a monster. You're not responsible for the actions of the god-king and his men. I blame you for nothing."

"But—" She cut herself off with a choked sob. Her body quaked and conflict raged within her. I held her tighter.

I closed my eyes. "I was born without a curse to parents who loved me, in a small town with a sturdy wall and food for us all. I was born with magic, a gift from the gods themselves. Artemis, it's my duty and honor to stave off the darkness with what blessings I can."

It was everything my mother and father had taught me. A world without suffering could never be achieved, just as there could never be a garden free of bugs or weeds or disease. But that didn't mean one shouldn't keep a garden.

I inhaled, hurting as the air filled my lungs, but I was content to feel Artemis relax against me. "Darkness encroaches every day. It took my mother from me, but I won't let it take anyone else."

"What if—" Artemis began, her voice shaky as she spoke directly into my cloak, "—what if *I'm* the darkness?"

"You're not."

"How do you know? How can you be sure?"

"Let me prove it to you."

"But how?"

Artemis looked up at me, her eyes wet and red with anguish. I stroked her black hair—beautiful hair, silky and straight—hoping to soothe her, and she quivered under my touch. The way she looked at me—it was unlike anyone else. I didn't know if it was reverence or trust, but she didn't have the same expression with others. It reminded me of how my father had looked at my mother.

"Come," I said.

I guided her down the cave path. Artemis followed in silence, and it didn't take long before the trickle of water reached my ears.

We entered a cavern, one aglow with boulders of light, and in the center was a shallow lake, no more than three feet deep in the middle. On the opposite side rested a massive corpse of bone and half-rotted flesh—so massive, in fact, it could have swallowed our mountain lodge.

The corpse had once been a creature, something akin to a fish or a snake, perhaps a hybrid of both, and it had had lustrous white and blue scales, now cracked and falling apart.

It had once gone by the name Vahltera, the Temperance God.

Artemis craned her head back, her mouth agape.

The Temperance God rested with her head over the lake, propped up on rocks jutting from the side of the cavern walls. Her eyes were gone—rotted away—leaving holes of darkness in their place. From the left eye streamed a continual waterfall, like a fountain of tears running down her serpentine face and splashing into the lake.

My father walked out into the shallow water. Wulf waited at the shore. I kept Artemis close and directed her attention to the lake.

"Mariana," my father said, his voice echoing throughout the cavern. "It… It took a long time. Too long. But I brought you home."

He pressed his lips against the black skull in a delicate kiss. After a long exhale, he placed my mother's remains into the lake.

The clear waters obscured nothing. Bones rested beneath the surface. Hundreds of skeletons, from animals to people, all gathered around the god as though they had chosen their final resting place. When the black skull sank to the bottom and hit the rock of the mountain, it broke apart and dissolved, leaving a cloud of darkness. A few moments later, the particles disappeared.

"What happened?" Artemis whispered.

"The Forsaken don't venture here," Wulf replied. "Nor do the sinister. The water destroys them. It destroys evil."

I stepped into the lake and splashed the water across the injury on my chest. I breathed easy. The soothing touch of cold relief washed over me, taking any pain and filling my mind with a steady calm. The mystic water mended the injury, but not completely. Once the wound was sealed, the water stopped its wonders.

I stood and held my hand out to Artemis. "Come," I commanded. "If you're part of the darkness, the waters will kill you, but there's no need to fear."

Artemis stared at me, her eyes wide. "What if—" her voice failed for a moment. "What if the waters do kill me?"

"They won't."

She gulped down air, her gaze flicking between me and the edge of the lake. I wanted her to see that her fears were unfounded, but I couldn't force her. When Artemis stepped back, shaken, I dropped my hand.

Wulf stepped close to Artemis and placed a hand on her shoulder.

"This is the Temperance God," he said. "She wouldn't harm somebody like you."

Artemis stared up at the god. "She's dead. And water has no will. It'll destroy me like it did your mother's skull."

"She's not dead." Wulf frowned. "Our mother spoke to her when she was still, well, when she was still herself. That's why I wanted to bring you here, Artemis. I thought—because you know magic so well—that maybe you could speak to the god."

Artemis shook her head.

Wulf continued, "Do you see the waterfall? There used to be a second one. It ran from the god's other eye. But lately, the lake has grown smaller, and the scales of the god have become duller. I fear something's wrong."

She shook her head again. "I can't. Not me. I shouldn't even be in a place like this. I soil it with my presence."

It pained me to hear Artemis say such things.

"Wait here," I said. "I'll return shortly."

I turned and trudged through the water, my cloak trailing behind me.

My mother had come to the Boneyard on many occasions. She had said she had heard the voice of Vahltera herself. She had said the god had given her peace. And after my mother had turned, my father had come here to seek guidance. He had said the god had given him a curved piece of bone—a bone straight from the god's body—and a great quantity of scales.

My father had fashioned the scales into a cloak for me and crafted the bone into a bow for Wulf. He had said the god had given us protection in this world, for we were her children. And there was no material in the world that matched the might of the old gods. Her scales warded off all manner of attack, even divine fire, and the bone bow carried with it a blessing that slayed the Forsaken. I suspected the bow could even kill a god-king, and I was certain something similar must have been used on the god-king in Saileer.

The day my father had received his gifts, however, was the day the second stream of tears had stopped. In my heart, I knew why.

The old gods were not like mankind. They didn't age or perish like we did. The Temperance God was a creature of power beyond our comprehension. She was giving her essence away until there was nothing left to give. Sadness tainted the water of the lake. Death was welcome to her. Only when she had given everything would she know peace.

I stepped between piles of bones and made my way to the waterfall of tears. I stood within the stream and wished Artemis would join me. The water calmed all rage. Even my hate for the decrees and the god-king were no more.

I closed my eyes.

Please, Vahltera, as your child, I'm uncertain of what I should do. My mother championed a fight against the darkness, but in the end, she was consumed by it. How can I stop this? How can I save people like Thea and Steen? How can I save Artemis, a woman who has done nothing to warrant punishment? How?

The longer I waited in the water, the more my desire to stay intensified.

My father walked out of the lake and headed for the cave entrance. He would return to the lodge and confront Uncle

Bryn. I didn't wish to be part of their struggle, so it was best he went ahead of us.

I drank the cool water as it splashed down on me. Then I exhaled.

Understanding struck me. There was a time for temperance, and a time for rage. If I stayed here, like my father wanted, the lake would quell my hate each time I came seeking guidance, as it always had. It would keep me complacent. If I wished to change the world, I had to have a passion for it—I had to know the burning desire to right injustices—and I wouldn't find it in Ludlow or the mountain lodge.

"Is this epiphany your doing?" I asked, staring up at the god.

There was no answer.

I once again closed my eyes. "Please. Help me. I need wisdom. Once you're gone, I'll carry on in your stead, but without purpose, it won't mean anything."

The cavern quaked, sending small waves across the surface of the lake. Rocks fell from the ceiling, splashing all around me. Bones under the surface of the water toppled and mixed together.

"Rylion!" Wulf cried.

He jumped into the water and sloshed my way.

I glanced over my shoulder and shook my head. Wulf stopped midway and relaxed his shoulders as the quaking gradually became a slight tremor.

Water gushed from the Temperance God's mouth, pouring into the lake with a loud crash. Bits of bone and chunks of rotted flesh plunged into the shallow depths, but the stream never touched me. In the last wave to be expelled, a long shard of bone fell straight down.

The bone shard was so sharp and hardened that when it landed, it pierced the stone bottom of the lake like a javelin in dirt. It was five feet in length and straight, protruding from the surface of the water once the shaking died down.

"Are you hurt?" Wulf asked.

"No," I said.

I waded through the smaller bits of bone, mucus, and chunks of flesh. When I reached the bone shard, I knew I had the wisdom I sought. I risked cutting myself if I even tried to take the shard. The keen edges gleamed in the light of the glowing boulders.

This wasn't the same type of gift the god had given my father. The Temperance God had given him scales and a curved bone—objects that could be used for defense and to keep one safe from a distance. This was different. It was a weapon and *only* a weapon.

But what did the Temperance God want me to do with it? I feared I didn't even need to ask the question. My heart already knew the answer.

The waterfall of tears lessened to a trickle.

"Artemis," I called out. "Join me."

She stood at the shore of the lake, clutching the scarf I had given her.

Wulf turned to face Artemis. "You'll be all right. I promise."

Artemis scrunched her eyes closed and hesitated. Before I called out again, however, she stormed into the water, splashing herself up to the chest in her rush to enter the lake. Then she stopped and stared.

The water didn't harm her. She touched it with a bare hand. Nothing.

"I told you," Wulf said, half-smiling.

Artemis exhaled and headed for me. When she drew near, I stepped aside and motioned to the trickling waterfall. She stood in the stream of water, allowing the waterfall to run through her raven hair and down her spine.

Wulf shuffled over and examined the bone shard. He

reached out to touch it, but I stopped him. *I would pull it from the stone, and no one else.* I would rather Wulf not hurt himself on my account.

Artemis rubbed at her eyes. She was crying.

"What's wrong?" Wulf asked.

Artemis exhaled a ragged breath. "There's so much sadness."

"Sadness?" Wulf glanced around, his eyes wide. "I don't feel sadness. Just… calm."

I had found that there were certain people who felt more of the god's presence than others. Wulf had never been one to feel or hear the magic of the old gods, but I suspected he was happier for it. The sorrow in the water ate at me, but in a slow and subtle way.

Artemis shook her head. "I saw it. Caprice was right." She turned to me, her eyebrows knitted together.

Artemis saw something? In the water?

"What did you see?" I asked.

"The god…" Artemis rubbed at her eyes again. "She had buried herself alive."

INTERLUDE

THEA YELLAHJAR

"Just a little farther, Deana," I said as I stroked her sorrel coat.

Deana nickered. The presence of the sinister horse still bothered her; I saw it in the way she flicked her tail and snuck glances at the other beast. I was sure the monstrous horse could kill and eat Deana if it wanted. The sinister ate flesh, no matter the breed or type, even if they could also eat vegetation.

But the black mare didn't attack or lash out. She followed behind us, watching over her rider as he slid along the snow on my makeshift sled. Binding a few branches together had taken time, but it had done the trick.

Deana pulled the man along, leaving a furrow in the snowbanks, and I guided her toward the Boneyard.

The sunlight waned as the day came to an end. Although there had been fighting earlier, the land now had a stillness that followed death. I hoped it was just the Forsaken who had died. I couldn't stand the thought of the others getting harmed, even if we barely interacted. No one deserved to be mauled by the creatures created by the curse.

We exited a grove of trees, and I spotted the sheer wall of rock that hid the cave to the Boneyard.

"Wait," I whispered.

Deana snorted and stopped her march.

Footprints marked the snow all around the cave entrance. There were so many, I suspected a good number of people had entered, especially since the prints were different sizes. Had Osmund and Rylion come here? They were the ones who had shown me this place, so it would make sense.

I waited and listened.

Nothing.

Perhaps they had left?

"Let's go," I said.

Deana ambled forward, still glancing over her shoulder from time to time. I stroked her muzzle. Everything would be fine once we got inside.

When we reached the cave, the black mare came to a halt. It didn't surprise me. The sinister didn't approach the cave, for whatever reason. She backed away and growled, her head lowered and her ears back.

"We'll be back," I said to the mare. "You guard the entrance."

They said sinister animals were intelligent—more so than any animal—but I was still taken aback when the sinister horse seemed to understand my words. She paced the front and turned her attention to the woods. I gathered her master's halberd from the snow and tied it to her saddle, resulting in a makeshift jousting lance strapped down and pointed forward.

Deana moved into the darkness of the cave. The path was narrow, not accommodating for a horse, but she managed despite the cramped conditions. It didn't take long before we reached the glowing rocks, and I knew we were close. The gentle blue illumination calmed Deana, and I breathed easy.

Once I heard the trickle of water, I smiled, jogging into the massive cavern.

Some people were unsettled by the bones. This place was a graveyard, after all, but I felt as though the past individuals had come here because they wanted to, not because this was a battleground or ritual of death. They came to be with Vahltera, their god.

Perhaps they were even her children. That was what I liked to think, anyway.

Deana walked into the cavern, her hooves clopping on the rock and echoing all around us. I guided her to the edge of the shallow lake and urged her to drag the injured man in.

She locked her legs, unwilling to move forward.

"I need to get him into the water," I said. "Please, Deana. Don't be afraid."

Deana waited for a moment, staring with her giant horse eyes. I stepped into the lake and splashed my arms.

"See?"

She snorted and then stepped forward, pulling the man into the water. I walked over to make sure he didn't go too far, but I caught my breath the moment his armor began melting.

The black plate he wore—it was made of the King's Stone —dissolved in the water, bleeding away into an inky cloud that tainted the lake. I had never seen anything like it, and I didn't know what it meant. Would the man melt away as well?

I untied him from my makeshift sled and grabbed him by the armpits. He had clothing under his armor—a simple tunic and trousers—and they didn't disappear. Only his armor.

I rested him back on the shore, allowing most of his body to stay in the water. His ribs carried a deep gouge, and there was a puncture wound on his hip. A misty cloud of scarlet blood soiled the otherwise pristine waters.

Deana moved away from us and drank from the lake. I

allowed her to do what she pleased while I contemplated the man's fate.

"What's wrong?" I asked myself aloud, confused.

The water usually healed wounds. I had seen Wulf recover while resting here. But the man continued to bleed, and it seemed worse without his armor.

I glanced back at the massive corpse that had once been a god. The waterfall that poured from her eye was nothing more than a trickle now. Had something happened to the Boneyard?

The man didn't move. I leaned over him and lowered my ear close to his mouth. His breath was weak and fading. I was surprised he had made it this long; it would be a shame if he died now.

I took a deep breath and grabbed him under the armpits once again. With a huff, I dragged him further into the lake, allowing the water to help take him along. The bones got under my feet, and twice I almost fell, but I waded on regardless. The waterfall had always been special, perhaps it would help.

Once under the tiny stream, I hefted the man's head underneath.

I felt the calmest here, like life wasn't so terrible and painful. This was a kind place. One of compassion. If the man was good—if the man deserved to live—this place would help him. I felt it.

"Please," I murmured.

For a moment, nothing happened. But then the cavern rumbled, sending ripples over the lake. Deana whinnied and rushed for the shore, kicking up water as she went. I held the man close, glancing around at the ceiling, fearing that stones might fall on us at any second.

But it never happened. Instead, the waterfall dried up, and the glowing stones waned in intensity. One by one, they went out, blanketing the cavern in darkness. Two boulders remained lit at the end of the quake, but they weren't enough to give the entire cavern light. It seemed like the dead of night, and everything had become a silhouette.

The man coughed and gasped. I flinched and almost dropped him, but I kept my heart inside my ribcage and took another deep breath.

I walked the man back to the shore, both relieved and a little terrified that he was doing better. He was still a member of the Holy Guard, but at least I knew for certain he wasn't one of the evil men I feared. Even his steed had stayed by his side, the first sign I knew he must have been a compassionate individual.

Another tremor drew my attention. I glanced up just as the skull of the old god dislodged from the rocks. It came crashing down into the lake, splashing a wave of water over the cavern. I was submerged and carried a few feet before the water receded back into place. I kept hold of the man and listened to him choke on the water. After a few hard coughs, he returned to breathing.

It took a minute for the cavern to settle. I eased the man onto the shore, his waist and legs in the lake, and then I took a seat next to him.

He opened his eyes. I pulled my clothing tight around my body. My spiderweb mark wasn't visible—it was on my left shoulder blade—but I still worried.

He turned his head and stared. He said nothing.

"Are you feeling well?" I whispered, my voice unsteady.

The man stared a bit longer before replying, "Where am I?"

"I brought you to the Boneyard to rest."

He coughed and spat up a mouthful of water. Once he regained his composure, he asked, "Why?"

"Your steed."

His eyebrows knitted together.

"I wouldn't have pulled you from the snow if it weren't

for your steed," I said, looking away. "She trusts you. And she's concerned about you. If you had mistreated her… I doubt she would have stayed by your side."

He closed his eyes.

I didn't like the silence.

"What's your mare's name?" I asked.

"Kelphy," he said, his voice quiet.

Kelphy. It was a pretty name for a horse. It was a pleasant surprise to hear he hadn't named her something wicked or disgusting, just because of what she was. I liked Kelphy—I was certain she still guarded the outside of the cave.

I shivered. I hadn't noticed it before, but the cavern had always been a pleasant temperature. Now it grew colder by the second.

"What's *your* name?" I asked, a little embarrassed I hadn't thought to ask it first.

"Alexavier Lowell."

I forced a smile. "The Temperance God saved you, Alexavier Lowell. You were dying, but then she brought you back."

He remained silent, his eyes still closed.

Although I was soaked, I didn't want to leave the cavern. Instead, I scooted up to the wall and rested my back against it. Alexavier needed time to heal. Maybe in the morning, he would be fully recovered.

Then we could go our separate ways.

INTERLUDE
OSMUND NASOS

It was a fine day to find one's final resting place.

The sun bathed the world in an orange glow, highlighting the wonder of the mountain before finding rest of its own. Mariana would have said the same thing. She had found the beauty in everything. Any day would have been a good day for her, but I was happy it was this day, and not one filled with rain and storms. I didn't know if I could've kept my composure then.

The winter wind rushed by, returning my attention to the task at hand.

"You're certain she's at peace?" Bryn asked.

I nodded.

My younger brother had always doubted, but I could tell he had taken my word as the truth. He straightened his robes and exhaled. The cliff edge we stood on overlooked a great valley of snow-covered trees, creating a tranquil landscape of evergreen and white. It was a decent view, even for my blurry eyes. This, too, made for a fine final resting place.

Bryn ran a hand over his face.

I gritted my teeth, unable to look at him for long.

We were old—older than I liked to admit—but I had

thought we would always face the world together, as family. I had never thought I would have to bury him. I figured he would be there at *my* deathbed, reading me his damn stories, with Mariana rubbing my knuckles and reassuring me we would meet up again in some great beyond.

That was what I had imagined. That, and a few more kids. Three or four more. All there to say goodbye.

But that would never happen. It was a reality that had disappeared along with most of my eyesight.

"I'm sorry," Bryn said, his voice strained.

"Don't bother."

"I should've turned long before now. It would've been easier then."

"It's better you get to know it's all over," I muttered.

Bryn let out another long exhale. "You'll take care of Wulfric?"

"I always have."

Nothing would change that. I had raised Wulf as my son. I never thought of him differently from Rylion.

Again, the wind picked up, taking a flurry of snowflakes along for the ride. The dusting of snow fell down the hundred and forty feet to the valley below, adding to the white. Soon the sun would disappear beyond the horizon.

"We haven't much time," Bryn whispered. "You should do it while there's still light."

Ice gripped my chest.

I walked away from my younger brother, a few yards at the most, and then turned back to face him. He stood at the edge of the cliff, his back square to me. Even with my miserable aim, it was a decent target.

I hefted Calavandi and nocked an arrow.

This was it. The agreement we had made. Once Mariana knew rest, I would send Bryn to join her. It was my duty to make sure it happened before the curse took him, before I had to hunt my brother as well.

But still, my hands trembled, and my arms threatened to quit. I remembered when Bryn had been born—how my mother had said it would be *my* responsibility as an older brother to look after him—how we had made our way in this world together, despite our modest beginnings in life. The memories felt like curses themselves, one day meant to consume my thoughts and fill me with despair.

I pulled back the string and held it.

Bryn was my advisor, the man who knew everything compared to the uneducated farmers of our hometown. And when my strength had failed, his knowledge had won. But that had been a lifetime ago.

My forearms burned as I tried to keep the bow steady. I could point it away. I could. But that wasn't our agreement. This was a kindness. And a punishment. Only I could deliver it with any justice.

I released my hold and the whistle that followed hurt my ears. The arrow punctured Bryn through the chest, drilling between ribs and exiting the other side of his body in a spray of crimson. He staggered forward from the force of the blow and then collapsed, choking on blood. After a thick gurgle, he crawled to the edge of the cliff. Once he fell, I took a ragged breath, the chill burning my lungs, perhaps an empathic pain.

Today I had killed the love of my life and my little brother.

I would never be the same man. Pieces of me were gone forever.

I wished I could apologize. I wished I could've made it right. I had never wanted this. All I had wanted was for us to be a family—a fine, happy family—free of hardship and concern. To be a good father, to be a good man, to be the strength they all sought.

The agony in my chest spread to the rest of my being. There was no physical ailment, just sorrow so deep, I gave the edge of the cliff consideration.

I could join Bryn and Mariana and end this life of

shattered dreams. Rylion and Wulf were men now. They had no need of me.

But then I touched my gut and remembered the fear I'd had after Alexavier had cut me open. I had been afraid to die—that I wouldn't finish my duty to her—that I wouldn't see Rylion and Wulf through to their own happy families.

Mariana must have known. She had always known when I had been unhappy, and she'd always known what to do to make it right. Even… Even as a mindless beast, she…

I pressed my fingers over my eyelids to stave off the tears. I loved her. I still loved her. How could I spit in the face of her last gift to me? She had given me back life, even when I had been taking hers. I wouldn't waste it. I couldn't.

I steeled myself to my new reality and headed back for the lodge.

"I've made up my mind," I said, my voice the only one in the lodge.

The others regarded me with intent stares. Wulf, Caprice, Steen, Lydia, and Artemis—each waiting, their breath bated. They wouldn't like my decision, but it wasn't up for discussion. It was a choice I had made, and I wouldn't turn back.

I exhaled and said, "I'm going to speak to God-King Eliezer."

The silence that followed was colder than the snow outside.

"The god-king won't grant you an audience just because you ask," Steen finally said. "And what would you say to him, anyway? You know he could curse you with a single utterance."

I tensed at the thought. "My father was once a member of his Holy Guard," I said. "I think I'll be able to gain an audience with him on that fact alone."

Lydia pushed her braided hair over her shoulder and frowned. "What're you gonna ask for?"

"I'm going to ask him to rescind some of his decrees," I

said. "And I'm going to ask him to remove the curse from Artemis."

The entire room turned to face Artemis. She stepped back, her shocked expression locked on mine. She seemed incredulous I had brought it up, or maybe conflicted, I didn't know, but her curse was the most unjust of them all. If anyone deserved to have theirs removed, it was her.

"Can the god-king even do that?" Lydia asked in a hushed tone. She glanced to Caprice. "Can he remove curses?"

Caprice frowned. "I don't know."

"Can he even remove decrees?" Steen asked. He stood from the table and paced in front of the hearth—the never-ending fire flicking behind him. "I've never heard of that! Not once. Not in any tales."

Lydia reached out and took Caprice's hand. "Please. You must know something. Priestesses always have tales of the old god-kings and god-queens. There must be something."

Again, silence descended. Lydia wasn't the only one who was curious. The crackle of the fire reminded me that time flowed, but otherwise, I waited for Caprice to finish mulling over the question.

"There is the Ruined Kingdom," she said.

Steen sighed. "That's a fairy tale. And what does it have to do with our current situation?"

"You asked for stories. I know of one. Do you wish to hear it?"

Lydia nodded. "Of course."

"Yes," Steen added with a sigh. "Forgive my… impatience."

Caprice steadied herself with a quick breath and then said, "The Ruined Kingdom was once ruled over by God-King Kyrin. He wanted to be the purest god-king of them all—remembered for all time as perfect and wise beyond all others. He made hundreds, *no*, thousands of decrees, right down to the appropriate price to sell bread and lard. He thought that if he controlled everything, he would bring about a perfect utopia."

I clenched my jaw to prevent myself from speaking. There was too much pain and suffering in this world to have a god-king instilling fear over every tiny action.

Caprice continued, "Less than five years later, the kingdom ate itself because of the monsters within. The Forsaken didn't yield, and Kyrin's Holy Guard fell, one by one."

A pop of flame from the hearth punctuated Caprice's terrible story.

"The tales say that God-King Kyrin refused to do anything about the outcome," Caprice intoned. "He wanted his citizens to suffer, for they were truly evil if they couldn't follow his rules. The story implied he *could* have done something, but he chose not to. Perhaps there really is a way for a god-king or god-queen to rescind decrees. Maybe even remove curses."

Lydia jumped up from the table. "I think we should try," she said, excitement in her tone and her bright blue eyes. When nobody replied, she continued, "God-King Eliezer should know his citizens are sufferin'."

"He'll never listen," Steen stated. He glared at the fire, his jaw tight. "Why would he grant reprieve to criminals? He has no incentive. He'd only be flooded with millions of requests—and then people would break his decrees more and more. It undermines his rule!"

"But what if we explained your situation to him?" Lydia walked over to Steen and took his hand. "You didn't know you were stealing from a member of the god-king's court. And you killed the summer lioness to protect my li'l brother. Maybe you could repent. Maybe then the god-king would forgive you."

Steen ripped his arm away from her. "That's not how the decrees work, and you know it."

"You're already cursed. There's no harm in speakin' to him now."

"Why're you so fanatical, woman? You're a fool if you think it'll change anything!"

"I don't want to lose you," Lydia said, her voice hushed. Her statement quieted Steen. He turned away, glowering at the floor. She continued, "Do you want us to end like Osmund, one of us a monster and the other huntin' for a decade of their life? I already gave thought to seein' the god-king. I… I was gonna do it myself, but now that Rylion is goin', I don't see why we shouldn't join him."

Wulf stepped up close to me, his gaze searching mine. "Do you intend to leave now, Rylion? It's the start of winter. The storms are coming." His eyes shifted to the window and the winds blustering outside. Tonight we would be visited by black clouds.

But the cold didn't bother me. I could traverse the sleet and ice with little trouble. Then again, if Artemis and Lydia joined me, we would need to take a safer route.

"We can wait until the storms blow over," I said. "Then we leave Mount Regel and head for the capital. Will you join me?"

My brother nodded. "Of course."

The capital city, Luthecia, was a hard week's ride during the summer, but the winter would make it harder. Although the entire Kingdom of Luka wasn't covered in snow like Mount Regel, the rains and winds would create trouble. This wasn't the best time of year for travel, but I couldn't wait forever, not when Artemis or the others could turn into Forsaken. My protection—my ability to prevent them from turning—was a boon, but what if they wandered too far away? It would be like with my mother all over again. I couldn't stand the thought.

I should've come to this conclusion long ago, the day I

had pulled Artemis from the streets, but now I had wisdom from Vahltera, and there was no excuse to delay.

I stared at the bone shard resting on the table. It had been swaddled twice over, and secured with leather belts to prevent anyone from cutting themselves, but I could still tell it had the keenest of edges. Before I headed to Luthecia, I would need to see the same smith my father had visited to craft Calavandi. It would add time to the trip, but it was a step that couldn't be overlooked.

Weary and exhausted, I headed for the stairs. The others muttered among themselves, no doubt debating the usefulness of visiting God-King Eliezer. I would hear what they had decided in the morning.

When I reached the top step, I glanced over my shoulder. Artemis hid in the shadows of the main room, her back to the wall. She didn't look at me, or anyone else, her gaze drilling into the floorboards. I thought she would have had more to say about my announcement, either for or against, but instead, she had become quiet, like the first few days after I had met her.

Her dark hair and skin reminded me she was from the capital. The rings on the collar of her robe also reminded me of her years of study—she had once lived a life of luxury. Perhaps she had even met the god-king at one point in her life. Most noblemen saw the god-king, either at soirées or through political forums.

I would have to discuss the matter with her. She might know more about my chances of success.

INTERLUDE
THEA YELLAHJAR

Kelphy, the sinister horse, growled and shook her head. Her black mane, cut neat, had escaped the armor plating and shifted in the winds of the stormy morning. She refused to come into the cave, no matter how hard I called and pleaded.

I thought the magic that kept the sinister at bay had disappeared, but a sliver must have remained, keeping the last few boulders glowing and dispelling anything born from the Forsaken.

My stomach grumbled. Snow covered everything from the roads, to the trees, to the corpses of sinister birds that hadn't made it through the night. I needed to return to the lodge before I met a similar fate, but I couldn't travel in such conditions.

Kelphy's breaths came out as rivers of steam. I didn't know how she had survived as long as she had, but the sinister horse didn't seem ready for death. Her human eyes had a glazed-over white that matched the snow, and I wondered if they were frozen. Did they even blink? I hadn't seen it, but they did move occasionally, and I tried to avoid looking at them directly.

"You can't stay out here," I said. "You should find shelter."

The Holy Guard halberd caught my eye. I grabbed Kelphy's reins and pulled her close, shivering back the snow. I unstrapped the weapon from her saddle, hating the cold bite of the strange metal each time my fingers grazed it. The halberd was a terrible tool of war. If the cave retained some of the old god, even a tiny bit, I wanted it to destroy this blighted weapon once and for all.

I returned to the cave, my steps uncertain as I traveled through unyielding shadows. No matter how long I held the halberd, it burned my hands with an icy extreme. Only when I entered the cavern was I greeted with the calm blue glow of the Boneyard, easing some of the pain. It saddened me there wasn't much of the god's presence left, but I was glad a little remained so that I could continue to return here.

To my surprise, Alexavier stood at the edge of the lake. He kept Deana close and stroked the length of her back. He was a man of impressive stature, with the physique of a warrior. Even in the dim lighting, I could tell he had recovered from his battle—there was nothing hindering him now.

"Um," I said.

Alexavier turned to face me. "You've returned."

"Yes." I held the weapon close, hesitant. When he walked to my side, I bunched my shoulders to my neck. "Kelphy refuses to take shelter in the cave."

He said nothing for a moment, before asking, "May I have the pleasure of your name, my lady?"

The etiquette of his words and the regal manner of his speech—I couldn't help but blush. I was no noblewoman. I had been born on the edge of a small town to two poor goat herders. No one had called me "my lady" before.

"Thea," I said once I had found my voice.

"And your surname?"

"Yellahjar."

"Lady Yellahjar," he said as he held out his hand, palm up. "You have done me a great service."

I gingerly placed my hand on top of his. He bowed deeply enough to touch his forehead to my knuckles—a sign of a knight's fealty to their masters, lieges, and royalty, a formality used in courts to show the utmost respect.

I ripped my hand away and dropped the halberd. The metal weapon clattered on the floor, filling the area with a rattle. Deana neighed and retreated a few feet away, her eyes wide.

"Is something wrong?" Alexavier asked.

But I could barely find my breath. I stepped back and turned away, my body trembling. When I glanced at my hands, I saw a red line of irritation left behind from when I had held the halberd. He was a member of the Holy Guard, chosen by the god-king to slay the wicked.

I was one of the wicked.

"You needn't thank me," I said in a strained voice. "The Temperance God found you worthy of saving."

"That's the second time you've said that."

"It's the truth."

Alexavier scooped the halberd off the cavern floor. "The old gods are dead. Your quick thinking brought me in from the snow."

I glanced out over the lake. The terrible lighting shrouded the edges of the cavern in thick darkness. Even the corpse of the god sat beyond the impenetrable shadows, just out of sight. Had he not seen the glory of the old god when I had brought him here? He had been wounded. Perhaps he never had.

"But your injuries," I muttered.

"Divine fire courses through my veins," he said with an easy smile. "It sustains me. I recover quickly when not in the snow."

But his magic had failed. I had seen it. He had worsened

each second I had cared for him until I had brought him to the lake. He attributed to himself what the Temperance God had given him—though it mattered little. Alexavier would live whether he knew the truth or not.

"Once the storm dies, you can return to the capital," I said. "Kelphy is eager to see you again."

"I will. Thank you."

"That's good to hear."

Alexavier moved closer, his easy smile never fading. "I would be honored if you joined me."

I held my breath and waited.

"Do you have family?" he asked. "I would take them all to the capital and give them a new life. My position as God-King Eliezer's Scourge grants me many luxuries. Caring for you and your family is the least I could do to repay your kindness."

The sheer cold of winter filled my veins. He was the god-king's *Scourge*? I hadn't known that.

When I didn't answer, Alexavier continued, "You seem distressed. Have I done something to offend you? If so, it was never my intention. You're the first bit of light I've come across since I crossed our kingdom's southern river. A true virtue."

A true virtue? Me?

How could he say such things? He didn't know what I was. What if he found out? Would he… would he still think of me the same way?

His words—everything about him—I felt so conflicted. He was a knight from my childhood stories, here to whisk me away and give me a life I never could have imagined. A fairy tale made flesh.

I loved fairy tales. I would've given anything to have had this happen when I was younger. Anything! But now circumstances were different. Life had ruined my dreams and made sure they could never come true.

Or perhaps the Temperance God had revived him because he was the man who would finally put my haunting thoughts to rest. Maybe he would give me back a life with the answer of but a few simple questions. Questions no one else had had the knowledge to properly answer.

I matched my gaze to his, my brow furrowed. "Can I ask you something?" Even though I whispered, my voice reverberated around us.

"Anything," Alexavier said.

"Are people who are cursed… Are they evil?"

Now *he* was silent.

I persisted, "Are they soulless, like my mother told me? Do they have a darkness that breeds in their beings until they become monsters of their sins?"

Alexavier gave me a curt nod. "They are evil."

"No matter what? What if they don't feel evil? What if they… want to be virtuous?"

My voice slipped from me as I remembered how my mother had described the cursed. She had said they were always monsters—hiding and waiting to destroy the world with their malice—and it was the god-king who showed us who was wicked and who was just by making his decrees.

She'd said she had known I was evil the moment I had been born.

"If they wanted to be virtuous, they would have respected the decrees of the land," Alexavier stated. "There's no need to fret over such questions, however. I will—"

"Are there no circumstances that justify breaking a decree?" I asked, regardless of his statements.

"Never."

His response had a finality about it that sent a shiver up my spine.

Alexavier narrowed his gaze. "Why would there be circumstances for breaking the decrees?"

"Everyone f-faces hardships. What if they had to?"

"The god-king is only asking men not to kill, steal, or be unfaithful to their spouse. Is that truly unreasonable? Are you implying that mankind is so fundamentally evil that asking them to abstain from such activities is abhorrent?"

"No," I said, shaking my head. "I just... I don't understand. Men kill each other all the time. You've killed. Soldiers have killed. Yet when..."

"There are a total of three decrees against killing," Alexavier stated, his tone heated. "*Only three*. Killing a god-king or god-queen is like striking at the divine itself. The only other decrees are for one's mother and father. Again, is it unreasonable to ask someone to respect the individuals who gave them life? Has mankind fallen so much that this is impossible?"

I ran my hands over my face and held back the flood of pain burning in my being. Tears threatened to spill from me, but I chased them away with deep breaths.

Perhaps I was evil after all.

Alexavier stepped closer. "Lady Yellahjar, why do you ask such questions?"

I moved away and splashed into the shallow part of the lake, my knees shaking. Deana trotted to my side and nickered, my distress bleeding into her. The cool water soaked into my clothing. Chills ran across my skin.

"What if," I said as I held tightly onto Deana, my voice ethereal as I slipped into terrible memories, "what if there were a husband and wife who argued?"

Alexavier didn't move from his place on the shore. He simply stared, his dark eyes searching mine.

"What if that husband drank all noon and night? What if he became angry when he allowed liquor to consume his thoughts? What if... What if the liquor drove him to violence?"

I took in a ragged breath. I could still smell my father's

ale-laced breath when I closed my eyes. He had lived to drink. No amount of persuasion could keep him from his liquor.

"Is harming your wife not an evil act?" I asked. "He's not breaking a decree, yet he causes the world such suffering. How can you justify that?"

Alexavier tightened his grip on his halberd. "The decrees are not the sole measurement of evil, they are simply the limit. A line one must never cross."

"He would have killed her!" I shouted.

The echoes added to my frustration and guilt. He would have! Every night, it had gotten worse. And when my mother hadn't moved, when she had given in to the suffering, my father would turn his fists to me. Hatred had filled his eyes and actions. He had hated a great many things—himself most of all.

I didn't trust men. I didn't trust them when they poisoned their own minds and believed it to be reality. I didn't trust them when they knowingly decided to make such alterations to their perception because they liked reality better in a world where they were uninhibited from decency and empathy.

Silence once again descended over the cavern.

I whispered, "She wasn't moving."

Alexavier said nothing.

"It was the worst night. He was so consumed with drunken rage; I don't know what he thought. He hit her again and again. I… I love my mother. Of course I respect her. It pained me to see her hurt, like any who care for another trapped in agony. And, well, I couldn't bring myself to watch. And I couldn't bring myself to look away, either."

"Don't," Alexavier said in a low voice. "You know what I am. I'll leave. You can go back to your life."

I stared, needing to hear his answer to my dilemma more than anything else. The Temperance God thought him worthy

—he must have known the answer. He could save me the self-torment of never knowing.

"I killed my father," I said. "Before he could snuff out my mother's life." Silent, hot tears streamed down my face. "He wouldn't have been cursed for killing her. *His* sin could have been forgiven. But mine… Tell me. Tell me why mine cannot."

"You force my hand," I said, staring at the woman huddled close to her faithful horse.

"Answer me," Lady Yellahjar pleaded. "You said I was virtue, but you also say the cursed are evil, beyond forgiveness. Am I evil?"

The god-kings and god-queens were divine vessels blessed with the power of the old gods to rule the world in their stead. The god-kings and god-queens dwelled among us to keep humanity from slipping into the darkness. Their decrees served as guidelines to a path of righteousness. That was what the new priestesses said. That was what I had always known.

Tears slipped from Lady Yellahjar's face. She never looked away, even when I readied my halberd.

"I don't want to be evil," she whispered. "But I couldn't allow such hatred to take my mother. What should I have done?"

"There are others with the authority," I said, my voice unsteady, much to my own surprise.

I had killed so many of the cursed. It was a service to the world to stop the Forsaken—the monsters were a punishment to the populace for not policing themselves. A punishment for good people standing by while others fell to corruption. But I offered them relief from their secondary punishment. I was saving them.

Lady Yellahjar shook her head as her horse stepped closer.

"I tried," she said. "But my father worked for the guard. They never listened! None of them."

I didn't know what to say. There shouldn't be—no, there *wasn't*—a reason to break the decrees. If mankind couldn't abide by a few simple rules, perhaps they should be destroyed, just as some of the old gods had intended.

"Am I evil?" she asked again.

"Run," I told her as I stepped out into the lake. "Your horse can take you far from me."

That was what I told those whom I loathed to kill. I told them to run. If they ran, and I pursued, at least I was still carrying out my order. *Kill all the cursed.* Lady Yellahjar had saved my life. For that, I would allow her what little time she had left, even if I risked fighting a monster at the end of my chase.

Lady Yellahjar gripped the mane of her steed. "I didn't run from my father," she whispered. "And I won't run from you."

My mouth went dry. What kind of father hurts his child? What kind of man brings nothing but suffering to those around him?

I knew the answer.

Lady Yellahjar wiped her face with a shaky hand. "No matter how many times I... I relive the memories in my mind... I know, without doubt, I would always do the same thing." More tears streaked down her cheeks. "But when I'm about to turn... when I'm about to become a monster... Rylion comforts me. He says I'm not evil. He s-says I did the right thing. And then the t-turn stops. I'm not a monster."

She caught her breath and trembled.

"So which is it?" Lady Yellahjar asked, her voice raw with emotion. "Am I a monster? Put my troubled mind to rest."

I waded through the knee-deep water until I was a few feet away.

I hadn't been endowed with the right of rulership by the old gods, nor was I in line to be the inheritor of such a power. I wasn't so arrogant as to think I could judge someone for the content of their soul—but God-King Eliezer could. That was why... That was why he had the power of the decrees. That was what the old gods had wanted. They had wanted mankind to administer their own justice.

"Why won't you answer me?" she whispered.

I couldn't bring myself to speak to her. My throat burned, and I hadn't taken a breath since I had told her to run. She didn't avert her gaze, or flinch away, or even attempt to escape. She just waited. But I didn't have an answer to her question, and that realization disturbed me most of all.

Once the rippling of the water stopped, a cold silence set in.

I stabbed forward with my halberd, the blade slicing through Lady Yellahjar's flesh with little difficulty, piercing her heart in one swift strike. She stumbled back from the blow and collapsed into the water, her horse neighing in protest. When the beast turned to kick, I swung the halberd, frightening it with the whistle of a honed edge. It trotted away, grunting and snorting.

The dim lighting prevented me from seeing the blood— and the outline of her body—for which I was grateful. I turned on my heel, leaving the horse to the cavern lake. My troubled mind wouldn't stop examining the details of the encounter.

I didn't have an answer for her. Lady Yellahjar had helped me, kind and gentle in all regards, yet she had been a monster. Finally, I inhaled, but it only added to the fire of my suffering. She hadn't been a brigand or corsair. She hadn't been a blight to mankind.

The narrow passageway to the outside was difficult to navigate. I held my hand on the wall and continued forward, determined not to look back.

It was better this way. If I hadn't killed her, I would have been cursed as well. And those blessed with magic who later became Forsaken were far worse than any other, like the bird Forsaken who had controlled ice and wind. It was an extreme punishment. Those with divine gifts should be held to a higher standard than others. I could not disobey God-King Eliezer's command. Ever.

So why didn't that put me at ease?

"Kelphy, to me," I called out the moment I stepped into the snow.

My mare jumped to my side, her coat and tail frosted with ice. I ran my hand down her neck despite the chill. Kelphy had always been loyal, and I vowed to care for her forever.

"Take me to Ludlow," I commanded.

She growled as she turned to allow me to mount.

I needed to speak with God-King Eliezer. Only he could quell my endless doubt. Until then, I wouldn't be right—I would keep reliving my attack against Lady Yellahjar—my body trembling with uncertainty.

I *had* to speak with him.

CHAPTER TWELVE

Dawn broke on a new day, casting light over the world once again.

I waited by the fire for Rylion, Osmund, Wulf, and Lydia. They packed their supplies in silence, and a melancholy atmosphere permeated lodge. Thea and Bryn had never returned. No one asked about Bryn, and I suspected he was dead at the hands of his own brother, but I refused to inquire.

Thea, on the other hand, had the others worried.

No one had seen her. Not throughout the night, not yesterday, not today. Even one of the horses had gone missing. Had she left Mount Regel? Rylion didn't think so. He insisted we needed to search for her—that she was somewhere on the mountain.

I had been the cause of her disappearance. I had accused her of impropriety, and she had left the safety of the lodge to escape my presence.

This was my fault.

Caprice and Steen waited at the table, both stitching up old clothes that needed mending.

"Are you ready?" Osmund asked the others with a grunt.

Wulf, Rylion, and Lydia nodded.

"Good. We should break into two groups and search along the roads. There are caves and thickets Thea could have stayed in to keep warm, especially if she has Deana with her."

"Artemis and I will check the Boneyard," Rylion said, fastening his cloak around his shoulders. "There's a chance she went there to avoid the harsh weather."

Osmund nodded. "All right. Meet back at the lodge by sundown."

Again, everyone agreed.

I stood and took my place next to Rylion, surprised that he wanted me and me alone for the trip. Not that I would complain. I wanted his company, but conflict still raged inside me, especially after his declaration.

Seeking an audience with God-King Eliezer was the last thing I would've done.

We exited the lodge together and crunched through the powdery snow. Rylion moved with utter confidence, neither slipping nor shivering as he made his way to the road toward the Boneyard. I shuffled after him in his tracks, using the packed snowbank for ease of movement.

It only took a few minutes of travel before he stopped and glanced over his shoulder.

"Artemis," he said.

I walked up to his side. "Yes?"

"You've been to the capital."

Ah. He wanted to talk about my past.

"I lived in the capital," I said. "But it feels like a lifetime ago."

"Did you ever meet God-King Eliezer?"

I clutched my scarf close. "Yes."

"How would you describe him?"

We continued our walk as I mulled over the question. I had seen God-King Eliezer on multiple occasions. Three times

I had spoken with him, but they were in passing, nothing substantial. At least, not until the last time.

"I would say he's cold, but I may be judging him poorly. Everyone acts skittish in his presence. They duck away, hide when they can, or engage in short bursts of conversation, as though fearful they'll be cursed at any second. Even the members of his court—even his advisors—shrink away in the shadows when he twitches his lips into a frown."

Rylion stared straight ahead, his eyes unseeing. "Would you say he's an emotional man, ruled by anger?"

"I never saw him display anything other than contempt, passive contentment, and dissatisfaction. Even when—" I stopped myself short. Even when he had sentenced me to death. He had kept himself from rage even then, despite my mother's treachery and insubordination.

"Even when?" Rylion asked.

I shook my head. "I've never seen him happy, let's leave it at that."

"I see."

"I doubt he'll grant your requests. He's... not a man who would admit mistakes."

Rylion clenched his jaw and narrowed his eyes. "Fear keeps otherwise honorable men from doing the right thing. I won't let fear stop me from seeking his audience. Even if God-King Eliezer will curse me for seeking reprieve."

The mere thought of Rylion becoming cursed sent cold anger flowing through my veins.

"He has divine powers," I whispered. "Stronger than a Lord of Flame and Cinder. More potent than your mother's. It's a gift from the old gods to all god-kings and god-queens."

Rylion tensed. "I know."

Walking to the Boneyard in the morning chill woke me more than anything else. I took brisk steps and enjoyed the fact that my fire kept me warm no matter the situation. I could only imagine the hard time Thea must be having. Then again, the cavern had been pleasant when last I saw it. If Thea was there, she should be fine.

"Are you a noblewoman, Artemis?"

I almost slipped on the ice when the question registered in my thoughts.

"Not anymore," I forced myself to say.

"Are you the daughter of a duke or duchess?"

"I… That's not my life anymore. I'm someone different."

"You never told me your surname."

These were questions I never wanted to answer. Rylion must have sensed my distress because he gave me a sidelong glance.

"Take your time," he said. "But when you feel as though you can trust me, I would like to hear more about your history."

"I trust you," I blurted out.

Again, he gave me an odd look.

"I do, I swear it. But speaking about my past would make it real all over again. Perhaps… when we're alone… where no one could possibly hear. I'll tell you anything you want to know."

"Hm."

We continued in silence, our only companion the crunch of our footsteps. Dead birds littered the open fields of snow and twice I spotted sinister snakes—much like the giant viper Forsaken Alexavier had killed—poking around the corpses. Sinister animals weren't normal. I wouldn't be surprised if they didn't feel the cold at all.

"Have you known Thea long?" I asked. There was a possibility she had transformed into one of the Forsaken. I didn't want to ask the question outright, but perhaps it was time.

Rylion nodded. "My father found her several years back. Thea's mother had tried to kill her."

"I see. She hated the fact her daughter was cursed?"

"Yes. My father pulled Thea from a burning barn."

Not an unusual practice—fire cleansed everything, after all—but family members were typically kinder than a live pyre.

"Did she break one of the more violent decrees?" I asked.

"She's too gentle to be violent without provocation. And the moment I met her, I knew she was like us. I insisted we care for her until she turned."

"Like us?" I mulled over the statement and then snapped my attention to him. "What do you mean? She has divine fire? She's a Lord of Flame and Cinder?"

"No. Nor is she like my mother, with healing waters. But there's something about her. I can always tell. Just as I knew when I found you on the side of the road. Thea's a descendant of an old god. It's in her blood."

The tone in Rylion's voice, and the way he spoke, it made me think he was intrigued and wondering—like he had feelings for her. I found my breath coming in short bursts and my heart tightened in my chest. I raked a hand through my hair, trying to quiet my anger, but it was difficult. Every day I spent with Rylion, I knew he was someone I wouldn't want to live without. No one compared. I had never felt this way with anyone else.

I wanted him to be mine, but what if he fell for someone else? I felt as if I had enough unbridled hate to scorch the world.

We reached the cave before I could dwell on the situation further.

"Something's wrong," Rylion muttered.

I glanced around. The snow had been disturbed by a large animal, and there was a chill to the area that hadn't been present before.

Rylion strode forward and I shuffled behind. The dark cave entrance had no light, so I snapped my finger and sprang forth a tiny ball of flame. It illuminated our path as we continued inward.

"Shouldn't there be glowing rocks?" I asked, examining the once-mythical boulders.

Rylion picked up his pace.

No light greeted us as we entered the cavern. None at all. And when I glanced down, I spotted another black sinister serpent sliding its way along the stone wall. I held out a hand and lit it ablaze, killing the creature before it could get too far. The sinister serpent squealed and curled in on itself, but I still heard a faint slithering echoing off the walls. There must have been more.

"Since when can sinister animals enter this cave?" I asked.

Rylion walked to the edge of my light and crouched. I jogged to his side and caught my breath.

The lake was gone. No water anywhere.

Just hundreds of bones.

Nickering echoed off the walls. Rylion and I turned to spot a horse standing in the darkness. We walked over, and Rylion pulled out his short sword. The closer we got, the more the bones were cracked and broken, some even deteriorating into dust. When the light of my fire shone on the horse, which lifted its head and snorted.

"Deana," Rylion said.

Deana trotted over, snorting and grunting with a nervous energy. She appeared emaciated, her ribs jutting from her body. Had she always been this unhealthy? Could being trapped in a cavern for a handful of days do that to a horse?

"Where is Thea?" Rylion asked.

"Rylion?" a meek voice asked from the darkness.

I held my palm up, allowing the light of my flames to reach out further.

Thea sat huddled on the stone floor of the cavern. She clutched the collar of her simple dress, keeping it up despite the open cut through the chest of the fabric. Blood stained her clothing, but I saw no injury. Thea trembled, her gaze locked on her knees.

Rylion jumped to her side and undid his cloak. In one simple motion, he covered her from the shoulders down.

"What happened?" I asked.

Thea shook her head. "He killed me," she whispered. *"He killed me."*

"You're fine," Rylion said, examining her with narrowed eyes. "Everything will be all right."

Thea shook her head. "He didn't answer me. I thought he would know. But he didn't answer me."

"Shh, shh. No one else is here. It's just us."

Rylion lifted Thea with ease, one arm under her legs, one wrapped around her back. She placed her forehead on his collarbone and took in a ragged breath. The sight set my blood on fire.

Thea shivered. "I'm so cold."

Rylion turned to me with a hard stare. I held out my hand and summoned a never-ending fire, maintaining it like a campfire blaze. It hovered an inch off the icy stone floor, swirling with an inner power no one could detect but me. Rylion set Thea down by the edge of the heat.

"I'll round up Deana," he said. "Keep Thea warm."

The horse clopped around in the darkness. Why wasn't it attracted to the light of my flame?

But before Rylion could return, I stared at Thea. She was pale and shaken. Her skin glistened with a fresh coat of sweat. Whatever had happened, it had disturbed her.

"Are you... all right?" I asked, my tone lame and my own voice betraying my hesitation.

To my surprise, she met my gaze. For a moment, she said nothing, and then muttered, "I asked him if I was evil."

"Who?"

"The man in the snow."

"Hm. Well, with a title like that, he's obviously a definitive source of information," I quipped.

"He wouldn't answer."

I crossed my arms. "If you wanted the answer, you should've come to me. *Everyone* is evil. It runs in our veins. All we can do is fight against it."

"He killed me," Thea muttered again. "He stabbed me through my heart."

Odd that she kept using the word *killed* when it was clear she wasn't dead. If Thea had been stabbed through the heart, how was she here now? Perhaps she was shaken and delusional. Our surroundings were soaked with an ominous sadness. It could mess with the mind.

But the flickering fire calmed me a bit. I admired my work as Rylion returned with Deana in tow. The horse snorted, but otherwise did as it was told, soothed by the warmth of the flame.

"I'm sorry," I said, looking away from Thea. "This all happened because of me. I shouldn't have questioned you about your intentions. I was curt, and it wasn't appropriate."

She held Rylion's cloak close. "No… I brought the man to the Boneyard."

"Still. There's no excuse for my behavior. Please, forgive me."

"Now isn't the time, Artemis," Rylion said. "Let's return to the lodge."

He walked close, the light casting harsh shadows over his body and armor. He was imposing, even when I knew he wouldn't harm us, and I was reminded he was a warrior first, no matter how he comforted Thea.

Again, Rylion scooped Thea into his arms. She no longer shivered and instead closed her eyes. The sight—them together in a tight embrace—intensified my hatred. Every gesture. Every comment. Every touch. Like oil on a flame.

I followed Rylion, my breaths shallow.

Tonight, I would tell him of my affection for him. For better or worse.

Winds howled beyond the sanctuary of the lodge, disturbing the darkness of night. I paced the main room, waiting for Rylion to come downstairs.

Thea had stayed in her room all day. She wanted to rest. That was what she had said. Rest. Although I regretted speaking to her in such a harsh manner, at no point had she been cross with me. That fact comforted my thoughts, but it didn't ease the growing heat in my blood or the curdling of my stomach.

I didn't want to be the source of someone else's suffering.

The creak of the staircase accelerated my heart rate. Rylion stepped down, his expression crestfallen. I stood at the edge of the last step and waited until we were together before I followed him into the kitchen.

"Is Thea all right?" I asked.

Rylion nodded. "She's healthy and content. Her biggest concern was for Deana."

"Did she say what happened to the Boneyard? What happened to the water? Why were there sinister snakes inside the cave?"

"I don't know." Rylion narrowed his eyes as he opened the pantry and took out a bottle of wine. With the drink in hand, he took a seat at the table. The sturdy piece of furniture didn't bend or creak under his weight. "Thea said there had been water in the Boneyard when she arrived, but after she woke up, there was none."

"And what of the man?" I asked. "The one she said killed her?"

"It was Alexavier. The Scourge."

"He's here?" I asked, breathless.

Rylion broke the seal of the wine bottle. "Thea said he mentioned returning to the capital. And if he hasn't made it to the lodge yet, I doubt he will. He's either frozen in the snow or he's made it beyond Mount Regel."

"The capital…"

"You needn't travel to the capital with me," Rylion said as he eyed the glass bottle. "I understand you left Luthecia for personal reasons."

I could tell him my history—about my family, and my upbringing—but those were all things of the past. I had forsaken them. I had surrendered my old identity and I wanted to move forward.

No, that wasn't true. What I wanted was to move forward *with* him. I wanted Rylion as my source of strength, and no else's.

But how could I say such a thing? Confessing my adoration could come across as forced and awkward. Where would I start? What would I say? Was it appropriate to talk about it now, while we were alone? Was it even appropriate, as the woman, to voice my need for a man? I could already hear my mother's snide remarks, the word *whore* on the tip of her tongue.

Rylion took a swig of the wine and then placed the bottle on the table. He said nothing and barely gave me a second glance. Exhaustion rolled off of him like sap from a tree.

When would we have another moment of quiet solitude? Soon we would be traveling to the capital as a group, and then there would be no privacy.

"Rylion," I said as I took a seat next to him at the table, limiting the distance between us so I could keep my voice low. "I… have something to say to you."

He turned to me with a weak smile. "Speak your mind." He had bags under his eyes, and the energy of his speech was nonexistent, but I couldn't wait any longer.

"Are you smitten with anyone?" I asked, my face

painfully hot. I couldn't bring myself to look into his eyes. Instead, I spoke to the tabletop, glaring at the wood like *it* was to blame for my cowardice. "Or are you betrothed? You're the son of a knight from the Holy Guard, after all. I'm sure your father could've arranged something."

Rylion chuckled. "No. I'm neither smitten nor betrothed."

I wrestled my hands together, my fingers lacing and then unlacing a dozen times. Why was this so difficult? I hated problems I couldn't just burn to the ground. Surely Rylion understood what I was trying to get at? But he said nothing. He just waited for me to continue.

"You're different," I said, my voice strained. "I've known so many people in my lifetime, and they share the same taint. I rarely enjoy the company of others. But you... I feel different about you. The feelings I have... They're passion. And jealousy."

Even uttering the two statements caused me to cringe. How would Rylion react to such declarations? Or perhaps he had experienced this many times before. He brought comfort and reassurance to everyone he knew. Surely, it was common for someone to declare their secret love for him.

"I never wish to part from you," I said, forcing out each word, though my mouth was dry. I had to speak my mind. I had gone too far to back down now. I focused on the dark wood of the table, glowering at the smooth surface, unable to look up at Rylion.

No reply.

With my jaw clenched, I continued, "Every day my feelings for you grow. I want to accompany you to the capital. I want to be with you when you speak to the god-king. At all points, no matter the danger to myself, I wish to be by your side."

"Artemis—"

"*I know this isn't proper etiquette,*" I said, cutting him off, desperate to explain. "And my family won't offer you anything for a marriage, nor can I guarantee you land or prestige. But ever since you first spoke to me… your voice has been ingrained in my thoughts."

"Artemis…"

I held my tongue this time, waiting for his response. Rylion fidgeted with the wine bottle, his thoughts so scattered I swore I heard them. After a prolonged moment of silent suffering, he finally took a deep breath.

"You want us to wed?" he asked, his words slow.

"I want *you*. I don't care how that happens."

Rylion nervously chuckled and then took a long swig of wine. When he placed the bottle down, he said, "You're forceful and confident in everything you do, I see."

I finally found the courage to tear my gaze from the table. I stared into his calm brown eyes and found worry looking back at me.

Just as I feared. He didn't feel the same about me.

I quickly turned away, focusing my attention on the far wall. "If you cannot take me as a woman and a lover, please don't… send me away because of this. I swear I won't make this public knowledge."

"Artemis, I wouldn't send you away."

"But you don't want me as your wife either?" I demanded, wanting the damn answer.

"I don't think you understand. It's not that simple. I—"

The door cracked open, and I leapt away from Rylion on instinct. To my surprise, I was trembling, uncertain of what I should do with my hands, so I tucked them into my armpits. The encounter with Rylion had taken a toll on my willpower. The fear of his rejection weighed on my mind more than I wanted to admit.

"Rylion?" Osmund asked as he stepped into the kitchen. He looked just as exhausted as his son. "What're you doing, boy?"

Rylion stood from the table and straightened his tunic

with unsteady hands. "Artemis and I were having a discussion. Do you need me?"

"Yes. There are things I need to tell you." Osmund faced me and nodded. "You'll excuse us, Artemis. You two can resume your discussion another time." He waved his hand and Rylion followed, not bothering to offer me a glance and leaving me to the chill of the barren kitchen.

I stood from the table and paced, cursing myself while I did so.

A *discussion*? I confessed my adoration of the man and Rylion said we were having a *discussion*? Rylion had the gift of understatement.

And he never gave me a proper answer. *Feh.* I had known something like this would create a rift between us. He probably thought I was touched in the head or just unfit for companionship. Maybe he thought my confession was a jest at some level.

First confronting Thea, now Rylion. What if he asked me to leave?

What a fool I was! I should've left well enough alone. Had I not said anything, I could've stayed by his side, even if I couldn't have him for myself.

I placed my hands on the edge of the table, attempting to clear my thoughts. Smoke stung my nose. When I glanced down, I noticed I had burned hand-shaped imprints into the wood with my fire.

Gods damn me.

CHAPTER THIRTEEN

I paced my room in front of the window, watching the flurry of midafternoon snow. I hadn't seen Rylion since last night, and I was unable to sleep. All I wanted was his answer. If he insisted I leave, I would travel away from Luka and attempt to start again elsewhere. I had come to terms with the worst outcomes—I could handle them—but waiting for his decision was worse than nails through the foot.

Knocking at my door broke my thoughts.

I hustled over and swung it open. To my disappointment, Caprice stood before me, her long black hair straight and shiny, even in the dim hallway.

"Yes?" I asked, curt.

"I saw the table in the kitchen was damaged," Caprice said, no hint of irritation about her. "Burned with two handprints." She smiled as she stepped into my room.

"What of it?" I allowed her in, though I gave a brief thought to sending her away. I restrained my rage-fueled desires.

"I came to see if you needed company, Artemis. You've

spent most of your free time alone since joining our eclectic family."

I crossed my arms. She wasn't wrong. I had been solitary. Up until recently, there was no reason to trust anyone here but Rylion. But all of them had taken a risk by harboring me, especially since they knew about Alexavier's quest to kill me. It was unfair to treat them as scum.

"I don't think now is the best time for company," I forced myself to say, attempting niceties before anger.

"Now is the perfect time for company."

Caprice ambled around my room, examining the walls and washbasin, as if looking for more scorch marks.

I shut the door. "If now is the perfect time, I assume you have an idea for conversation?"

"No."

"Fantastic," I quipped. "You can sit there and watch me pace, then."

Caprice chuckled. "No. I think it would be best if you prayed with me. It's a form of meditation. It will help clear your thoughts."

"I've prayed to the gods of old on many occasions," I said. "It's never cleared my mind, that's for sure."

"At my temple, we learned ways to pray in peace. I'll show you some of those techniques."

She took a seat at the end of my rickety bed.

A part of me was curious. I sat next to her. Caprice grabbed my hands and set them in my lap, positioning me in just the right way for prayers. Before I could ask her what she was doing, she faced me and crossed her legs, motioning that I should do the same. I followed along, stiff and anxious.

"Close your eyes and focus on your breathing," Caprice said.

I did so, though my breathing was hardly anything worth taking note of.

"You have to focus on each breath. Don't force anything.

Breathe naturally. Follow the air as it goes through your system. Take note of your rising and falling chest."

Caprice had a melodic voice. I hadn't noticed before.

I did as she instructed. My breathing was the center of my attention. The longer I focused, the more I also realized how tense I was.

"Relax," she whispered, as though she could read minds.

This was a lot less praying and a lot more meditation. Then again, it did what Caprice said it would do. I was more at peace than I had been ten minutes ago, and the time since now and seeing Rylion didn't seem that long. He was the type of man that would think hard before making decisions—I should have known. Even if he enjoyed my company, he would take time to think everything over.

There was no reason to fret just yet. There was much to deliberate on.

"Anger comes easily for you," Caprice said.

I opened my eyes and glared, my anger—ironically—returning in full force. "Are you going on about my lineage again?"

"Just a statement of fact."

She didn't open her eyes. Instead, she sat straight and tall, a little more regal than I would have assumed.

Her stories returned to my mind. For a moment, I wanted to believe everything Caprice had ever said. Was I a descendant of the old gods? I would like to think so. Then again, apparently my ancient ancestor—the War God, Ravintus—fought on the side to destroy all mankind, making me the daughter of a traitor with a bloodthirst for genocide.

"Caprice," I drawled, my thoughts scattered. "Why did the War God want to cleanse the world of man?"

"It depends on the story you believe."

I needed a distraction. "Tell me these stories."

"One states that Ravintus trusted the God of Truths, and when the God of Truths declared that mankind was inherently evil—that they could not be saved—Ravintus took it to heart. He wanted to purge the world of darkness wherever it could be found."

Mankind *was* evil. I supposed that was a reason to kill them off.

"What's the other story?" I asked.

"That Ravintus was jealous."

"Jealous?" I said, caught off guard by the word.

Caprice opened her eyes and lifted an eyebrow. "I told you he was in love with Vahltera, the Temperance God."

"And?"

"And he thought her love for mankind was greater than her love for him. He wished to be her one and only, and sought to destroy all other objects of her affection."

Jealousy did drive men to do irrational things. But were the gods of old susceptible to the same emotions as mankind? I hoped not. Then again, there had been a war fought between the gods on whether to destroy mankind or save it. Some emotions must have played a part.

"Well?" I asked.

Caprice tilted her head. "Hm?"

"Did she love mankind more than him?"

Caprice laughed. "That's what you wish to know? I'm sorry, there is no definite answer. However, if you want my opinion, sometimes people confuse duty with love, and vice versa. Just because she protected mankind does not mean she loved them more."

A creak outside my door silenced the conversation. Was someone waiting outside? They didn't knock.

I stood and walked over, my mouth dry. Had Rylion returned? I opened the door and flinched back. Wulf waited outside, his back against the wall, but he jumped to attention the moment our eyes met.

"Ah, Artemis," Wulf said, forcing a smile. "Forgive me. I came to speak to you, but you were busy, so..."

"So you decided to listen in?" I asked, lifting an eyebrow. He had obviously just been listening at the door.

"Like I said, forgive me." Wulf rubbed at the back of his neck and avoided meeting my gaze. "But I came because I wanted you to teach me about... Well, about your divine magic."

"Why?"

"I want to wield mine." Wulf ran a hand through his curly brown hair. The tiny curls got wrapped around his fingers. "I want to fight with it, like you fight with your fire."

I stepped into the hall and closed my bedroom door. Caprice continued to meditate without saying a word, and perhaps that was for the better. I moved closer to Wulf and sighed.

"I'm a Lord of Flame and Cinder," I muttered.

He nodded once. "And?"

"It's different. Lords of Winter Stillness aren't known for their destruction."

"Ice is death itself," Wulf stated. "Fire is alive, but it, too, will eventually die." He held up his hand and ice coated his palm. "Nothing survives the cold, and ice doesn't live, breathe, or consume. It just kills. So, why can't my magic be used for combat? I should be able to wield this against the Forsaken."

I hadn't thought of ice in that way.

Perhaps Wulf was right.

After a quick glance over my shoulder, I fidgeted with the rings on my robe. "Very well. I'll teach you what my father taught me. But not here. His methods for learning magic... They were extreme."

Wulf's eyes lit up. He leaned in closer to me, and when he breathed, I felt a chill rolling off him. "When do we start?"

"Artemis?" Caprice called from my room.

"Later," I said to Wulf. "For now, I need to meditate, apparently."

"Can I join you?" he asked. Wulf gave me the once over. "I'd like to learn more from you, if you wouldn't mind."

I replied with a curt nod. "Do as you want."

How was it that everyone wanted my time today? I huffed, opened the door to my room, and then stepped aside, motioning Wulf in. He jumped at the opportunity. He walked into my room and took a seat on my bed, next to Caprice. His gaunt frame made it easy for him to fit on the mattress, but he was so tall, it made things awkward.

After I shut the door, I retook my seat, straining the weak bedframe even further. It would be a miracle if the furniture survived the meditation session.

"We should return to our praying," Caprice said. "Again, close your eyes and focus on your breathing."

Wulf leaned forward, and I was reminded of how much taller than me he was. "Do you think this will help improve my understanding of divine magic?"

"This may help," Caprice said. "As a Lord of Winter Stillness, you must master yourself. Calm. Tranquility. Your magic is at its height when you are devoid of heated emotions."

I shook my head. "My father taught me that my magic stems from strength, practice, and passion. Sitting on my bed and contemplating your breath won't help you."

Caprice chuckled. "Perhaps that was how your fire improved, but I assure you that the children of Vahltera did not learn their skills in such a fashion."

What did Caprice know? Had *she* studied magic for years, improving her craft? My anger came so quick, it almost startled me. I took another breath and allowed myself to calm.

"The Temperance God was enigmatic to most, and her children were the same," Caprice said. She stared at Wulf. "Rylion has a deep connection to his magic because he studies in quiet solitude."

The bed groaned as Wulf fixed his posture. "Well, my

brother has mastered powers of defense. The cursed don't become the Forsaken around him, and he's sturdy and strong." Wulf gritted his teeth. "*I* want powers that will help us rid the world of the Forsaken."

Caprice frowned. "Is that wise?"

"Of course it is," I snapped. "Stop trying to convince us that pacifism is best."

It wasn't.

Wulf gave me an appreciative glance.

In a world full of monsters—and individuals trying to control us—the only salvation and freedom was power.

But Wulf's talk of magical powers got me thinking. Could Lords pursue different routes to their magic? Could Rylion train for defense while his brother trained in a different style? I had only known one way, and that was from my father. He had been taught by his father, and so on—I had thought it was the only way.

Another question drifted into my thoughts.

"Caprice," I whispered. "What kind of Lord is Thea?"

Her powers... I hadn't seen them. Was Thea a Lord of Winter Stillness? She seemed too anxious to have any tranquility in her.

Caprice held her breath and contemplated my question. The three of us—myself, Wulf, Caprice—all on this single, tiny bed, made it impossible to hide any shift in our bodies or expressions. Caprice frowned at my question, but hid her discontentment a half second later.

"Thea is a Lord of Desolation," Caprice whispered.

"Pleasant," I quipped.

"What god's bloodline does Thea descend from?" Wulf asked. He leaned in even closer, rapt attention on Caprice.

"She descends from Casseda, the Despair God."

Even hearing the name disturbed me. I shivered and rubbed at my arms. I was *never* cold, not when I had my fire, but I didn't care for the name *Casseda*. It felt as though I had known this person at one time, but had forgotten.

Wulf cracked his knuckles, his gaze lingering on the bed. Was he mulling over stories of the old gods in his head? How had Casseda died? I couldn't remember.

"The Despair God was thought to be the most powerful," Caprice whispered, as though she heard my thoughts. Her narrow face, pale and smooth, reminded me of a porcelain doll as she recited the tale, her expression aggressively neutral. "Casseda couldn't be harmed or killed, not even by her fellow gods. She is the epitome of bleakness and blight, and she ruled through fear and destruction. So do her descendants."

"She couldn't be killed?" Wulf repeated, almost in awe.

Caprice shook her head. "Whenever the Despair God died, she rose again, stronger than before."

"But... I thought the old gods all died? Doesn't that include Casseda?"

"The old gods will return once the era of mankind is over," Caprice stated. Then she held up a finger. "Casseda *was* defeated on the battlefield. During the war of the old gods, she fought on the side to exterminate humanity, and many thought Casseda was unstoppable. But in order to save the last kingdoms of man, Justinus, the Hope God, forcefully merged himself with Casseda, their flesh intertwining into something disgusting and unspeakable. The abomination fled the battlefield and was never seen or heard from again."

I hadn't expected *that*.

What twisted lives the old gods had led. Their war over mankind had destroyed their power and capabilities. I still didn't truly believe Caprice about people being descended from the old gods, but since I had no way to disprove her, I allowed my imagination to wander. Had Thea inherited the Despair God's power? Was that how she had been "killed" by Alexavier, but lived to tell the tale?

Under no circumstances could we allow Thea to become a Forsaken. With her magic, she would make a terrifying beast.

"Enough of this talk," Caprice said, holding up both her hands. "This has agitated you both, and that isn't our goal here. You need inner reflection. As a matter of fact, if you two commit to praying like this, at least once a day, you'll find peace with your problems, and the gods of old will reward you for it."

Her insistence seemed genuine, so I exhaled, took my seat again, and then closed my eyes. With the snow continuing outside, perhaps this was the best way to calm my doubts.

Five days. That was how long the snow lasted. When the storms ended, we were supposed to head for the capital to confront the god-king, but no one spoke about the matter. I suspected some were hoping Rylion would change his mind.

Wulf wanted me to train him in magic, but I couldn't focus.

Seven days. That was how long it had been since I had spoken to Rylion.

He was avoiding me. There was no other explanation. He didn't seem like the type to avoid conflict. He had engaged Alexavier without hesitation, and fought several Forsaken, even at the peril of his own life. Yet he wouldn't speak to me. Perhaps I should have saved him the discomfort and left the lodge forever.

"You don't look so good," Lydia said. "You've been real quiet for some time now."

I paced the front room of the lodge, waiting for the stew that had been promised for dinner. Steen stirred the contents of the pot, the thick aroma of meat and onion wafting over the area. The flames in the fireplace crackled and popped, creating a song of ash.

"Didn't you say Rylion would be returning soon?" I asked, ignoring Lydia's question.

"Yeah, I did say that."

"I need to speak with him."

Steen sipped at the broth. "You know who else has been quiet? Osmund. The man has barely left his room. He sends Rylion to do all the maintenance around the mountain."

The information sank into my thoughts. Osmund had been at the lodge more often than before. He didn't speak, except to Rylion, and then locked himself in his room. But I had enough to worry about. Osmund's dilemma would have to wait.

Rylion would return for dinner. There wouldn't be any avoidance if he was here.

The horses outside whinnied as a series of loud bangs issued from the front door. Lydia and Steen exchanged worried glances, but I headed straight for the door and opened it. A middle-aged man swaddled in heavy furs stood before me, frost coating the edges of his clothes and face.

"Can I help you?" I asked.

He pulled down the fur over his mouth. "Is Osmund Nasos here? I-I must speak to him. At once." The man held back his chattering, but not completely.

I turned to Lydia and motioned her to the stairs. She went to Osmund's room, dashing up the steps two at a time. Steen huddled closer to the pot, a glare on his face and suspicion rolling off him thicker than the stew.

Was this new man a hunter? He carried an axe and several skinning knives. Perhaps he was a woodsman.

Osmund lumbered down the steps, a deep frown set into his older face. "Who's there? Why has someone come all the way to Mount Regel to find me?"

Lydia walked to the railing of the stairs and leaned heavily against it.

"Osmund!" the man said the moment they spotted each other. "Thank the gods. We need you, more than ever."

"What's happened, Rowland?"

"It's a Forsaken. One from the Kingdom of Saileer." The woodsman, Rowland, walked into the lodge, almost pushing me aside to do so. I allowed him, since he was an acquaintance of Osmund, but his frantic manner of speech had me worried.

Osmund reached the bottom of the steps, his frown never letting up. "From Saileer? How would you even know?"

"This one is far worse than the others, my friend. Whispers have reached us, even in Ludlow. The Forsaken that crossed the border is the *King Killer*. The man who killed the Saileer's god-king."

I shivered.

Every Forsaken took on characteristics of the decree they had broken, but there was another catch. The first few decrees uttered were the most powerful—they created the most devastating monsters—because they were the most important, at least according to the god-king or god-queen who spoke them. The further down the list of decrees, the weaker the curse, and thus, the weaker the Forsaken created from them, though they were still frightening and vicious.

A decree against regicide was always the first one muttered. Always. Meaning the Forsaken would be deadly beyond belief, and an embodiment of slaying god-kings.

"The King Killer?" Osmund muttered. He stroked his stubble-covered face. "Why did it come to the Kingdom of Luka? Why didn't it stay in Saileer?"

Rowland shook his head. Snow melted off his body thanks to the fire, and droplets of water pooled at his feet. "I've heard rumors," he said. "The new god-queen ordered the Forsaken to be lured to the border."

"Why? Why not appoint her Scourge, and have her guard kill the beast?"

"It's different than the rest!" Rowland continued. "The King Killer has an aura about it, Osmund. A presence. It's a king of monsters, it is. When anyone cursed gets close to this beast—they transform. Right then. Right there. It's evil magic. The King Killer rampages across the hills, turning bandits into a blighted army."

The King Killer forcibly transformed anyone who was cursed? I placed a hand over my shoulder, my heart rate increasing with every second. I felt my pulse through the black mark on my body.

Osmund ran an unsteady hand over his face. "No. It can't be."

"It's true. All hunters are to slay the beasts and destroy the King Killer as quickly as possible, before it's too late. Please, Osmund. There's word it's heading north of Ludlow. What if it comes to us? Our town would never survive."

Lydia turned to Steen, her brow furrowed. I didn't even bother glancing over to Steen. I knew what he was feeling. This King Killer would destroy us all.

"I… I'll talk to my boys," Osmund said, his voice almost a whisper. "Head back to Ludlow and tell everyone to fortify the wall."

"You know it's not complete."

"Fortify what they can."

"I'll do that. I'll deliver the message. Please hurry and meet with the other hunters. This blight must be destroyed."

Rowland gave several awkward bows before he headed out of the lodge. No one spoke once he was gone. What was there to say? The news settled over us like heavy dust. What would we do? Steen, Thea, Caprice, and I were all cursed. Were we going to wait here while Osmund and his two sons attempted to slay the King Killer? They might as well commit suicide. The outcome would be the same.

"Are you really intending to fight the beast?" Steen asked, breaking the tension between us.

Osmund shook his head. "No."

Steen exhaled and half smiled. "Thank the gods."

"We should fight this beast," Lydia said. "What if it comes here? Steen, what would you do?"

"Become a monster, obviously," he quipped.

Lydia placed her hands on her hips. "Ya know what I meant. We shouldn't sit and wait for it. We should do somethin'."

"No," Osmund snapped, an edge of finality to his voice. "The King Killer will likely follow the trade roads. The Forsaken are drawn to towns and villages that have the most life, and our mountain has little."

"There are plenty of Forsaken here," Lydia said. "Perhaps the King Killer will—"

"Those are brigands who transformed here, girl. They would have left the mountain and headed for Ludlow had we not stopped them. But what we should do now is allow the King Killer to continue on its way."

Lydia shook her head. "If the King Killer is headin' for Ludlow and beyond, we really should do somethin'!"

"We aren't the type of hunters who can handle such a Forsaken. Half our members are cursed! This is too dangerous. We should leave this to the younger hunters. Or the men who have nothing left to live for."

"I'm goin'," Lydia said as she descended the last few steps and stood by Steen's side in the front room of the lodge. "I'm good with a bow, and I've wanted to help you for a long time now."

Steen stopped stirring the food. "No. Absolutely not."

"I'm doin' this for you, Steen," she said. "If the King Killer comes here, I'll lose you. I won't stand by while that happens."

Her words were heated, and her conviction evident. But Steen stood and walked away, distancing himself from her, his jaw clenched.

"You can't," Steen snapped. "Even Osmund is worried, and he was once part of the Holy Guard. You say you don't want to lose me, but I don't want to lose you either, woman!"

"What're you sayin' I should do, then?"

"Let someone else handle this. The Scourge. Other hunters. Anyone else but us. We don't need to be involved."

"That's craven and heartless and short sighted," Lydia said, red in the face. "You heard Rowland. He came here pleadin' for help. If I can help, I'm goin' to. I'll protect you and Ludlow." She turned to me, her hard gaze set. "What about you? What're you goin' to do?"

I already knew the answer, no matter the circumstance.

"I'll help Rylion in whatever course of action he takes," I said.

Osmund regarded me with an odd look, his frown deepening. "Rylion won't be making any decisions. He'll stay here, with me. I won't lose any more of my family, do you understand me, girl? And my sons are all I have left."

Lydia huffed. "You know Rylion will want to fight."

"I won't allow him. Not him. Not Wulf. Other men can handle this."

"What about when we head to the capital?"

"We *won't* be heading to the capital, not with a king of abominations roaming the countryside."

Steen turned his glare on me. For some reason, it felt as though he blamed me for the incident, like *I* was the reason the King Killer existed. "No matter what fire you may possess, you should thank Osmund for keeping you here. A monster with your fell flames would kill us all, even Rylion."

"You don't know what you're saying," I growled. I knew of Rylion's aura to protect the cursed. Would it prevent the King Killer's aura? It was a mystery, but I would risk everything to help him fight the monster.

"The King Killer will force you to become one of the Forsaken." Steen motioned to my being as though I couldn't comprehend his statement without a visual aid. "Yet you glower at me like a shrew. Every day I see your arrogance shining through. You're a monster wearing the skin of a woman, and if you ever think anything else, you're deluding yourself."

"Such audacity," I said with a sneer. "You wish to see my arrogance? My monstrous side?" Embers wafted in the air, spinning on an invisible breeze of hate. Even the flames in the fireplace intensified with my rage.

Steen stepped back, his eyes wide.

Osmund moved between us, his face red. "*Enough,*" he bellowed. "We will have no more talk about this. None! We won't hunt the King Killer, and we won't leave the lodge either. Steen, you'll keep your idiotic comments to yourself. Artemis, you'll not burn down my lodge."

I turned away, forcing breaths and willing my anger back under control. The embers died. The fireplace returned to a calmer state.

"We'll all get along, understand?" Osmund snapped.

The silence that followed spoke magnitudes.

The King Killer.

The conversation floated up into my room like a terrible steam, suffocating me with the new knowledge. I wished something so awful didn't exist, but that wasn't the world we lived in.

I examined my tunic and pressed my hand to my chest. The memory of Alexavier's halberd lingered. It had sliced through my heart, and the haunting sensation of my heart not beating filled my thoughts. It had been just like the day with my father. When I closed my eyes, I could picture everything with perfect recollection.

I had killed my father. I couldn't let him place another hand on my mother.

But what I had done was unforgivable. I had broken a decree, so afterward—after I had been marked as one of the cursed—I had pulled the blade from my father's corpse and then turned it on myself. Stabbing the knife into my body had felt different from than what I had imagined. The searing had lasted for every second my blood spilled out of my throat.

I hadn't regretted my actions, I'd just wished…

I had known more happiness in my life.

But after the blood had drained from my body, I had awoken, my house twisted and warped, my neck no longer slashed. I had stood, healthy and uninjured, and the next thing I had heard was my mother's screams.

Just like in the Boneyard. Alexavier had slashed my heart, but then I awoke, healthy and uninjured. The Boneyard had been just as twisted and warped as my house—like my surroundings had paid the price for my recovery.

But *how* had I come back to life? Why had I been denied my escape? Was I so evil that even the freedom of death was denied me?

That was what my mother had said. I was evil.

Evil.

I couldn't kill myself to escape the curse. Somehow, for some reason, I had been resurrected. Caprice had said I was descended from an old god, but what kind of fell magic would keep me trapped in a life I didn't want? What kind of Lord was I? I didn't have Rylion's calm cold, or Artemis's flame.

My mother had tried to kill me. She had locked me in the barn and set the outside ablaze. I hadn't fought against her. After all, if I were evil, what was the point of living? I should save everyone the trouble and leave.

So why hadn't Alexavier answered my question?

I covered my face with my hands, frustrated by my inability to die. Other cursed individuals had killed themselves, and no one had ever reported a false death, like mine. I had thought maybe the Scourge could kill me. His halberd had stung like any death should. But nothing.

Was my body even flesh and blood? Rylion's body stitched itself back together far faster than others, and he said it was a divine gift, but mine didn't feel like a gift at all.

But perhaps there was another way.

The King Killer.

It would transform me, and I wouldn't have to wait

anymore. I could take fate into my own hands. I could force myself to stop existing. Maybe then, if hunters were nearby, they could finish the deed and burn my corpse, sending the ashes to the winds.

A fitting end for evil.

I had to find the King Killer.

INTERLUDE
ALEXAVIER LOWELL

Winter travel broke even the hardiest of travelers.

For days, I had waited just short of Luthecia, the winds and rains flooding the roads. Kelphy had gone through worse treks, but her waning health prevented me from reaching my final destination.

God-King Eliezer would no doubt question my absence. Every member of the Holy Guard I had taken with me was now dead. All but one. Charles Gregom had turned back when I had told him to flee. He should have reached the capital days ago. I worried what Eliezer would do upon hearing Charles's report, but there was nothing I could do about that until the weather calmed.

Sleep eluded me. So did tranquility.

If Lady Yellahjar was correct—if she was a virtue who had saved her mother at the cost of breaking a decree—then there could be others like her. Others who shouldn't bear the mark. Others whom I had killed without a second thought.

The breaking of the day pierced the unforgiving darkness of the night. Colors shone on the horizon. Today, I would make my way to Luthecia.

I exited my inn room and closed the door. Already there

was movement throughout the building. Day brought with it all manner of activity, but I ignored the maids and apprentice boys. No one recognized me as I walked past. Normally people sang my praises, or jumped to fetch me luxuries, but today they turned away and continued their work, certain I was no one of importance. It was because I wore simple clothing and not my Holy Guard armor. Dressed as a ragged traveler, they didn't spare me a second thought.

Once outside, I headed for the north end of town. Kelphy wasn't a creature to be kept among gentle horses and mules, so I had left her outside the gates of the city. She had the blood of the Forsaken in her veins, giving her a tendency toward violence. In the hands of a skilled trainer, I wouldn't worry, but this tiny town didn't have the resources or understanding sufficient to handle her.

Light shone off the town's King's Stone, catching my eyes. I squinted and held a hand up, surprised to see a crowd of people forming near the base of the obsidian pillar. They murmured and pointed and whispered. I jogged over, my heart seizing up with each beat. Had God-King Eliezer issued a new decree? It had been a while since the last—the day of his most recent wedding, to be specific.

I tried to march through the crowd, but there were dozens of people in front of me, each trying to touch the King's Stone to understand the new decree. I didn't blame them. Checking the King's Stone every day was basic due diligence. Anyone who wasn't rushing for the King's Stone would be a fool.

But I wasn't just anyone. I was the Scourge. I needed to know the decrees at the core of my being, more than anyone here.

"Step aside," I said to the man in front of me.

He elbowed my arm and offered a glare over his shoulder.

"Wait your turn," he said with a grunt. "I got here first."

I gritted my teeth and remained silent. Without my armor

and halberd, I appeared to be an average citizen. Rather than reveal my identity, I waited.

"What's happening?" a woman shrieked.

Panic spread through the crowd like an illness, jumping from one person to the next. I stepped back and steeled myself for a fight. The man in front of me—the man I had spoken to—turned his attention to his arm.

A black mark spread from his elbow to his wrist, ending only once it reached the tips of his fingers. It was spiderwebbed and hideous—the mark of the cursed.

"W-What is this?" he asked, his voice unsteady.

Everyone backed away, some with their hands over their mouths. The man shook his head, mumbling statements of disbelief and shock. I didn't know which decree he had broken, but God-King Eliezer had given me a direct command to kill those who were cursed.

"Everyone," I said. "I am Alexavier Lowell, the god-king's Scourge. Stand back and I will handle this!"

Panic transformed into hysteria.

The crowd broke apart, everyone rushing toward buildings, some screaming to hide the children. The cursed man blubbered something incomprehensible and ran for the King's Stone.

I held up my hand and called forth my divine fire, lighting up the city square with a holy pyre. The man stumbled in his haste and drowned in the fiery red of my flames. He flailed and cried, but my magic consumed him faster than anything made with flint and iron. Once charred, his corpse shriveled in on itself, the smell of cooked meat thick in the air.

I lowered my hand and took a deep breath.

Then I glanced around. Every door was closed, every window blocked. None had stayed to cheer or applaud. The stench of fear overtook the burning of hair.

I walked forward, past the embers and the cinders. The

King's Stone was unharmed, and I cast my gaze to the top of the list and read the most recently issued decrees.

My heart stopped for a moment and all feeling left my body.

Three new decrees.

They read:

Cursed be the man who disobeys the orders of the Holy Guard.
Cursed be the man who attacks a member of the Holy Guard.
Cursed be the man who hinders the work of the Holy Guard.

Within a fraction of a second, I knew why these had been uttered by the god-king. Charles had made it back to God-King Eliezer and no doubt reported there were hunters on the mountain hiding the cursed. In an attempt to help us—to make the search easier, or for me to return to Eliezer's side—the god-king had issued these three decrees.

The man in the crowd…

He hadn't stepped aside when I had told him to.

That was when he had become cursed.

It was difficult to think. Noise buzzed in my mind. Did the man deserve to die because of his minor transgression against me? He hadn't even known who I was. How could Eliezer do this? These decrees gave the Holy Guard a vast amount of power—too vast, too ill thought out.

And that was why the townspeople weren't flocking to thank me. No one wanted to risk a command issued from my lips. None of them trusted that I would keep them safe.

Winter winds blew through the empty town square.

What was Eliezer thinking? How could he do this?

I walked away from the King's Stone, my breath ragged.

CHAPTER FOURTEEN

I waited in the snow, around the side of the lodge, my breath coming out in visible streams. Rylion and his father argued not far from my location. I stayed out of their sight, though they had been wrapped in their discussions for hours.

"—and if we join other hunters, we'll have a greater chance of bringing down the King Killer," Rylion said, never angry, always calm.

"No," Osmund growled. "I don't care about the odds. That beast is far worse than the nightmares roaming this mountain."

"I disagree."

"The Holy Guard can handle the King Killer."

"You saw what happened to the Holy Guard when they fought here on Mount Regel. What if they aren't enough for the King Killer? What if the other hunters fail? Luka could suffer. Weren't you once a member of the Holy Guard? Don't you feel any sort of—"

"*Rylion*," Osmund said, curt. "I've lost my brother, I've lost the love of my life—what more do I need to give up to prove I've fought for this kingdom? Do I need to lose my sons as well? This isn't our battle. Others can pay the price. I've lost enough."

"We're talented hunters. Wulf and I are Lords. We won't fall."

"Wulf is inexperienced, and you can't defend everyone, even if you try. We don't have the tools or the warriors needed for this task."

"Artemis's divine flame would rid the world of that beast."

"Artemis will become a beast herself if she gets close to it!" Osmund's yelling almost overtook the entire mountain. "Don't bring up arguments that are impossible, boy."

Rylion exhaled, and although he could quell his anger like a saint, it didn't mean he had an infinite amount of patience. "You know my magic will stop the change. Artemis won't become one of the Forsaken while I'm around."

"And what if you falter? You aren't perfect with your abilities, you never have been. Why don't you look at your mother's corpse and then tell me you can guarantee Artemis won't change? Maybe then we can talk."

The biting comments left me trembling.

Who did Osmund think he was? How could he say such a heartless thing to his own son?

Rylion had no reply. He had already said he blamed himself for his mother's transformation, and it seemed Osmund kept that belief healthy. But Rylion hadn't cursed his mother. He wasn't to blame for her transformation, at least, not as far as I was concerned.

I tensed at the sound of snow crunching underfoot. Osmund's heavier breathing betrayed his identity as he walked back into the lodge. The slam of the heavy door rang out into the trees. Rylion never joined him. Rylion never moved.

With a huff, I walked around the building and headed for Rylion's position. He stood near the snowy tree line that surrounded the lodge. When I reached him, he gave me an odd glance. Apprehension? But he said nothing and allowed me to take a place at his side.

The heavy winds and flurry of powdered snow covered everything in white. Even Rylion's shoulders carried small mounds of ice. His skin never paled, and his breath remained hot. For once, I felt the chill, especially now that I was close to him.

Was the ice... his doing? He was a Lord of Winter Stillness, after all.

I pulled my cloak close and willed my inner fire to flood my veins.

The longer the wind coursed between us, the more I realized Rylion's only option.

"You've lived under your father's rule long enough," I said. "You're your own man."

"My father is a talented warrior," Rylion muttered. "I cannot do this without him."

"Depression has stolen the last of his prime. Besides, his eyes will hinder his usefulness."

"No one else can wield Calavandi."

"Wulf could, with practice. And my fire is far more effective than the bow."

Rylion met my gaze. "Is this what you want, Artemis? For us to fight the King Killer?"

His direct question gave me pause. After a long inhale, I said, "You've been distant lately. Troubled. Unhappy. I feared it was my doing, but you've been arguing with your father the entire time as well. What I want is for you to pursue your own course of action. I'll help you any way I can."

Rylion looked away, his attention set on the darkness between trees, but the vacant stare told me he saw nothing. "You haven't made me unhappy."

"Yet you avoid me."

"I..."

His lack of an explanation grated.

But I pushed down the feeling and said, "You mentioned speaking to God-King Eliezer. Will you still travel to the capital to meet with him? Or are you also going to give up on that because your father doesn't want you to leave the mountain?"

"Traveling to the capital will no doubt entangle me in the hunt for the King Killer. And if I set out to slay the King Killer, I'm certain the god-king will take note. I cannot do one task and avoid the other."

I glowered at the snow. "Why do you hesitate? This isn't like you. I've seen you charge the Forsaken—even Alexavier, the God-King's Scourge—without a second thought, yet here you are, fretting over your next course of action. If you truly believe you'll slay the King Killer, like you said to your father, what does it matter if he gives you his blessing? All he wants is for you to continue living." I threw an arm in the air, my anger creating ambient embers. "Slay the beast, speak to the god-king, and return to your father's side a hero of legend. Everyone wins!"

Rylion half-smiled and then chuckled. "You make it sound so effortless."

"I'll help you," I said. "With your aura, I'll approach the beast and use my fire. The monster will never stand a chance."

Rylion didn't reply.

His pensive attitude reinforced my belief that he was distancing himself from me. Did he think I was bad luck? Had I offended him in some way? Did he despise my personality and brash demeanor?

"Or do you want me to leave?" I asked, holding onto the scarf, twisting my fingers into the warm fabric. "Enough of your silence. I can't handle it. If you avoid me for another moment, I'll be driven to flames." I gripped the sleeves of my robes, my fingers twisting into the fabric. I wanted to be honest and direct, but Rylion made everything complicated. Why couldn't he just say what he wanted?

"Walk with me," Rylion said, a somber hint in his voice.

The twinge of depression quelled my rage. I relaxed and followed him into the woods, wondering what could possibly upset him.

The branches held mounds of snow above us, creating a false darkness despite the noontime hour. We crunched through the thick shadows at a steady pace, heading further and further from the lodge. Rylion kept his gaze forward, but again, his vacant stare betrayed his deep thoughts. I stayed at his side, determined to hear him out, no matter where he decided to take us.

His blue cloak, heavy with the scales woven into the fabric, disturbed the snow, creating a shallow furrow. Rylion had sewn a new piece of cloth over the damaged areas from our fighting, but I saw the glimmer of the Temperance God's beauty whenever I looked at it.

Then we reached a frozen stream. Pillars of sunlight shone down through a few broken branches, creating a dazzling shimmer across the slick ice. There were enough trees around us that it seemed like we had entered the womb of the woods, protectively encased and given insight to a magical location for new life.

"I didn't know how to tell you," Rylion whispered. "So I avoided you while I dwelled on it. I only want to say what I mean, and your insistence we be together isn't something I've experienced before."

I exhaled, enjoying the warmth of my own breath. "Women have never been attracted to you?"

"That's not it. Most women take my subtle rejection as a knife to the heart or ego. They typically refuse to speak to me afterward. I've never met anyone who... continually pursued me, even after I indicated I wanted no such relationship."

I smoothed my long, black hair. "Are you trying to say you don't want to be with me?"

"That's right."

I turned on my heel and clenched my jaw tight.

Was I not good enough? Did he think me simple and untalented? Ugly? Unfit to be a mother?

Or was it the curse?

My anger faded with each new breath. *My curse.* It haunted all of my actions. It wasn't unreasonable that Rylion would want to avoid a fate like his father's—killing his own wife.

"Artemis," he said with a sigh. "Please hear me out."

"I've pieced this together," I replied, curt. "No need to drag out an apology. I understand you want nothing to do with a cursed woman."

"It's not your curse."

His denial brought my rage back in full force. I whirled back around, desperate to hear his feeble explanation. "Then speak."

Rylion faced the frozen stream with a grim expression. "I cannot be with *anyone.* I've never spoken of this before, but my mother explained it to me before she had transformed. You see... she was a descendant of Vahltera, the Temperance God. As punishment for killing her lover, the War God, all of Vahltera's children are doomed to have relationships that end in tragedy."

I waited, my heart the loudest noise for miles.

"My mother said her parents met a similar fate when my grandfather killed my grandmother." Rylion shook his head. "And you saw what happened to my mother, father, and uncle. None of them found happiness like in fairy tales. My father had to kill my mother... It's the fate of all Vahltera's children, and I've come to terms with it."

"So, you believe you'll hurt the person you love because

of your blood relation to the old god?" I asked, almost relieved to hear it wasn't *me* he had a problem with.

"Yes," Rylion replied, the melancholy of his expression bleeding into his voice. "And I cannot bear the thought of harming my wife or children. Surely you must understand." He turned and faced me at last. "If my relationships are doomed to end in tragedy, why should I have any? I've avoided them my entire life to protect others from this ill fate."

"I don't care," I said, more forcefully than I wanted, but I couldn't help myself. "A few months ago, I thought the cursed could never stop the transformation, yet here you are, protecting us from turning. If magic exists to stop such a powerful and terrible force in the world, then there must be magic that will prevent you from harming your family. We will find it. Together."

For a moment, Rylion didn't reply. Then he chuckled, his dolor breaking away into a slightly cheerful expression.

"You wish to fight all magics in the world?" he asked, one eyebrow raised.

"I will do whatever it takes to have you," I stated.

I probably sounded obsessed, but I didn't care. Rylion was unlike any man I knew. Just being close to him put me at ease.

I placed a hand on his arm, admiring the solid muscle under the fabric. He was a force to be reckoned with.

Rylion stared down at me, his gaze searching mine with a hard intensity. "Artemis…"

My heart beat fast and my face heated with each moment our gaze remained locked. I found his earnest nature and gentle disposition so appealing. His body—a man of hard labor, strong, yet composed and civilized—I enjoyed it as well, but it mattered less than his character. It was his tranquility and noble demeanor I loved most.

I wanted to tell him, but I felt foolish even thinking such

poetic words. Only twittering ladies of the court said such compromising statements.

But I felt the poetic words. Deep in my chest. They swelled and clogged my throat, threatening to spill out at any second.

"Do you want to be with me?" I asked, my voice unsteady, but only for a moment.

"What if we can't find a way to stop my ill-fated destiny from coming to fruition?" Rylion asked in a whisper.

"I would rather be with you than never attempt out of fear."

"You say such things without hesitation," he said with a single huffed laugh. "I've never known a woman like you."

"You don't like my demeanor?" I asked.

Rylion leaned closer to me. The simple act of limiting the distance between us added to the knots in my body. I wanted him to embrace me, but he stilled himself.

"Am I worthy enough to be your wife?" I asked.

"You have it the other way around," he whispered. "You were once a noblewoman. You're a Lord of Flame and Cinder. You're youthful and vibrant. Confident and filled with passion. Intelligent. More learned and world-wise than any I know. Am *I* worthy of *you*?"

"I..." It took me a moment to breathe. I hadn't known he thought such things of me. When I found my words I whispered back, "I'm cursed."

"If you can overlook my dark fate, I can overlook yours as well."

"Then... you're the only man worthy of me."

Even muttering those words came at the cost of my composure. I trembled, fearing he would laugh at my statement and reject me outright. I would've given anything to hear his thoughts—to know for sure how he felt.

When Rylion tepidly wrapped an arm around my body, and I felt his trembling as well. His uncertainty only emboldened me. I completed the embrace, wrapping my arms around his muscular torso, happy to know what it was like to hold him tight. He smelled of the woods, so pleasant and relaxing, and I pushed his chainmail cloak aside to nuzzle the soft tunic underneath.

Rylion stroked my hair, his hand unsteady but gentle.

"Artemis," he muttered, half-chortling and half-apologetic. "Forgive me, but I denied myself companionship for so many years I barely know where to begin."

I, too, had pushed such thoughts from my mind before I met Rylion. That didn't matter. I knew what I wanted now.

I stared up at him, enjoying the soft brown of his eyes as he gazed back.

"Kiss me," I commanded.

Rylion hesitated a moment, but then cupped the back of my head with his hand and leaned down until our lips were a hair's distance apart. He slowed only a second before gently connecting. The chill of his skin surprised me, but the warmth of my body dispelled the cold. I pressed harder against him, eager to know what he tasted like—enjoying sensations I had never experienced—wrapping my hand around his neck and combing my fingers through the base of his hair.

Such intimacy left me breathless and weak in the legs. I wanted to know everything about him. To know every inch of his flesh. To feel every pleasure another person could offer me.

Steam wafted up around us. Rylion broke our embrace and glanced around. The ice of the stream had melted slightly, and sloshy snow dripped from the trees. We stood in a puddle of water, the snow receding at a rapid rate.

I blushed and forced a single laugh. "I must apologize. My divine fire—"

Rylion pulled me back into his arms, and I swallowed the last of my words. His heart beat heavy and fast. Did he feel as I did? Had the moment left him wanting more?

"I'm going to fight the King Killer," he said. "And I'm going to speak to God-King Eliezer about your curse."

I nodded against him. "Then I will accompany you."

"Along the way… we can be wed."

Marriage happened quickly in the Kingdom of Luka. Either a noble family would promise their child to another house in exchange for favors or wealth, or the commoners would arrange marriages the instant their children came of age, all in the hopes of avoiding an accident that led to someone becoming cursed for a single night of weak willpower. Rylion's offer to wed immediately didn't surprise me, but I enjoyed it more than I should have.

I twisted my fingers into his tunic. "I would have it no other way."

CHAPTER FIFTEEN

The sun pierced the cold, creating a window of warmth comfortable enough for us to travel.

Lydia, Steen, and Wulf prepped the cart while Thea prepared each of the horses, complete with blankets, saddles, and packs. Rylion loaded the weapons, including Calavandi and his new giant bone shard. Although I hadn't witnessed the discussion between Rylion and his father, I knew Osmund's absence was a gift. Animosity poured from the lodge, but at least Osmund had allowed his sons to take his divine weapon.

Caprice and I waited in the shade of two snowy pines. Too many hands could cause chaos, and we had already gathered up the blankets and clothing for the trek.

Once finished, Rylion sat at the front of the cart. I leapt onto the cart bench and took a seat next to him, eagerness apparent in each of my steps. Rylion offered me a reserved smile, and I wondered if he had informed the others of our relationship. No one had commented, and I suspected they knew nothing.

That was fine. I didn't want or need their approval. And even if they disapproved, I wouldn't care.

However, Rylion's story about how his bloodline was doomed to have tragic relationships *did* bother me. I dwelled on it, even after I thought I had gotten over it. What if it happened to us? What if I was sealing his fate by demanding to be with him? Would our fate be our undoing?

Did Rylion think the same way?

He stared at me with a mix of emotions deep in his eyes, everything swirling together into something unreadable. But he never regarded me with disgust or hate, for which I was thankful.

"Come," Rylion said. "We should leave Mount Regel while we can."

While everyone hopped onto the cart or readied themselves for a walk, Osmund exited the lodge. The atmosphere on the mountain chilled another few degrees when no one spoke. After a long moment, both Wulf and Rylion slid off the cart and approached their father.

Their voices died in the gentle winter breeze. I heard nothing of their conversation, but Osmund's grim expression told me everything. He was trying one last time to convince his sons to stay. It wouldn't work, though. Rylion's conviction was steadfast, and Osmund had become a different man now that his brother wasn't here. Osmund was haggard. Worn. Like he had aged a decade overnight.

To my relief, Osmund offered his sons a quick embrace before heading back to the lodge. He would be alone while we were away, but he had said he wanted it that way.

"Something is different about you," Caprice said, ripping me from my musings.

I turned to her and narrowed my eyes. "What do you mean?"

"You're less agitated. That bodes well for our trek."

Wulf nodded with the sentiment. "You do seem much happier than before."

Caprice smiled. "It will be easier to watch over you."

Watch over me?

I looked away, remembering her comments. She had said it was her duty—her obligation—to help the children of the old gods. Thea, Wulf, Rylion, and I were all her charges. She would be there to tell us stories and offer us guidance, but I didn't want her watching over my actions. If anything, I would need to protect her. I hadn't seen Caprice do much of anything outside of meditating and wandering around the lodge. What skills could she possibly hope to bring to this excursion?

Rylion leapt back to the front cart seat, and everyone quieted down. Lydia and Steen sat close together in the back, practically in each other's laps, huddled like only lovers would allow. Envy ate at me. Although Rylion had agreed to all my demands, I still wanted more. I didn't want to wait. I wanted him in my arms at all times.

Was this how all people felt when they found someone they adored? Or was I obsessed beyond reason?

Thea urged the horses forward, and we headed down the main path of Mount Regel.

We reached the edge of Ludlow well after nightfall. Although traveling the roads at night was dangerous, camping near the mountain was worse, so we pressed forward.

Before we rested, Wulf pointed us toward the King's Stone. The decrees shone in the night, glowing blue and illuminating the black pillar for all to see. To my surprise, three new decrees rested at the top of the list. My chest tightened, panic flooding my thoughts. These new decrees could be anything. They could even prevent us from seeing God-King Eliezer.

We rode the cart close, and everyone gathered around the King's Stone to touch it.

Dread replaced my panic the moment I read each new decree.

Cursed be the man who disobeys the orders of the Holy Guard.
Cursed be the man who attacks a member of the Holy Guard.
Cursed be the man who hinders the work of the Holy Guard.

The next we saw Alexavier, everyone in our hunting group would become cursed.

Everyone.

He would simply order us to surrender, and if we didn't, we would all be marked by the curse.

Rylion turned to me, shock apparent in his wide eyes. "Why would God-King Eliezer make such decrees?"

My mouth was dry, and it was difficult to formulate an answer. When I glanced around, I noticed the rest of our group had their attention on me, as though they, too, needed an answer.

"Alexavier probably told him of our battle on Mount Regel," I said. "And this angered the god-king. He's not a man to let things go, and he probably thinks this will help all future hunts by the Holy Guard."

"Do you know God-King Eliezer well?" Wulf asked.

I crossed my arms and huffed. "I know him enough."

"My father said God-King Eliezer was stoic. Is that true?"

"True to a certain extent."

Steen glanced from the King's Stone to me and then back to the stone. "If you know him, why don't you tell us what you can about some of these decrees? Why did he make so many around marriage? Why did he focus on punishing carnal desires?"

He motioned to the six decrees that revolved around lust and faithfulness.

Cursed be the man who lies with another before marriage.

Cursed be the man who lies with an animal.
Cursed be the man who lies with a corpse.
Cursed be the man who lies with the Forsaken.
Cursed be the man who lies with a child less than the age of ten.
Cursed be the man who commits adultery.

I was shocked Steen didn't know the answer, but it was apparent the noble gossip didn't reach places like Ludlow.

"God-King Eliezer has taken several wives," I said. "Five in total. None of them ever produced a child. In his frustration, he had them put to death, but everyone suspects the fault must lie with him. They say he's barren, but God-King Eliezer puts to death anyone who says so in his presence. In order to prevent his new wives from cuckolding him and becoming pregnant by another, he crafted these decrees."

"These were all made to prevent his wives from being unfaithful?" Steen asked, his eyebrows lifting to his hairline. "Is that really why?"

I nodded. "Yes. He wanted to make sure any children they had were blood-related to him. That's how a new god-king or god-queen is chosen. Through blood. He wants an heir."

"I thought the god-king had sisters," Steen said. "Doesn't he? Can't they have heirs?"

Even mentioning the god-king's sisters sent chills down my spine. The faster I explained this, the faster we could move on to a different subject. Perhaps, if I was succinct, there would never be any further questions.

"He has sisters," I stated. "And their children can inherit the power, but God-King Eliezer doesn't want that. He's personally forbidden his sisters from having children—and breaking his command would result in them being cursed."

"He's more controlling than I ever suspected," Wulf said. He walked back to the cart, his face set in a heavy frown. He muttered, almost too quiet to hear, "Rylion's request to remove the decrees is a fool's errand."

God-King Eliezer would never do it, but I was curious to see how Rylion would handle this. Perhaps the god-king could be shown reason…

We entered Rylion's family home in Ludlow.

Everyone agreed to stay until dawn. Steen and Lydia claimed one room, Caprice and Thea claimed another, and Wulf claimed the last, leaving Rylion and me to the front room.

The home brought back memories, even though I had only stayed in it for one day after Rylion had taken me from the streets. I dreaded returning to the capital, especially now that I had people and things I hated to lose, but that fear wouldn't deter me from my set course.

I stood idle as Rylion prepped the couch for sleeping. We didn't speak, but nothing felt out of place or unnatural. The fireplace was lit, and the room was pleasantly alight and warm. Rylion stripped down to his tunic and trousers before glancing in my direction.

"Shall you take the couch and I'll take the floor?" he asked.

"I'll stay awake."

Rylion lifted an eyebrow. "There's no need. Ludlow isn't dangerous."

"I don't think I'll be able to sleep."

My pulse had run fast since Rylion had agreed to be mine. Something about getting the feelings off my chest had changed my perspective and given me a second wind. Perhaps Caprice and Wulf were right. Perhaps I was much happier now.

"Artemis." Rylion threw back the blankets, creating a cozy

bed on the couch. "Tell me, what do you expect of me as your future husband? I must admit, I had thought I would die alone, probably fighting one of the Forsaken."

I hadn't contemplated a perfect husband before.

"We should wait to discuss this until after you've spoken to God-King Eliezer."

"Why is that?" Rylion asked.

"There is always a chance something will go wrong. If the god-king wants us killed, we will be killed. It's best to leave these hopeful conversations for when we return."

Rylion, still in his clothes, sat on the couch and exhaled. The furniture creaked underneath his mountain of a body. He stared at the ceiling while the fire crackled in the hearth. The soothing scene allowed me to breathe easy. But I also feared I would never get to experience such a tranquil moment ever again. Once we embarked on our journey, there wouldn't be many chances to be alone again.

"Does your family maintain any heraldry?" I asked, wanting to hear his voice.

"I'm not sure. What is *heraldry*?"

"Heraldry is the family's crest and coat of arms," I said matter-of-factly. "Noble houses have them, of course. They display them through banners or signs. The Holy Guard wear the symbol of the king etched into the black armor."

Rylion mulled over the statement for a moment. "I have no family crest."

"You may make one," I said. "Or if you want, I may make one for you. There are several specific requirements for heraldry in Luka. I know them all. I studied it for two months one summer."

"Didn't you say heraldry was only for nobles?"

"*I'm* a noble." I touched the rings on my robe, reminding him of my many years of education. And while I didn't have any money or land to my name, my noble status still entitled me to my heraldry. "Once we wed, you will be one as well."

"Wouldn't we use your family crest?" Rylion asked, half-smiling. Then his expression hardened into something serious. "You never did tell me your surname."

I had dreaded this moment for a variety of reasons, but if I was going to marry the man, I had to tell him. I had kept my lineage a secret for most of my life. Only a few knew now, and that number dwindled with the passage of time.

The flicker of flames in the fireplace emboldened me.

"I'm a member of House Petrelis," I said. "My full name is Artemisia Heim Petrelis."

Rylion grew stiff and quiet. Then he stood up from the couch, so tense he looked ready for battle.

"*Petrelis*?" he repeated. "The same as *God-King Eliezer Petrelis*? You're a member of the god-king's house?"

I held up both hands to quiet him. "Shh! Please. I beg you. No one is to know." I walked closer to Rylion, my gait stiff. "My mother is the god-king's sister. I'm Eliezer's niece."

Rylion stared down at me, his eyes searching my gaze as though he was hoping this was all a jest. *I* wished it were a jest, but this was my unfortunate reality. God-King Eliezer hated me—he had ordered his sisters not to have children, but that had happened *after* I was born. My mother, fearing Eliezer would give her a direct command never to have a family, had stayed away from the capital city for over a year. She and my father wed, and then I was born...

Too bad for my mother I was born *cursed*. She had never let me forget it. She had never let me forget anything, including the agony and shame she had to endure to make sure I had life.

"My mother kept me hidden because of my curse," I whispered. "That's why you've never heard of me."

Rylion took a breath and held it for a prolonged moment. "Are you... the heir to the throne of Luka?"

I hated his question.

This was why Eliezer hated me so.

"Yes," I said, my voice barely audible. "But it won't matter," I quickly added. "God-King Eliezer has sentenced me to death. His Scourge will hunt me for the rest of eternity, or the curse will eventually transform me into one of the Forsaken. I'll never become the next god-queen."

Eliezer wanted *his* children to inherit the throne, and until he had some, *I* was nothing more than a terrible reminder.

"What will happen when we go to see the god-king?" Rylion asked, his voice as low as mine, but colder. And terse. "Will he insist on killing you?"

The fire crackled and then waned, as though quickly dying. I waved my hand and gave it more fuel, but the room suddenly had an icy chill that hadn't been there before.

"I don't know," I whispered.

"One of the reasons I wanted to see him was so that I could get your curse removed."

"I know."

Rylion's voice grew louder as he asked, "Why didn't you tell me your lineage then?"

I shook my head. "I don't know. I... I didn't want to tell anyone. I figured the god-king would tell you *no*, regardless of my identity."

The empowered flames in the fireplace licked out onto the bricks, searching for more fuel to consume. I controlled the fire with my magic, forcing it to become smaller once again. The heat didn't dispel the chill.

"Let's... not speak of this right now," Rylion eventually said.

I placed a hand on my shoulder—the one with my own curse mark. It halted my thoughts.

Rylion took his seat back on the couch, and he pulled me onto his lap. I didn't resist, even though I was startled by the action. Then Rylion lay down, his back on the cushions. He kept me on top of him, and I curled up on his chest.

The difference in our size was apparent. I felt like a cat as I rested my head on his collarbone, my ear to his body. The sound of his heartbeat through his tunic was reassuring.

He was so warm and muscly—it was like lying on top of a warm rock.

Rylion stroked my long hair, his attention on the ceiling. His tense movements betrayed his growing anger. If he weren't so upset, I would've enjoyed the moment for what it was.

Unable to think of anything to say, I closed my eyes and allowed the melody of his heart to sing me to sleep.

I prayed to the old gods I would have a hundred more nights with the same soothing lullaby.

Steen fussed with the bed, smoothin' the blankets and fluffin' the pillows. Wulf had given us an extra blanket, one with stars stitched across a night sky. It was meant for Steen to sleep on the floor, since the bed was too small for two people, but he refused to take it. He put all the blankets on the mattress, creatin' a fluffy nest for me to rest in.

Steen patted the bed, urgin' me to get some sleep.

"You don't have to do that," I said.

"My wife should have all the comforts," he said, throwin' back the blankets so I could easily get tucked in for the night.

"Won't you be uncomfortable on the hard wood floor?"

"I can tough it out." Steen huffed, like even suggestin' he couldn't was an insult.

It made me smile. I turned my attention to the window and watched Steen in the reflection. My pappy had tried to tell me Steen would be a selfish lover—a man who would leave me the moment he had what he wanted. But Steen had never left, not even when I was ill. He took his wedding oath to heart, he did. Every luxury we had, though there were never many, he always gave to me.

Now, if only I could improve that prickly personality of his. He was always so cross, like he was in an eternal argument with the universe, and it colored his mood.

"It's ready," Steen said, irritation in his words. He wanted me to get as much sleep as possible.

He motioned to the bed a second time. I moseyed over and took a seat. The fluff of the blankets hid the hard mattress and jagged frame. Steen meandered over to the washbasin, splashed his face, and then headed to the corner.

Steen sat with his back to the wall. He had slept leanin' against a wall many a night. He rubbed at the stubble on his jaw, and I knew he wanted to shave, but couldn't. His straight edge razor was at the mountain lodge. Then he patted at his oak-brown hair, obviously focused on his disheveled state.

Steen had lived among nobles for so long that appearances mattered a great deal to him, even if they didn't matter to anyone else.

"Thank you, Lil Piglet," I said, smilin'.

Steen snapped his attention to me and glared. "I *hate* that nickname."

"I only use it when no one's around."

"If you're not careful, I'll give you an irksome nickname." Steen crossed his arms.

I chuckled into my hand. "What would it be?"

"You wouldn't want me to say."

"I wouldn't mind if you called me *Princess*."

Steen snorted out a couple of laughs, *just* like a lil piglet. "Princess? You? The one always wearing trousers? The one raised with the animals in the barn?"

"You may call me *Barn Princess*, then."

"Barn Princess," Steen mumbled as he leaned his head against the wall. "Preposterous. Can you imagine your japes in front of noblemen? They would have me beaten for using such titles with flippant disregard to their station."

I rested back on the bed, still smilin'. Steen would call me Barn Princess before he fell asleep. I knew him too well. He denied me nothing.

But his mention of the noblemen festered in my thoughts. They weren't like the people of the farmlands—people who instilled in me a sense of love for the world, and a sense of jolly merriment. Noblemen were foreign to me. Would God-King Eliezer free Steen of his curse?

I had kept the coins Osmund had paid me over the years. I had thought, if I saved enough, I could pay the noble who Steen had stolen from, and the god-king would have to listen. Perhaps I still could, but...

I curled up under the blankets and slid a hand over my stomach. No moon's blood twice in a row. My mother had said that was the herald to the quickening—the time when a woman would feel the child move in her body. Steen and I had tried for years, but nothin' ever came, like trying to grow crops in the dead of winter.

But now I knew this was different.

Why *now*?

Grandpappy would've said it was a sign from the gods. I had to see God-King Eliezer before Steen turned into one of the Forsaken. I had to save Steen, so he could be a father to our child. If I had to grovel for Steen's forgiveness, I would. Anythin' to keep him with me.

"Are you ready for sleep?" Steen asked.

"Yes," I said, my voice somber, hoping he would mistake it for exhaustion.

Steen stood and smothered the candle flame with a nickel-plated snuffer. The darkness blanketed us and added a chill I hadn't noticed before. I held the blankets close, aware Steen had nothing.

"Goodnight," Steen said as he returned to the corner of the room. And then he muttered, "My precious Barn Princess."

Ah. I knew it.

Steen…

Goodnight, my Lil Prince, father of my unborn child.

Once he was asleep, I would get up from my bed and throw one of the blankets over his shiverin' body.

I sat on the edge of the rickety bed, my thoughts wandering.

Caprice brushed her long black hair and then tied it back in a loose braid. The people of Saileer had myths about the length and care of their hair. Cutting one's own hair was the same as self-mutilation. Each strand of hair represented a memory, and each hair that fell out was a memory one would never recall.

I had never known of such legends until Caprice told me. Even the men had long hair in the Kingdom of Saileer, though Caprice said there were people attempting to throw off the old traditions. Travel between the kingdoms was so rare, since so many of the god-kings and god-queens forbade leaving, that I suspected I would never know the culture of anything outside Luka, even with Caprice weaving so many fantastical stories.

But what did it matter? Sometimes I daydreamed of a world different than reality, but it would never change anything. I was foolish for thinking I could escape through delusion and fairy tales.

"Are you well?" Caprice asked.

I nodded once.

"You've been sullen for days."

I turned away from her and rested on the flat pillow of our bed. We were both so thin we could share, but I didn't know if I would be able to sleep.

Caprice took her place on the bed next to me. Her soft skin and warm touch were a comfort. Whereas men brought back terrible memories, I found the gentleness of Caprice's presence to be a gift I didn't deserve. Sharing a bed with her relaxed me.

I rolled to my side, my own brown hair tangling in front of my face. If I thought hair really did contain memories, I would rip mine all out.

Caprice snuffed the light in the room, and the noises of the owls beyond the window grew louder. I held my blankets close, listening to the uneven rhythm of my heart. What would it matter if it stopped? I would rise again afterward, cheating death a third time.

"Thea," Caprice whispered. "I worry about you most of all."

I said nothing.

"Please speak to me."

I had no words. What was there to discuss? Talking about nightmares did not make them vanish.

"I want to help you, Thea. You're wayward and drifting. Can't you see? Allow my teachings to aid you. As a child of despair, I know you're prone to self-doubt and suffering."

"Why did you leave Saileer?" I asked, steering the conversation away from my dark thoughts. I didn't want to discuss *me*.

"I left Saileer because the god-king ordered the destruction of all churches. He wanted the heads of all high priestesses, and he wanted the books written about the old gods to burn."

"Why do you keep repeating the tales if you know they will bring you disaster?"

"It is important to help the lost return to the road. The old gods left children, all aimless and afraid. They must know their heritage—born of gods and mankind. Passing wisdom from one generation to the next is a higher calling."

Such virtue. I wondered what Alexavier would say if he heard Caprice's speech. She wasn't like me. She wasn't allowing the darkness to fester in her. Even though she was cursed, she carried on, bringing to the world order where there was chaos.

"Thea," she said, gently. "Don't hide behind questions. As a Lord of Desolation, you have a responsibility to care for yourself. What if you hurt others with your magic? It could happen by accident."

I held my breath. Did she know of my false death in the Boneyard? Or the time I had risen again after slaying my own father?

I suspected she must.

"You have blood far more ancient than theirs," Caprice whispered. She placed a hand on my shoulder. I tensed, but I didn't attempt to move it either. Caprice continued, "Casseda, the Despair God, was born before light itself. She came from the darkness—the black you see between the stars at night."

"And Casseda is my kin?" I whispered. "The Despair God?"

Despair.

The word stuck with me. I dwelled on it longer than I should have. Despair. Was that what I felt? Yes. Despair. Ever since I had killed my father. Ever since I had risen again from the grave. That was all I felt.

"Casseda's magic flows through your veins," Caprice said.

The house was quiet, which made my thoughts seem loud and overbearing. Our room was cold. I shivered at an uncontrollable rate.

"Do you know much about Casseda?" I asked, dreading the answer.

"The Despair God had a deep-seated evil in her heart. When I'm close to you... I can feel the same terrible darkness. It's the kind of evil described in all my texts. Please, Thea. Let me help you rid yourself of it. If you embrace despair, it'll consume you."

Evil?

I stopped listening the instant Caprice uttered the word.

Evil.

I sat up and threw off the blankets. Sweat dampened my skin, soaking into my tunic, causing it to cling to my body. I stood and rushed for the door, unconcerned with my lack of modesty. Caprice told me to wait, but it was a faint cry to my numb ears. I slammed out of the room, unable to breathe, unable to focus.

Rylion and Artemis slept in the front parlor, both piled on the couch. I ran past them, my dark shadow dancing across the wall thanks to the fire in the hearth. I barreled through the front door and found Wulf pacing outside. He, too, asked me something, but his words were just as distant as Caprice's. He grabbed my elbow and held me back.

"Don't touch me," I shouted, breathless.

Wulf released his grasp in an instant, his face sown with confusion. I turned away and raced toward the horses, fueled by my desperation.

Caprice could sense my *evil*? That was what she had said. Just like my mother. I knew it had to be true. I knew it. That was why Alexavier couldn't answer me. That was why I had killed my father. I was a blight—worse than one of the Forsaken.

"Deana," I called out with a weak voice as I stumbled across the cobblestones. My hands shook, and my vision blurred. "Help me."

The clop of her hooves put me at ease. At least she wasn't

afraid. I could hide my wickedness from the animals, but not priestesses.

Why had I returned to Rylion and the others? I had sought his comfort. I had sought his wisdom. I had sought his protective aura. But all he had said was *you're not evil.* He didn't know. I had fooled him, too. Now I had to leave and find the King Killer on my own. I couldn't hurt everyone here with my vile presence.

Deana allowed me onto her back, despite my ill-suited attire.

"Go," I commanded.

And she trotted toward the city wall, north toward our destination.

CHAPTER SIXTEEN

Wulf prepped the remaining two horses. Normally, two animals pulled the cart while one rested, each rotated out to avoid undue fatigue, but without a third horse, the routine was impossible. Lydia and Steen agreed not to ride on the cart unless necessary, to avoid exhausting the animals prematurely.

I paced outside Rylion's family home—pacing was my first comfort in any troubled situation, but it didn't always help. Not even the morning sun eased my nerves.

I had thought Thea had recovered from her trauma in the Boneyard, but it seemed both Rylion and I were mistaken. She had run off in the middle of the night, according to Caprice and Wulf, and left no note about her intended destination. Wulf said Thea had been distraught, her eyes filled with panic.

"I'm to blame," Caprice said as we all prepared for the trek. "I tried to help her, but I handled it poorly. Thea's delicate and I should've been more understanding and softer. Fear caused her to leave us, and I should've explained that we could chase away the fright."

Rylion shook his head. "Don't blame yourself. Thea was

distressed. She spoke endlessly of dying and a question the Scourge couldn't answer."

A frown formed on Caprice's face, an expression I hadn't seen from her. But she offered no explanation, and we didn't have much time to dwell on it.

"She couldn't have gone far," I said. "If we hurry, we'll likely find her before she finds the King Killer. At least, I hope so."

"We should let her do as she pleases," Wulf said as he finished tying down the horses. "Thea knows she's safe in our midst. If she feels strongly about leaving, we should let her."

Steen huffed. "What about Deana? We need our horses!"

Wulf shrugged. "My father gave Thea that horse. It's hers."

"Then should we buy another?" Steen tapped the side of his head. "Think about our situation. We can't let this problem go."

"We'll ask every rancher from here to the capital if they have a spare horse for sale," Rylion said. "But we cannot dwell on this if we're going to reach the King Killer."

"Let me find a horse," Wulf said.

The eagerness in his voice couldn't be understated. His brother regarded him with a frown.

"You sure you can handle it?" Rylion asked.

"I'm old enough to deal with coin, and strong enough to protect it. And I know the cost of an animal. I even know where the traders are."

"It might take you a while to find a rancher with a spare horse."

"But once we do, it'll be easy riding back to you all," Wulf said, smiling.

Rylion took a few moments to mull over the statement. Finally, he relaxed and replied with a curt nod. "Very well. I'll give you the coin, and you return with the steed. And get a mare, if you can. I've always had better luck with the mares over the geldings or stallions."

Rylion walked back into his house, leaving the rest of us outside. I wanted to follow him, but he was just gathering the last of the supplies. The anxious need to leave gave everyone a restless tic. I resumed my pacing.

But Wulf hesitated. He walked over to me, and I stopped to stare. What did he want? He obviously had something heavy on his mind. Something pressing. I feared he might have more information on Thea he had failed to disclose.

Wulf brushed himself off. "Come with me. On my trek to get a horse, I mean."

His demand took me by surprise. "The cart has our supplies."

"Steen can watch the cart."

I couldn't argue with that. I knew what he wanted—some sort of magical instruction.

Once Rylion returned with the coin, I straightened my robes and followed Wulf away from his family's home. He smiled and brushed back his curly hair, clearing it of loose snow.

We headed down the road, and I gritted my teeth. This was where I had first encountered Rylion.

"Watch this," Wulf said. He waved his hand—exactly how I would—and a swish of ice fluttered through the air, straight off the tips of his fingers. The sparkle of frost disappeared a second later, long before any of the townsfolk could see. "I've been watching you practice your own magic."

I touched the rings on my robes. "You need to pay more attention, then. My father said my divine fire was part of my body. I assume your divine frost is the same way. Don't let it disappear once it leaves you."

Wulf nodded once. "I'll try." Then he held his hand up, ice coating his fingers and palms. "Why does *this* happen? You never light yourself on fire, do you?"

Once upon a time, I had caught myself on fire. My father had been by my side, so he had snuffed the flames out in an instant, but the event had left me with nightmares. For a short while, I couldn't even create fire, I had been so afraid. I hadn't wanted to hurt myself.

"Keep in mind that you're a *Lord*," I said, mimicking a speech my father had given me. "You *control* the magic. You *decide* what it'll do. Never let it rule you, or else it'll cling to every movement."

Wulf took a deep breath and rubbed his frost-covered hand against the side of his trousers. Then he offered me half a smile. "You're beautiful when you offer instruction."

I opened my mouth and then closed it, my face hot. When I shot him a glare, Wulf just laughed.

"I've seen you with Rylion."

"What of it?" I snapped, startling a woman on the side of the main road.

"He's my brother."

"And? This is no concern of yours."

"We're family. It's always my concern."

His voice shifted from playful to serious in an instant. He wanted to scare me? Warn me away? Take me for himself? I wasn't sure, but I didn't care. His magic was weak when compared to mine. Anyone—or anything—that tried to take Rylion from me would burn.

"I don't want Rylion to get cursed," Wulf said with a shrug. "So, ya know, perhaps you two should keep your distance. I mean, I could just as easily show you around. My brother isn't one for talking much, anyway."

"Rylion and I are to be wed," I stated, no room for discussion or argument. Wulf held his breath. I continued, "I spoke with Rylion, and he agreed. So, you have nothing to fear. Rylion will never be cursed, so long as I have a say."

Wulf stopped walking. "You two will wed?"

Then he doubled over in the middle of the road, both his

arms wrapped around his torso. He groaned and clenched his teeth, his body trembling. I stopped and turned to face him, my eyebrows knitted, my body tense. What was wrong?

Rime formed over the ground beneath his feet. Frost spread across his boots and trousers, and then coated some of his skin. The winds kicked up around us—it reminded me of his Forsaken mother. As a bird, she had created painful winds filled with ice and hail. Now her son was doing the same.

"What's wrong?" a citizen of Ludlow called out from a nearby building. "Isn't that Osmund's boy?"

"There's nothing to see here," I said as I stepped close to Wulf, trying to block everyone's view of his ice-covered body. "It's just, uh, the weather. Return to your homes." Then I placed a hand on Wulf's shoulder and immediately regretted my decision.

He *burned*.

I jerked my hand away, shaken.

"Please, help me," Wulf muttered through gritted teeth, his breathing ragged. He trembled as he fell to one knee. The ice continued to spread from him, coating more of the road and snaking toward me. "I… I can't seem to control it."

Angry at the cold, I created fire around us. Gasps rang out afterward, some from the nearby buildings, some from the horse-drawn carts just a dozen feet away. The denizens of this tiny town didn't know what they were dealing with. I doubted they had ever seen a fully trained Lord of Magic, and they *definitely* hadn't witnessed the might of a Lord of Flame and Cinder.

Wulf's hoarfrost grew worse with each passing second.

"You'll be okay," I said, washing the road in a light amount of heat. Ice melted off the cobblestones and my flames thawed the dirt. "Wulf, please. Remember what I just told you. If you're a Lord of Winter Stillness, act like it. Take control of the magic. Bend it to your will."

The wind picked up around us, adding to the frigid sensation of winter.

Wulf forced himself to nod and then took shallow breaths.

Slowly, but surely, the ice around him faded. Then the frost fell off his body and the wind in the city died down.

What had caused *that*? Had Wulf become so wrapped up in his own thoughts that he had lost control of his magic? That had happened to me a few times. My father had said it would happen if ever I became hysterical.

I held out a hand, and Wulf took it in order to stand. He was heavier than I had thought, and I almost toppled over.

"I'm sorry," he breathed.

"Forget it." I waved my hand, steam wafting from the tips of my fingers. "Luckily for you, I was here to deal with the situation if you couldn't."

Wulf ran a shaky hand through his curly hair. "I didn't know that would happen. Truly, I'm sorry."

"Listen. Forget this misstep and let's focus on acquiring a horse." I pointed to the narrow road of Ludlow. "We aren't far, correct? We need to find Thea. We need to find the King Killer. And most importantly—we need to reach the capital. None of that is made easier with your apologies."

My speech must have motivated him, because Wulf smiled and laughed like he always did. He patted my shoulder and motioned forward. "Thank you, Artemis."

It hadn't taken us long to secure a horse.

Wulf didn't want to talk about his magic, though. Not after he had lost control momentarily. He remained quiet the entire walk back, guiding the new mare with a gentle touch, and occasionally whispering sweet reassurances to her, but never anything to me.

When we reached Wulf's family home, he secured the

horse to our cart and immediately headed for the front door. His irritation rolled off him like water off a leaf, but I didn't know what to say.

"You should train some more with Caprice," I called out to him.

Wulf said nothing. He entered the house and then slammed the door shut.

I wondered if *that* was the difference between Wulf and Rylion. Whereas Rylion knew no deep emotions, Wulf seemed steeped in them. Odd for a child of temperance. Perhaps Wulf's own rage and frustrations fueled his hoarfrost magic.

Rylion emerged from the house, and I straightened my posture. He was dressed for the trek, swaddled in heavy furs and leather. I had something I wanted to show him, and while I had been in town with Wulf, I had secured some charcoal and parchment.

"Rylion." I cleared my throat and inhaled to wash away the building excitement. "Come here. There's something you need to see."

It had been troublesome finding a spare piece of parchment in such a tiny town, and even more troublesome finding a piece of charcoal of sufficient quality to draw. I had managed, though, and it had all been worth it for Rylion's heraldry.

I held out the parchment. Rylion took it and his eyes went wide.

Most heraldry had three components. There was an animal that symbolized the nature of the house, and the personality of the nobles. There was a weapon, or object, often found on the knights or men of the house. And then there was something that represented the deed of nobility— the reason the house had been elevated to aristocratic levels to begin with.

The heraldry I had designed for Rylion and me had a

white bird in the center. I had used birch bark for the coloration. And it wasn't just any bird, but a four-winged bird. Two large wings and two smaller wings.

Rylion touched that part of the picture with a gentle graze of his fingers.

"You honored my mother," he said under his breath. "This is… This is her."

"I thought it fitting," I said. "And it's the reason you deserve nobility. You and your father hunt the Forsaken in the name of the god-king. It's both symbolic and relevant to the heraldry."

In her claws were two objects. One was a bow and the other a bone. Mariana only had two children, after all, but the bow not only represented Wulf, but the unborn daughter Osmund had told me about—Calavandi.

The bone was a gift from the Temperance God. It should be remembered throughout history that the god had found Rylion worthy to have such a gift. It would create myths, and legends, and make for grand tales.

"I'm honored," Rylion said, his voice still on the verge of breathlessness. "I didn't think you'd give it such forethought."

I waved away his comment. "I won't ever fail you."

"I thought no one could know of your nobility?" he asked in a whisper.

"Even if that's true, I still enjoyed designing this. We can keep it in our eventual home—probably above the mantle."

"We should go," Rylion said as he motioned toward the door. "The faster we head north, the sooner we'll reach the King Killer. And there is a city we must stop at before the capital." Then he carefully tucked the parchment into his pocket, treating it as though it were frail and precious.

"Which city are we going to head to first?"

"The City of Gourna."

Gourna was the second largest city in all of Luka. It was on the edge of the God Graveyard and the Lake of the Damned, and many nobles made their residence there. I had passed through it on my way to Ludlow, but the experience had been less than pleasant. The sewers under the city made a vast network of catacombs. All manner of cutthroats, robbers, and criminals made their homes in the sewage, and my father had to fend more than a few off before we escaped the city walls.

"Why Gourna?" I asked.

"Gourna has a blacksmith who fashioned my father's bow. I wish to speak to him about my bone shard, and now I want a set of heraldry made using this design."

"What about Thea?"

"Honestly… I don't know. I hope we find her soon, but I fear she might've headed back toward Mount Regel."

"I'll keep an eye out as we travel."

Rylion nodded. "I appreciate it, Artemis."

We walked together to the cart. Caprice, Wulf, Steen, and Lydia were already waiting for us, and the moment everything was set, we headed off in relative silence, with only the clopping of hooves as white noise for my thoughts.

***

Our trek had little interruption. We weren't accosted by brigands or stopped by any knights or members of the Holy Guard. It was uneventful in a pleasant way.

Except for the basket of silk cloth we had seen on the side of the road. The woven basket had been tied shut with a leather strap and sat in the winter weeds beside the well-beaten path. Traders who walked past gave the basket an odd glance and then hurried on their way. We did the same. No one wanted to take silk for themselves, for fear the basket belonged to someone in the god-king's court.

Cursed be the man who steals from a member of the god-king's court.

If it had been a basket of apples, it would've been taken immediately. The nobles in the god-king's court rarely dealt with or traded simple produce. But silk was a different story. The basket had likely fallen off the cart of a merchant carrying samples to show to other nobles before a trade.

So... the basket remained untouched. Better than becoming cursed.

The day waned and the sun set in the distance.

My feet bled from the walking, but I refused to ride in the cart if Rylion was walking. Even with his armor and cape, he made no mention of discomfort or exhaustion. I kept my suffering to myself, as I always had, but it took the better part of my willpower to do so. I thought of nothing else besides trudging forward as the slick blood in my boots made every step difficult. Luckily, I had gone mostly numb from the ankles down.

No one else spoke as we walked the northern road out of Ludlow. Groups of trees dotted the landscape, and the grass once grew to waist height, but during the winter it was a barren landscape of dirt and thick-rooted weeds. Thankfully, the dirt road was packed and smooth from frequent use.

As the sun set, I spotted multiple campfires ahead of us. We had almost made it to Torta, a small town not too far north of Ludlow. Tents were pitched in the open fields around the town's wooden walls, some tents large and others so small I wondered if they were even intended for people.

"What are those?" Rylion asked.

I unclenched my jaw and took a shallow breath. "Those are circus nomads."

"From other kingdoms?"

"They have no kingdom. They're outcasts from lands now under water."

Rylion frowned. "Are they cursed?"

"No. They aren't bound by the decrees until they settle in a kingdom, which is why they're always on the move."

I didn't know much about the nomads, other than what my tutors had taught me. The circus nomads traveled between kingdoms in small packs of forty to fifty people. They set up shop, sold exotic goods, and performed scandalous shows before leaving town and heading to the next destination. People attempted to get information about the outside world from them, but the nomads were notorious for "sticking to their own kind."

I had never been to the circus, but I had heard many a story. Half the time they ended in robbery, or a snake oil salesman that ran out of town the moment his wares were proven to be faulty.

"We should stop there," Lydia said, her smile bright enough to chase away the night. She walked around the cart and pointed to the largest tent in the shadowy distance. "My grandpappy would take us to the circus any time they came through town!"

"We're searching for a monster of monsters," Steen said, holding a hand up in exasperation. "Do you really want us robbed blind by a group of swindlers?"

"They aren't swindlers." Lydia rubbed at her stomach, and then her lower back. "You should see their dances and colored lights."

"These people live by no decrees. Without rules to hold them in place, obviously they would be wild and without remorse."

For once, I agreed with Steen. We couldn't trust anyone who lived without laws. We needed laws to keep peace among the populace, lest our monstrous natures consume us all.

Rylion stopped walking, his mood shifting to something colder than before. I happily stopped with him and rubbed at my neck. I was sweating, and the feeling irritated me.

"What is that?" Rylion asked, his voice low.

I followed his gaze.

Torta stood in the distance, silhouetted by the sun. As I stared, the wooden walls trembled and shook, and wood splintered, sending debris into the sky. Screams echoed in the twilight.

Such destruction only ever had one source. A Forsaken was here—perhaps the one we were looking for. The King Killer.

My heart froze and I couldn't breathe.

What if we got too close?

I stepped back and almost stumbled. Damn the gods. My feet somehow regained their feeling. Pain flared with each new breath I inhaled.

"A Forsaken is in the city," I whispered.

Rylion nodded. "Just as I thought. We should go to meet it."

"I'll go with you," Lydia said as she jogged around the side of the cart. Although her back obviously bothered her, determination flared in her eyes.

Wulf stepped forward, but Steen lingered behind. The look in Steen's eyes matched my own. I knew he feared transforming—who didn't?—but this was sooner than I had thought it would happen.

Where was Caprice? Had she gone and hidden herself?

Wulf walked past Calavandi and shook his head. "I'm no good with the bow. I'll use my magic against the Forsaken."

"Now isn't the time," Rylion said.

"My hoarfrost is deadly. You'll see."

"The bones of the Temperance God quell the rage of the monsters. We should use the bow."

Wulf gritted his teeth, his anger turning cold. "*You* use it."

Loud bells chimed from the circus people, warning everyone away. Panic had a distinct sound, and it was the hundreds of feet stomping across the ground as people ran for their lives.

Riders galloped past our cart in pairs, their colorful clothing betraying their nomad origins. Blue, purple, and yellow coats were bright, even in the harsh light of the sunset. Rylion held up a hand, and one rider slowed his steed.

"*Run,*" the nomad said. "A Forsaken has spawned inside the city."

Rylion frowned. "The King Killer?"

The nomad shook his head as he urged his horse forward. "The King Killer ran his blighted army through the farmlands and continued north. Hunters are chasing it as we speak. None are left in Torta. We have no protection here. *Run,* I said."

"We're hunters," Rylion stated. "Spread the word that we're here. We'll deal with the Forsaken."

The monster here wasn't the King Killer. The information gave me new life.

A terrible shriek pierced the area. Rylion clenched his jaw and then turned around. He grabbed his father's bow and three bone arrows, and then rushed toward the city, his heavy cloak barely fluttering behind him.

I hobbled after, determined to scorch the beast with my own two hands.

Wulf and Lydia chased after.

CHAPTER SEVENTEEN

The streets of Torta pulsed with life and fire.

Crowds of people clogged the paths to the Forsaken, preventing us from taking the cart as we made our way deeper into the city. Buildings had been covered in oil and set ablaze. The flames were meant to slow the Forsaken, but those monsters had little sense of self-preservation. And even if the beast was hurt, it would always regenerate until the human skull was removed from its grotesque body.

The people of Torta obviously didn't know how to handle these nightmare creatures. The Forsaken would run amuck until we handled it.

"We stay together," I commanded.

Rylion, Wulf, and Lydia all replied with silent nods.

The farther into town we ran, the more I noticed burrows in the dirt roads. They reminded me of snake and rabbit holes —deep and precise—but these were large enough for a man or horse to tumble into. And the holes were everywhere. Near each home. Near the wells. Near the tavern. The ground was raised up in some areas and cracked in others. Nothing looked right.

Through ragged breaths, I said, "It'll be underground."

Rylion held Calavandi close. "Are you sure?"

"Yes."

I had seen this before. Forsaken reflected the decree they had broken. Anyone who attempted to leave the kingdom was cursed, resulting in a Forsaken with evasive mannerisms, born from their desire to escape the borders of their nation. The fell magic twisted them until they became creatures who dug, flew, or swam with unrivaled capabilities.

Smoke wafted on the evening winds, stinging my eyes. The embers from the flames danced into the sky, becoming a new set of stars that twinkled with a deadly inner light. With a mere thought I extinguished them all. An ember to the eye could harm our chances, and I would rather not risk it.

The moment the fires died, the city became darker. The sun had almost set, resulting in a blood-red sky half-covered in smoke.

We reached the market square and found it riddled with the Forsaken's burrow holes. A man ran by one and a spindly arm reached out of the darkness—an arm black as the void and more than six feet long. It grabbed the terrified man by the throat and punctured his neck with four-jointed fingers that ended in sharp bone talons.

The man choked and hit the dirt, blood gushing from his severed arteries. The monstrous arm grabbed the man's leg and dragged him to the hole, his wet shouts of terror barely heard over the commotion of the fleeing citizens.

Rylion, Wulf, Lydia, and I stayed away from the edges of the Forsaken's holes, but I knew any monster lurking underground would sense the tremors from our feet.

"What should we do?" Rylion asked, his attention on me. Despite his anxiety, his voice remained calm and confident. It helped me maintain my composure.

"You don't have a plan?" I asked. "You've been a hunter for years, not me."

Wulf stepped close and shook his head. "Our father was the one who trained with the Holy Guard. He knew what to do in these situations. He was the one giving the orders."

I hadn't trained with the Holy Guard, but I had read enough about the Forsaken to fill three libraries. If Rylion and Wulf didn't want to devise a plan, I would.

"I'll burn it out," I said, touching the vibrant red scarf and knowing my path to be certain. "You three will wait by the hole and attack when it flees."

I normally didn't use my flames in front of vast crowds because of my father's long-standing rule to never expose my gift. But I couldn't worry about that now.

Rylion pinned back his cloak and dropped Calavandi, along with the three arrows. With the Forsaken underground, there was little need for it. He then unsheathed his short sword and headed for the hole where the man had disappeared. Wulf followed close behind, his gaze on his hands. Would he use his hoarfrost correctly?

Only Lydia remained behind. She held her bow and kept her distance, no doubt hoping the beast would spring out of the ground.

I wished Rylion had heavier armor for these types of tasks. At least his cloak protected him from terrible magic effects. When he drew near one of the holes, I worried for his safety.

I stepped forward and gritted my teeth, determined to kill the Forsaken no matter how little in the way of reinforcements we had.

Rylion and Wulf stood at the edge of the monster's hole.

I held my hand over the nearest burrow, and a torrent of fire washed into the darkness. Hunters—normal hunters who sought regular animals—used similar methods to scare out foxes and rabbits that had holed up to avoid their dogs. Would this method work with the Forsaken?

My flames flooded the underground tunnel. After a long

moment of heat and blaze, the monster rumbled through its hideaway and finally burst out from a hole awash in fire.

I caught my breath and jumped back. The beast had the body of a giant black centipede, its exoskeleton reflecting the flickers of flame. It had two human arms, long enough, and with enough joints, to stretch a good ten feet from its body. The centipede's face reminded me of a twisted spider, with mandibles and a spindly tongue soaked in blood.

The beast must have been twenty feet in length, and weighed the same as eight horses. Its hundreds of centipede legs squirmed as it dragged itself into the town square.

Rylion attacked the Forsaken the moment he could. His short sword pierced through a section of the exoskeleton and slid into the center of the monster's centipede body. Human limbs and organs spilled out from the ruptured stomach, splashing onto the dirt like a cracked egg over a skillet. The Forsaken crashed onto the ground, but it was clear from its writhing legs that it wasn't dead.

Rylion lifted his blade out of the monster's stomach and then ran for the head, careful never to step into the monster's blood. With one powerful swing—stronger than any man I had ever seen—Rylion slammed his blade into the Forsaken's head, busting open its skull and exposing its brains.

The red sunset died in the distance, blanketing the city in darkness.

The Forsaken collapsed to the ground. Lydia and Wulf stared with wide-eyed disbelief.

Was that it? The ease of our victory got me smiling. *Thank the old gods.* At least no harm had come to Rylion.

I wiped sweat from my face as I ambled over to Rylion. He hadn't lost sight of our goal. He cut into the Forsaken, looking for the skull of the human who had been cursed. We needed to remove it, or else the monster would return.

But then, as my eyes adjusted to the night, I noticed

something moving in the dark. A second hand reached out of one of the many holes, and it went straight for Wulf.

There were two!

I almost didn't find the words before it was too late. *"Behind you!"* I shouted.

There wasn't even a moment's worth of time to correct his actions. Wulf whirled around, and in a split second, was clever enough to hold an arm up to his neck. The Forsaken tried to puncture his throat, but Wulf's arm blocked the attack.

Ice flared around the market square, coating the Forsaken, the dirt, and some of the nearby holes. It wasn't enough, though. Wulf's hoarfrost had slowed the monster, but not killed it. The Forsaken grabbed his leg and yanked hard. Wulf fell to the ground, the back of his head slamming on his own ice.

"Brother!" Rylion yelled.

He dropped the centipede before he completed his task and ran for Wulf. But he wasn't fast enough.

Wulf was dragged across the frost-covered ground. Then he was sucked into the tunnel, a bloody trail the only evidence he had been here.

Although I risked harming Wulf, I ran to the nearest hole and sent a torrent of flame shooting into it. If the creature remained underground, Wulf would die for sure. A few burns were a small price to pay for his life.

The second centipede Forsaken burst out of its hideaway, screeching as it scuttled into the square on needle-knife legs. It dragged Wulf along as it hissed and undulated its grotesque mandible.

It headed for another hole, but Lydia was clever. She let loose an arrow, and it slammed into one of the Forsaken's many eyes. The beast screeched and came to a halt. Then it released Wulf and rushed for Lydia.

Rylion tried to cut it off, but the beast was too quick and

too large. It dashed around Rylion and then lashed out with its human hand. The bone talons caught Lydia's forearm and shoulder, and she screamed as she tumbled across the ground.

Rylion stabbed the centipede's body. The monster thrashed its backend and hit his side.

Most men would've fallen, but Rylion wasn't most men. He held his ground and stabbed again. The Forsaken rushed away, its centipede body scuttling across the ground at frightening speeds.

Then it headed for me.

I held up a hand and unleashed divine fire.

"Die," I whispered through gritted teeth.

The monster reached through my flames and slashed me across the side. The bone fingers were sharper than any knife I had ever known. My robes didn't stand a chance. They were shredded, along with my skin.

"Face me!" Rylion stepped forward and swung with his sword. He gouged a chunk of the monster's flesh from its backend.

The Forsaken whipped around. The beast swung wide with its bone claws. It sliced Rylion's upper arm, splattering his blood across the town square. Rylion growled back a curse, and when the creature swiped again, Rylion slashed with his sword, slicing off three of the monster's fingers. Black blood splashed across Rylion's on the ground, creating a painting of gore and mayhem.

The centipede grimaced and hissed.

Wulf staggered to his feet and a terrible chill blanketed the area. The air itself froze. I couldn't even take a breath. I grabbed at my neck, the pain of the hoarfrost more intense than I had been expecting.

I forced an exhale, and fire left my lips. I stumbled back a few steps, startled by my own flames. Clearly, my magic wasn't going to let me get frozen. I took a breath, the icy snow in the air burning my lungs.

Wulf ran for Calavandi. He scooped the bone bow and a single arrow off the ground.

With all his might, he pulled the drawstring and fired. The arrow whistled through the air and then pierced the monster's "neck" just below the head and burst out the other side, creating a gaping wound. The frozen air returned to normal, but a crust of rime still marked the market square, despite my fire, like ice itself had locked everything in place.

The Forsaken twisted as it fell to the ground. But the fell beast wasn't dead.

I stepped forward to finish the bastard.

My flame burned hotter than before as I aimed the blazing torrent at the monster's open wound. I didn't know why, but the thought of it existing—the thought that it represented all evil in this world—ate at me. Maybe I hated it because it could be *me* one day, but I tried to push the thoughts from my mind as I burned the creature to cinders. Right now, it was evil incarnate, even if it had once been a person.

The beast screamed, and it unnerved me for a second, only because of how similar it sounded to a woman on the edge of death. Once the shrieking stopped, I quelled my fire.

Rylion walked to the tail-end of the beast, his breath heavy, and cut out the second skull.

I had no idea we would be facing *two* Forsaken. A piece of me wondered if there would be others. Perhaps a group of people had transformed all at once. Both of these Forsaken had been disgusting centipedes, after all. They had both broken the same decree, no doubt in my mind.

I gritted my teeth when a plausible explanation came to mind. These were people who had traveled with the circus nomads. They were cursed, but they had hidden it well. Had the King Killer caused their transformation? I couldn't know for sure.

"Wulfric?" Rylion asked as he rushed to his brother's side.

"Damn Forsaken," Wulf muttered, his breath coming out as an icy mist. "That's twice my leg has gotten wounded. *Twice*."

Wulf held his leg with unsteady hands, his face red and coated in a fresh layer of sweat. The claw wound was a series of deep punctures that exposed the muscle of his leg. He held it as best he could, stifling the blood flow. While it was deep, it looked small enough to heal. He was luckier than most who encountered such beasts.

Wulf forced a smile. "I think the gods have it out for my calf."

While the two brothers shared a dark chuckle, I headed for Lydia. She hadn't gotten to her feet, and I worried she was unconscious. To my surprise, she was awake and holding her side, but unwilling to move.

I leaned down to help her. "Are you okay?"

Lydia trembled. "I'm afraid."

"The Forsaken are gone." I glanced around, my eyes on the holes. "Nothing here."

"Not for me. For my babe."

At first, I wasn't sure what she was referring to. Then it dawned on me. I faced her with a look of incredulous anger. "You're *with child* and you came here to fight the Forsaken?" I couldn't control my voice. The whole damn town knew my every word. "There's a time and place for everything. This is neither the time nor the place for an expecting mother!"

Lydia's eyebrows knitted, and her body went stiff. "My mammie did everythin' when she carried her babes, and I'll be no different."

"Then get to your feet!"

Lydia didn't reply. She remained on the ground, unable to stand. She wouldn't look at me either. Was her child still alive? She had taken a hard fall.

Rylion offered his brother a shoulder. Wulf took it, but he

needed bandages and care, or else he could bleed to death. The same for all of us, but Wulf was the worst. His injuries were clogged with mud, and his eyes were unfocused. Rylion must have known the urgency, because he hurried back to me, and pointed to the main road.

"We can get back to our cart if we head this way."

"There could be other Forsaken," I said, motioning to the holes. "We must employ caution."

"Very well. Tell me your plan, and I'll do it."

"Can you carry Lydia as well?" I asked.

Rylion leaned down, scooped Lydia into his one arm, and helped her to her feet. She squeaked as he held her close, his strength undeniable. I suspected Rylion could carry all three of us out of town and never break a sweat.

"We should stay close and leave as quickly as possible." I went a short distance ahead. "Follow me."

Rylion kept his gaze forward and hurried through the empty streets, ignoring his own minor injuries. Torta had grown eerily silent after the Forsaken were slain. The fires were gone, thanks to my magic, and the deserted houses sat idle, some with their doors still open and swinging on hinges. I watched every shadow and every movement, ready to use my flames should the need arise.

"I need a weapon like Calavandi," Rylion said as we neared the wall.

Wulf had kept the weapon in his grasp. "It is useful."

"Your current weapon lacks power," I said. "Even Alexavier, despite being a Lord of Flame and Cinder, relied on the King's Stone halberd to slice through the flesh of the Forsaken. Without either, you are merely an obstacle for the monsters. I know you wish to hold the front lines, but these monsters grow bolder year after year. You'll be putting yourself in senseless danger without a weapon."

"That's what I'm seeking in Gourna," Rylion said. "A weapon crafted from the bone shard the Temperance God gave me. I think… the god wanted me to take this path. What do you think is best?"

I held my breath for a moment, pleased he came to me for advice on such an issue. I mulled over the information. "I think it's a splendid idea. A weapon crafted from the Temperance God's bone will likely slice through any Forsaken. It's large, however. It could be unwieldy if you don't find the right weaponsmith."

"Trust me. The smith in Gourna will craft a weapon worthy of legend."

My excitement for Gourna rose with his enthusiasm.

Outside the wall of the city, Steen and Caprice waited for us patiently. Then I spotted something interesting. Another horse was tied to our cart, but it wasn't anything normal. It was a magical beast, like the summer lioness.

When we approached, all I could do was stare at the animal.

A pure white horse stood before us. It wasn't just its coat that was white; its hooves and even its eyes were too. Its mane shimmered in the evening darkness, despite the plumes of smoke rising from the city and blotting out the moons and the stars. And the horse had six legs—four in front, two in the back. Truly a majestic beast.

"What is this?" I asked.

Caprice placed her hand on the white coat of the animal. "I stumbled upon a great find as everyone fled the city. This is a hailstone stallion. They're rare, and from the Kingdom of Oliad, running wild in the Everfrost Mountains. Fear not. These are gentle creatures from the time of the old gods." She stroked its snout and the horse snorted.

The stallion had my respect, but I didn't wish to touch it. The icy presence it had conflicted with my fire. I would allow Wulf and Rylion to handle the animal.

Rylion barely gave the new mount a second glance. He set to work gathering the medical supplies for Lydia and his brother. The hailstone stallion stomped a hoof, restless. It might have sensed the presence of Forsaken, or perhaps it was agitated by all the people nearby. If Thea were here, I was sure she could have calmed the beast.

The gaze of its white eye tracked Rylion and me for a second. I wondered if magic could speak to magic. Did the animal know we were different from the others? While I admired the beauty of the horse, Rylion gently set Lydia down on the cart and then wrapped his brother's leg.

"Where did you find it?" I asked.

Caprice smiled. "It came to see the hoarfrost." She pointed to the walls of the city. Ice had covered some of the wooden posts. "It seems Lords of Winter Stillness aren't common to these lands."

Wulf glanced at his legs. Blood wept onto the dirt, and frost speckled every inch of his skin. Although he could summon his magic, he had little control over it. If the city hadn't been deserted, he would've killed people with his uncontrolled power.

"What's his name?"

"Equinox."

The people of Torta celebrated into the night.

No more Forsaken appeared and the two we had killed were cleared away and burned. Eating the flesh of the Forsaken was like consuming poison, and none of the townsfolk wanted to risk their livestock becoming ill. Everything was thrown onto a massive pyre.

The circus nomads celebrated with the people of Torta. They put on a show, dancing and singing, and the atmosphere became saturated with merriment. Despite the darkness of night, everyone frolicked and drank. The denizens of Torta were happy about the dead Forsaken, but also about the fact the King Killer had moved further north, avoiding them altogether. They had much to cheer for.

Wulf and Caprice joined in the festivities. Wulf didn't move around much, not after his leg was bound, but the music seemed to lift his spirits. Although I would normally be worried if someone had an injury like his, Wulf was a Lord of Magic. He would weather this injury better than most.

Lydia and Steen didn't celebrate. They sequestered themselves away from everything, and I suspected they were still worried about Lydia's unborn child. She hadn't been *too* injured, and I hoped she hadn't lost her babe.

Rylion and I sat at the edge of the celebrations, on the winter-torn fields. A bonfire raged only thirty feet from us, and I enjoyed the flicker of the gigantic flames. I didn't want attention, so I sat half-behind Rylion. While I enjoyed the fluid movements of the dancers, and the melody of their simple instruments, interacting with them left a sour taste in my mouth.

Rylion clapped after a particularly fevered dance. The performers sweated waterfalls, and when they bowed, droplets splashed off their skin.

"Artemis." Rylion glanced over his shoulder. "Can you see anything back there? Sit closer. By my side."

Reluctantly, I scooted across the ground until I was at his side.

Everyone in our hunting group received special treatment from the town and the circus nomads, even Equinox, our new six-legged steed. The townsfolk brought us food, the circus nomads performed for us specially, and everyone sang songs about our fight with the centipede Forsaken. The attention was pleasant, but the only reason we had become the saviors was because of circumstance. All the other hunters were out looking for the King Killer.

A set of fair maidens moved in front of Rylion and offered another energetic dance. They were beautiful women, much like my mother. Athletic and striking. Each had pale skin and blonde hair, unlike anyone from the Kingdom of Luka, as we were known for our bronze complexions. The dancers had dark eyes—on the verge of coal black—that stood out against their pale features, drawing attention to them like a dot of red on clean linen.

One young girl got closer than the rest. She moved her body like water, graceful in all regards, her fine clothing clinging to her body. She offered Rylion a smile and twirled in closer than before—close enough I could smell her damn flower-oil perfume.

It took all of my willpower not to wash the woman in flame.

Rylion clapped along with the song and gave the girl a smile. I placed my hand on top of his leg and leaned against him.

Jealousy wasn't becoming of a lady—that was what my mother had said—yet here I was, stewing in livid emotions that threatened to burn me from the inside out.

One of the other dancers shimmied in my direction, perhaps to offer me the same adoration and attention. I turned away, my shoulders bunched at my neck. They should have showered their gifts on someone else. I had no eyes for anyone but Rylion—I had come to terms with it. No one had earned my trust like he had.

Yet…

I wanted to think everyone around us was controlled by greed and selfishness. I wanted to think the dancer sought nothing but coin and favors—to use us. But that didn't seem to be the case. The nomads denied us when we offered to pay for the food, and they insisted on giving us beds in their tents and warm baths before we headed out.

We had already saved them. There was nothing to gain by helping us now.

"Ah. Here are our saviors!"

Rylion and I turned to a man dressed as a jester. Tight leotard, colors stolen from the rainbow, a tiny top hat, one eye painted with a black star. He embodied everything foolish and fun.

"Let me formally thank you on behalf of my troupe," the jester said with an exaggerated bow. "I'm Ringmaster Christofle. Perhaps I can fetch you both wine?"

The dancing women stopped their performance and bowed their heads.

Rylion smiled. "That would be appreciated, thank you."

"No," I interjected. "We don't need any wine."

Both Rylion and Christofle lifted their eyebrows.

I gripped Rylion's sleeve. I leaned close and kept my voice a soft whisper. "Even if they've been kind, we shouldn't let our guard down. Wine makes even the noblest of men a buffoon."

"Worried?" Christofle asked. Had he heard me? He chuckled when I glowered in his direction. Then he motioned to the crowd celebrating around the bonfire. "We're nothing but simple folk. We have no intention of robbing a fine group of hunters, *trust me*. I saw what you did to those monsters."

The dancers giggled and snickered.

"You live a life wandering from town to town," I said. "Clearly you lack common sense. Which means you might try to rob us once we're liquored up."

"Ah, I see. That's a good idea." Christofle motioned for a dancer to come closer. "Are you hearing this? Write it down. No one has ever thought of that before! What a flawless scheme!"

His sarcasm didn't impress me.

Christofle laughed and then half-shrugged. "Forgive me, fearless hunters. I specialize in laughs, not larceny."

"Heh. You aren't ruled by any nation or subject to any decrees. You could be any manner of person, including a brigand." I held Rylion even tighter. "It's just best that we take no chances."

"Living under decrees doesn't make one virtuous." Christofle danced back a bit and offered another deep bow. "However, if you want no wine, then your wish is granted." His lithe body made it easy for him to hop back among the performers and cartwheel around the open field.

I watched him until it became impossible.

"I've thought long and hard about your actions, Artemis," Rylion said, his gaze on the fire before us.

"Me?" I asked. "*My* actions?"

"Yes. You always say people aren't to be trusted, but tell me… who has harmed you more, a farmer tending his land, or the god-king himself?"

I held my breath for a moment before replying, "God-King Eliezer."

"Then why do you fear the peasant folk?"

"I don't fear them," I snapped.

But I did. Oddly. I realized it just then.

I feared anyone I didn't know.

Rylion shook his head. "I understand people are capable of evil, but the people I fear more are the ones with power to do something substantial. I'm… *afraid*… of the god-king."

He refused to look at me, but he spoke the truth. I heard it in the way his voice drifted.

"I'm afraid of Alexavier as well," Rylion murmured. "Especially with these new decrees. They have so much power, and we barely have anything. I don't fear men like Christofle, yet you always advise I stay away from them."

"You're afraid of power?"

"Men with power have the potential to do great harm. Maybe they won't, but what if they do? It seems far more frightening than a man dancing in a field." Then Rylion faced me and forced a smile. "I'm sorry. I don't mean to be sullen.

We should celebrate and then rest. Tomorrow we'll reach Gourna."

His words floated through my mind.

I had only ever known people with great power. And all of them wielded it with little regard for others. I held Rylion closer, enjoying his warmth as my thoughts drifted to odd and unexplored places.

Celebrating. Ha!

There were thousands of cursed throughout the land. Some bandits, some in hiding, some on the run—and hundreds of Forsaken stalked the roads and dark corners of the kingdom. We had killed two and the town celebrated? What fools. Their campfires, music, and dancing could attract more monsters. Those beasts rushed toward merriment and life without hesitation. It was as if they needed to snuff it out, no matter the cost.

And without Osmund, it was only a matter of time before we met with a casualty. Rylion and Wulf relied on Artemis to act as their sword, but I still didn't trust the woman. Sure, she wielded fire. Yet when they had faced two monsters, Lydia had been injured.

And what if Lydia had died? She was my wife—if anything happened to her, I didn't know what I would do with myself.

It wasn't entirely Artemis's fault. Lydia did whatever she wanted. Stubborn, like her old goat of a father. Reckless. Lydia thought she was a man, she did. No matter how many times I tried to dissuade her from action, she felt she needed to be part of it. And logic had no sway with her. None at all. I would have a better chance of changing Lydia's mind if I cried rather than articulating coherent points.

I walked in the shadows of the nomad's tents, shunning the festivities as I made my way back to Lydia. I cradled two bowls of hot soup, careful not to spill any on my tunic as I hustled from one dark patch to the next.

Lydia sat on the far edge of the encampment. She clapped her hands to the music and spoke with the performers, an ease to her speech and mannerisms. It didn't surprise me that she mingled well with the nomads—Lydia was baseborn, no etiquette among any of them.

I approached from the shadow of a tall tent, silencing my own grumbling before I got close. Lydia hated my observations, no matter how true they were. I hesitated when I reached the edge of the darkness. Lydia spoke with two dancers, and I didn't want to interrupt. Most of the circus people didn't care for my snide glances or curt remarks.

"You take such good care of yourself," one dancer said as she stroked Lydia's sandy blonde hair. "Such fine qualities for a hunter."

Lydia smiled. "I fletch the arrows and gather the supplies and whatnot. I don't do the actual huntin'."

"Still. Such luster. I've only seen such shimmering hair on noblewomen."

The second dancer threw herself down on the grass, taking a seat like a feather landing on the surface of water. She smoothed her silky garments and frowned. "You're injured?" She touched Lydia's arm, over a few hastily done bandages.

Lydia nodded. "A scratch."

"But you're with child. Are you both okay?"

Lydia paled, her faint freckles becoming visible with the wan complexion. "I... Well, how'd you know?"

"I've known many a woman who glowed like you."

The first dancer nodded. "Yes. I can see it, too."

I turned away, a cold shiver washing over my skin. I almost dropped the soup in my haste to distance myself. But I kept quiet, unable to voice my anger.

Lydia was with child and had said *nothing*? To me? The father?

With a slight smile, Lydia nodded to the women. "My pappy said circus folk saw things others didn't. I never figured you'd guess. Even Steen hasn't noticed. Please no whispers or barn talk. I don't want to tell Steen until after we see the god-king."

The noblemen I had served in Gourna had joked and said that worthless men were sterile. They had called me all manner of clever names, from *cur* to *dullard*, but I had always consoled myself with the thought of a family of my own—a household where I kept them as a king would. Yet Lydia had never birthed a child. I knew it wasn't her fault. *She* wasn't worthless.

I was.

Another punishment to go along with my curse mark. At least, that was what I had thought.

I continued walking behind the tents, my pace picking up the longer I went. Lydia was with child. I had never thought I would see the day. Finally, I would have a family all my own!

Except we still needed to face the King Killer. And then what would happen? Knowing my fortune, Lydia would be killed first, and then I would die a slow, painful death right after her. I had known we shouldn't have gone after the monster. I had known.

Lydia would never turn around, however. She thought she was saving me by helping Rylion and Wulf.

Gods curse them both! Since when did they defy their father and hunt creatures without him? They had never acted out before. Never. They had always been faithful, always—

My thoughts and feet both halted. I knew the problem

before my mind started churning. Artemis. She had been a plague from the start. A complication that had brought us more trouble than we had ever deserved. She must have convinced Wulf and Rylion to fight their father's wishes.

Artemis was a witch.

And she would kill Lydia with her insistence we fight the King Killer. Artemis would rob me of the few remaining joys in my life. She would rob me of a family.

Gods damn her. It wasn't fair!

She was a noblewoman, too. It all made sense, then. Those damn nobles weren't as affected by the decrees as the average man. The Holy Guard even wielded the power to curse people now. They couldn't be trusted.

I would have to protect Lydia and my child all by myself. I couldn't rely on those so-called *Lords of Magic*. They weren't going to risk themselves for Lydia. I would be the one who defended my family from the darkness of the world, even if everyone turned their backs on me.

I threw my soups to the ground, leaving the swirling bowls in the grass.

No matter what happened, I would make sure Lydia never had to carry this spiderweb marking. I had already been cursed twice—who cared if I broke more decrees now? I'd do anything to keep my family out of harm's way.

INTERLUDE
ALEXAVIER LOWELL

I had finally made it to the capital, Luthecia. Once I was through the massive walls that surrounded the city—walls so large they housed citizens themselves—I was met with cheers and smiles. The knights brought me to Luthecia Castle, and the citizens of the capital celebrated in the streets.

The god-king's Scourge has returned. He will slay the King Killer.

The squire boys attended to my armor, making certain it was secure. The castle steward gave me updates about the state of the kingdom, droning on about taxes, travel, and the King's Stones. A couple of handmaids brought me refreshments and smiled brightly whenever I turned my eyes to them.

But I barely heard a word, my mind and body numb.

My father had told me: *Beware those who know remorse, good men have no need of the emotion.* If one conducted himself with purity, then there was nothing to regret. And by every standard by which I judged my life, I had been pure. I had never broken the decrees. I had served my god-king without question. I had killed hundreds of monsters roaming the countryside.

Yet I was steeped in remorse—drowning in it by the second.

With my armor fitted, I sent the boys away. My black-matte armor had been crafted from King's Stone. It would repel the Forsaken and keep me protected from evil. Where had my first set gone? Lady Yellahjar hadn't stolen it...

The steward attempted to say something else, but I ignored him and headed for the god-king's parlor. All day, I had dreaded speaking with him. God-King Eliezer had returned from his border trip and there could be no delay.

Luthecia Castle, at the heart of Luka, had stood for 500 years and served as a personal estate for the god-king, surrounded by massive gardens. Walking from one location to the next was like traversing a city. Walls enclosed the entire property, but each section was separated so that they did not touch. As the god-king's Scourge, my accommodations were among the most luxurious in Luka, and before I had met Lady Yellahjar, I had thought my privileges had been justified by my exemplary service.

The morning sun graced everything with its touch, from the glimmering water in the fountains to the sparkle of the dew on the winter trees. Truly, Luthecia Castle was a sight to behold, but I barely paid attention to my surroundings. I just didn't care.

I strode along the brickwork path, the servants bowing to me when I passed. Without stopping to see the new recruits for the Holy Guard, without even visiting the stable to check on Kelphy, I entered the god-king's wing of the castle.

History marked the walls in the form of paintings and maps. Every god-king and god-queen of Luka had a portrait of themselves and their family mounted somewhere within the castle. And all the kingdoms in all the lands had their territories marked on vast banners. When I had been younger,

I had wondered how such maps could exist if people were forbidden from leaving Luka, but as an adult, I knew now the god-kings and god-queens had not always existed. There had been a time before—the time of the old gods—and it was then that the maps had been created.

So long ago…

I approached the god-king's parlor, and two doormen greeted me with deep bows at the waist. I motioned them aside, and they jumped to open the door. Normally, the parlor would greet me with a harsh orange light from the fire in the hearth, but not today.

Darkness enveloped the room, strangling the glimmer of light from the tiny windows on one wall. My eternal flame, the one I had created for the god-king and his fireplace, had died when I had fallen unconscious on Mount Regel. The cold and uninviting atmosphere didn't offer me any strength, but I marched forward regardless.

God-King Eliezer stood in front of the dead hearth, staring down at the bones that lined the inside. So many bones. Some large. Some small. They weren't all human, but most were.

The king's five advisors sat on the far side of the room, their postures stiff and their eyes open for unnaturally long periods of time.

"My liege," I said as I stepped inside.

The doormen shut the door behind me.

God-King Eliezer motioned me over with a quick wave of his hand. "Approach."

His voice shook with an inner power, gruff and forceful. He was imposing—not as striking or intimidating as his portraits would lead future generations to believe—but tall and broad of shoulder. The most striking feature, the one all god-kings and god-queens shared, was his crown.

The crown grew from his skull, black and shiny, like ebony.

It twisted around through his stained-blond hair, similar

to thorns, but rose up past his forehead, creating two horns that angled forward. They weren't long, a mere four or five inches, but the point and jagged thorns had keen edges. They said the moment his mother, the late God-Queen Elaina, had died was the moment the crown had jutted from his head and spiraled into shape.

I walked to God-King Eliezer's side and knelt on one knee before taking his hand and pressing the knuckles to my forehead—a gesture of fealty. No one spoke while I submitted myself to my liege, and I barely breathed as I stared down at the black and gray stones of the castle floor. I couldn't stand until the god-king allowed me, as was custom.

"I have come to speak with you," I said, keeping my posture stiff, his knuckles flush against my forehead. "Serious matters plague me."

God-King Eliezer turned to face his advisors. "Leave us."

The words of the god-king were absolute, which bred fear in most who dined with him. If he gave a command, even a simple one, it had to be followed or else the insubordinate would be cursed. Because of that, God-King Eliezer tended to use gentle phrases such *you may leave* or *I have no need for your services*. They weren't commands, but suggestions. The astute would understand.

But a command such as *leave us* demanded immediate action. All five of his advisors jumped from their seats and offered minimum farewells as they exited the parlor. One dropped a sheet of parchment, but he left it on the floor in his haste to comply with the god-king's command.

The doors slammed shut behind the god-king's advisors.

God-King Eliezer removed his hand from my grasp. "You may stand." He exhaled and turned away. "I had thought you dead. I'm pleased to see you've returned."

"Thank you, my liege."

I stood and tried to relax, but no part of me would listen.

Eliezer's deep voice rumbled in his chest as he chortled. "Tell me, did you slay Artemisia?"

"No," I said as I met his hard-set gaze.

He was older, and his face was lined with his usual expression: an intent scrutiny, as though he were examining everything with his full attention. His raven-colored clothing had a sheen similar to the feathers of the bird. Unusual—he typically wore gray and silver, in accordance with the new church's approved colorations. That had been why he dyed his black hair. His dark skin didn't quite match the fair blond of his locks.

"What happened?" the god-king asked.

"I found her on Mount Regel, living with a group of hunters, one of which was Osmund Nasos."

"A former knight of the Holy Guard?" The god-king's voice was laced with irritation—I was always aware of his mood.

"The very same."

"Traitor," God-King Eliezer said with a sneer. He looked away from me, narrowing his gaze and returning his attention to the bones of the hearth. "He should be put to death as well."

"There's something else I wish to discuss," I said, needing to get the doubt off my chest. "Please, my liege. This is important. There was a woman I met who—"

"There are more pressing matters at hand," Eliezer said, cutting me off. "Saileer's King Killer roams *my* countryside. While the Kingdom of Valopa carves out chunks of Saileer's territory, my soldiers and citizens are terrified of this roving blight of a Forsaken."

That was an important matter, but I couldn't focus. Eliezer continued speaking, and I clenched my fists as I held in my words.

"If I'm ever going to expand Luka, now is the time. Saileer

is at its weakest, their new god-queen on the eve of her twelfth year. A thirteen-year-old god-queen won't know how to command an army. You, my Scourge, should've killed Artemisia when you had the chance, and then you should've turned your fury on the King Killer."

"Forgive me. But there was a woman who asked me—"

"I don't care about some *woman* you found on the mountain."

Tension stretched between us. Obviously, Eliezer had a lot on his mind. His kingdom was in turmoil, and Saileer was crumbling at our borders. But that didn't matter. I had to speak with him about the decrees.

He must've sensed my determination, because when he glanced back, his eyes were narrowed in a harsh glare.

"If you have a question, you may ask it," he said.

I gritted my teeth and shook my head. "My question has no significance unless I speak to you about Lady Yellahjar. Please, grant me but a moment."

God-King Eliezer mulled over my request before replying with a curt nod. "So be it. Tell me your story."

"Thank you." I breathed easier and then gathered my thoughts. "I met a woman on the mountain—Lady Yellahjar —who nursed me back to health after my confrontation with several Forsaken. In every way she was a saint, but when I revealed my identity, Lady Yellahjar told me she was one of the cursed."

"She knew your identity and still spoke to you of her sins?" the god-king asked.

"Yes. She had killed her father, a man who had abused her and her mother. Lady Yellahjar said if she hadn't killed him, the man would've killed her mother. Lady Yellahjar claimed there was no other choice, because the city guards would not intervene. And then she asked if she was evil for her actions."

God-King Eliezer waited, his calculating eyes never leaving mine.

"I couldn't answer her," I said, my voice strained. "I didn't know what to say. I'm not a priestess of the new church, and I don't understand the nuance of the church's teachings. Tell me, do you think Lady Yellahjar is evil?"

"No."

His immediate answer caught me off guard. He didn't even flinch or ponder. His answer was definite and without hesitation.

"But, then, why the decrees?" I asked. "If you know Lady Yellahjar isn't evil, why are you punishing her for—"

"Don't be naive, Alexavier," the god-king snapped. "You are my Scourge; you should know this better than anybody. The decrees are not meant to cast moral judgments. Good men can become cursed. Evil men can live their whole lives without knowing the mark. The decrees are there to *create order*. They protect Luka from chaos and nothing more."

It took me a moment to process his statement. When I was younger, I had been taught that the decrees were divine protections, meant to keep evil at bay. If morality wasn't behind their creation, how did the god-kings and god-queens determine what was right?

"Why must people die for breaking the decrees?" I asked. "Surely death and destruction are counterintuitive to order."

God-King Eliezer frowned. "The decrees would have no weight if the punishments were not extreme. Mankind is inherently lazy, and they need the spur of death to keep them on the right path."

"But… good men are being punished…"

"In the grand scheme of things, *order* is more important than *good*. Look at Saileer. Their god-king was murdered and now their citizens will suffer. Kingdoms will attack Saileer from all sides, and they will be ruled by a child until their ultimate demise. Had they maintained order, none of this would've happened. That's why death must be the penalty. Order must be maintained, *no matter the cost*."

Again, God-King Eliezer didn't hesitate or question his answer. He just knew. This was how it had to be.

I shook my head. "But Lady Yellahjar—"

"Did you kill her?"

The memory still haunted me. "I killed her," I whispered.

"Then it doesn't matter if the woman was good or evil. All that matters is that you maintained order and upheld my laws. You are the backbone of our society. You have saved us from becoming another Saileer. Do you see how this is noble?"

He spoke as though lecturing a child, and I almost felt foolish. Morality had helped me cope with the reality of killing hundreds. Without it, my actions felt… cold. Merciless. I didn't feel noble with this new explanation.

"My liege," I said, my voice low. "You hold the title of *god*. Even my father said the decrees were just and good. They're the powers given to you by the forces that created the universe. I'm certain the citizens believe as I did—that the decrees are meant to stifle evil, not chaos."

"Chaos is the garden that grows evil," God-King Eliezer said with a dismissive wave of his hand. "Yes, I am a god. And as such, I see the larger ramifications that mere mortals do not. But to craft decrees fighting only evil is folly. Mankind breeds evil and only order keeps such urges from destroying us all."

God-King Eliezer walked away from the hearth, his hands clasped behind his back, his agitation apparent in the way he tensed his shoulders.

Then he stopped by the wall and ran a hand over the black-bone crown jutting from his skull and blond hair. "It seems everyone must question me lately. What happened to the days of faith? The citizens must have faith in their god. They cannot understand my workings."

"I just want to know I'm working for the greater good," I said.

"Everything I do is for the greater good. I want Luka to be powerful and stable. I want to be a ruler remembered and venerated as much as the old gods. My decrees are simple and fair." God-King Eliezer snapped his attention to me. "Have you also lost faith in me? Is that why you're plagued with abstract questions of good and evil?"

A vast space separated us, and I stepped closer to limit the distance. As I thought over his question, I held my hand over the hearth and set it ablaze once again. The room was so cold, and the crackle of the new flames gave me the courage to speak my mind.

"I had to kill another man," I said as I watched the fire twist and pop. "In a city outside the capital. I hadn't seen the new decrees, so when I ordered him to step aside, he became cursed. I don't wish to kill people for violating my word, even if it maintains order. Surely, there can be a different punishment, or perhaps the decree can be removed."

"So you *do* question me."

The statement chilled me. My blood ran icy. I didn't want to argue with my lord, my king, my god, but what else could I do? The troubles wouldn't leave me. "I want to do what is just," I said. "I apologize if that comes across as faithless."

God-King Eliezer sighed. He ran a shaky hand over his face, rubbing at his prominent nose and then across his smooth chin, clearing away the newly formed sweat brought about by the fire.

"If you could slay a madman before he kills ten innocent victims, would you?" the god-king asked.

"Of course," I said.

"And if you could prevent a thief from ever stealing, would you?"

"Yes. Definitely."

"*That* is the essence of order," God-King Eliezer stated matter-of-factly. "That is *righteousness*. That is why we must have decrees that instill fear. Why we must have absolute punishments. It's to protect the greater populace. It is to hold them accountable for all their actions, even if some *good* individuals must suffer in the process."

"They are sacrifices for order?" I asked.

God-King Eliezer nodded. "Every man who avoids wrongdoing because they fear my punishment is a victory. Each god and god-king must think of their nation as a whole and make decisions toward order. Mothers and schoolteachers and nurses think of individuals and how each person is affected by day-to-day happenings. They coddle. True rulers will lead. *You* are one of those rulers, Alexavier."

After a deep breath, I forced myself to nod once. "I understand."

"The citizens of Luka simply need to follow my orders and obey so that our kingdom may thrive. And now, they must also follow *your* orders as well. You will watch your words, as I always have, or I will find a new Scourge."

Perhaps it was because I was simply a *man* and not a *god*, but Eliezer's answers didn't quell my doubt. Lady Yellahjar had been gentle and kind. The look she had given me when she had demanded answers still rocked me. I wished I could've righted the wrongs of the world and fixed her grief, but perhaps God-King Eliezer was correct. I was just naïve.

"Forgive my questions," I muttered. I bowed and forced myself to take even breaths, dispelling the chill still lingering throughout my body.

"You will find Artemisia and the King Killer, and then you will destroy them both," God-King Eliezer commanded.

"I understand."

"And you will also bring Osmund Nasos to me, so that he may pay for his betrayal."

"As you command."

The smell of burning flesh stung my nose. I turned my attention to the hearth and knitted my eyebrows. Luthecia

Castle had many fixtures made of bone and flesh—gifts from the old gods before their terrible war—but such objects did not burn with ease. Which meant the flesh in the hearth wasn't from the old gods. It was people. Fresh people.

"My liege?" I asked, motioning to the smoke. "Should I—"

"There is no need to worry," Eliezer said as he strode to the table where his advisors had once sat at. It was a narrow table for paperwork and books, made comfortable with cushions. "The smell will soon leave us, and I will have the parlor aired. My sister disobeyed me for the last time, but she had the blood of gods in her veins, so this was the only place fitting for her remains, to become one with Luthecia Castle."

I caught my breath and looked away from the fire.

His sister had ignored Eliezer's commands on many occasions. Having children, marrying a man whom God-King Eliezer had disapproved of, making deals with other noblemen without her lord brother's permission—but I had never thought he would make her pay the ultimate price for such transgressions.

"I will be on my way," I said. "Thank you for your insight, my liege."

With that, I left the king's parlor, my pulse uneven and my mind gnawing at intangible questions.

I had not considered the dilemma before: Which was more important, virtue or order? If all the kingdom was made better with unforgiving decrees that harmed a few innocent people, was the sacrifice worth it? Had Lady Yellahjar died to keep order? Was that what I had done?

Why must the two ideals be at odds?

Or was I simply eliminating choice and funneling the citizens of Luka into the most desirable route? Like a herd dog, I was instilling fear and ushering them toward a future the god-king deemed the best.

But I shook the thoughts from my head. God-King Eliezer

had given me commands and I had to follow them. I was a keeper of order—*his* keeper of order.

I would slay the King Killer and Artemisia and then turn my attention to Mount Regel.

CHAPTER EIGHTEEN

The King Killer wanted to be found.

It left a trail of destruction so deep and wide that it would scar the land for years to come. All the cursed it transformed with its aura traveled with it, laying waste to anything and everything in their path. They toppled trees. They left rivers of blood. We found mountains of rotted vegetation mixed with bone and flesh. I had seen nothing like it.

Fortunately, or unfortunately, the monsters continued to head north, past Gourna and to the capital city, Luthecia.

"The last of the Holy Guard will be in Luthecia," Steen said. "If the King Killer has at least the wits of a stump, it'll head in the opposite direction."

Caprice ran her fingers through her oiled, black hair. "The King Killer is looking to add to its sin."

"What does that even mean? It's heading for God-King Eliezer?"

"Yes."

The information didn't surprise me, but it also didn't bring me any relief. God-King Eliezer wouldn't fall to the King Killer, not when he could order everyone close to him to fight the creature or become one of the Forsaken. And if Alexavier had returned to the capital, I was sure he would be able to slay the beast.

Rylion placed a hand on my shoulder. I straightened my posture and glanced up at him. "Is something wrong?"

"Look there."

He pointed to the horizon, to the silhouette of Gourna backlit by the rising sun. The smell of cooked fish and tilled earth wafted across the breeze, bringing back memories. The city was waking, and soon it would bustle with life. And although the King Killer had run through the nearby fields, the city proper still stood strong and tall. Somehow, they had managed to avoid the wrath of the monster army.

"We're almost there," I said.

Rylion rotated his shoulders. "There's a weaponsmith here who will know how to shape the bone from the old god."

"We should head straight there. I don't know how long it'll take this smith to forge you a weapon, so we shouldn't waste time."

"I agree."

Caprice jogged to my side. She pointed off into the distance, to where the sun reflected off the surface of a massive lake. While most water ran pure and blue, the Lake of the Damned ran scarlet, like blood. Fish overpopulated the waters. Giant fish. Some so abyssal that rumors said the fish were somehow descended from a mother Forsaken at the bottom of the lake.

"That's the Lake of the Damned," Caprice whispered.

"I'm aware," I drawled.

"It's a sacred and divine place."

Steen scoffed. "As sacred and divine as a piss bucket."

Ignoring his quips, Caprice kept her gaze on the distant red lake. "The Temperance God fought the War God in the skies over this area. The lake is where the heart of the War God fell after his lover ripped it from his chest. When it hit the ground, it created a crater. Then it beat its last few pumps of blood, filling the lake."

Although I had never given the lake much thought, the story left me intrigued. If I were the descendant of the War God—though I would never truly believe that—what would happen if I went to the lake? Rylion seemed to have had a special connection with the corpse god in the mountain. The crying skull had answered his plight. Would a torn heart resonate with me?

"Why do you always tell me such stories?" I whispered.

Caprice leaned in closer to me. "I became a priestess because the stories intrigued my child self. I could think of nothing else but the struggles of the gods long past. Now that I have found so many descendants, I feel like I'm a participant in one of those tales. What role will I play? I hope it's a useful one. Something to guide the lost children back to their path."

"You fancy yourself a character in a tale?"

"I have the comprehension to realize history is being made."

"All decisions shape history," I said, thinking back to my studies of god-kings and god-queens.

"But some more than others." Caprice held up a long and delicate finger. "Careful—the more power one has, the more one impacts history."

Her cryptic statement had me rolling my eyes. I wasn't a fool. I understood power's importance in the world. Only power shaped people and societies, and those who wielded it often found themselves corrupted by its influence.

I had never met anyone in power I liked.

For a moment, the revelation hit me hard. I slowed my steps and stared at the ground. But what would I do with such information? What *could* be done? Nothing. It was just a fact of reality. A terrible, horrible fact.

Steen passed us breakfast pouches, filled with jerky and

biscuits. We ate in silence as we traveled down the thoroughfare. Our new hailstone stallion, Equinox, caught the attention of merchants, paupers, and traders. I wondered if they would approach us for our horse, but no one ever did.

Caprice stayed at my side for the rest of the trek, her gaze locked on the distant lake. I wondered what other stories she would tell me before we reached the capital.

The City of Gourna sat at a slant, the roads angled toward the lake, and some of the buildings leaning to a heavy degree. Not the stone buildings or large houses, but the rickety shacks near the walls made with shoddy construction. We stayed on the main road, cobblestone the entire length, and the denizens gave us odd stares.

Wulf rode through the streets on Equinox, enjoying the attention. Gods, he was having fun with it. He wore a smile like a king wears a crown, and any fine lady he spotted, he offered her a quick wave.

His injured leg remained bandaged, but his trousers covered everything, giving him the appearance of a strapping young hunter without flaw. When the white of Equinox's coat shimmered in the new light of day, a chorus of swooning echoed between the buildings. The women loved the majestic beast.

Three King's Stones were inside the city walls, each black pillar rising higher than the tallest building. Scholars and new priestesses worked for a few hours each morning around the monuments. The City of Gourna hired them to answer the questions of the townsfolk. Although the King's Stone explained the decrees to anyone who touched them, the scholars and priestesses would answer questions of faith and service to the kingdom.

My tutors had often told me about God-King Eliezer's

great contributions to Luka's success. And they also spoke of Eliezer's many wives. He wanted an heir, but one never came. People around the kingdom were expected to pray for him until a child was born.

Kingdoms without a god-king or god-queen would be devoured by the stronger kingdoms.

Rylion placed a hand on my shoulder and pointed. "There. Do you see those smokestacks? That is where the weaponsmith works his wonders. You and I will take the cart while Wulf procures us accommodations at the local inn."

"What about Steen, Lydia, and Caprice?"

"I think they deserve some rest before we depart."

The way he said those words—he had some ulterior motive. I had known children with better subterfuge skills, but I waited until we had separated from the others before voicing my observations.

Rylion took the giant bone shard from the cart and carried it over his shoulder. The sharp edges were covered with a blanket, which leather belts held in place. Although it looked heavy and unwieldy, Rylion didn't struggle with it. We walked through the town, across the slanted cobblestone roads, and the passersby gave us odd looks.

"Why is it just us meeting with the weaponsmith?" I asked once we had traveled down two full roads away from the others.

Rylion chuckled, his face slightly red. I had never seen him flustered like this before. I held my breath, anxious to hear his explanation.

"I want to spend as much time alone with you as possible before we're wed." He gave me a quick glance before returning his attention to the road we traveled. "Forgive me. I should've said something, but I didn't want the others to have improper thoughts about the situation."

Sometimes it felt like a fire lived inside me, burning with life, keeping me alive. When Rylion said even simple pleasantries about wanting my company, the fire burned warm and forgiving, like it could stave off any hardship so long as I heard those statements. I enjoyed the feeling, more than I wanted to admit. I stepped closer to him as we walked.

We could have spoken about our mission to see the god-king or our upcoming fight with the King Killer, but Rylion just smiled, dispelling such tense thoughts with a bit of levity.

"Do you have a favorite flower?" he asked.

What a fairytale question. Flowers? I had hardly had the time or home life to admire flowers.

My face grew red regardless, wondering what kind of flower he would present me on our wedding day. That was why he was asking—to discover what he should give me.

But I didn't actually have a favorite flower.

"The first flower you give me," I said. "That will be my favorite."

Rylion hesitated for a moment. Even his steps slowed, but he recovered quickly and smiled. "Have you never been given flowers?"

"They were of no consequence to me when I was younger. My mother wanted me to wield fire so much that anything flammable was used for practice. I've burned more flowers than a funeral home, I'm afraid."

"Do you not care for flowers? Would something else—"

"No," I said with a slight smile. "I want flowers."

I liked the idea of having something traditional. My life had been anything but traditional, and I had figured all the normal life experiences would slip by me. Maybe, for a single moment, I could pretend I lived a quiet life of happiness. It would please me.

"I shall think of something, then," Rylion said, his voice as distant as his thoughts.

We continued through the city, passing groups of merchants and workers alike. A few times, I feared pickpockets would attempt to steal from us, or that there were cutthroats in the crowd, but no one approached.

"You needn't worry," Rylion said.

"I'm not worried."

"Your gaze flits around as though every shadow will harm us."

"Better to be on guard than fall victim to a scoundrel."

"Heh. All that fretting will take its toll. Best to rest when you can so we'll be ready for when the real monsters show up."

We reached the weaponsmith's before I could ask anything else. The massive building stood apart from the others, with an open wall to allow the heat from the furnace to bleed into the streets. Immediately, my gaze turned to the blazing fire. It… wasn't normal.

Although there were apprentice boys running to and fro, and despite the weaponsmith shouting when I stepped inside, I walked straight for the fire. It called to me, like a low whisper caught in the wind and taken before it could be heard. I thought Rylion called my name at some point as well, but it faded from my perceptions.

The furnace—so massive, three horses could have stood inside of it—raged with divine fire. I knew the moment I neared. The flames were like mine. There was no wood at the bottom, only large scales, as if from a reptile or fish. Scales large enough to be sleds.

Rylion grabbed my shoulder and jerked me around. "Artemis, what're you doing?"

Shaking away the daze, I said, "I… just wanted to see the fire."

The weaponsmith hustled over to us, his solid body of muscle coated in a fine layer of sweat. He wore a heavy apron and thick pants, but his face was clean and his head bald. His eyebrows had seen better days—both were singed into tiny lines.

"What's your problem?" he barked. "Bargin' in here? Get out!"

"Please, Cuthbert," Rylion said. "She didn't mean to cause problems. We've simply come here to ask for your services."

Cuthbert stepped back. He was nearly as tall as Rylion, and certainly as capable. "You're Osmund's boy, aren't you?"

"That's right. I'm Rylion Nasos."

"Ah, it all makes sense now." The weaponsmith slapped his bald head. "I was wonderin' why Osmund had come to town. You've come here to get that bow repaired?"

"My father is in town?" Rylion asked, disbelief in his voice.

"That's right. Came in yesterday on a speedy horse. Said he was lookin' for someone."

Rylion exchanged a glance with me. There was no doubt in my mind why Osmund had raced to Gourna. Osmund didn't want to live out the last of his days in a lonely mountain cabin. He wanted to be with his sons, no matter what foolish path they walked. Especially considering the death of his brother.

"So, where's the bow?" Cuthbert asked.

Rylion shook his head. "No. Not Calavandi. I want you to forge something new from bone. Something like you did for my father."

"You have more bone? Sacred bone?" Cuthbert lifted both tiny eyebrows, his eyes alight with shock and delight.

"That's right. Let me show you."

While Rylion unwrapped the bone shard, I lingered back. The fire still called to me. Although two apprentice boys watched me with curiosity, I approached the furnace and rolled up my sleeve. The orange and red danced in my vision. I loved the flames. So beautiful and perfect.

Much to the horror of the children, I reached in and touched it. But divine fire didn't harm me. It licked at my skin, warm and pleasant.

When I had stood under the waterfall of tears in the Boneyard, I had felt the Temperance God's emotions. Now, holding my hand in the flames, I felt it again. Powerful. Resonating with my soul.

And there was so much *hate*.

I ripped my hand from the fire and staggered back. The scales in the furnace had been torn from the War God during his battle. The agony he had felt fueled the fire that forever blazed off the surface of the scales. The War God had wanted to end humanity for daring to take his lover's affection. The realization shook me, and I turned away with sweat rolling down my wan skin.

I didn't feel well. My stomach twisted in knots.

While Rylion gave Cuthbert the bone shard, I stumbled into the streets and held on to my side. All I needed was rest. The empathetic vision had disturbed me. That was all.

Rest.

CHAPTER NINETEEN

No amount of rest helped.

A full day in bed, and all I did was toss and turn. My room in the tavern consisted of a bed, a washbasin, and a desk. That was new—I hadn't been in a room with a proper desk since I had lived in the capital. I would often read and write for long periods of time then, and I had missed that.

Someone watched over me at all times. At first, Rylion was with me. Then Wulf. Now Caprice. She sat next to my sweat-soaked bed, her eyes on me like a thief eyes a purse. Every movement I made, she watched with stalkerish intensity.

I coughed and rolled to my side, my chest hot. "You can leave me. I promise I won't die."

Caprice half-smiled at my joke. "Rylion said you were bothered by the flames in the forge."

I groaned.

"They are the flames of the War God."

"I'm aware," I drawled. "I felt them."

"They will empower you. Anything from the War God

will resonate with your magic and with your mind on a deep and personal level. *That* is why you feel this way, child."

Child?

I gripped the blanket and held back my contempt. Could a *child* kill one of the Forsaken with their bare hands? But I said nothing. Best to just let Caprice tell her tales while I sweated away my ailment.

"What did you feel when you touched the flames?" Caprice asked.

"Anger. Hate." I scrunched my eyes shut. "A view of the world not so... dissimilar to my own." Perhaps we *were* related. The War God had felt disillusioned in the same way I did.

My vision at the forge returned to the forefront of my thoughts. Hate fueled the flames. A never-ending hate. It felt familiar, somehow. I'd always found the world so distasteful and disgusting. Especially humanity.

Caprice frowned. "A world view?"

"You heard me. The War God knows the frustrations of life. He knows the world is filled with darkness and betrayal. It angers him. It angers *me.*"

Caprice waited a long moment, mulling over my statements. Then she placed one hand on my bed, her touch gentle. "Tell me, Artemis, how would you describe this room?" With her other hand, she motioned to our modest surroundings.

I didn't know why, but my thoughts were filled with a painful fog, so I didn't want to protest. With a heavy sigh, I opened my eyes and glanced around, slowly taking in every detail.

Sun shone through the sole window, warming the small space. The washbasin was made of porcelain—much fancier than the wooden bowls I often found in taverns and inns— and the desk was a solid piece of oak, crafted with loving care around the legs. Images of silver hares and summer lionesses were carved into the side.

Even my blankets were made from soft wool and stitched in such a way as to create small scenes of sheep huddled together in fields. I hadn't noticed before, as the thread was the same color of off-white as the blanket itself.

For some reason, it reminded me of the first day with Rylion. I had been so scared then...

"The room," I muttered. "It's quaint. Cozy. A satisfying stay for what we paid. We have a comfortable bed and a clean window. A place to read or write. I would describe it as *high quality*, and a perfect example of Gourna."

"An example of Gourna?"

"In the capital, it's known as the *city of craftsmen*. All the artists and craftsmen have guilds here." I rubbed at my face, clearing the sweat away. "So, tell me, *priestess of the old gods*, what does *describing the room* have to do with the War God's flames?"

Caprice leaned in closer to me. "You have nothing else to describe?"

I wanted to slap her and tell her to leave. But I bit back that urge. "I have nothing else to describe. Now tell me the significance."

"You didn't want to mention the dust piling in the corners? Or the cobwebs attached to the back of the desk?"

With a tired gaze, I examined both the desk and the corners. Caprice was right. Dust. Webs.

"You didn't want to mention the slight crack in the glass of the window?" Caprice pointed to the upper part of the glass, right where it met the wall. A hairline crack was visible when I squinted.

"And?" I whispered.

"Some might describe this room as a shoddy. A poor-quality room pretending at comfort."

"What of it?"

When Caprice smiled this time, it felt precise and careful, like she wanted to say more, but held back at the last second. "You spoke of the War God's view of the world, and I wanted to show you—in no uncertain terms—that the world is only as dark as you think it is."

I wanted to offer some sort of protest, but I couldn't think of anything. The first night I had stayed with Rylion, I had worried I could transform or die or something far worse. I had even worried the others would kill me or turn me in for a few quick coins. The world had seemed darker then.

So much darker.

"Rylion helped me…" My words were barely audible, but Caprice leaned forward to hear. "I just… As long as he's here, I feel like the world is different."

"Careful," Caprice said in a motherly tone. "I'm the certain the War God thought of life differently when he was with the Temperance God." She brushed her knuckles across my blankets and said nothing else. "Don't let the War God's contempt taint your vision."

I hadn't thought of that before.

The world was only as dark as I thought it was.

But Caprice wasn't right. She couldn't have been. The actions of men were outside my control—my thoughts—and their darkness leaked into everything around them.

After a long sigh, I turned over on the bed, facing away from Caprice.

Why did I listen to her foolish stories?

Three days and it only became worse. I tossed and turned in my bed, sweat soaking the sheets. The nightmares were frequent and bizarre, fevered, and without direction. Sometimes they involved the King Killer, sometimes they involved Alexavier, but they all ended with Rylion's death. I blamed Caprice and Rylion. They both had told me terrible stories about lovers losing their significant others. I didn't want to think such things, not after I had finally found someone I wanted to call *lover*.

Rylion sat in my room at the small desk, his hand on a feather quill poised over a piece of parchment. The desk, positioned next to my bed, was low enough for me to see the writing. Although my head burned, I watched over Rylion as he attempted his letters.

Shaky and terrible, but each attempt was better than the last.

"My tutors would strike my knuckles if I made an error," I whispered. "I learned quickly, but I never much cared for my tutors."

Rylion chortled. "I'm glad our relationship won't take the same dark turn."

I smiled and rested my head on the side of the desk. Rylion was much too large for it. His legs didn't fit all the way under, not with the height of the chair. He sat at an odd angle, his bulk useful in most situations, just not scholastic ones.

"I'm educated enough for the both of us," I said.

"That may be true, but we need to wait for the weaponsmith regardless. And I'd rather be by your side while you recover, so I figured I could practice my letters."

I placed my hand on top of his and smiled. Rylion waited for a moment before pulling away, allowing him to finish his practicing. But his affection didn't quell the churning in my stomach. I rested back on the mattress.

"The fires in the forges," I muttered. "They're divine."

"So many people have said. That's why I needed to take the bone to Cuthbert. He can craft material that otherwise cannot be molded or warped with normal fire."

"Why didn't you ask me to help you craft a weapon? We could've avoided a trip to Gourna completely."

"I'm no weaponsmith," Rylion said as he started another

line of letters, his face twisted in half-concentration as he attempted to maintain a conversation. "Even with your divine fire, I wouldn't be able to craft a sword."

"Does Cuthbert wield flame?"

"No. He found the scales of the War God on the shores of the lake. They burn forever, without waning, and many thought they were ill omens. Cuthbert took them. So far, they've only brought him business, so I would say he made the right choice."

"How is his work now?" I asked, my voice low.

Rylion tapped at the desk and regarded me with a slight smile. "He's almost completed it. Soon, the hilt will be crafted, and I will have a new weapon."

"Hopefully it'll be enough to fight the King Killer." Hopefully, it wouldn't be infused with the hatred I had felt.

I grabbed my sweat-soaked blankets and held them close, my eyes scrunched shut.

What if... Caprice was right? What if I was blood-related to the War God, and his hate—the same hate that fueled the fire of the scales—ran through my veins? What if my contempt for the world around me stemmed from the War God's contempt? Could my life and personality really have been affected by my blood ties?

I rolled to my side, my head burning, my stomach twisting.

I loathed the idea that I harbored feelings and traits from a long-dead god. His struggles weren't my struggles, yet he dared to influence my behaviors? I wouldn't be controlled. I wouldn't be swayed. I would overcome his delusions and I would finally be free from the myriad of lunatics attempting to steer my destiny.

Only *I* would be the master of my fate! *Only me!*

"Artemis?" Rylion asked.

With my fingernails cutting into my palms, I asked, "Yes?"

"What's wrong?"

The question stuck with me for a moment.

What was wrong?

So many people had tried to control my life. My mother had wanted me to kill for her—become a master of fire to act as her tool. My father had wanted me to behave and listen to everything he'd had to say. The god-king wanted me dead, and so did his Scourge. The curse wanted me to become a monster and plague the lands. And now I saw that the War God influenced my actions, puppeteering me from within.

Every single person with authority in my life—from the gods to my parents—thought they could control me. I was too unruly. Too disobedient. Too troublesome. Always me. *I* was always the problem. Never *them*. My mother had claimed she had been a saint. My father had said it had been for my own good. The god-king had said life would be better if I were a corpse. The curse only took those who were *evil*.

"Artemis?" Rylion asked again.

"I'm sorry," I said through gritted teeth. Then I forced a calming breath. "I just want… to be free."

"Free of what?"

"Everyone. I want to make my own life."

It was all I felt. It consumed me, like whatever was consuming my insides. But how would I get rid of it? I didn't know. But a part of me didn't want to dwell any longer. I wanted to have a conversation. I wanted Rylion to comfort me.

Maybe I should ask him something fun.

"If you were god-king," I whispered, "what decrees would you utter?"

Rylion stopped writing and hesitated. I waited, hugging myself tightly, wondering what he would say. Curiosity ate at me. I started thinking of hypothetical decrees I had made in advance just to mull around in my thoughts.

"I don't know," Rylion said. "What would you utter, Artemis?"

"I'm not sure. It seems everyone gets it wrong or abuses the responsibility."

"People with power tend to abuse it."

"Isn't that ironic?" I asked with a laugh. It did strike me as wickedly funny. The god-kings and god-queens were supposed to care for their citizens. Protect them. Grow their nations.

"You're more educated than I am." Rylion shook his head. "I figured you would have something clever or insightful to decree."

I *wished* I had something clever or insightful.

"When a new person becomes a god-queen or god-king, the first thing they utter must be a decree," I whispered. That was what the tutors had told me. "All god-queens and god-kings *have* to have at least one. Almost all of them had forbidden regicide as the first decree. It makes the task easy. There's no need to think about it."

Rylion nodded along with my words. "I see. Is that what you'll utter, if you become god-queen?"

I didn't want to think about that. Eliezer would make sure that never came to pass.

"I don't know…"

"I've thought of one," Rylion said. He leaned back in the tiny chair, and the wood groaned, threatening to break. *"Cursed be the man who torments the cursed."*

"What does *torment* even mean in this context? Physical torture?"

"No. I meant *treating them unfairly.*"

I sighed and then shrugged. "People often keep their curse marks hidden. Someone might not even know they're dealing with the cursed, and then they'll accidentally break your decree."

Rylion furrowed his brow. "I hadn't thought of that."

"Uttering a decree requires thought."

"Cursed be the man who doesn't find you beautiful." Rylion offered a smile.

"That's preposterous," I said with a scoff. "Beauty is subjective. And besides, in a few decades, I'll objectively be a crone. That would doom the entire kingdom."

Rylion tapped his knuckles on top of the tiny desk. "Er, yes. Of course. I meant it as more of a compliment. I'm... not very good with loving remarks or comments."

I held my blankets close, cursing myself for being so obtuse. "Yes. I, uh, I, I'm not concerned about that. I just wanted to make sure we both knew that was a terrible decree. For logical reasons."

He touched my black hair for a moment, caressing me. I leaned into him and returned his smile, hoping he would forgive me for not grasping his compliment. After a short moment of affection, Rylion removed his hand and then turned his attention to his letters. "You still look unwell. Perhaps you should rest a bit longer."

"I will."

His voice put me at ease. I rested on the bed, allowing my muscles to uncoil. When I exhaled again, sleep took over. I would worry about my dread another day. All I needed now was rest.

When I woke, it was to Steen handing me a bowl of stew. He stared down at me like someone staring down at a bloated corpse in the gutter. I sat up and took the bowl with sweaty hands.

"Thank you," I managed to rasp.

"You look like shite," he said, no apology in his tone. "Get yourself together."

"Such kind words from a compassionate man," I quipped.

Steen wore a dirty tunic, a heavy coat, and long trousers—

too long, they draped over his boots. Had he borrowed them from Rylion? I wasn't certain, but I'd be willing to bet. What made him think he could chide me for my appearance?

"I'm not your mother. I'm not going to coddle you." Steen watched me sip the gravy, his gaze more intent than ever before. I stopped eating, and he lifted an eyebrow. "Don't you like it?"

"It's fine," I said. "Why are you fussing?"

Steen rubbed at his stubbled jaw. For a long moment, neither of us said anything. I blew on the stew, trying to cool it down, but fearing my magic might heat it up again.

While I fidgeted with my bowl, Steen regarded me with a deep frown. Then he glanced over his shoulder and then to the door. What was he waiting for? Obviously, the man had thoughts in his head.

In a quiet tone, Steen muttered, "I think it would be foolish for you to fight the King Killer."

"This is why you don't make decisions," I growled, keeping the stew close. "I won't allow Rylion to fight the beast on his own."

"If *you* become one of the Forsaken, you'll burn the kingdom to the ground."

"If you don't get out of my room, I'll give you a preview of that destruction."

Steen glowered down at me, his face twisted in irritation. I didn't care. The man pissed his pants over every slight problem. I wouldn't be shaken from my path. Not now. Not ever.

"This isn't a game," Steen said, strained.

I glared at him while I sipped more of the stew. Then I nibbled at the shreds of fish and chunks of potato. Lydia had been right. Steen was an excellent cook, especially with ingredients native to Gourna. The warm stew had a powerful fragrance of herbs, and each bite I enjoyed more than the last.

My stomach protested, however. I couldn't eat much

before I had to put the meal down. And my forehead burned more than ever, perhaps twice as painful as the day before. I wiped away the sweat with the back of my arm.

"If you want to survive an attack from the King Killer, you'll stick close to me and Rylion." I exhaled and rubbed at the side of my head. "There is no other alternative."

Something about the way Steen glared down at me—I didn't care for it. At some level, I had lost this man's trust. Or perhaps I had garnered his contempt. Either way, he despised me more than usual. Was it my duty to mend this rift? I liked to think it wasn't, but Rylion wouldn't sit by and do nothing if it were him, so I inhaled and then exhaled, frustrated.

"Rylion and I can handle the King Killer, and Rylion's magic will prevent the turn." I narrowed my eyes. "Stay with us."

"You should finish your meal and rest," Steen stated, never even acknowledging my plea. "Wouldn't want you to get any sicker."

"You're *concerned* about me now?"

"Maybe I'm hoping you'll stuff yourself full and then sleep through the King Killer's attack. That way, your own arrogance won't put everyone's lives at risk."

I gritted my teeth and forced myself to take a breath. After a quick calming chant in my thoughts, I asked, "Is there an apothecary in town? Someone who knows medicine and remedies? I need something. Someone."

"I know Gourna intimately. I was born here. I can find you an apothecary."

"Thank you."

Steen turned on his heel and left the room without another word, not even a goodbye. Perhaps I was just sick and annoyed, but his rude behavior grated on my patience. I had been working on my charisma—why couldn't he? Lydia made friends without effort, yet Steen still disgusted me. How could they have a romance? How did they find love?

I ate half my soup and put the bowl off to the side. No matter how much I forced myself to eat, nothing helped. I stared at the blankets for a long time, hating the way everything swirled in my vision.

Someone tapped on my door, and I lifted my head.

"You don't look good, girlie," Osmund said as he stroked his beard.

I hadn't seen Osmund since I had heard word of his arrival in the city. When he stepped into the room, he reminded me how old he was. Graying hair, a slight limp to his walk, his eyes lined with dark bags. His muscular arms and protruding gut made him *wide*.

"What're you doing here?" I asked—probably not the most pleasant of greetings.

"Is visiting you a problem?" Osmund held his hand on the doorknob.

"I mean, why are you here in the city?"

Osmund released the handle and then hobbled into the room. With a sigh, he replied, "I couldn't stay put. It's not my way. Bryn could read for months on end, but I have the warrior's itch. I'll die with a weapon in my hand, not a pillow."

Then I had been right. Osmund couldn't stand being away from the frontlines. He wanted to be with his family—with the action—and he had ridden here at an outrageous rate in order to catch up with us.

"Do you mind if I have a moment of your time?" Osmund asked.

"That's fine."

He walked to the desk and took a seat on the chair, his large frame, like Rylion's, straining the wooden legs. "Can I do anything for you?"

"I sent Steen to the apothecary."

Osmund leaned on the desk and crossed his arms over his chest. He examined Rylion's letters for a long while, a look of soft appreciation in his age lines. Then Osmund returned his attention to me. "Mariana… She was a Lord of Winter Stillness. Few people knew she could heal all sorts of ailments."

"I saw what she did for you on the mountain," I said, holding back my sarcasm.

"But did you really *see* it?" Osmund asked. He tensed in his seat and glared at the far wall. When he spoke again, it was with a distant voice. "My guts were spillin' out faster than I could catch 'em. And she still healed me. One touch— my body never felt as good. Do you understand now? She had a beautiful gift."

I hadn't thought about it before, but Osmund was right. Mariana's healing had been powerful and wondrous. Still, why tell me this now? She was gone and incapable of helping me recover.

"Is there a reason why you came to see me?" I asked.

"My son told me everythin'."

For a brief second, I thought he knew who I was—who I *really* was. I forced myself to inhale and calmed my beating heart.

"What do you mean?" I asked in a quiet voice.

Osmund glanced over and stroked his beard. "I've never heard of a woman demanding a man marry her. Well, I saw it once in a play, but that hardly counts. Plays are just fantasy tales. All make believe."

"I didn't *demand* that Rylion marry me," I said, my voice strained as I tried to think of a better way to explain it. The memories of the event *were* colored with my desperate need to have him to myself, however. "Did Rylion describe it that way?"

"Rylion told me the story, but I read between the lines."

"Well, it was… Er, it wasn't…" I gripped my blankets and shook my head. The scarf Rylion had given me was hung over the foot of the bed, reminding me of his affection. "It wouldn't have been that way if he didn't think his love was doomed to tragedy. I had to convince him, or else he would've lived his whole life without seeking anyone else."

When Osmund frowned, his beard drooped a bit. "He's still afraid something terrible will happen, isn't he?"

I didn't reply. I couldn't deny Rylion's claims—his mother was dead, and so was the god who had spawned his whole line, apparently—but his *doomed love* still seemed preposterous. I wouldn't let anything happen. My whole life had been filled with ill tidings. I wouldn't let such things hinder me any longer.

"I should tell you a story," Osmund said. "Back when I first met Mariana. She saved me from the side of the road. Bryn and I had run afoul of a Forsaken, and the beast gored me with its horn before chasing after a merchant and his horses. It was a bad wound. Bryn talked as if I were dying."

With even breaths, I listened to the story, picturing my own circumstances more than Osmund's. Why did Mariana's bloodline have an aptitude for helping people? Or perhaps I was reading too much into it.

Osmund continued, "I was a sellsword then, and Bryn was my know-it-all little brother. When he started learning with tutors, he taught Mariana on the side, and they both became masters of knowledge. After Rylion was born… Well, that was when I joined the Holy Guard."

The story drifted in and out of my thoughts. I closed my eyes and relaxed. Osmund had a gruff voice, but it soothed me to hear him talk about happier times. Everything in the past felt like a dream—different and special—and I liked imagining what it must have been like to be someone with a new family and in love.

"We lived outside the capital," Osmund said, his voice growing quieter with each word. "It was a small plot of land, but it was ours."

"Hm."

"Mariana always wanted a daughter. She spoke of it nonstop." Osmund didn't get to the point of his story. He just stared at the desk, his gaze unfocused, his voice trailing off.

I shifted around in my bed, my body hurting. "Why did you start this tale?"

"Oh." Osmund shook his head. When he returned his attention to me, it was with a slight frown. "Rylion has always been more like his mother. He could… in theory… heal you, just as Mariana once healed me."

I hadn't thought of that. Rylion hadn't been interested in developing those types of magic, and Wulf obviously wanted something destructive. Perhaps Osmund was right. Perhaps I could ask Rylion to try—and then I wouldn't feel this way.

Horns trumpeted outside. The racket grew louder and louder, until it rattled the windows. Then the horns stopped, leaving me anxious.

Osmund got up from his seat and stomped over to the window. He stood at the sill, his hot breath steaming across the glass. I forced myself to sit up, but I couldn't see the city, not at my angle. What was he looking at? It was hard to even tell what was going on.

"Someone lit the emergency fires," Osmund muttered in a grave tone. "See that colored smoke?"

A line of red mist wafted into the sky. The afternoon sun shone through it, creating a crimson shadow that covered several blocks of the city.

"I see it," I said.

"It means the King Killer is heading back for Gourna."

Although my stomach churned and protested, I bolted upright. "The King Killer? It's coming here?"

"That's right."

I threw the sweat-soaked blankets off my body and slid off the mattress. I wasn't wearing much—simple trousers and a thin tunic—but I didn't care. Rylion would be heading for the monster. I needed to be by his side.

For everyone's sakes.

"You're gonna sit here," Osmund stated as he rushed for the door. "I'm gonna find my sons and we're going to join the forces to fight it."

"I need to fight," I said as I smoothed my hair with shaky hands. "My divine fire is too important."

"You're sick," Osmund snapped. "You've been shakin' this whole time, barely eatin' your food, bedridden. Wait for Steen to return from the apothecary. Rest. We'll deal with the monster."

He stormed out of the room, leaving me alone by the edge of the bed. My forehead burned, and my vision tunneled.

My fire…

They needed it. There was no way Osmund's bow would be enough for something as terrible as the King Killer. And there would be dozens of other Forsaken surrounding the beast.

Although my body protested my actions, I hobbled my way to the dresser. I would get dressed, find Rylion, and then help him fight the King Killer. I didn't care what condition I was in.

INTERLUDE
THEA YELLAHJAR

I stood at the edge of the field, where the flatland met the woods, my gaze focused on the gigantic meadow in front of me. A horde of Forsaken ran across the winter-torn field. The shade from the nearby trees shielded me from view, but as soon as the wind shifted, the monsters would know my whereabouts.

There it was.

The King Killer.

A lion.

The beast was ten times the size of any other Forsaken, its fur black and its mane made of writhing worms—thousands of them. They danced in the wind, each one reaching, grasping, and looking for anything to grab and drag toward the mouth of the massive feline. The lion monster's eyes were tiny, but they glowed an insidious red, brighter than any star in the night sky.

And the King Killer had horns. A twisted thorn crown grew out of its skull and two spikes jutted forward, like a goat's. When the beast roared, its mouth opened so wide that it ripped its own skin, splashing blood onto the Gourna countryside. The lion's fangs were jagged and hooked.

So were its massive horse-size claws.

Twenty other Forsaken swarmed around the King Killer, each much smaller than the lion. And since most Forsaken born of a similar decree looked alike, I recognized a few of the blighted monsters. There was a lizard—elongated and disgusting, with many hands and speed unparalleled. A thief. That was why it ran so fast, and had so many grasping claws.

And then I noticed three boars, each with tusks and genitals large enough to be seen from afar. They were creatures who lusted for flesh, never satisfied until they had their barbed erections deep inside the warm bodies of anything that moved.

I wasn't familiar with them all. The other creatures twisted and turned, following the King Killer without much thought to their actions. Giant snakes and blobs of flesh with little definition mixed together in a pile of flesh and blood.

Lords of Magic who became Forsaken transformed into the most dangerous of monsters. Mariana had been a Lord of Winter Stillness, and while she had been a Forsaken, she had created storms across Mount Regel. What would I become?

Forsaken fought over everything. A group of sheep, trapped in their pen, couldn't escape the destruction. One Forsaken grabbed a sheep's leg, another grabbed the sheep's head, and then they pulled in opposite directions until the farm animal was torn in half.

The rest of the sheep met with similar fates, their bleating so panicked and terrifying, it sounded as though they were screaming.

But where was the King Killer heading? The beast pressed forward, its eyes on the red lake in the distance. His army of Forsaken monsters followed him, some trailing sheep carcasses behind them.

If I stayed in the shadow of the woods, I'd be safe.

Deana waited for me in the woods, stomping and snorting. She wanted me to return to the city with her—she wanted me to escape the Forsaken—but I couldn't. I waved her away, hoping she would save herself from a needless death. The Forsaken would happily consume a horse, but I didn't want that for her.

I stepped out into the field and headed toward the abominations. At first, I was slow, but then I picked up my pace until I was running. My memories taunted me as I went. My father beating my mother. My mother trying to kill me. Even Alexavier—they pushed me forward, their voices in my ears, telling me this was the correct choice.

The harder I ran, the hotter my body became. My lungs hurt by the time I reached the ruined sheep ranch. I almost slipped in the blood, but I managed to keep my footing as I continued.

When I became a Forsaken, would the memories leave me? Would I die and become a monster? Or would I retain my thoughts? Soon, I would find out.

My curse mark was on my shoulder. It burned stronger the closer I got to the King Killer, almost as much as my legs. Blood wept from the mark, soaking my shirt and causing the fabric to cling to my body. I gulped down breaths and closed my eyes.

A part of me heard whispers from the Forsaken.

Was I a Lord of Monsters? Was that my magic? I had never attempted to use it. I had never wanted it. All I had wanted… was to avoid hardship… People like Artemis and Wulf and Rylion were capable and powerful, and I had always felt… Not like that.

I couldn't die, but hopefully, as a Forsaken, I would.

My mark pulsed with agony. The stench of the Forsaken clogged my nose and throat. I choked as I tripped on my own feet. Without warning, I hit the ground hard. The roar and rumble and growls of the Forsaken danced around me. Had they come to consume my flesh?

More blood ran from my mark. I grabbed at it, barely

enduring the pain. My flesh bubbled under my fingertips, my shoulder bulging outward. I yelled and curled in around myself, lying on the dirt in the fetal position.

The Forsaken gathered around—even the King Killer. The midafternoon sun shone around us, but the giant Forsaken cast dark shadows.

They didn't eat me. They just watched. My body twisted and morphed. My bones broke. The sensation of my skull —*my face*—rearranging itself, was unlike anything I had imagined. My spine trembled, my ribs jutted outward, and my organs rolled around my insides, like apples in a burlap sack.

My eyes melted in their sockets, the jelly-ooze running down my face, across my cheek, over my nose—some dribbling onto my lips. I hadn't realized I wasn't breathing until that moment. Darkness invaded all my thoughts, and the salty taste of my own flesh left me terrified.

The Forsaken grabbed me, pulling and prodding, but not in a malicious way. They were helping. They freed me of my clothing, and then my old skin. Little by little, my new form escaped my old one, growing from my curse mark.

But…

At least nothing hurt anymore.

My mark didn't hurt. My thoughts didn't hurt. I started breathing with ease. And then my heart beating harder than ever before. The Forsaken were speaking to me. They whispered encouragement, told me to get up, help them.

Lord of Desolation.

Help us.

Mankind no longer deserves to rule over the land.

Destroy them.

Although I could no longer see, my path was clear. Freed of agony, I knew the Forsaken were right. The time of mankind was over. Swimming in a sea of darkness, my second body searched for life—searched for the object of my hatred.

My father…

Any and all like him would be the first to die.

As a Lord of Desolation, I would ravage the land.

CHAPTER TWENTY

The citizens of Gourna funneled into the street from every building, creating a river of bodies that threatened to drown me. I pushed my way through the desperate denizens, heading toward the danger. The King Killer and his army of monsters were beyond the walls of the city, but the dirt and debris they kicked up created a pillar of dust in their wake.

The King Killer was heading toward the Lake of the Damned, but why? The mountain lake, created by the tears of the Temperance God, had melted the Forsaken and dispelled the sinister creatures.

Did the monsters want the War God's heart hidden within the crimson depths? Could they even reach it without being destroyed?

The red lake glittered in the afternoon light, but the panic in the city didn't allow me to enjoy the sight. I made it to the weaponsmith's forge, though it took all of my willpower to stay conscious and focused. The forge raged with fire, but no one was around. I stumbled through the workshop, searching for any signs of people. Most of the weapons had been taken, but raw materials were still in their containers. Tin, iron, bronze, and quenching water sat in stacks by the far wall, obviously gathered to be taken but later abandoned.

"Rylion!" I shouted. "Rylion!"

The scales in the forge flared, crackled, and sizzled with greater intensity than I remembered. I didn't want to get close, lest I grew weaker. The hate from the scales would poison me.

"Rylion!"

"Artemis?"

I turned and found Rylion on the cobblestone road. His new bone sword, nearly five feet in length, was hefted over his shoulder, the hilt of the weapon another foot in length. The double-edged blade had a keen edge, sharper than anything I had seen before. The guard and pommel of the sword were crafted to resemble feathers.

Was it the heraldry I had made for Rylion? Had he asked the weaponsmith to incorporate the details into the design of his new weapon?

A word was carved into the bone—*Justice*—Rylion had picked a name.

Rylion motioned for me to join him.

With weak steps, I hurried to his side. Rylion wrapped a protective arm around me while dozens of Gourna citizens ran down the street, passing us with wide eyes and panicked breaths.

"What're you doing here?" Rylion asked. "If something had happened…"

"I'm fine. Now that I'm with you, everything will be fine."

"Where are the others?" Rylion glanced around, his eyes wide and searching the crowds of people who rushed by. "Where are Steen and Caprice? Both are cursed… They shouldn't get anywhere near the King Killer."

My thoughts briefly went to Steen, and the irritation, if not hatred, in his eyes whenever he glanced in my direction. Had he intentionally run off to avoid us? I hoped not.

"Your father and brother are heading out to confront the beast," I said. I gripped his arm and held him close. "I'm not sure about the others. Rylion… My fire can slay the King Killer. But…"

"What do you need from me?"

Osmund had said that Rylion should heal me, but we didn't have time to use trial and error. We couldn't train. We couldn't meditate. I couldn't rely on his magic.

Perhaps Rylion sensed my doubt and worry, because he kept me close as he spoke. "I have an idea," he whispered.

I searched his gaze. "What is it?"

"The Lake of the Damned."

I didn't need him to explain. If the waters of the Temperance God could help Rylion, perhaps the blood of the War God would help me. Then again, the flames on the War God's scales had driven me to weakness. The roar of the forge's fire had stolen my attention. Perhaps the War God wasn't as forgiving as the Temperance God. Perhaps the Lake of the Damned would hurt me further—even kill me.

I held on to Rylion, uncertain of the best course of action. Fear had almost prevented me from entering the lake in the mountain. I had thought the waters there would kill me, but I had been wrong. Perhaps I should trust my *long-lost progenitor* and allow the blood red waters of the nearby lake to help me.

No.

I was struck with a different realization. The flames and the red water weren't comforting places. The lake would be filled with the same type of hate and rage the fire was, but that didn't mean it would hurt me. I had to embrace it, just as Rylion and the others had embraced the calm of the mountain lake.

Just as Caprice had spoken about world views. I needed to use the War God's view of the world to help fuel my divine magic. I was a Lord of Flame and Cinders. I could use his might.

"Okay," I whispered into Rylion's clothing. With a weak grip, I clung to him, never wanting to stray far from his side ever again. "Take me there."

Rylion gathered me up with one arm and carried most of my weight against his body. "Let's go."

Before I could say anything more, we headed down the slanted roads of Gourna. The families rushing from their homes and businesses didn't give us a difficult time. They avoided Rylion as much as possible, streaming around him like water flows around a rock. Everyone who got a glimpse of his sword ducked away. A few even gasped and headed down an alleyway.

Rylion's strength and confidence…

I relaxed a bit in his hold. Although we were about to face a monster of legend, his calm determination spread to me. We could do this. His sword, made from the Temperance God, would kill the Forsaken just as quickly as Calavandi.

I just needed my health back, and I could help him.

We rushed down the last of the roads next to the city's wall. Normally, the gates would be closed, but in certain emergencies, they were thrown open so the citizens could flee. Rylion carried me toward the lake, his body growing tenser the closer we got to the danger.

A terrible odor filled the sky. Rotting flesh. I gagged as we continued, but nothing unsettled my stomach as much as catching sight of the King Killer.

The Forsaken always took on features of their sin, and the King Killer epitomized that. A black lion—master of his domain, legend of the animal kingdom, surrounded by a pride. The other Forsaken swarmed around the lion, tripping over themselves as they rushed to stay close to their monstrous king.

The lion was much larger than the rest, and I suspected it was because of the decree. Since the prohibition of regicide had been the first decree uttered in Saileer, it was the most powerful, lending more of its fell magic to the transformation of the man. The gargantuan beast moved forward, barely paying attention to the other Forsaken. With his giant lion paws, he stalked toward the Lake of the Damned, occasionally crushing a small part of another Forsaken as he traveled.

The King Killer had a mane that writhed, a mouth wide enough to scoop up an entire horse and carriage, and a pelt as dark as night.

I wanted to ignore the other Forsaken—they were beasts of varying sizes and shapes, some familiar, others distorted animals, like silver hares or boars—but one other Forsaken stood out as frightening.

Was it a horse?

A twisted horse with more legs than it needed. It had a long face and a white mane that grew from most of its back in fine wisps. Teeth—human teeth—jutted out of the creature's body at random locations. Its shoulder, the bottom of its jaw, its flank. Bloody snot leaked from its nose, and white fluid oozed from its eye sockets. When it screamed, the other Forsaken cried out in chorus.

The horse-Forsaken had a mouth filled with all sorts of teeth, some human, some horse, some fangs. It was a beast of many things, but it disturbed me how well it ran with its many legs.

And its hooves…

They destroyed everything they touched. Altering the ground, killing the weeds, the trees, and even other Forsaken, if they were foolish enough to be trampled.

The pack of Forsaken wasn't far from Rylion and me. They were at the edge of the Lake of the Damned, a few hundred feet from the city's docks. The King Killer led them to the water but stopped before stepping into the red waves.

They weren't far from the walls of the city—less than two hundred feet—and the moment they neared, someone inside

Gourna screamed. A black beast rose up between two buildings, its body bulging and twisting, red blood splattering across bricks and wood until it ultimately turned black and stunk of rot. A new Forsaken was birthed right before our eyes, this one snake-like and crying.

The new monster smashed the nearby buildings and quaked as it tried to rush over the wall. The Forsaken broke the bricks by slamming its head against the barrier, heedless to its own health. The beast cracked its face and skull in the process of escaping Gourna, and the moment it was free, it rushed for the King Killer, eager to join the apocalyptic army.

Would I transform that way? I clung to Rylion, hoping his magic would shield me from disaster, like it had at the winter lodge.

Rylion carried me to Gourna's piers. I held on to him, but I never took my eyes off the Forsaken. The moment they turned toward us, we would have to fight.

Fortunately—or unfortunately—the monsters were focused on the people who were hiding in boathouses on the edge of the water. The foolish Gournan citizens had obviously thought they could outsmart the beasts. They hadn't been educated. My tutors had taught me countless times that the Forsaken could smell life from a mile away. They sought it out to destroy it, as all Forsaken were fueled by an undying need to consume, destroy, and obliterate.

The Forsaken smashed the wood of the boathouses and clawed around inside until they had dragged every last person out into the daylight. Women, small children, elderly men—they stood no chance against the ravenous beasts.

Rylion held his breath as he ran down the pier. Even his attention was glued to the Forsaken, his jaw clenched. When he reached the end, Rylion stopped next to one of the many boats. I gripped his shirt, urging him to let me go.

"I should get in the water," I said, my voice raspy and soft. "You should defend the people of Gourna."

Rylion tightened his grip on me. "I'm not leaving you."

"But—"

"The King Killer's aura... You'll transform if I'm not nearby."

I nodded once. He was right. Then I motioned to the red lake. It was an eerie sight—the lake was the color of blood, but it wasn't thick. It was water, splashing against the wood of the pier, just tinted scarlet.

At least, I hoped it was.

Rylion slowly lowered me over the edge of the pier, never letting me slip from his grasp. When my legs plunged beneath the surface, I stifled a gasp. It wasn't cold or hot. It was warm. An odd temperature that caused me to shiver in disgust.

"Wait," I whispered. Then I pulled off my red scarf and carefully wrapped it around Rylion's neck. I didn't want it soaked in the odd lake water.

Rylion lowered me the rest of the way, submerging my body in the warm waters. I grabbed hold of the pier, hating the scent of fish, oil, and copper. Something about this lake drove my imagination wild. I couldn't see beneath the surface, and when something tickled my leg, my mind played tricks on me. What if there were Forsaken already in the lake? What if there were dead bodies adding to the bizarre coloration?

What if...

The Lake of the Damned soaked my clothes entirely, and just like at the forge, I felt a deep and unabating hatred oozing from the waters. I closed my eyes and held my breath, allowing the waters to speak to me. The War God, Ravintus, had fought his lover. She had chosen humanity over him— she had refused to take a place by Ravintus's side, even when he offered it to her.

Their fight had been brutal. Vahltera, the Temperance God, had tried to curb Ravintus's rage, but nothing had worked. They had ravaged the land, toppled mountains, and incinerated forests during their long-fought battle. Ravintus hadn't wanted to kill her…

He had held back.

And she had ripped out his still-beating heart and thrown it to the ground. It still beat, deep at the bottom of the lake. The pulse of the War God dictated the flow of water.

Suddenly, his rage felt justified. Why had Vahltera done that? Why had she turned her back on him? Humanity hadn't been hers to protect—she'd had no duty to the race—but as Ravintus's lover, she'd had a duty to respect his wishes.

In the end, Ravintus had refused to kill her, but Vahltera didn't return that courtesy. She had taken everything from him. If she hadn't sided against him, there probably wouldn't have been war in the first place.

Then again, if Vahltera had sided with Ravintus, all humanity would've been wiped from the planet.

I held on to that hate and rage and allowed it to infect me. I gulped down some of the lake water and then coughed it back up. The water tasted of decayed meat. I hacked and then groaned, my lungs burning and my nose leaking in protest.

"Artemis?" Rylion called down from the pier.

"I'm fine," I wheezed.

"It's not that." He reached down and grabbed my wet robes. Then he unceremoniously yanked me from the lake. I collapsed onto the pier, my body shivering from the chill of the wind.

The King Killer leapt for the lake, slamming into the red water, sending a wave of gore toward the dock. Rylion threw his scaled cloak around me, shielding me from the worst of the water. I coughed up another mouthful of lake water, and I silently cursed at myself.

The King Killer didn't die while within the lake. The War God's blood didn't kill the Forsaken like the Temperance God's tears.

I needed to drink some of the lake in order to truly connect with the hate of the War God. Would he help me? I didn't know, but the monsters were quickly approaching. Either the War God helped me, or everyone would be killed, so I couldn't allow anything else to happen.

A Forsaken with the form of a twisted boar charged around the lake's edge. Its tusks were long and jagged, with sharp spines. It snorted and stomped, and the skull of the man it had once been jutted out of the beast's shoulder.

Rylion hefted his new bone blade. The yellowish white of the bone shone beautifully in the afternoon light, the ivory practically glowing.

The boar headed straight for the docks. Gourna wasn't a gigantic city. The docks consisted of a warehouse, four piers, and a loading platform for crates and merchandise. Far on the other side of the lake, around a stunted mountain, was another city. The smarter citizens of Gourna had taken the fast vessels and headed across the lake the moment the trumpets had sounded. The remaining boats, tiny and slow, were tied to the piers, all of them stained red by the lake water.

The Forsaken didn't care. It smashed through the wood loading dock and then plowed into the warehouse, snorting and shrieking the entire time. Shouts and cries for help rang from the building.

More people hiding.

What fools.

Rylion stepped toward them but then stopped. He maintained his place by my side, his hands shaking, his gaze fixed on the boar Forsaken—only a few hundred feet away.

Then a snake-shaped Forsaken shot for the docks as well, its black scales flashing in the daylight, its fangs long enough to skewer a man.

Then another Forsaken headed toward the docks.

And then another.

Rylion and I were at the end of one pier, and we had

nowhere to go. Swimming across the Lake of the Damned was impossible. We would have to fight. Rylion had his new blade, but I needed…

I turned my attention to the water, my heart beating so hard, it was difficult to hear anything else.

"Rylion," I whispered. "If we don't make it through this, I'm sorry. All of this… It's my fault."

"Don't apologize," Rylion stated, cold and calm. "We *will* make it through this."

"If I hadn't stumbled into Ludlow, you would be in the winter lodge."

"My life has a greater purpose now." Rylion said everything without the slightest hesitation—his strength and confidence in his conviction, as much as his body. His sword required both his hands to wield, and he held his weapon at the ready, his feet apart in a combat stance. "Before you, the world seemed small… Now I know its vastness. You showed me that, Artemis. Stand with me. We'll face this together."

I glanced back at the water. It called me. I needed its hate and rage.

After a long sigh, I slid off the pier into the warm water. "Wait, Rylion… Please. I just need a little time."

The City of Gourna practically destroyed itself during the mass exodus.

I knew this town well. Once the trumpets had sounded, I had headed straight for Lydia. I didn't want to find the others. Not that priestess, Caprice, not the Nasos brothers, not Artemis or Osmund—I wanted nothing to do with them. I had Lydia, and she had our child, and that was all I cared about.

And the King Killer in the distance clearly wouldn't be stopped by a single arrow.

I held Lydia's hand, tighter than I ever should have, and led her down the narrow alleyways between buildings. Every cursed individual in the city was desperate to get away from the King Killer, and I counted myself among the panicked. My vision tunneled. All I could think about were the walls around the city.

"Wait, Steen," Lydia called out behind me.

Although it was midafternoon, the tall buildings on either side of us created dark shadows that kept us hidden. Sweat dappled my skin and created rivulets of salty water that went straight to the corners of my mouth. As a chef, I valued my sense of taste, but sometimes I wished I couldn't detect the sourness of fear. Fright came to me a bit too easily. My greatest shame.

"*Steen*, wait!"

A pile of discarded laundry half-blocked our path. I stopped and kicked the clothing to the side. Mold stained the underside of the garments.

Lydia yanked my arm. "Ya can't be like this!"

I pulled her back to me. "Stop, woman! We have to go!"

"The others—we need to get to them."

"They can protect themselves."

I guided her around the discarded clothing and continued through the alleyways. When I had been an apprentice chef, the noble houses would send us boys to the market to gather the freshest ingredients for the day. The quickest ways through the city were always in the shadows—in cracks between the wrought-iron fences. I squeezed myself through the old haunts, my thoughts focused on the wall. We were getting close.

"We should find Rylion," Lydia said as she touched the quiver attached to her leg and waist. She only had a few arrows. "He'll keep us safe."

"If we get out of the city, we'll be safe then, too."

We exited onto a back street, one made of dirt and covered with horse manure. We passed groups of people, and I only got a glance of them, but that was enough. Cursed individuals were being beaten to death. Their spiderweb marks were visible, and four to five people had picked up rocks and were bashing in their skulls, preventing them from turning into monsters by caving in their heads. Blood and brains marked the streets.

Lydia looked away, her lips quivering.

We passed the groups of people and then turned down an

empty street. I kept my grip on Lydia's hand tight as I raced for the gates. Then the unthinkable happened. One of my curse marks—the one on my shoulder—pulsed with agony. I stutter-stepped and grabbed at my arm, horrified as blood soaked into my tunic and coat.

"Steen?"

I couldn't turn around and face her. My fate was sealed.

Although I loathed to do so, I let go of Lydia's hand. "Run."

She stood in the alleyway with me, unmoving and silent.

"*Run,*" I shouted, keeping my back to her. "You need to get away from me."

Why now? Why did I have to turn *now*? Was the King Killer so close that I was being affected? Or was I just unlucky?

In reality, I had made a fool's mistake. By taking the back alleys and roads, I had guaranteed we would never run into Osmund, Rylion, or Wulf. None of them knew the city like I did. They would've stayed on the main streets and followed the crowds, and if I had done the same, perhaps we would've met up with them.

I was such a narrow-sighted dullard. I had thought myself so clever, but in reality, I had brought this upon myself. Artemis was right. Rylion *could* prevent the turn, and I should've clung to him like a child, whether or not Artemis was with him.

"Steen?" Lydia wrapped her arms around mine. "What is it?"

Once she touched the warm blood on my sleeve, she stopped talking. Lydia knew. We *both* knew. This was the first sign of the turning. In a few moments, I would become one of the Forsaken. And if Lydia didn't hurry away, I would kill her. And our unborn child. All because I had thought I could get us out of the city a few moments faster than everyone else.

What hubris. What arrogance.

I almost laughed.

"Head toward the main—" Another wave of agony cut me off. I gasped and fell to my knees, the blood of my curse mark flowing as though I had been cut. Blood even wept from my nose, and all I could smell was the stench of copper.

Lydia knelt next to me. "I'm not leavin' you."

I shoved her away, my chest twisting with both regret and magic. "Get. Away. Go."

"Get up," she said, never leaving my side. "We can get to Rylion! You'll see. Get up. Come now. We have to go!"

With my teeth gritted, I shook my head. "Go, woman. I can't… I can't make it. You need to go."

Talking hurt my throat, like the words were barbed and pulled up from my stomach.

Lydia grabbed my arm and tried to help me to my feet. "Come," she sweetly said, half a sob and half a laugh in her voice. "You're not turnin'. You're not. Everythin' will be fine."

I shook my head, unable to speak.

"C'mon, lil piglet."

I hated that nickname, but in this moment, it had me smiling. I didn't know when I had begun crying, but the tears were hot on my face. They dripped onto my trousers, causing me to shiver.

Why wouldn't she just go?

Lydia yanked on my arm.

I jerked out of her grasp, practically hissing in outrage. "Go." With what little strength I could muster, I shoved her away. "Protect our babe. Go."

The thought of the child gave me hope. Maybe it wouldn't lead a life like mine. Maybe it would have something better. Lydia would be an excellent mother—I had always known that. I wanted so much to see the child, to tell them I was proud and cherish every minute they were in my arms.

I would never know that feeling now.

Another round of agony flared through me. And then another.

Lydia returned to my side, clinging to my coat.

The only wish I had—my final wish as a man—was that she would run far from here and never look back.

INTERLUDE
LYDIA CALLOWS

"Steen, please," I begged, holdin' on to his dirty coat. "You're not one of the Forsaken yet. Get up. Please."

Steen took in sharp breaths, his whole body tremblin'. The more blood that wept from his curse mark, the more panic I felt. The King Killer hadn't frightened me. Neither had the Scourge. But losin' Steen… I didn't know what to do. He meant the world to me.

And he knew about our child? Since when?

It didn't matter none. Steen knew now.

He kept tryin' to push me away. Again and again, even when I tried to heft half his weight. I couldn't lose him. His child couldn't lose him. Why had we left Rylion and the others?

I wiped tears from my face. Steen couldn't stand. He just couldn't. And then his second curse mark began bleedin', soakin' the back of his tunic and coat. Not only had he stolen from the god-king's court, but he had also killed one of the summer lionesses to protect me and my lil brother. Steen had always been there for me, and now he wanted me to leave him?

"I won't abandon you," I said, my voice soaked in tears.

Steen grabbed my hand and tugged me close. I leaned in and listened to his raspy breathin'. Blood poured from both his nostrils.

"You're not abandoning me," Steen said, his voice rough. "You're protecting our child." He pushed me one last time. "Now go." Through the pain, somehow, he managed to give me a smile. "I love you, Barn Princess."

Curse the gods! Why did it have to be this way? Why couldn't they have mercy on him? Had Steen really done so much evil that he deserved all this sufferin'? All I wanted was mercy for him.

I shook my head. "I l-love you, too. Wait h-here. I'll bring Rylion back. You'll see. Just wait. Take deep breaths. It'll be okay. Everythin' will be okay."

Was I talkin' to him or myself? I wasn't sure.

I stood and hurried back the way we had come. Steen wanted me to head to the main road. That was best. Wulf's new horse—the hailstone stallion—could be seen from any gutter in the whole city. The white coat glittered, it did. I would spot it, find Rylion, and drag that man to the alleyway, no matter what the cost.

With determination in my steps, I leapt around a pile of discarded clothes and then straight for the streets. My legs burned, but I kept pushin'. When my belly hurt, I wrapped an arm around my gut, hopin' it wasn't too serious.

"We're almost there," I said between breaths, my trembling hand on my stomach. "Almost there."

I had no idea if I was *almost there*, but the chant helped me continue forward without losin' hope. After all, I was almost there. I couldn't give up now.

The townsfolk of Gourna had mostly fled. The main streets were empty when I reached them. I half-tripped on the cobblestones as I turned my eyes on the Lake of the Damned. The city was built mostly on the side of a hill, creatin' a weird slant. It allowed me to see over the northern wall—I was starin' down at it, after all. The lake… The red jewel glittered in the midafternoon sun. And there it was! The King Killer. Splashin' through the waters. And so were the other monsters.

I took a moment to catch my breath.

It was quiet.

I had hunted for years, and nothin' was as unsettlin' as unexpected quiet. Why? What was happenin'? A house crashed in the distance, and I whipped around, quiverin'. The streets rumbled and the houses shook. Somethin' was headin' my way.

After I gulped down some air, I took off down the road. The cobblestone was uneven from the turmoil. People and their animals had come through this area, disturbin' the stones. I tried not to trip, but it was difficult.

Another crash behind me.

When I turned, I couldn't breathe.

One of the Forsaken came tearin' out of the alleyway. It was mix of a summer lioness and a lizard with many hands. The fell beast had a coat of black fur and patches of scales all over its twisted body. Its head had the ears and forehead of a lioness, and the bottom jaw of a lizard, complete with two gullets.

A skull jutted from the beast's chest. A man's face—Steen's —was twisted in agony, frozen in place. I wanted to cry, but the terror wouldn't let me. There were no other folks on the broken road. The winds shifted and twisted. Was this the doin' of the King Killer? Had Steen transformed because the wicked beast was near?

I had been too slow. If only I had gotten to Rylion faster.

The lioness-lizard rushed down the street, its claws scrapin' against the stones as it shot for me. I had a bow. I had an arrow. But my arms wouldn't cooperate. The Forsaken beast screamed like a man and then lunged for me, its body bigger than three oxen. The monster slammed me with its massive shoulder.

I hit the street on my back, my head crashin' down on the cobblestone. My vision went black for a moment. The Forsaken was above me, smellin' foul of decay and disease. Like flesh that had been left in the sun.

The monster's two mouths were open wide, its tongues lashin' outward. The twisted beast held me down. This was the end. But instead of cuttin' my throat or bitin' my face, the Forsaken moved its claws over my gut.

The beast pressed its claw into my body, just below the ribs.

"No!" I screamed, unable to free myself from its weight.

Why? Why was it comin' for my unborn child? Wasn't this Steen? Was it his twisted wish to see his babe that the monster would do anything to fulfill that? Would he cut our child out of my body and hold it in his twisted monster hand, just to see it one time?

I closed my eyes, and a chill came over me. This was it. Although I had known Steen could transform, I had never thought he'd turn out this way. I had thought we'd make it. I had thought I would be strong enough to take us the distance, despite what my pappy had said.

Then I couldn't breathe. The air was too cold.

I snapped my eyes open, and snow filled the air. It reminded me of Mount Regel. Where was I?

Ice blasted across the streets of Gourna. Hail and frost covered everythin'. My nose burned. My fingertips went numb. The Forsaken screeched and jumped away from me. The beast yelled with both mouths and then turned its attention to the source of the cold.

Wulf and his new horse, Equinox, stood on the shattered cobblestone road not too far from us. He rode the animal bareback, and the hailstone stallion didn't seem to mind. Wulf held out a hand and smirked.

"You're facing a Lord of Winter Stillness." Then Wulf waved his hand and another wave of chill washed over the area.

But what happened afterward? Ice clung to his hand. Wulf jerked it back and held it close to his chest, the ice crystals slinkin' down his arm and causin' him to bleed. The man gritted his teeth and stuck it out, but I had never seen anythin' like that. Artemis didn't hurt herself with her divine fire.

I wanted to cheer for him, but I still couldn't take a deep breath. The icy crystals on the air hurt. I grabbed at my throat, wonderin' if I'd make it through this fight.

Equinox leapt forward. The horse had six legs, and it made it easy for the beast to turn, pivot, and jump without much trouble. The Forsaken moved with incredible speeds and managed to leap to the side, avoidin' the hailstone stallion. I had heard that the stallions had icy hooves capable of cuttin' flesh and inflictin' frostbite, but I had never seen it.

Wulf held out his frosted hand and unleashed his magic another time. The ice filled the air, like snow, and then ripped between the cobblestone, breakin' the street further. When the rime touched the Forsaken, it clung to the beast's flesh, rottin' away some of its black skin and fur.

The monster screamed with both mouths, but all I could do was stare at the face in the chest.

Wulf urged Equinox forward, and the stallion galloped across the ice without problem. It was a creature created by the Temperance God, and no amount of chill would stop it.

The Forsaken lashed out with knife-like claws, ready to shred everythin' to death. It clipped Equinox, marrin' his beautiful white coat. The horse tripped and hit the road, red blood streakin' across its white body. Wulf hit the ground and tumbled, the ice clawin' at his body just as much as the Forsaken.

I had my bow.

After another deep breath, I repeated that to myself.

I had my bow.

With shaky hands, I held it in front of me. Then I pulled an arrow from the quiver on my hip and nocked it on the string. My arms were jam. My conviction dead. This was still Steen. A nightmarish version of him, but still him. He had wanted to see our child. He had wanted to protect me…

Wulf stood and used his hoarfrost another time, but that was too much. He bled from his palm, elbow, and the cracks in his ice-covered lips.

I took aim—not too long, I had learned my lesson through huntin'—and fired an arrow. I caught my breath, stunned. The arrow went straight for the Forsaken's chest, but fire sprouted from the black fur.

Summer lionesses were known for their heat. Had this monster stolen that capability? My arrows were wood and feathers. They would always burn to magic.

Wulf shouted, *"Lydia! To me!"*

The Forsaken lunged for Wulf, but he used his magic again, creatin' enough ice that spines jutted from the ground, sharp and ominous, cuttin' up the Forsaken's many hands and paws. The beast couldn't run straight to Wulf without crossin' a field of broken glass.

I hobbled to Wulf's side, the back of my head bleedin'. I grabbed his arm and then jerked my hand away. He was cold. Too cold. Frozen beyond the surface of his skin. Wulf grimaced as he shook his head, and when he exhaled, icy air went with it.

"The arrow," he muttered, his voice almost inaudible. "Here."

Wulf held out his frozen hand.

Without further explanation, I understood. I placed one of my arrows in his frosted palm. Then he used his hoarfrost and coated my weapon. With a shaky hand, I picked up the frost-covered arrow and then nocked it.

The Forsaken scurried around the spikes of ice and then headed for us, both mouths opened wide. I aimed and then fired. The icy arrow went straight into one of the beast's throats, and while the fire tried to stop it, the frost protected it from the flame.

The arrow cut straight into the Forsaken's throat.

Into *Steen's* throat.

The Forsaken thrashed its head and slammed into a nearby house. The wall cracked and stones crashed onto the road. The beast lashed out with a lizard tail, shatterin' nearby windows and cuttin' through wooden street signs.

My hands shook as Wulf beckoned me for another arrow. For some reason, it became easier to breathe. Was this drainin' Wulf? Was he tired? Could he continue at this rate? Would we both die here?

I handed the arrow to Wulf as the Forsaken turned its red eyes on us. Still, all I could focus on was Steen's twisted face. What was I doin'? Was this right? Should I help him? Or were these arrows just easin' his sufferin'? I didn't want to think about it. I wanted to forget.

Tears streaked down my face as Wulf struggled to hand me the arrow. He could barely move, like a man covered in snow. With water in my eyes and my heart in my throat, I nocked the other icy arrow.

The Forsaken came for me, its red eyes alight with hunger. I fired before it reached me, my aim not for the mouth, but for the chest. Flames licked off the black pelt, but it didn't matter. Wulf's hoarfrost kept my arrow shielded from the worst of the heat.

The arrow shattered Steen's skull, which then broke apart.

Without the skull, the Forsaken wasn't whole. The beast jerked and flinched, its eyes wide but somehow lifeless. Without the skull of the person who had sinned, the Forsaken were no more. Normally, the skulls didn't break as easily—

they didn't break at all—but Steen's had shattered without much effort.

Had it been Wulf's divine magic? Or had it been Steen wantin' to end his life? He had been the kind of man who would allow me to kill him, just so I had known it was over. His last gift had been resolution.

When I turned back toward Wulf, I frowned.

"What happened?" I asked as I knelt by his side. He, too, had collapsed to the road, unable to move. Despite the fact that I sounded confident, nothin' could be further from the truth. The quiet streets of Gourna reminded me of a graveyard, and Steen's monstrous body oozed black blood into the cobblestone grooves, creating a scene straight from my nightmares.

I couldn't look long. I needed to focus on somethin' else. Anythin' else.

Wulf's teeth chattered. With shaky breaths, I glanced around. The deserted road was covered in rubble, glass, and bits of meltin' ice. Roars and screams echoed up from the Lake of the Damned. A battle was happenin' near the docks, and I didn't know if I should attempt to help or just flee for my life.

Someone needed to help Wulf, though.

Equinox picked himself off the stone and limped toward us. The horse's pure white eyes haunted me. He looked like a corpse—a soulless vessel looking for a rider. I couldn't bring myself to touch him, but I knew Equinox wanted to help.

"Here," I said to the horse. "Help me. I'll get 'im on your back. We can ride together."

The divine beast snorted and stomped his three good hooves. The back leg had been twisted durin' the fightin', and I doubted the beast would be able to gallop away.

With some effort, I managed to help Wulf to his feet and then help him onto the hailstone stallion. He could barely move, and some of his skin had deadened. His left arm—the one he had been channelin' his magic through—looked like it couldn't move. Wulf kept it close to his chest, his fingers curled in on themselves.

"I'll be fine," he said through his chatterin'. "L-Let's go."

I pulled myself onto the stallion, my arms shaky. Once I was situated behind Wulf, I gripped his coat and closed my eyes. Whatever happened now, I didn't want any part in it. All I could think about was how much Steen had wanted to have a life and a family. How much he would've given anythin' to have the curse mark removed from his body.

I would have to tell God-King Eliezer. I had to.

Even if it meant… me and the babe would join Steen in the end.

CHAPTER TWENTY-ONE

I floated in the red waters of the Lake of the Damned, my hands shaking.

One of the Forsaken rushed the pier, its body heavy and the wooden boards weak. The monster destroyed everything it touched as it attempted to rush toward Rylion. Fortunately, it also slowed the monster as it practically tripped over the broken wood. Rylion hefted his weapon, and although the pier shook, he moved forward with confident steps. When the boar was near, Rylion stopped to attack.

The bone sword, Justice, was heavy—I could tell from my position in the water—but Rylion was a strong man, perhaps the strongest I had ever met. When Rylion swung the blade, it *flew* through the air, a frightening *swoosh* heralding his strike. Justice slammed into the Forsaken's shoulder, cutting through its boar-like black hide. The monster squealed, but not for long.

With a powerful jerk of its head, the Forsaken gored Rylion with a jagged tusk. Rylion kept his footing, even as the monster tried to knock him into the water. And then, with another quick strike, Rylion planted the blade deep in the monster's throat.

The boar toppled to the side, gurgling on its own black blood. Then it fell into the lake, crashing beneath the water and tainting the lake further. The commotion drew the attention of the other Forsaken, including the twisted horse that rotted everything it touched.

Three more headed our way, trampling over the destroyed warehouse and heading for our decimated pier. Rylion lifted his blade again, his clothing stained with blood from the boar's attack.

Even if Rylion could defeat each of these Forsaken individually, he couldn't handle twenty of them at a time, or even in a row. They would take their price from him, gouging his face, killing him with a million cuts.

Rylion probably knew that, but he stood his ground regardless. With Justice in both hands, he braced for the next Forsaken—some freakish snake with two human arms limply jutting from its serpentine body. The arms dragged along the dock, lifeless and barely moving, both large enough to compare to a full-grown man.

There wasn't time to watch. I held my breath and ducked beneath the sickening red water. Fish swarmed me as I pushed my way deeper into the lake. They didn't bite or bother me, the fish simply swam close and nibbled at my robes, seeking sustenance. They were larger than I had expected, some the length of my arm. I ignored the fish as I went even deeper, my ears hurting.

The beat of the War God's heart helped me relax, even though I could still sense his rage. Once I was substantially submerged, I gulped down water.

My body tried to cough it all back up, but that was why I had gone so far underwater. I wanted there to be no other option—I would swallow this water and gain whatever insight I needed to help Rylion.

The warm fluid slid into my belly, roiling through my insides. I curled in on myself, fearing the lake water was some sort of poison. I tried to remember Caprice's words, about perceptions and allowing the War God to help me.

Was that it? Did I have to believe the War God was my progenitor? The being who had sired one of my previous ancestors? Did I have to accept him as kin before his waning magic would help me?

I didn't care about him. I didn't care about any of that.

All I cared about was protecting Rylion and ridding myself of this curse once and for all. If I became the next god-queen, if I lived beyond today, *then* I would think about that future.

And if the War God wanted to see his long-lost grandchild escape the horde of monsters, he would help me now.

The warm lake water filled my nostrils and lungs, and at first, I thought I would drown. But once I closed my eyes and allowed the anger to fill me, the pain vanished. I swam back for the surface, the anger of the War God permeating my body. Just as the Temperance God had lent her healing magic to Rylion and the others—and parts of her body to be used as weapons against the Forsaken—the War God lent me a small fraction of his remaining power.

It was fuel.

Fuel for my divine fire.

When I broke the surface, I coughed up the warm water, chunks of fish and fibers of… something… caught in the liquid. With my teeth gritted, I pulled myself out of the lake, yanking my lean body up onto the pier, my fingers burning from the effort. My robes and the metal rings dragged me down, but not enough to stop my ascent.

Rylion had been fighting with the Forsaken the entire time I had been beneath the surface. Three more Forsaken bodies littered the lakeshore, the fell beasts stinking up the landscape with their foul odor. Rylion had moved his position to the docks, somehow leaving our broken pier behind.

When another boar charged at him, Rylion cleaved

through the neck of the monster with a fierce swing. The creature choked and sputtered, and its frothy saliva spilled from its massive pig mouth and fell onto the broken docks.

But Rylion wasn't able to lift his weapon after that. The bone blade was too much. It stuck in the shattered wood, and even from my place on the pier, I saw him gulping down air, unable to catch his breath.

I was a Lord of Flame and Cinder. And these animals were *nothing*.

I held up a hand, and hot flames shot forward. Embers spilled onto everything. In a matter of moments, the whole dock was a pyre. Heat, anger, exhaust—the power of the War God was mine. When I exhaled, smoke and ash spilled out, as if I were burning my insides like incense.

When my flames torched the Forsaken, they melted the creatures' flesh like cream. I caught five of them with a wave of fire, like a tsunami of destruction and heat. The black scales of the snakes curled in on themselves like burnt leaves. The disgusting pigs smelled of cooking oil.

But the twisted horse with man legs and human teeth jutting from random places on its body... That abomination didn't burn like the others.

It didn't burn *at all*.

While my enhanced flames brought destruction to everything they touched, the horse monstrosity defied logic. It screamed like a banshee and then "galloped" toward Rylion. Unable to lift Justice, Rylion couldn't defend himself, and when the horse neared him, their size difference became startlingly apparent.

The twisted horse was ten feet at the shoulder, and Rylion seemed like a child in comparison. The horse's human teeth, poking out of its shoulders, neck, knees, and spine, all wiggled and writhed, like they were trying to escape the Forsaken's cursed body.

The Forsaken slammed Rylion with one of its decaying

hooves, and the rot of monster transferred to Rylion. His arm, his body, his armor—it blackened and then weakened. He stumbled backward, dropping his bone weapon and then hitting the dock.

"Fell beast!" I yelled. I ran across the rickety pier and leapt over a wrecked portion. Then I unleashed another torrent of flame. *"Away!"*

Rylion had already killed five of these Forsaken by himself. As he was injured and now weakening, it was my turn to help him, but when my fire touched the horse Forsaken, it glided over the top, never even singeing its mane. I widened my eyes, unsure of what was happening.

The human skull jutting from the Forsaken…

I recognized her. For some reason, her face wasn't twisted in agony or regret. It was happy. She smiled wide. Wider than any person should have been able to.

Thea.

What was this?

Caprice had said… that Thea had been a Lord of Desolation. Had Thea's blighted magic transferred to this grotesque beast? This Forsaken was also a Lord of Desolation, unable to be killed?

"Artemis, get back!" Rylion shouted.

I ran the rest of the way to his side, unwilling to leave him. I placed a hand on his shoulder, and he flinched away.

"You're hot," he said through gritted teeth.

I pulled back my hand and grimaced. The fuel from the War God still coursed through me. I imagined my body was much hotter than before.

A whistle pierced the sky. A bone arrow slammed into Thea's Forsaken. It cut deep into her flesh, right where her shoulder met her neck, sinking all the way to the feather. The Forsaken horse turned its eyeless face toward the archer in question: Osmund Nasos.

Osmund stood near Gourna's wall. He nocked another

arrow, but his arms shook. It was a miracle he had hit the gigantic monster in the first place, what with his eyesight. Could he do it again?

The Forsaken charged him.

I wanted to intervene, so I launched another cataclysmic level of fire. Flames covered the dock, turning our surroundings into an active volcano. I caught the city's walls on fire and torched the guardhouse by the gates. I could've decimated an entire army with my divine inferno, but the monsters were my only target here.

There had been twenty-one Forsaken with the King Killer, but now there were only two—the horse and some sort of lizard that jetted out of the way of my flames. Everything else had either been sliced into pieces by Rylion or burned to the bone by my intense blaze.

The grotesque horse went for Osmund with a bizarre gait. It ran with its many legs, its mouth opened wide. Thea's smiling face made the whole beast scarier in my mind.

The horse slammed into Osmund. He hit the ground and tried to brace himself on his arms, but the horse kicked again, shattering one of his hands and sending him sprawling. Blood from his face and gut smeared across the cobblestones. When the Forsaken came for him a third time, I thought he was finished, and I could do nothing.

"Father!" Rylion cried.

A halberd flew through the air and struck the horse, cutting through its black skin and white-wisp mane. The halberd was made of King's Stone, and it cut through the Forsaken with ease. A man galloped out of the city. I knew him well.

Alexavier. The god-king's Scourge.

He charged for the horse and fought it off, protecting Osmund from the abomination.

The King Killer roared, his lion-like voice sending ripples across the red lake. Alexavier could handle the Lord of

Desolation. I would handle the lion and the lizard by myself. When I went to face them, Rylion forced himself to stand and then placed a hand on my shoulder.

"Don't go far," he breathed.

I replied with a curt nod, but I didn't know what to do. I had to destroy those monsters before the War God's gift left me. Without it, I wouldn't be able to handle the towering monstrosity.

"Come," I commanded. Then I held out my hand. "Feel the rage with me."

Rylion hesitated. Obviously, it wasn't in his nature to feel such furious passions, but I didn't care. If the War God's magic could improve mine, it could improve Rylion's as well.

He took my hand. I gripped him tightly, and he breathed a bit easier. The Temperance God had healed him, but I couldn't do that—I just give him fuel. The War God wanted death, and we would give it to him.

With enhanced strength, Rylion hurried with me to the edge of the lake. I stepped over the charred corpses of the Forsaken, all while holding our breath. Eating the Forsaken wasn't possible, but the amount of meat on this beach could've fed the whole city.

The lion and his worm-mane stared at us with red eyes. He glanced between me and Rylion, and then settled on me alone. I knew why. I was an heir to the throne—the next god-queen. The beast somehow knew. He could smell the taint of the throne in my veins.

And he hated me for it.

I didn't blame the King Killer. The decrees were often too harsh, and Saileer had been one of the worst nations. The King Killer figured I would be the same. Another link in the chain. Another fool who didn't know how to wield a god's power.

He was probably right. Even now, standing before the monster, I knew I could kill him, but I didn't know if I could lead a nation. I didn't even know if I could utter a decree I thought was fair.

But that didn't matter.

I wouldn't be stopped.

The lion lunged for me with his giant mouth opening wide. I held up my hand and unleashed a torrent of flame. It washed over him completely—over his mane, into his gullet, over his red eyes—and it burned everything. The King Killer stood no chance against my empowered fire.

The War God wanted this.

For a moment, that startled me.

The War God *wanted* the King Killer dead. Why? The War God wanted all humanity to die? Shouldn't he have wanted the Forsaken to take over the world?

My momentary distraction cost me. The lizard—black in color, with giant eyes like a toad and claws as sharp as hooks—leapt at me from the side, avoiding my embers.

Its fangs sank into my gut, piercing me deeply. The pain was white and blinding. My legs gave out from under me.

CHAPTER TWENTY-TWO

Rylion growled and then curled his hands into fists and struck the lizard in the face.

He wasn't calm and collected, like usual. The War God's influence urged him to violence. But... he didn't have hoarfrost like Wulf. For a brief moment of clarity, I understood some simple facts.

The War God and the Temperance God had been lovers.

If we were their children, descended from their loins, and there was a good chance this was true, their bloods had mixed. Wulf—whose father had to be Bryn, and not Osmund —must have had the blood of the War God in his veins, but Rylion—whose father was Osmund, and not Bryn—did not. Wulf's lineage was mixed. Bryn hadn't been a full brother of Osmund, and he had some blood of the War God in his veins, but was unable to manifest powers. And *that* was why Wulf summoned hoarfrost with his fury and emotion, and why Rylion could not.

But the clarity left me after that. I didn't fully grasp the magic or how to use it at its peak. I needed more time. More study. More clarity.

Regardless of my understanding, I hit the ground, the

Forsaken on top of me, its fangs still in my side. Rylion grabbed its head, and with his enhanced strength, he forced the monster's jaws open, and then ripped it away from my body. With frightening power, Rylion yanked the monster's jaws apart. He kept yanking until the monster was screaming with agony and blood wept from the corners of its mouth.

Then Rylion finished his pull, his muscles bulging as he tore the jaw of the Forsaken away from its head. With a gasp for breath, he threw the jaw to the side, the black blood coating him from head to toe. He turned his gaze to me, his gaze focused on my injury.

The King Killer burned under a pyre of my eternal flame.

The last of the Forsaken were dead.

Except for Thea.

When I turned my attention to her, I saw that Alexavier and the Forsaken were caught in a struggle. The horse monster wouldn't die. Alexavier stabbed at it from every angle, his sinister steed running circles around the massive Forsaken. With his King's Stone halberd, he sliced the monster's flesh, but no matter what he did, the damage was never enough.

Then he used his divine fire, and just like with me, nothing happened.

When Alexavier finally stabbed the Forsaken in one of its white eyes, the creature reared up and thrashed about.

The horse shrieked, and then buckled and its hooves slammed into Alexavier's sinister horse, knocking Alexavier from his saddle. He hit the road near the walls and then spun. His steed was dead upon impact, its head crushed by the hooves of the Forsaken.

Alexavier, dazed, barely moved. He struggled as he reached for his halberd, not far from his fingers.

INTERLUDE
ALEXAVIER LOWELL

I tried to reach for my weapon, but my vision swam with lights and shapes. Halberds were the perfect weapon to wield from horseback. A halberd was long, with a pole-like grip, and the top was a hybrid of a spear and axe. No matter how I attacked—either through a charge or a swing—the length of the halberd and the variety of points at the end would slay most enemies.

But the halberd wasn't as useful without a mount.

Kelphy's blood pooled around me. The kick to her head had been too severe. Although she was a sinister animal, I had taken a liking to her. Her two sets of eyes, both the human and the horse, were busted and squished. Her back legs twitched as I tried to focus on grabbing my halberd.

The Forsaken with the shape of a many-legged horse turned away from me. Through my foggy vision, I finally caught sight of the human skull jutting out of its body.

Lady Yellahjar…

My mind had to be playing tricks on me. It couldn't have been her. I had killed her and left her body in the mountain lake.

Or had she risen again?

The faces on the Forsaken were typically ones of pain, their expressions horrific. Lady Yellahjar's smile disturbed me more than any of those. For some reason, I knew that I had played a part in this.

She stepped around me, her horse-like visage writhing and squirming. She was disturbed by my presence. Lady Yellahjar didn't want to hurt me. Or perhaps seeing me brought back memories.

The Forsaken headed toward Artemisia and Osmund's son. I managed to pick up my blood-soaked halberd, but my concentration wouldn't return. My head throbbed. Would Lady Yellahjar kill everyone here?

I didn't know how she continued to live through my attacks. Even my fire—*my divine flame*—had done nothing.

Artemisia tried to use her fire, but her blaze washed over Lady Yellahjar as well, the Forsaken's fallen form unable to burn. The beast lunged for Artemisia and effortlessly knocked her to the ground. Artemisia bled from an injury to the side, her robes soaked in crimson.

Osmund's boy—a warrior through and through—stood and leapt in front of Artemisia. When the horse Forsaken attacked, it kicked with its hoof. A normal horse could knock a man out. A monstrous horse could easily kill a group of people. Fortunately, Osmund's son dodged the blow and then stepped to the side, drawing the Forsaken's attention away from Artemisia.

Was he trying to save her?

He would kill himself in the process. The man was in terrible shape, and he had no weapon. Was his plan to die and be a distraction? It had to have been. There was no other way the girl could escape. Perhaps, if the man distracted the beast long enough, Artemisia could run.

A whistle broke through my thoughts.

A bone arrow shattered the flesh of Lady Yellahjar. Another arrow was planted in the beast's neck, drawing its attention away from Artemisia and the man.

Osmund had pulled himself from the ground, and with a crushed hand and twisted fingers, he had somehow fired his bone bow. The arrow cut deep. The Forsaken snorted and whipped around, ready to kill Osmund.

The old man looked like he was prepared, just like when he had been fighting the bird on Mount Regel.

Lady Yellahjar…

She charged at Osmund, her smiling human face just as disturbing now as the first time I had glimpsed it. Weapons made from the King's Stone had the ability to destroy the flesh of the Forsaken. If I cut Lady Yellahjar's head out of the Forsaken's body, she would die. That was what I needed to do.

Addled and shaken, I held my halberd with both hands. Lady Yellahjar would have to rush by me in order to reach Osmund. The ground shook with each beat of her hooves. She ran with intensity, her ghoulish horse face and wisp mane a thing of horror. Lady Yellahjar didn't meet my gaze. She kept her attention locked on Osmund.

Ideal.

I widened my stance, and although my vision still shook, I hardened myself to my attack. Lady Yellahjar rushed by me, and the long reach of my halberd allowed me to slash into her chest. I gouged a chunk of her flesh straight from her disgusting body. The skull—the one with a face stretched over the black bone, smiling wide—popped from the Forsaken's chest like a ruptured pimple.

The beast shuddered and then crashed onto the road that led into the city, shattering the cobblestone. A tremor from the impact sent me to the ground. I hit the hard surface on the side of my knee, and a flash of pain spiked through my body.

With deep breaths, I waited.

The body didn't move. I had been correct.

Lady Yellahjar's head sat on the ground just beyond the road. Still smiling.

CHAPTER TWENTY-THREE

The City of Gourna had seen better days.

The docks were on fire. The homes and stores had been wrecked by the panicked mobs and the few Forsaken that had spawned within the walls. The farmlands and walls had been crushed by the army of Forsaken led by the King Killer.

Our battle had stretched the limit of iron and magic, but at least we had won.

I stood next to Rylion on the outside of the ruined northern wall, my hands shaking. The King Killer was a charred mess, and Thea's destructive Forsaken was no longer moving. Although Rylion had a difficult time moving, he forced himself to his feet and then rushed to his father's aid.

My side bled, but not much. I kept my hand over the puncture wounds, stifling the blood flow. My body would keep me alive—I was a Lord of Flame and Cinder, after all—but I feared I'd be incapacitated again.

When Rylion didn't leave his father's side, I hobbled over, curious.

The sun set in the far distance, casting an ominous red hue over the battlefield. The bodies of the Forsaken littered the ruined docks and banks of the red lake. To my surprise, the Lake of the Damned didn't look as scarlet as it had before. Was it similar to the mountain lake? Was the War God's magic waning? Leaving this area forever?

Rylion knelt and cradled his father close to his chest. Rylion was wet from the water of the scarlet lake, and splattered with both my blood, and the Forsaken's. Yet somehow, he still retained his noble presence. His hands, though calloused and powerful, held Osmund with an infectious tranquility.

When I approached, I held my breath and said nothing.

"You're strong," Rylion said. "Stronger than me."

Osmund slowly shook his head. "No, my boy. No. I was afraid. I'm just... a cowardly old man made great by his family."

"Mother saved you," Rylion said, his voice breaking at the last word. He inhaled and steadied himself. "You have to hold on. For her."

"She saved me." Osmund held Rylion's cloak with a weak grip. "She saved me so I could be here. At this moment. To make sure you were safe."

"No. No—you're wrong. She wanted you to live."

"Mariana knew me well."

Rylion took off his cloak and wrapped it around his father's injured body. Osmund bled from every location, especially his arm and head. With such injuries, he would bleed out soon.

"She knew I'd never rest in peace if my son died to a Forsaken I had protected," Osmund said. "Thea... I never wanted this for her. I should've been... more watchful."

"It's *my* fault," Rylion whispered. "If I had been closer to her, I could've—"

"You didn't curse them, boy." Osmund closed his eyes, his brow furrowed. "You don't hold any blame."

Rylion lifted him up, holding Osmund gently against his chest.

"You're going to be okay," Rylion muttered.

Osmund shook his head. "Mariana knew me well."

"You said that."

"She knew… I'd rather die with my family around me… than die alone on the mountain. And she granted my wish…"

I couldn't watch this unfold any longer. I turned away, my insides twisted into a mass of worms. I held my injured gut and glared at the road. Alexavier was there, cradling Thea's skull. Was he talking to it? I was too far away to hear. It seemed odd, the way he looked at the smiling face. Was he… remorseful?

The battlefield of Forsaken would rise again unless all the black skulls were collected. I stumbled from one to the next, locating the skull in each monster and burning it away from the creature's flesh. I took my time. Rylion walked his father into the city. I didn't fear being apart from him. For some reason, I knew the power Ravintus had given me in the lake would stop the turn for a short while. I focused instead on the task at hand.

The King Killer's skull was the most important of all. There was a huge bounty on this head, and we needed to keep it close. I separated it from the others, taking careful precautions to preserve it. The skin stretched over the bone had the face of a man who had lived a long life. Wrinkles. Lines. His expression was contorted in agony.

Once the other skulls had been gathered and piled near the shattered docks, I spotted Wulf and Lydia exiting the city on Wulf's hailstone stallion. They were both injured—Wulf covered in ice and rime. They headed for me, the stallion limping. When they approached, Lydia pointed to Wulf, her hands shaking badly.

"Please," she whispered. "He's cold. Too cold. Ya have to do somethin'."

I hurried over and touched Wulf's arm. I almost jerked away when I felt his frosted skin. He was ice, all the way to the bone. With a deep breath, I closed my eyes and focused on heating him, one bit at a time.

Wulf managed to take in a deep breath, but he grimaced at the same time, like ice crystals were in his lungs. Blood leaked from his nose, and he shivered at a constant rate.

"Where is Steen?" I asked.

Silence.

Neither of them said anything. Lydia rubbed at her stomach, her gaze vacant. I didn't need any other clue. I knew. Just like Thea, Steen had turned on us.

Lydia surprised me. She kept her composure and even turned her attention to Rylion, who stood by the gates of the city. "Wulf, we should go see your brother and your pappy." She patted the side of the white horse. "C'mon, boy."

The steed took them straight to Rylion.

The sun dipped below the horizon, blanketing us in a new night. The chilly winds whipped over the warm lake, creating tiny vortexes of wind. I rubbed at my arms, shaken for a moment. The last of the war God's gift faded from me.

The only loose end remaining was Alexavier. I didn't want to face the Scourge. He had dogged me for miles—*for months* —and his unwavering devotion to the crown would be the death of me, if I let it.

To my confusion, when I turned to face him, Caprice was by his side!

Where had she come from?

I glanced around, startled and questioning my own perception. I hadn't seen her. Caprice hadn't been at the docks. But now she was *here*? In front of me? Unharmed and in her simple but beautiful white robes?

She circled close around Alexavier, her inky hair flowing behind her with ethereal grace. When she touched Alexavier's shoulder, it was with a gentle graze.

"Thank you for putting Thea to rest," Caprice whispered.

I walked closer, my injuries bothering me, but not enough to mask my inquisitiveness. When I was but a mere ten feet away, I stopped and held my breath. Would I need to slay Alexavier? How would I even do it? I had no weapons beyond my fire.

Fortunately, Alexavier didn't seem concerned about me. He only had eyes for Thea.

"Lady Yellahjar," Alexavier murmured. "Did you know her?"

Caprice frowned. "Thea was a lost child. She struggled daily."

"I... I thought she was dead."

"Lords of Desolation are friends with death itself." Caprice touched Thea's skull and then frowned. "She ran to the King Killer seeking her final death. She wanted to wash away her evil from the world."

"Evil?" Alexavier asked, his eyebrows knitting. "She said she was evil?"

Caprice didn't answer.

I didn't know what to add to the conversation. Thea *had* been lost. She had lived in the past, haunted by her decisions and unable to leave them. Why was Alexavier so distraught over this? Had he known her? Perhaps in another life. It worried me, though. Would he blame us for what had happened?

Did it matter? Alexavier was about to stand, and then we'd be in another fight. He couldn't leave without trying to kill me. That much, I knew.

Alexavier used his halberd as a crutch as he got to his feet. His knee was twisted in a bizarre fashion. Would he ever walk correctly again? His sinister steed was dead—he had nothing but his injured body to carry him into the city.

Despite my close proximity, Alexavier didn't look at me. He held Thea's skull against his side. A storm raged in his eyes, clouding his gaze. It was like he was lost in a dream of his own musings.

Caprice reached for Thea's remains. "I can give her a proper burial."

Alexavier jerked the skull away from her grip. "You won't touch it, woman. This is mine."

"She needs to rest."

"I'll handle whatever she needs." Alexavier then turned his hard and dark gaze to me. For a moment, he regarded me with a harsh seriousness. After several seconds of silence, he exhaled. "God-King Eliezer wants you dead."

"Come at me, then, *dog*," I said, wanting to face him myself. Rylion was injured and dealing with his father's death. *I* would find a way to end this. "I'm done running."

"Such audacity," he growled.

"For what? My *sin*? I have none. I was born this way, yet here I am, being terrorized by a madman." I waved my hand at the destruction around us. "I stopped the Forsaken from raging out of control when I killed the King Killer, yet *I'm* the priority? *I'm* the nightmare terrorizing the people of Gourna?"

Alexavier had nothing to say.

"Nothing I do matters, right?" I barked, unable to hold back my anger. "Why should I even bother? I should've let the monsters rampage through the streets. *I should've joined them, like Thea.* She had the right idea. Why bother struggling once you're cursed? Why bother trying? You'll always be *evil.*"

I didn't know exactly why, but something changed in Alexavier after I made that statement. He held his breath, his eyes searching mine. We had a moment—he realized I was right. Something about the lack of redemption bothered him.

With a gentle hold, he brought Thea's skull higher up. "I can't… seem to shake this feeling of regret. Something in my soul won't release my guilt."

"What're you talking about, fool?" I asked, my eyes narrowed. "You're not cursed. According to the god-king, you're a saint."

Again, my words impacted deep. Alexavier dwelled on my statements and never turned back. His grip loosened on his halberd. He didn't want to fight. He didn't want any of this. His conviction left him faster than the leaves on the fall trees.

"I see now." Alexavier exhaled harder than before. Then he clenched his jaw and his body tensed. He laughed once, half-smiling, but never let his grip loosen on Thea's skull. "Artemisia, thank you for articulating what my heart felt before. I now have the words to explain how I feel." He continued to chuckle, and it bothered me.

"You think this is funny?" I asked. Did he not understand the severity of his actions?

"It's very funny." Alexavier laughed again, this time dark and cold. "What's the punishment for disobeying the god-king?" he asked Caprice.

With a frown, Caprice replied, "Ultimately, it's death."

"And what's the punishment for treason?" Alexavier asked me.

"Death," I said.

"Well, then..." Alexavier smiled wider. "I've got news: I've disobeyed the god-king's orders. And since it's the same punishment no matter what, my next course of action is clear."

And before my eyes, I witnessed the worst thing possible. A black spiderweb marking appeared on Alexavier's skin, starting at the base of his left ear and spreading to his cheek and neck. The curse mark appeared like ink soaking into parchment.

He was now one of the cursed.

I stepped away. "Why?"

Alexavier reached a hand up and touched the mark. Had

he felt it appear? "Because you helped me come to a terrible realization. I don't want to kill you."

Caprice's sudden appearance hadn't bothered everyone else like it had me. Every time I asked her about it, she refused to answer, but since it was a low-priority item, I didn't push the matter. Caprice had been useful, after all. Helpful, even. Although I hadn't trusted her before, that wasn't the case anymore.

Once the citizens had returned to the city after the chaos, we returned to our room in the tavern. It was colder than before. My thoughts colored everything black. The others acted the same way.

We had lost Steen and Thea.

And Osmund.

Rylion and Wulf didn't want to discuss it with us. They stayed in a separate room for a full day. Then at night, they wrapped Osmund's body in multiple layers of clean, white cloth. I didn't know where they had procured it, but I didn't ask, either.

The brothers carefully loaded the body onto our cart and then attached it to our hailstone stallion. Lydia and Caprice sat on the back of the cart. Lydia needed the rest. She was certain she hadn't lost her child, which surprised me. After all the fighting, I figured it would've been the first casualty.

Wulf and Rylion walked with our cart out of the city. We headed for the road around the Lake of the Damned—the ferries across weren't returning anytime soon. Additionally, Wulf and Rylion insisted on visiting the God Graveyard to put their father to rest.

The last person joining us was someone I had never expected.

Alexavier Lowell, the God-King's Scourge, traveled with

us on a normal horse steed. Rylion had accepted the man into our ranks, but I didn't know how I felt about it. The Scourge had always been feared by the cursed, and now he was riding with us in silence, his gaze straight ahead, his expression devoid of emotion.

Alexavier's reasoning had been sound. He questioned the god-king's orders, and now he couldn't go back. Since we were going to speak with the god-king, Alexavier wanted to accompany us so he could question his liege one final time. I didn't know what Alexavier hoped for, but it seemed like he had resigned himself to some sort of death.

I sat at the front of the cart, allowing my side to heal. The fangs of the Forsaken had gone deep, but none of my organs had been fatally damaged.

The walk around the scarlet lake was quiet and relaxing. At a few points during the journey, I thought I heard the beating of the heart under the water. Perhaps I was mistaken, but it occupied my thoughts for several hours.

When we reached the God Graveyard, we stopped the cart and removed Osmund's body.

"This is a sacred place," Caprice whispered. She motioned to the gates and then to the hallowed field. "Be careful what you say and do here."

The God Graveyard was a massive field of graves and fences. Colossal stones jutted from the ground, each gray and white, like marble. From afar, they appeared like ribs, and I wondered if they were actually bones. The gargantuan stones surrounded the outside of the graveyard, defining the perimeter.

The graves were made of polished granite. Six statues were in the center of the graveyard, each one representing one of the old gods. Ravintus had the visage of a dragon and the horns of a rhinoceros. Vahltera was also a dragon, but more serpentine and elegant than the bulky War God.

Sella, the God of Truths, had a single eyeball and the body

of a worm. Norrus, the God of Falsehoods, had *six* eyes, his body the same worm-like shape, though his had spines on the back. They were twins, or so the legends claimed. They looked it.

The Despair God and the Hope God were different. Their statues had been smashed. Half of each statue remained, but not enough for me to get a mental picture of what they looked like. Instead, it reminded me of their terrible fate.

Only god-kings and god-queens were supposed to be buried in the graveyard, but the City of Gourna had stopped that practice centuries ago. Since then, the only people buried in the God Graveyard were people who weren't cursed.

Technically, we weren't allowed to bury whomever we wanted here. The gravekeeper was the one who dug plots and determined where bodies went, but Rylion and Wulf didn't care. At night, the gravekeeper was in his tiny house on the edge of the massive field. Light flickered in the window, but he never came out to confront us. I assumed he didn't want trouble, not after the horde of Forsaken had crashed through the city.

Wulf and Rylion buried their father on the outskirts of the God Graveyard, in a grave and coffin that had originally been meant for someone else. To keep him from being dug up again, Wulf used his hoarfrost to coat the coffin.

"If you give it part of yourself, you can make the ice eternal," I said.

That was how my flames worked. I could maintain them forever, regardless of fuel. I figured Wulf had the same ability, but instead with his winter powers. No one would ever be able to remove that coffin, not so long as Wulf persisted.

Then I gave Wulf and Rylion their space and returned to the cart with Caprice and Lydia. Once I sat down, I brushed off my robes and turned to Caprice.

"If someone was both a child of Ravintus and Vahltera, what kind of Lord would they be?" I asked.

"Their blood and magic would mix together," Caprice muttered. "They would be a Lord of Vengeance and Verglas."

The words rolled in my thoughts. Was Wulf one such Lord? What a rarity. Perhaps, if we lived through our time in the capital, I could practice more with Wulf. I'd help him study magic just as much as I would help Rylion study his letters.

"I sent word to the god-king," Alexavier said from atop his steed. His voice had all the emotion of a corpse. Thea's skull remained in a pouch tied to his saddle. "I told God-King Eliezer I was bringing him the man who slayed the King Killer."

"I'm no man," I said.

"You're a man like the decrees mean—a member of *mankind*." Alexavier managed a small smirk. "The god-king will be expecting us. He will order us to the throne room, and then ask to speak with you. He'll offer you a great reward for your service to the Kingdom of Luka."

"I have no intention of taking his rewards." Not from the god-king, my absent uncle.

Alexavier faced me with a frown. "I don't care what you do. All that matters is that I speak to the god-king one last time."

"Before you kill him?" I asked.

Alexavier turned away. "I don't know what will happen. But if *someone* kills the god-king, Osmund's sons must strike down the person who committed regicide. We need to prevent the appearance of another King Killer."

I nodded once. "As you wish."

Regicide was a terrible crime. If Alexavier wanted to take it for himself, I would let him.

He returned his attention to the far road. "It'll only take us a couple of days to reach the capital. It's almost time."

Alexavier was right. A few days on the road, and we would finally be face-to-face with God-King Eliezer himself.

For some reason, when I had been on the snowy peak of Mount Regel, time crawled by, slowed by the chill. Now time sped forward at an unusual rate, heated and filled with tension.

I didn't want to face the god-king, but nothing would stop that now.

CHAPTER TWENTY-FOUR

A day into our travels, we stopped at a small town at the base of a mountain. Rylion and I approached the keepers of the new church, and they agreed to wed us that evening.

Although optimism was low, and most of us were injured, we went ahead with the ceremony regardless. All new churches in the Kingdom of Luka were built upon hilltops, to represent humanity's journey to self-autonomy. We no longer needed the old gods—our human god-kings and god-queens would lead us to prosperity, or so the chants and hymns claimed.

I was somewhat familiar with the new church's rules and customs, even though my mother and father had kept me hidden away from the world. The tutors had taught me many things, and the practices of the new church had been among them.

It was enough for me to gain an audience with a priestess and convince her we were devout followers.

The small church on the top of the hill had exactly eight people inside. Wulf, Lydia, Caprice, and Alexavier sat in the pews. Although Alexavier's curse mark was on the side of his head, he had hidden it by wearing a wrap over most of his head. Nomads typically wore a similar headdress, and some knights wore cloth under their helmets to protect their scalp. Although it looked odd on Alexavier, it wasn't completely out of place. The folds of cloth covered the spiderweb marking over his ear.

Rylion and I stood atop a circular platform in the middle of the room, as was custom. Again, more symbology for hilltops. Those to be wed would stand upon an elevated platform to symbolize moving out of childhood and into adulthood.

The last two people in the small church were the two priestesses—an elderly woman by the name of Norma, and a younger woman by the name of Gane.

Although I disliked most people, I counted myself lucky to know everyone around me. Even Alexavier, who hadn't said much since accompanying us to the capital. He intrigued me. While killing me would've been the smarter move, he had refused. I had never thought I would see that happen.

Priestess Norma circled our platform, reading the traditional notes for couples who wished to bind themselves together.

"The difference between good men and evil men is whether they act on impure thoughts," Norma said, her voice wavering with age, but she kept her volume high. Her words reached the vaulted ceiling. "Unfortunately, some men lack the willpower to restrain themselves from evil."

Rylion and I held hands, staring at each other while the younger priestess sang a song with no lyrics. I wore my scholar's robes, which wasn't traditional, but I also had Rylion's red scarf, and that brought me joy. Rylion had his armor and hunting gear, and it suited him well.

The thirty copper rings on Norma's robes jingled as she walked. They weighed on her robes, but the gray garment had been triple sewn and reinforced, preventing the rings from tearing the cloth.

Gray—or silver, if the church had been built within a wealthy city—was considered the most humble and honest color, used by most priestesses of the new church. It was a mix of white and black, and represented the complicated and dueling nature of humanity.

"Tonight, we celebrate two individuals who wish to unite their lives and conduct themselves within the proper guidance of God-King Eliezer."

Although the sky was black outside, the many lanterns within the church were lit. Each was made of glass and wrought iron, some with designs on the sides that cast shadowy figures across the walls. Each lantern was a piece of history, and the shadowy figures were individuals riding horses, or others assuming the throne.

Norma smiled wide, her wizened face alight with genuine happiness. "Now that you are wed, the god-king has granted his blessing upon you. Go forth. Be intimate and gay."

Gane sang a bit louder, her voice straining as she tried to keep the melody slow and joyful without taking a long breath.

Once the ceremony was over, Rylion leaned down and brought his lips to mine. He was colder than I liked, but my inner fire was enough warmth for both of us. Typically, there would be cheering, and if this were a *proper* ceremony, Rylion and I would plant a tree.

Planting a tree was a way of giving life to the kingdom. Even if a couple couldn't bear children—such as a union between two men or two women or two of the elderly—they were still expected to help grow the Kingdom of Luka. The trees, according to tradition, were children of the soil, and each couple would raise their tree throughout their marriage, making sure it was strong and healthy when they died, symbolizing a life well lived.

But Rylion and I had to face the god-king. Our tree would likely never make it beyond its sapling stage, so why even bother planting it?

With our ceremony concluded, everyone stood up from the pews and regarded Rylion and me with gentle smiles. Lydia also wept silent tears, and I suspected her ceremony with Steen was fresh in her mind.

I walked out of the church and down the hill, my pulse quickening with each step. Though I still hurt from the battle with the Forsaken, my heart didn't care. Rylion held me close as we strolled down the chilly streets back to the town's sole inn. The tiny bedrooms were positioned above a stable, resulting in pungent smells wafting through the windows.

We retreated to our cramped accommodations and locked the door.

When we were finally alone, I hesitated with my clothes. Although I had been cursed my whole life, I had never been intimate with another. I had considered it on several occasions, but disgust had prevented me from ever acting on any carnal urges.

Now, I was alone with someone who I admired and cherished. Rylion was a man of quiet strength and perseverance. I went to the window, shaky from the shoulders down. Should I undress and lie on the mattress? Should I wait for him to control the situation? Razing this town and reducing all the buildings to ash seemed like an easier task than allowing myself to be vulnerable.

What if Rylion didn't find my naked body alluring? I was still injured on my side, the puncture wound barely scabbed over. Not only that, but my shoulder and the skin over my heart carried my curse mark—the disgusting spiderweb design that I hated. I grazed the spot over the robes, nervous. Additionally, I didn't groom myself with much care. The noblewomen in the capital maintained themselves with fierce dedication. They used oils for their hair, to keep it smooth and luxurious. And once a day, they would lavish their skin in butters that prevented wrinkles and kept them soft.

Fire ran through my veins. I was ashen and warm, and my palms callous.

Rylion walked up behind me. I stared at his reflection in the glass of the window. Did he wish me to speak? Should I articulate my fears?

Never.

I swallowed my insecurities, prepared to hide them, no matter what.

But then Rylion placed his hands on my shoulders. My body betrayed me—I locked up, stiff and unmoving, unable to breathe. In that moment, I felt like such a child. Was I frightened of this moment? Was that the feeling that coursed through my body, chilling my flames?

"You needn't fret," Rylion said, his pleasant tranquility infectious.

"Do you find me beautiful?" I demanded, cutting straight to the heart of my hesitation.

"Very."

His quick response spoke to the truth. I allowed myself to relax in his grip. Rylion never rushed anything, not even this. He leaned down and trailed kisses up my neck, caressing my skin. With soft words, he whispered into my ear, his lips brushing against the shell.

"I love you," he said.

I caught my breath, stunned by the intensity of the statement.

There was a reply on the tip of my tongue, yet Rylion continued, "For my entire life, I resisted all urges of the flesh. But you invade my dreams, my thoughts, and my desires. When I'm with you, I yearn for the things I've never allowed myself to consider." He smiled. "Even my future seems brighter now—away from the ice of the mountain that I rarely left."

Rylion turned me around so that we were facing. Then he ran his fingers to the collar of my robes and undid the fastening. "Do you desire me, Artemisia?"

"Of course," I stated, almost haughty. "Your father said you described my pursuit of you as an obsession. Obviously, at some level, I find you desirable in more ways than one."

I shouldn't have sounded so offended, but I just couldn't believe he would even question my yearning. I wanted him. More than anything else in this world. I wanted him in my arms. I wanted him happy. Everything.

Rylion smiled as he pulled my robes open and removed my scarf, and then allowed them to fall to the wooden floor. With a few last motions, he removed the last of my undergarments, exposing my flesh to the chill of the inn room. Although my instinct was to cover my curse mark on my shoulder, I remained still and silent. Rylion ran his knuckles over my cheeks, and for some reason, it felt gentler than before. Weren't men lustful creatures?

"You have exemplary self-control," I said, soft and slow.

"You're not the type of woman who would appreciate being held down." Rylion brushed my hair with his fingers. "You've made that clear since the first day we met."

His confidence—in all things—still managed to rock me. He wanted me to feel secure? And free? Even in this moment?

"You're not disgusted by my mark?" I asked. "I still… have no idea why I have it. It could be because I'm… I'm a monster."

"You know you're not. *I* know you're not. And even if you were, I still loved my mother, even as one of the Forsaken."

His answer was damn near poetic. It was everything I wanted to hear. Tears welled at the corners of my eyes, and I had to wipe them away. Why was Rylion so perfect? Had my curse mark been the price I had to pay to find a man like him? If it was, I would pay it a hundred times over, in a hundred different lifetimes.

I grabbed at the belt of his trousers and unfastened everything. If Rylion could see me in the flesh, I would see him. We would have this moment together.

Rylion didn't stop me. I tore off his cloak and yanked off his tunic, surprised by his body. Although I had seen other men naked—by accident, or when I had been hiding out as a man—none compared to Rylion. In any way.

When I touched him, Rylion flinched, but never moved away. He was more surprised than anything. And while Rylion could maintain a calm demeanor, his body betrayed his excitement.

I never thought I would have a night like this, but I thanked whatever gods had made this possible.

In the morning, we left the small town and headed for the capital. If we made no stops, we would reach Luthecia by late midday. Rylion and I didn't speak much, but we didn't need to. Anytime I glanced in his direction, my face grew hot, and I couldn't suppress a smile.

Neither could he. I found his smile to be... the warmth of summer in the dead of winter.

Wulf was unusually quiet during our trek. He sat on the cart with Lydia, holding her close and whispering gentle encouragements. His usual bounce was sadly absent, and I felt it in the silence that lingered between us. Lydia was the only one who could keep his attention.

I sat at the front of the cart, guiding Equinox. The road to the capital was well traveled, and the trees had been culled for some distance, preventing cutpurses from hiding in groves and leaping out at small groups of travelers.

"You are a proud Lord of Flame and Cinder," Caprice said, breaking the quiet curse that the group had been under.

I shivered, fearing she was referring to me. Caprice's gaze was squarely on Alexavier, however.

Alexavier took a deep breath as he patted his mare—it was nothing like his old sinister steed. He had the riding skill of a man who had been born in the saddle, though. No matter what animal he rode, he had no trouble.

"I'm a nobleman," he replied. "I should have pride."

"Why do you clutch Thea's skull so tightly?" Caprice asked, not bothering to be coy.

Rylion, who walked alongside Equinox, glanced over his shoulder. He said nothing, but I suspected he wanted to know the answer. Everyone did. Even Wulf and Lydia paid careful attention to the terse conversation.

"What does it matter why I hold on to the skull?" Alexavier asked. "I'm here to escort you to the god-king and then… and then end this. You have nothing to fear from me."

Caprice frowned. "Did you know Thea? She kept to herself, in constant dread of men."

Alexavier stared straight ahead.

"Were you smitten with her? Taken by her beauty? Perhaps it was *you* she was hiding from."

Tightening his grip on the reins of his horse, Alexavier sneered. "The Lowell family tree does not entwine with commoners."

"So, you wanted nothing to do with her?"

Again, the silence curdled between us.

Wulf, pushed to anger, leapt off the back of the cart and walked around to the side, closer to Alexavier. Wulf's left arm —the one he had used his magic with—didn't move as much as the other. It had deadened slightly because of his hoarfrost, and I suspected he'd never be able to fully close his left hand ever again.

"You spoke with Thea, didn't you?" Wulf demanded.

"I did." Alexavier obviously didn't want the truth dragged out one question at a time. Instead, he scoffed and waved the lot of us away. "I spoke with Lady Yellahjar for a brief period of time. She... She saved my life. And now, I want to make sure her name is not forgotten. She did me a great service, and a man of honor should've repaid her efforts in kind. I haven't done that yet."

Wulf ran a hand through his curly hair. "Thea saved your life?"

"Are your ears as bad as your father's eyes?" Alexavier shook his head. "Lady Yellahjar deserved better than this. I wanted to give her a title and land. I wanted to take her from the tiny lodge on the mountainside and reward her for her virtues."

"I see," Caprice muttered. "She wouldn't be a commoner then, would she?"

Alexavier ignored Caprice's comment and continued, "The decree she broke is just, and while the god-king has a logical reason for its existence, I need to speak with him about circumstance. I can't stand by any longer."

Wulf, in a moment of curiosity, calmed himself and glanced up toward the sky. "What if the god-king ordered someone to break a decree? What would happen then?"

"The god-king's words are absolute," Alexavier replied. "Those who are compelled won't be cursed for following orders, even if the god-king ordered them to break a decree."

"I wasn't aware of that," Caprice muttered. "How very interesting."

Alexavier scoffed. "Wulfric has made a strong point, even if that wasn't his intent. God-King Eliezer has many tools to punish those who threaten his order. He decided not to use them. Perhaps he'll suffer for his choices."

The finality of Alexavier's statement left the rest of us without any further questions.

CHAPTER TWENTY-FIVE

By midday, we spotted the massive walls surrounding Luthecia. I knew them well.

Legend said the walls of Luthecia were constructed during the time of the old gods. The insides were long corridors, fortified rooms, and fortified stone. People *lived* inside the walls, some even ran businesses and kept small livestock. The walls were thick—forty feet deep—and they surrounded the entire city. My tutors had said that stone and clay had been brought in from every corner of the kingdom, but I doubted the kingdom had enough stone.

The walls were beyond any feat of architecture I had ever seen. They stood fifty feet tall, and they cast dark shadows over half the city, depending on the location of the sun.

No one wanted to live within the walls. They smelled as old as they were, and the guards patrolled the corridors with an iron fist. It was *their* territory. Their families and friends lived easy lives, but anyone they didn't care for would mysteriously disappear.

The walls were designed after the honeycombs of bees, and my tutors claimed it was to keep the citizens of the old gods' nations from ever needing to leave. They could all live close—surrounding their lords—with no reason to leave.

Getting through the walls was a difficult task. That was why I hadn't escaped the capital when I was younger. If it had been easy, I would've run away from my controlling mother and judgmental father, but nothing was ever simple in Luthecia.

When we approached the city-like wall, our stallion neighed and thrashed. Rylion touched Equinox and he calmed, as though by magic, and we continued through the massive gates. Once inside the wall, we had to travel the long pathway to the other side. There was no sunlight here, only torches and lanterns. They provided flickering light, but at any moment, the guards could snuff them, and then they could restrain us.

Well, they couldn't restrain *us*. We were Lords of Magic, except Caprice, but I now had my suspicions. How had Caprice escaped Saileer? How had she appeared after the King Killer had been slain? Was she a Lord of Magic and she just hadn't told us? In my heart, I knew it to be true.

I didn't question her about it, though. No need now. I had to focus on our goal.

The guards at the end of the black corridor crossed their spears and blocked our way forward. Alexavier urged his horse over to the men in heavy armor. The guards' steel plate shone in the torchlight, and their helmets had likely obstructed their view of his face until Alexavier drew near.

"Alexavier Lowell?" one of the guards asked, disbelief thick in his words. "The Scourge?" The guards stepped aside, their armor clinking as they moved. "Forgive me, Lord. I didn't recognize your steed."

The Holy Guard famously rode on sinister beasts. According to my favorite tutor, it was because the Holy Guard were supposed to be masters of the Forsaken. Sinister creatures were *half* Forsaken, nothing but twisted monsters, and therefore, the Holy Guard should have no fear of them.

"I understand your hesitation," Alexavier stated. "Now step aside. These hunters are the ones who slayed the King Killer. They've come to present the skull to God-King Eliezer."

"As you wish."

Once the guards leapt out of the way, Alexavier urged his horse forward and rode into the main streets of Luthecia. Trumpets blared from the wall, announcing his arrival.

Equinox snorted and his eyes went wide as we exited the shadow of the massive wall and continued down the main thoroughfare. I didn't understand the horse's panic, but it was adding to my own. The sun beat down on us with an unforgiving intensity. The people parted, allowing Alexavier to pass without hassle. Windows shut all around us, but the prying eyes of curious citizens never relented.

I tried to ignore them. It was impossible. Their stares…

I hated their stares.

"Someone is going to recognize me," I said, my voice breathless.

Rylion undid his cloak and threw it off his shoulders. Then he wrapped me in the cloak and pulled up the hood. The heavy garment weighed me down, but it was thick and obscured every portion of my slender body. With a gentle touch, he caressed my cheek.

"Don't fret," Rylion said. "I've spoken with Alexavier. We will speak to the god-king together. You needn't worry."

As Rylion stepped away, I grabbed the armored pauldron on his shoulder, holding him back. "God-King Eliezer has powers granted to him by the old gods. All god-kings and god-queens have the same destructive abilities."

"I'm not afraid of him," Rylion stated matter-of-factly.

"You don't even know what he's capable of." *I* didn't even know the extent of his powers, just that he had them.

Rylion smiled. "Someone in Saileer killed their god-king, didn't they? It can be done, no matter what magic Eliezer has."

I tightened my grip on Rylion's armor. "You don't know what the situation was in Saileer. Maybe the god-king was murdered in his sleep. Maybe he was choking on his stew when the assassin struck. Or maybe he allowed the other man to slay him." I shook my head. "Please. For me. Don't fight the god-king. If you must speak to him, do so in a diplomatic manner."

Rylion grabbed my hand and removed it from his armor. "Artemis—I came here for several reasons, but one of them is to get the god-king to lift your curse. I won't leave until that has happened."

My insides twisted and hurt, like they were wrapping around a thorn bush. What if the god-king killed Rylion? What would I do then?

I'd return to the War God's heart, steal the rest of its power, and raze Luthecia.

But I didn't want that.

More trumpets heralded our path. The beautiful brick roads, tall wrought-iron fences, and groves of trees planted in specific locations throughout the capital spoke to its wealth and stability. For over eighty years, the city hadn't known conflict. My tutors had claimed it was because the last couple of god-kings were so incredibly fierce. The other nations wanted nothing to do with us, for fear they would face the ire and wrath of the Kingdom of Luka.

Five King's Stones stood tall throughout Luthecia, the decrees glowing blue on the side of the black obelisks. Hundreds of people gathered around them, each trying to touch the stone so they could hear the decrees. No one wanted to be surprised.

Chimneys breathed smoke no matter the time of day, filling the gutters and covering the roofs in ash and soot. City cleaners worked nonstop to fight the grime. They stopped their work to gawk as we rode by. I heard whispers of our deeds. Everyone knew we were hunters. Everyone knew we had destroyed the King Killer.

Shouldn't they be happier? No one approached, and I blamed Alexavier. If he ordered them to do *anything*, and they refused, they would become cursed. No one wanted that.

I'd stay away from him, too.

Six members of the Holy Guard rode down the street in pairs. Their sinister horses were decked in armor, and they carried weapons made of King's Stone. Without a word, they circled our cart, formed a procession, and then trotted at our speed as we continued toward the center of Luthecia.

Wulf held Lydia closer and rubbed at her shoulders. Caprice pulled a hood over her head. She and I were the remaining cursed members of our group. Hopefully, the Holy Guard wouldn't discover our marks.

I kept my own cloak well over my face, trembling under the heavy scales woven into the fabric. I was a Lord of Flame and Cinder, capable of killing the worst of monsters, but the god-king still disturbed me. I feared more for Rylion than myself, and I prayed to the old gods that we would make it through an audience with Eliezer.

Perhaps he would listen to reason. Perhaps he would grant a pardon to Alexavier and me.

I doubted it. But nothing was impossible.

Luthecia Castle had been built over 500 years ago. It had been designed in the same style as all the castles in the neighboring kingdom. It was a smaller city inside the city, complete with its own wall. Unlike the massive city walls that allowed people to live inside of them, the castle walls were tall and narrow, topped with metal thorns. Luthecia Castle was separated into several buildings with gardens all around.

Married couples planted trees, but god-kings and god-queens were meant to keep lavish gardens around their castles as a metaphor for growing their nation. The greener and healthier the garden, the more just and caring the ruler, or so the legend said.

I didn't know if Eliezer believed in such tales, but I did know he cared about appearances. God-King Eliezer had knocked over several buildings within Luthecia Castle in order to expand his garden. It was now twice as large as the gardens created by the last god-king. Eliezer had even ordered the castle gardeners to build terraces for extra plants to hang from. The result was a luxurious estate covered in flowers of every color and greens of every hue, even in the dead of winter. Pine trees, coneflowers, and lilies of the valley bloomed everywhere. They defied the cold, and supposedly spoke to Eliezer's competence.

Alexavier dismounted once we entered the castle's estate.

The members of the Holy Guard did the same. A few approached Alexavier, and he spoke with them briefly, though I couldn't hear their words.

Rylion turned to the cart, his posture stiff and his eyes hard. He motioned me off.

"You should go without me," I whispered.

He shook his head. "I'm here to remove your curse." Then he motioned for me a second time.

"He won't do it. The god-king wants me dead."

"You slayed the King Killer," Rylion stated. "He will have to grant you a favor for your heroism."

Eliezer wouldn't grant anything. I held the cloak close. "*You* should claim you slayed the King Killer, Rylion. Eliezer might grant you a favor, but if he knows *I'm* here, he'll never listen."

Rylion nodded once. "If that's what you wish."

"All I want is for us to leave this place." I scooted to the edge of the cart's driver seat. "Please, Rylion. We can still escape. As long as I'm with you, I won't transform into one of the Forsaken. We should flee this place. We could live our lives on Mount Regel."

"I won't allow you to suffer," Rylion said, his voice gentle. "And what if… another situation happens like my mother? What if I'm away for a single day and then you turn? I would never forgive myself."

I couldn't promise him that wouldn't happen. But I would rather take that risk than see him die or become cursed, like me.

"It's about more than you," Rylion stated. "It's about all the others, too."

"You care about them more than you care about me?" I snapped, heat in my voice.

Rylion placed a hand on my shoulder, and his control seeped into me. "What about our children? What about the future? Please, Artemis. We shouldn't let fear dictate our decisions. You're the bravest, most determined person I know. If you stand with me now, we'll be successful."

Children?

Again, there were several experiences I had never thought I would have, and children was one of them. Now, it seemed like I could have everything, but I first had to risk it all.

Why was Rylion doing this? Why did he care about so many other people and things?

I gritted my teeth and shook away the thoughts.

I wouldn't allow the War God's mistakes to become my own. If Rylion thought this was important, then *I* needed to consider it important. We would stand together, no matter the outcome. I had already decided.

"Very well," I said. "Let us see God-King Eliezer. Together."

I stepped down from the cart. Wulf and Lydia got off the back, but the six members of the Holy Guard surrounded us. When Alexavier gave them a wave of his hand, the men backed away.

Wulf and Lydia turned to Rylion, their brows furrowed.

"Wait here," Rylion commanded. Then he grabbed the sack with the King Killer's skull and threw it over his massive shoulder. Once secure, Rylion dragged his bone blade off the cart as well. It was wrapped in cloth, but it was still clearly *a weapon.*

"Is there a reason you're taking the sword?" one of the Holy Guard asked. "Brandishing a blade in the god-king's throne room is a sign of disrespect."

Alexavier held up a hand. "This hunter has my trust. Question nothing. We will return shortly." His words were commands. No one could disobey.

"A-As you wish, Scourge." Then the Holy Guard motioned to Rylion. "How shall we announce them?"

"I'm Rylion Nasos, the man who slayed the King Killer," Rylion stated. "And this is my apprentice." He motioned to me.

The man nodded and hurried off, rushing to the building ahead of us.

Caprice never even tried to leave the cart. She seemed determined to transform into a statue. Perhaps if she didn't move, no one would notice her.

Together with Alexavier and Rylion, I walked toward the main building of Luthecia Castle. The winter garden provided pleasant smells, but nothing chased away my doubt. Alexavier's knee hadn't fully recovered, and he limped a bit, but after a while he sucked in air through his teeth and forced himself to match Rylion's gait.

It was impressive, but I could see the grimace on his face whenever he put weight on his injured leg.

Knights waited outside all doors of the main building, and they motioned us in as we approached. Once we stepped inside, the glitter of the polished stone floor caught my attention. We practically stood on a mirror, and when I glanced down, I shivered. The reflection told a tale of a thousand words, each a synonym for *anxiety*.

The long, intimidating hall led straight to the throne room. The average citizen of Luka probably thought the god-king spent the majority of his time somewhere in this main building, but they were wrong. The throne room, and the adjoining meeting rooms, were reserved for moments of importance and diplomacy. God-King Eliezer rarely spent time in the throne room, at least not while I had lived within Luthecia Castle.

The tall double doors, high enough to reach the vaulted ceiling, were opened by attendants. Then the throne room stretched before us. Alexavier and Rylion strode forward, no hesitation. I trailed behind, keeping the hood of Rylion's cloak over my head.

As long as Rylion was safe, I would be fine.

The throne room had a long carpet of purple and gold, that covered a portion of the mirror-like floor. The east and west walls of the room were missing. We could glance right and left and see the majestic gardens on either side of us. Gigantic balconies were lined by pines and flowers. It was a beautiful sight most never saw, and I loathed every second. At the far end of the room, a set of stairs led up to the throne platform, separating the ground floor from the god-kings and god-queens of Luka. The throne itself had always baffled me, however.

It was a seat shaped for something much larger than a man. It had no back, just a wide bench with piked armrests that would accommodate no man unless he loved to bleed himself. A horse could rest easy on the throne, and I had always wondered what went into its design. My tutors never had an answer.

Nine advisors and one scribe sat on pillow seats at the bottom of the stairway. They wore the robes of scholars, each with forty rings on their collars, the bare minimum years of study required to serve the god-kings and god-queens.

God-King Eliezer stood in front of the throne, a sword in one hand, the tip on the floor, the hilt pointed toward the ceiling. He held it like an old man held a walking stick. That would be improper for a normal weapon—the blade tip would become dull, and it was disrespectful to the weaponsmith who crafted it.

But this wasn't a normal weapon.

It reminded me of weapons wielded by the Holy Guard. It was made of King's Stone, and gilded in silver. Interestingly, parts of the silver had been etched, revealing the black core and adding an artistic flare to the weapon.

The sword...

It was ceremonial, but it would kill a man as well.

The attendants at the door announced us.

"God-King Eliezer, I present to you your Scourge, and Rylion Nasos, slayer of the King Killer. Rylion has brought his apprentice."

It relieved me that the attendant didn't know my identity. If anyone knew, they would have to pay with their head for my presence.

Was my mother here? I didn't see her, but she rarely visited her brother.

God-King Eliezer advanced to the edge of the first step at the top of the stairway. He wore gray and silver armor, harkening to the new church's love of the colors. His hair had been stained a blondish white, a process I had never cared for. His dark skin contrasted nicely against the fair coloring, though. It gave him a distinct appearance.

As did the crown growing out of his head.

The black bone was King's Stone, and it twisted around his head, on his forehead, and then two horns pointed forward. To hide most of this, he wore a silver crown over it, but the thorns of his "natural" crown could still be seen, if someone knew what to look for.

Eliezer embodied the word *intimidating*. He stood with such confidence and contempt that it was like our mere existence was a waste of his time. Eliezer's narrowed eyes glared down at us from on high.

"Step forward, hunter," God-King Eliezer commanded.

The whole room held their breath. If Rylion refused, he would be cursed. Thankfully, Rylion did as he was told. He strode the long carpet until he came to the seats of the advisors, and then he knelt down on one knee.

Alexavier and I waited a good twenty feet away.

Eliezer gave Rylion the once over. Then Rylion stood.

"Your Majesty, I've brought this for you." He placed the sack with the King Killer's head on the carpet. Rylion opened it so that everyone could see the black skull within. The skin of the assassin's face was still stretched over the bone, the man's expression twisted in agony.

"You've done a great deed for the Kingdom of Luka," the god-king said. "You shall be rewarded."

The single scribe wrote at a furious rate. He served the kingdom by writing down every word the god-king spoke. What a tedious job, but it made for wonderful records.

"Thank you, Your Majesty," Rylion said.

Eliezer forced a smile, but it wasn't natural, and the wrinkles on his face said he frowned more often than not. "I shall offer you a position within the Holy Guard. Your family name will be raised to nobility, and you will be given land here in the capital."

Rylion inhaled, and then spoke. "While gracious, I must refuse. I don't wish to join the ranks of the Holy Guard. I've seen enough of the Forsaken to last a lifetime."

The nine advisors, all in their fifties, exchanged glances. The scribe wrote small notes for Rylion's response. His words weren't as important.

God-King Eliezer's expression didn't change much. "I see. Unfortunate, but I understand that the Forsaken can take a toll on a person. The sins of the Forsaken mark the hearts of all men who encounter them." The god-king held up a hand, motioning to Rylion. "Perhaps gold and territory in your hometown would be a better reward for a hero such as yourself?"

"I have a different request," Rylion said, his confidence infectious, but my stomach wouldn't calm. Rylion stood a bit taller. "The Forsaken have taken much from me. My mother, my father, my uncle… And now they threaten to take my wife."

The scribe glanced up from his work, curious for the first time, and distracted from his duty. Even the god-king's advisors seemed more rapt than before. No one had been expecting this.

The god-king lifted a blond eyebrow. "Your wife? I see. I shall dispatch the Holy Guard to your home immediately. This plague of Forsaken shall be quelled."

"You don't understand, Your Majesty. It's not the monsters that plague me. It's the curse mark."

Ice filled the throne room. The advisors and the scribe paid close attention to the exchange. Rylion wouldn't stop, however. He continued speaking.

"My wife is cursed, and if you truly want to thank me for my service to the kingdom, then I humbly request you remove her mark."

The statement ended in silence. None of the advisors turned to look at the god-king. Even I was too afraid to see his expression. Not Rylion, though. He met Eliezer's stare with a hard look of his own. Rylion knew exactly what he wanted out of this exchange, and he wouldn't be deterred.

"Sinners must be punished," God-King Eliezer stated, no hesitation. "Those who break my decrees *deserve* the mark. There are no exceptions."

"Never?" Rylion asked, the heat of his voice almost sarcastic.

Eliezer scoffed. "The facts may change, and the evidence may change, but values should remain consistent. That is true justice."

"This is different, Your Majesty. There were no circumstances to my wife's curse. She was born with the mark with no sin to her name." Rylion tensed and asked again, "Will you remove her mark and set her free from the terror of turning?"

"She was *born* with it?" Eliezer asked.

"Yes."

At that, the scribe wrote a furious pace. The advisors whispered among themselves. Even Alexavier glanced over to me, like he hadn't been expecting such a statement. I held firm and tried not to betray my identity.

Eliezer openly laughed. It was cold, almost as icy as the room. "Your wife is none other than Artemisia."

The eyes of the advisors went wide.

Rylion nodded. "That's correct. If you know of her plight, why have you done nothing?"

"Plight? There is no plight." Eliezer slammed the tip of his sword into the stone floor of his throne platform. "My sister gave birth to Artemisia against my wishes. As punishment, I went and saw my sister's newborn a few days after Artemisia was brought into this world. I gazed down upon the wrinkled, disgusting form of my niece, and I ordered her to stop her beating heart."

The statement startled me.

It shook everyone else.

All my life, my curse mark had been a mystery. It had haunted my dreams and eaten at my self-confidence. I had thought my heart evil. And all this time, it was just because the god-king had given an order to *an infant*? A child who couldn't follow through with the order, no matter what they did?

What a horrendous act. It changed my whole world perspective.

I wasn't evil.

My suffering and self-loathing had been a farce.

"Since that day, Artemisia has been cursed," God-King Eliezer stated. "She must suffer as punishment for her mother's sins. Artemisia's life is an affront to me and this kingdom. I will not remove her curse."

Without warning, Alexavier strode forward, his gait betraying his anger, even with his injured knee. "Eliezer, please reconsider. In my opinion—"

"If I wanted your opinion, *I would give it to you*," Eliezer roared, silencing Alexavier before he could offer a tirade. "This isn't up for debate. If you want another reward, Rylion Nasos, you may ask now. Otherwise, kindly leave Luthecia Castle."

Alexavier ignored the god-king's orders. "I won't be silenced any more. I disagree with your reasoning. I disagree with your path. If you won't change the decrees—if you won't remove your mistakes from this world—I'll do it for you."

CHAPTER TWENTY-SIX

"Do you not remember to whom you're speaking?" God-King Eliezer asked. With a wave of his hand, he commanded, "Get out of my sight."

But Alexavier didn't budge. He ripped off his head wrapping, exposing the curse mark on his ear. Another mark appeared around his right eye, like a patch sewn into his skin. Alexavier touched the black webbing and callously smiled.

"Is that it?" Alexavier snapped. "If you have nothing else to attack me with, I'm going to insist you answer for your own sins, *god-king*. Everyone who suffers under your rule is *your* failing."

There was no turning back. The defiance in Alexavier's statements was absolute. The advisors each stood from their pillow seats and hurried out of the throne room, their panic apparent in their wide eyes and frantic retreat. The rings on their robes jingled the entire way out. The sole scribe rushed after them, clutching his parchment and quill close.

Once everyone was out of the throne room, I pulled the hood of Rylion's cloak off my head. Eliezer gave me a momentary glance, but he said nothing. What was there to say? We had nothing between us but bitterness and hate.

"Ah, I see now," Eliezer said as he picked up his blade and stepped down the stairway a single step. "You came here for a fight. Alexavier, I'm disappointed. I'm a *god*. You're a man. There is no competition, and a battle between us would go against the natural order of things."

Rylion unwrapped Justice and allowed the massive bone blade to hit the carpet. The sharp sword cut through some of the fabric. His act of aggression was enough to determine his intent.

"You, too?" Eliezer laughed. "Two men are nothing. Trust me—each new god-king and god-queen is tested." He waved his hand, his face twisting in rage. "My reign has been just and fair. None of my decrees are unreasonable."

"Cursing a child is unreasonable," Rylion stated. "It's tantamount to wickedness."

"Even the old gods were occasionally prone to jealousy and envy." Eliezer stopped, went a few more steps, and then stopped again halfway down the stairway. "One moment of weakness is hardly worth this treason. But I understand. Love makes men foolish. You don't want your wife to suffer—and I don't want your wife to live. Our goals are conflicting. The only thing I hate about you is that you're going to dress this up as a duel between good and evil. If you had any honesty, you'd admit this was petty."

Rylion didn't reply to Eliezer's taunts. He just held his bone sword with both hands, his stance wide.

Were they really going to fight? I remained rooted in place, my hate building. If God-King Eliezer hurt Rylion, I'd unleash my fury on the castle.

God-King Eliezer lifted his sword, slow and precise. "You face a god," he said. "I rarely have to show people my divine form, but for this, I think I'll make an exception."

Was he going to use magic? Did he have another body? Was this like the tales of the werewolf? I hadn't heard of this ability.

To my surprise—to *everyone's* surprise—Eliezer didn't charge down the steps and attack.

No.

Eliezer turned the blade on *himself.* With power and conviction, he stabbed the weapon into his gut and pulled the blade upward. The fiendish sword sliced through his armor without hinderance. It also opened his guts and allowed them to spill across the steps, hot and wet and slick with blood.

Alexavier and Rylion, taken aback, both stepped away from the crimson waterfall cascading down to the throne room carpet.

Eliezer laughed once as his body slumped to the steps. For a short moment, blood gushed from the open, gaping wound. His insides reminded me of a freshly gutted pig, pink and white and red.

Why?

Was he a corpse god? What did he think he was doing?

Everyone held their breath, even the rustle of the wind died down, as though the world wanted to know what was happening as well. Unfortunately, the god-king had the punch line this time.

Eliezer's blood boiled.

Then Eliezer's organs moved.

To my horror, the black horns of his crown emerged from the crimson blood, like something rising out of a deep lake. The horns... they weren't a crown anymore. They were just *horns.* Of a dragon. The reptilian creature rose from the god-king's blood puddle, its scales midnight, and its eyes white. The beast was enormous, and it exited Eliezer's guts as though they were a tangled door to another realm the dragon had been hiding in.

Had Eliezer's blood acted as some sort of summoning pool? Had this dragon been called here?

No.

The beast lifted its front claws and dragged the last half of his body out of the innards. When the dragon stepped forward, colossal and intimidating, its head almost touched the high ceiling.

This was God-King Eliezer. He had called forth his body from the realm of magic, ready to fight both Rylion and Alexavier.

Stunned, the two men stared on with wide eyes and shaky grips.

Eliezer wasn't disgusting, like the Forsaken. His dragon-form was majestic and everything I had heard about from legends. Large leathery wings, spines, and a tail that easily whipped around the room. A fearsome beast.

As a dragon, Eliezer lunged down the steps. He gored Alexavier with his horns immediately, and then threw him across the throne room. Alexavier hit the floor a few feet away from me, his arm breaking, and his blood splattering across the carpet.

Alexavier didn't move afterward.

Then Eliezer turned his attention to Rylion.

The god-king frightened me, but not as much as losing the love of my life. I forced myself to step forward. No matter what, I wouldn't allow Rylion to die.

Eliezer opened his mouth and revealed a black tongue, gums, and throat—like a void to the darkness. Flames sparked to life between his massive fangs, and when I reached Rylion's side, I threw his cloak over his body just before the god-king vomited fire. The blaze burned my robes, and singed Rylion's boots, but it couldn't cut through the cloak, and it couldn't damage my skin. As a Lord of Flame and Cinder, I feared no heat.

Obviously disgusted with my presence, Eliezer whipped his tail around and lashed me hard enough to send me tumbling. I rolled onto the stone floor, my reflection on the mirror-like stone enough to see I was dazed.

It took me a while. My vision swam.

Rylion fought with the dragon, his bone blade enough to cut through the scales of the beast. Eliezer roared and breathed flame again, but now Rylion had the cloak from the Temperance God.

I pushed myself to my feet and stood.

Eliezer slammed Rylion with his dragon-shoulder, and Rylion tumbled out onto one of the many balconies and fell into the vegetation. When Eliezer tried to give chase, I held up my hand and unleashed a torrent of fire. The god-king wasn't harmed. He, too, wasn't harmed by heat.

Eliezer slammed out of the throne room, leapt over the balcony, and met Rylion in the beautiful gardens that filled Luthecia Castle. I felt useless, even as a Lord of Flame and Cinder. Fortunately, Rylion's magic worked wonders against the dragon. Rylion was calm, and strong beyond belief. When he swung his giant sword, he managed to cleave chunks from the god-king's chest and ribs.

Fire roiled in my stomach. I pushed myself to my feet, my wound from the fight with the King Killer actively bleeding. Then I turned my attention to the castle garden. I unleashed a torrent of fire on the opposite balcony, away from Rylion and the god-king, setting the property ablaze. *This* would give everyone something to remember.

The blaze, fueled by my magic, leapt from one tree to the next, incinerating the lilies of the valley, and the beautiful pines. The red fire and black smoke invigorated me. Shouts from the castle spread just as quickly as the flame. Soon, the Holy Guard and the knights would rush to quell the inferno.

Rylion and the god-king continued their fight on the opposite side of the throne room. I thought they were alone, but when I examined their devastated surroundings, I noticed Wulf and Caprice racing down the path. Wulf leapt to his brother's side and ushered forth his hoarfrost. It coated everything—the flowers, the trees, the stone, and the balcony —but also his ruined arm and half his neck and face.

Caprice also held up her elegant hands. Glaring light sparked forth, harsh and unforgiving. Then specks of reflective surfaces appeared over the frost, creating harsh spots of radiance that caused me to close my eyes.

These were the tactics of deception—hiding behind the flare of the sun, like a summer hawk did before swooping into the lake to catch its prey.

Caprice was a Lord. This proved it.

Probably descended from the God of Falsehoods.

Caprice's lights blinded Eliezer. When I forced myself to open my eyes, Rylion was slashing recklessly, also blinded. He caught the dragon by surprise, and cut another gouge in the beast's chest.

Then Eliezer went berserk.

He thrashed around, striking Wulf with his tail, and half-crushing Caprice with his claw. Eliezer whipped his head around and hit Rylion, sending him flying. The massive dragon threw his head from side to side, his horns knocking over trees, his claws creating furrows in the flower beds. The beast just wouldn't be stopped, no matter how much he bled from Rylion's attacks.

I stepped forward, my heart racing. "I'm here!" I shouted. "If you want to kill me, here I am, Eliezer! The heir to the throne!"

I wanted Eliezer to focus on me, and only me. If someone had to die in this fight, it was my life I cared about the least.

With my fire ready, I set the rug of the throne room ablaze. Then the pillowed seats, and finally the awkward throne itself. It occurred to me then—the throne was shaped for a dragon, and not a man. This castle had been built with the god-king's and god-queen's divine form in mind.

My shouts drew Eliezer's attention, which was all I wanted. The beast charged at me, clambering over toppled trees, and then smashing through the balcony. I waited, prepared to take the blow, but then more ice coated his legs, hindering the dragon's movement. He couldn't bend his elbows, and he jerked to a halt just before climbing into the throne room.

The dragon was a mere thirty feet away, his hot breath stinking up the area. Smoke fumed from his nostrils and mouth, his black gums shiny from his own blood and saliva. Eliezer truly seemed like an animal in that moment.

"Eliezer! Face me!"

Rylion's voice uncharacteristically boomed out across the garden. Eliezer's long neck allowed him to turn his head all the way around and stare behind him. Rylion was there, waiting, Justice in his hands. He sliced at Eliezer's hind legs, taunting the dragon to attack.

Eliezer obliged.

With his dragon fangs, Eliezer bit at Rylion, but missed. The snap of his maw sounded like the crash of a building. Eliezer went to attack again. Then, with strength not found in the average man, Rylion stabbed up into the dragon's maw. The blade punctured the roof of Eliezer's mouth. In one frightening move, the dragon was shaken. Eliezer twitched and thrashed again, his leather wings stretched wide.

Rylion swung his blade and cut through the thin flesh of the right wing.

Such power and devastation. Blood splashed upon the once grand garden. Rylion thrust one final time. His blade went deep into the god-king's chest, right between the ribs.

Somehow, I felt the god-king's last heartbeat.

And then I tumbled to the floor of the burning throne room, unconscious.

CHAPTER TWENTY-SEVEN

When I woke, my throat hurt.

Somehow, even though my head felt like it was splitting apart, I knew I had to say something. This was it. My first decree. Whatever I said, it would become the new law of the land. Everyone would be bound to this directive, held hostage by the threat of becoming cursed.

But what should I say?

I could do what every god-queen had done before me—I could utter a decree against regicide. But I didn't care about my life. Perhaps I should utter a decree against killing Rylion? The thought brought a slight bit of laughter to my throat. It could be my wedding gift to him.

No.

I needed to form my decree properly. There was no passion in my veins for ruling Luka through fear. If I was forced to make a decree, then I would only have one. *Only one.* But what would it be?

What did I value? What did I think was just?

What problems could I solve by uttering a rule against them?

I gritted my teeth, struggling to find the answer.

Then it struck me. *Authority*. If used properly, it could lead a nation to greatness. But... That wasn't the case in the Kingdom of Luka. Authority was being used as a weapon.

It shouldn't be the citizens who feared those in power—it should be those *with the power and authority* who feared the weapons they wielded. A blade forgets, but the flesh remembers. Every cut and wound the god-king made against the people was remembered far longer by the average citizen than by him.

That was the problem.

But could I correct it? Could I reverse that fear?

Should 100 people live in fear and terror, or just a few people? By any metric I used to measure my decree, I understood I had stumbled upon my answer.

Now I knew what my decree had to be.

The final decree. The only one I needed.

"Cursed be the man who abuses their station of power," I whispered.

That was it. All I needed. Anyone who wanted to assume authority and control would have to answer to those they watched over. Those who became the captain of the guard would have to remember their oath to the city. Those who watched after children couldn't use them for their own lusts and gain. Those who wanted to lead our kingdom would have to do so without corruption or sacrificing the citizens.

Anyone who took power, and then abused it for their own gains, would be cursed.

Only a few people would be affected by this decree—the fewest number of people possible.

Because that was the root of my problems. Of Rylion's problems. It was those who sought to control us. No man was flawless, and their incompetence hurt us all. Now everyone would have to think twice before reaching for the mantle of *leader*.

Then my headache faded. I no longer needed to utter any decrees. I stood and my hand instinctively went to my head. A crown had appeared. Horns and thorns jutted from my skin and skull. I was the God-Queen of Luka. A terrible day.

Rylion hobbled out of the ruined gardens, past the dragon body of Eliezer, and straight to my side in the throne room. He had been harmed during the fighting, but the only thing I saw was the black spiderweb around his forehead—like a crown all its own. The black marks bled down his face. An upside-down crown, then. Ominous and bad luck.

Rylion had committed regicide. He was cursed, destined to become another King Killer Forsaken.

I took shaky breaths and got to my feet. When he approached, I held still, fearful of what he might say. My body—it didn't hurt anymore—and I suspected that becoming the god-queen had empowered me.

I was a dragon now.

"Artemis," my husband said. "It's over."

The flames, smoke, and blood told a story of destruction, but my crown—and my only decree—were the prizes at the end of the war.

"I'm sorry," Rylion concluded.

I touched the bone crown around my head. "Don't." Then I looked at my unsteady hands. "Can you go on? Are you badly injured?"

"Like I said. It's over."

"I see Eliezer's body."

"I meant—*this*." Rylion touched his own curse mark, the reverse crown. "I can't... I can't become another King Killer. I won't hurt the citizens of Luka. I must... tell you goodbye. And leave."

This was what I had feared the most. Ever since meeting Rylion—ever since he had pulled me from the streets of Ludlow—I had feared he would send me away. Now, in our most glorious moment, he wanted to kill himself.

I wouldn't allow that to happen.

"No," I said. "*No.*" I stepped close to Rylion and then gripped his cloak, my grip so tight I feared I harmed the scale mail underneath. "I won't allow you to leave me."

"It must be this way." Rylion's voice lowered as he added, "I tried to warn you. My family… Something always prevents us from being with our loved ones. I prepared for this eventuality in my heart many years ago."

"*No,*" I growled, flames in my body. "There is no magic or circumstance I won't fight to keep you."

"Nothing can remove my curse," Rylion said, stroking my hair. "You heard Eliezer."

"I don't care. If magic *can* bestow the curse, magic —*somewhere*—can remove it." I ripped my hand away from his cloak, fire building in my chest and burning me with hate for everything that wasn't him. "I will find it."

Rylion closed his eyes and turned away from me. "Don't make this difficult."

I was making this difficult? Rylion didn't understand his words sometimes. We stood in the half-ruined throne room of Luthecia Castle, because *he* had been determined to remove my curse. Now it was my chance to return the gesture. I'd ruin whole kingdoms to remove his.

"This matter isn't settled," I stated. "Your magic could prevent your turn."

"It might not," Rylion whispered.

"*I don't care.* We'll find a way. *I'll* find a way. As long as you're here—and not a monster—I'll use everything in my power to break this." I gestured to the throne room. "If the god-kings and god-queens can't remove curses, perhaps the old gods can. I'll find them. Or their corpses. I'll make them answer for this."

Rylion didn't reply. His presence calmed me. I loved him. That much fueled my desire to change reality.

"Give me time," I said. "If you start to turn, then I can end you, but until then, I don't want to lose you. Stay with me. Please. You're the only one… The only one I love. My anchor to life."

Rylion opened his eyes again and stared at me. "What do you mean?"

"If you die, I'll die, Rylion."

And I meant it. I didn't care if that made me weak. I knew myself well enough to understand my desires. My obsession chained me to Rylion, and I enjoyed every second. As long as I had him, I had the fuel for any flame.

Rylion stroked my long black hair. "Very well, God-Queen. We'll do it your way. We'll… We'll find a way to remove both our curses."

I held my breath for a long moment as I dwelled on our situation. Would I rule the Kingdom of Luka as the next god-queen? It would be easier to gather resources and information from the seat of a throne than the seat of an old cart.

"We'll stay here," I said. "I'll protect you, Wulf, Caprice, and Alexavier. I'll send scholars and priestesses all over the kingdom to gather information. I'll make it my priority to reverse the curses of the old god-kings. It'll be…" But then I stopped myself.

No.

My first decree. My only decree.

I couldn't use this power for myself. If I were to take the throne, I had to use my authority and power for the people, not my own selfish gains.

I shook my head. "I'm sorry. Rylion—we should leave this place. Right now. Before anyone finds us."

He frowned and held me close. "Why?"

"*Cursed be the man who abuses their station of power,*" I said. "My only decree." I stared up at him and smiled. "Once we've lifted these curses… Then we can return, and I can take my rightful place upon the throne."

Rylion nodded along with my words. "I see. Then, we

should go." He glanced toward the fires in the garden, and at the Holy Guard trying to snuff the flames. "We haven't much time."

"Let's gather your brother and Caprice."

"And Alexavier," Rylion muttered as he turned his gaze to the unconscious Scourge. "Perhaps we can save him as well."

Yes. That was what I wanted. I would return to the capital only when I had the right intentions to do so. And in the meantime, the only people who would take the throne were those who knew the risks of the power they wielded.

Until then, I would be free.

ABOUT THE AUTHOR

Shami Stovall is a multi-award-winning author of fantasy and science fiction, with several best-selling novels under her belt. Before that, she taught history and criminal law at the college level and loved every second. When she's not reading fascinating articles and books about ancient China or the Byzantine Empire, Stovall can be found playing way too many video games, especially RPGs and tactics simulators.

If you want to contact her, you can do so at the following locations:

Website: https://sastovallauthor.com
Twitter: @GameOverStation
Facebook: www.facebook.com/SAStovall
Email: s.adelle.s@gmail.com

www.ingramcontent.com/pod-product-compliance
Lightning Source LLC
Chambersburg PA
CBHW061343190726
48288CB00005B/1575